The Shadow Girl

The Shadow Girl

Cover Art: Jim Tetlow

Editor: Tamara Beach

ISBN: 978-0-9979395-6-9

Also available in digital (978-0-9996556-2-7)

Between the Lines Publishing

2515 White Bear Ave N.

Ste. A-8 #163

Maplewood, MN 55109

www.btwnthelines.com

Printed in the United States of America

Acknowledgements

Thank you, Stephanie, for letting me mix a hint of your truth along with a dash of mine, blending it all together with a hearty serving of fiction.

Thanks so much to Jill and Porsche for being my very first fans! Your encouragement has kept me writing when I wanted to give up.

A special thank you to Tamara Beach for being the best editor on the planet! You make me a better writer.

And of course, to my dear family, I appreciate all the advice, support and attempts at providing me a quiet space to work. I love you all.

This book is dedicated to the real Shadow Girl.

May she someday be noticed…

Chapter One

I have always known that I am invisible—even way back then, when it first started to happen. In fact, it goes back even further; in my earliest of memories and for as long as I can remember, the sense of being unnoticed was there. I think it started on a muggy day when I was six years old. I can still feel the excitement as my grandmother poked her nose through the living room drapes and announced that it was dry enough to make a trip to the neighborhood park. It had been raining for nearly a week straight, and I was glad to be free of the stuffy, dim rooms in our old home. It had become my prison that summer, a place where my older siblings would unleash their rainy-day boredom in the form of self-esteem-crushing torment.

We had watched as Grandmother pulled out the wagon from the shed and loaded it to the brim with goodies for a picnic lunch. It seemed like an eternity before we were finally following her down the cracked and uneven sidewalk. I was last in line behind my two older siblings as we passed by the familiar row of tall, skinny houses. Each home was built on a thin strip of a lot and looked identical to ours in structure and design. Grandmother had taught me that ours was the one with the black iron letters that read 3386. But I recognized it by the faded blue-gray paint and gaudy wrought iron shutters that overpowered the face of our family home.

Blossom Park was four blocks up the street, and—much to my disappointment—had never lived up to its name. There was not a bud, bloom, or flowering shrubbery anywhere to be seen. Instead, the postage-stamp-shaped piece of land was fitted between two brick buildings and flanked by a parking lot on one end and a tall chain-link fence that overlooked an alley on the other.

I was happy to be in the sun, nonetheless, even if it did happen to shine down in patchy pools of light over paint-chipped play equipment and a weed-encroached sand pit.

"Let's play house." It wasn't a suggestion so much as a command, spoken by my oldest sibling, Adonia. She had run ahead of the wagon, her caramel-colored ponytail was swinging like a pendulum with every step. She was only three years older than me, but the gap had always felt miles apart.

"House? Again? You promised we could play hot lava." Keane sighed impatiently, and adjusted the thick glasses resting on the bridge of his nose. He was just a year older than me, and sometimes I would fantasize that we could be best friends. After all, the exciting game of hot lava was something we both enjoyed much more than Adonia's boring, girly game of house. Who wanted to stir imaginary pots of stew with sticks when we could be dangling above fiery molten lava, holding on for dear life?

"We could play both," I suggested in a quiet voice, not wanting to cause an argument.

Adonia turned and sighed in an overly dramatic way as she rolled her eyes. "Well, if we can't agree, we will just have to play house first and *then* hot lava. There. Happy?"

I wondered if I would be paid attention to when I was older, like my sister. It was like my voice hadn't developed enough to be heard yet the way hers was, edged with authority and demanding attention.

"Fine; good idea. But I refuse to be the butler this time. Find some other kid," Keane said adamantly as he jogged up to the monkey bars, which everyone knew to be The House.

Grandmother was humming as she made her way to the benches that rested in the shade of a brick building. She parked the wagon after pulling out her book of crosswords and seated herself among the handful of other parents or guardians perched watchfully.

I found my six-year-old self feeling sorry for my grandmother and the other adults who weren't playing, but were only spectators. I wondered how many years I had left before I wasn't allowed to have fun anymore.

"Zylia!"

I jumped, startled at hearing my name being shouted so loudly. I suppose it was because I wasn't spoken to very often, unless I was in trouble for something. Adonia, hands on hips, with one of her pristine Keds tapping, was glaring at me from under the dome-shaped silver bars. I wasn't sure how long I had been holding up the game, so I hurriedly scrambled over.

"It's about time! You're the baby. Time for a nap." Adonia was using the toe of her sneaker to make a rectangle outline in the sand. "This is your crib."

I obediently curled up on my side as my older two siblings set out making further plans for the game. After a while I began feeling the sand press into the skin along my arm and the side of my face. I shifted and felt small pebbles slip into my shoes and the waistband of my jean shorts.

A girl I'd never seen before had jogged up and asked if she could play. She had coffee-colored skin and looked to be around Adonia's age.

"Of *course,*" Adonia said in a charming voice that I recognized immediately. I called it her *non-family* voice, the tone she used to fool strangers into thinking she was sugary sweet all the time. Fake as it may be, she managed to find and keep any number of friends while I had none, so I couldn't entirely argue with her methods.

Keane was looking longingly at a group of boys playing with a remote-control car. "I need to buy furniture for the house," he said suddenly. When I saw him wandering off, I knew he wouldn't come back to the game.

"Well, then, we should buy groceries while the baby is sleeping," the new girl said.

"Great! I'll just get my purse." Adonia looped an imaginary strap around her shoulder and turned to me. "Don't get out of your crib while we're gone." She said the last part in her *family* voice, so I knew she meant it.

I watched the pair of them walk off, the sound of their chummy conversation blending and fading into the other playground noises. I turned my head and looked up at the bluish-gray sky through the metal web of the playground structure. The storm clouds had gone, leaving a thin, dingy overcast. The sunlight perforated only portions of the hazy veil, and a memory popped into my head in that random way that memories do. Something about the way the light was playing down caused me to think of a flashlight shining beneath a worn blanket.

I remembered it from when Adonia and her sleepover friends had been telling spooky stories and I had crept in, uninvited. Whispers and giggles filtered out from under the blanket and into my envious ears. When had Adonia become so popular and well-liked, anyway?

There was a tickling sensation on my wrist that brought my gaze down from the sky and back to the present. I watched as a lone ant made his way over the back of my palm and up along my knuckles. I didn't make a dramatic move to flick it off me, the way my sister or mother would have done. I didn't even move at all. I just watched the little guy meandering along my fingers and wondered if he felt alone too, far away from his kind.

I could hear Grandmother calling, "Moss kids, get your lunch!" I guess she didn't want to chance stray kids grabbing at her peanut butter and apricot jam sandwiches. In my peripheral vision I could see her fishing around in the wagon, but I was uninterested in moving from my "crib" for the moment. I didn't want to lose track of the tiny black ant, which I had grown inexplicably fond of. If I moved, I might never feel this connection again.

Eventually I did move—or jolt, rather—as something rubbery bounced off my forehead, startling the wits out of me. I jerked upright just in time to see a pair of snickering boys rushing off with a big, red kickball. It was only then that I realized I had been asleep, not because of the sand pressed deeply into my skin or the string of drool wet on my cheek, but because my siblings and grandmother were nowhere to be seen.

I looked around once more, just to be sure, and prickling fear rushed over my body. "Grandmother!" I tried to call out, but my voice stuck in my throat and there was a pounding in my ears. What had happened while I was asleep? If my grandmother, Adonia, and Keane had been snatched away by kidnappers, the unworried children that were still playing at the park would at *least* appear alerted to the tragedy, right? So there had to be another reason they had left me behind.

There must have been an emergency! I thought. Who was in trouble? My mother? Father? Frankie, Keane's hamster? How was it that everyone but me had found out about this emergency?

I was pounding down the sidewalk, leaving the park and its ignorant visitors, dorky bullies, and my dear little ant all far behind me. I tripped once on the jagged concrete squares and fell against a tree. Even though I snagged my arm along the trunk, it didn't slow me down.

Before long, my house came in view, and I was that much closer to discovering the extent of this dreadful, life-changing tragedy. I bounded over the small, balding patch of grass and leapt over the short retaining wall and adjacent flower bed, not bothering with the four stone steps in the lawn that led up toward the covered entrance of our house.

I yanked open the iron screen door and stepped into the shade of the porch. Suddenly I was afraid to go any farther. What horrors would I witness inside?

I walked slowly along the long, skinny porch, breathing quickly. I stopped at the front door. It was open wide and I could hear voices coming from inside. My mother's chatty tone had never sounded so comforting. She was alive, at least!

I stepped into the entry hall, and the scent of frying food met my nose and made my stomach flop. I took a few steps down the hall past the stairway and peeked around the corner into the kitchen. There stood my mother, using a spoon to stir a large metal pot at the stove. She had a bright lipstick smile on her face and she was chatting happily into the phone, which was cradled between her neck and shoulder.

Grandmother was seated near her at the island counter, chopping vegetables while moving and puckering her wrinkled lips rhythmically.

Relief spread over me and faded into confusion. I backed out of the kitchen and ran up the wooden stairway to the second floor. Keane's bedroom was the first on the left, the scuffed door standing open. I looked in to find him crouched on the floor with his magnifying set.

"Keane!" I said loudly, startling him.

"What?" He glanced up, annoyed.

"What happened? Was there some sort of emergency? Is Frankie all right?" I was breathless and speaking rapidly.

"Why are you being so weird?" My brother drew up one side of his face, and I wondered if Adonia had taught him that expression because she wore it so frequently. It was a mixture of bewilderment and contempt. Thankfully, it didn't last long before he turned his face dismissively back toward his magnifiers.

"There wasn't an emergency? Why did you guys leave the park?"

Keane didn't even look up as he mumbled, "Uh, because Grandmother said it was time to go; duh. Why do we always leave the park?"

It was only at that moment the realization dawned on me that I had been abandoned at the park. They had left me there, asleep under the monkey bars with no one looking after me.

"But you left without *me*." I wanted to shout the words; instead, they came out very quietly through my quivering lips.

"What are you talking about? You were with us the whole time. Leave me alone already!" He jumped up and shut his bedroom door in my face.

My throat tightened and felt strained as I plodded back downstairs. Had no one even noticed I was gone? I wiped away tears before finding myself back in the kitchen.

"Oh, there you are!" my mother said brightly, looking at me for a split second. She had already ended her phone call, but her shiny blonde hair was still ruffled up where she had been clutching the receiver. "We were wondering when you'd come down. Why don't you go help your grandmother clear away the onionskins?"

I wordlessly slipped in alongside them at the island. My grandmother pointed a knobby finger and directed, "Bring that garbage bin over here; it'll be easier that way." She smiled encouragingly, as if I were being ever-so-helpful.

She really has no idea she left me, I thought, stunned, as I pulled over the grimy bin. Had I imagined the whole scene? Nothing seemed real anymore. I was suddenly aware of a stinging on the side of my arm. I looked down and saw that I was bleeding from a long scrape that stretched from mid-pinky to my elbow. It was the only evidence that I had been deserted, and the tingling pain was almost comforting.

That was over seven years ago, though—only the beginning of my descent toward being entirely undetectable. I had no idea that eventually I would fade away completely.

Chapter Two

I think things really began taking a turn for the stranger after the dream. In it, I was walking down a long, narrow path. I could see so many people alongside—everyone I've ever met or known. Random people, like the ice cream man who nearly drove over me when I was eight; my kindergarten recess aide; a nameless nurse I once encountered—they were all there. I called out, trying to get their attention Occasionally, someone turned their head and noticed me, but then immediately looked over my shoulder, gaping and gasping.

Their expressions made the dream feel like a nightmare. Their features twisted with such fear, I was horrified to look at what they saw. I knew something worse than terrible was just a few paces behind me.

So instead of glancing back, I ran as fast as I could, trying to put distance between me and the horrendous creature that must have been pursuing me. But the ground had become like a treadmill and I couldn't get anywhere. I felt the *thing* overtaking me; when it touched my skin, I understood what it was.

Blackness. Nothingness. It was in the shape of a giant, hazy shadow, enveloping me, swallowing me, and digesting me into the unknown. It was my biggest fear and my ultimate fate.

I woke up paralyzed with panic, clutching the sheet tightly at my throat. My eyes were wide, probing the dimly lit room. I could see from the corner of my eye that Ivy's twin bed was empty, the lilac-colored comforter smoothed neatly over the flowered sheets. Her side of the room was so orderly it was sickening. It was that inadequate feeling of being outdone by my seven-year-old baby sister, almost six years younger than me, that brought me back to reality.

I let the dream fade back inside my mind, receding into the realm of fantasy like a swilling tide. I tried my best to mentally keep it there while I moved my eyes over Ivy's bookshelf. The top shelf was full of glossy storybooks lined from tallest to shortest. Below that, her fancy display tea sets were gleaming. I knew she kept her less decorative play tea sets in a shoebox under her bed, behind the row of shoes that sat close together in easily accessible pairs.

Ivy was different from everyone else in my family. Not only because she was obsessively immaculate, but because out of all of them, she was the only one who truly noticed me.

And there were a lot of us living under that ancient roof. The narrow three-story house had been in our family for many decades and housed relatives from at least two generations for as long as I could remember.

There was Grandmother, who had recently been diagnosed with dementia; Mother and Father; Adonia; Keane; the twins, Mace and Bram; then me; and finally, Ivy. It was hard to believe I could feel such loneliness in a house so populated.

I flipped back my bedcovers as soon as the terror of the nightmare had subsided and put my bare feet on the cold wooden floor. It was mid-November and our ancient heating system probably still needed to be serviced.

I shuffled into the hall toward the bathroom that I shared with Adonia and Ivy. I purposefully woke up late every morning, because it was pointless trying to fight for bathroom time with two high-maintenance sisters.

This morning I was later than usual, though, so I quickly stripped off my mismatched pajamas and stepped into the shower. The stream was lukewarm for only a couple minutes before becoming chilly. It was just another consequence of making it to the bathroom in last place.

I scrubbed off as fast as I could but I was shivering uncontrollably as I wrapped up in a large, slightly scratchy towel. I could see myself clearly in the mirror over the sink. The shower water hadn't even gotten hot enough to steam over my reflection.

I saw myself as slim and plain as ever: long hair that looked like black ink when wet, oval-shaped face with a slightly pointed chin, and a small mouth outlined by lips that were colorless and much too thin.

The only feature on my face that could be described as anything beyond plain was my large emerald-green eyes surrounded by a fan of thick ebony lashes. It was the one part of my appearance that I allowed myself to feel a small amount of pride over. It was ridiculously vain, though, considering the fact that no one ever saw my eyes anyway. My gaze was usually cast downward, straight hair spilling in front of my face like a curtain.

I glanced over the countertop as I blow-dried my hair, taking in all the little pots full of pastel shadows and blushes that belonged to Adonia. I wondered who might notice me if I drew lines just above my lashes and covered my lips with that goo that made them shiny and sticky, just like my sister did every morning. People sure noticed her, especially boys.

Once or twice Ivy and I had tagged along behind her at the mall, and I had gotten this weird twist in my gut every time I saw someone looking at her. I couldn't believe how grown men would stare at her sixteen-year-old body from head to foot and back again. It caused me to feel angry and protective, even though she's the older one and is supposed to be in the responsible role. But then, after the annoyance had passed, I began to feel a sense of jealousy over those ogles that left me guilt-ridden and gloomy. No one would ever look at me, especially in an appraising, admiring way.

After it was dry, I parted my hair to one side and brushed it until it was shiny and sleek. I then quickly pulled on a pair of worn dark-wash jeans, a gray turtleneck, and my favorite hooded sweater-jacket that displayed a purple broken heart design across the front when zipped up.

Back in my room, I halfheartedly made my bed and shoved some clothes into a hamper, but there was still an obvious distinction between my domain and Ivy's. I slung my backpack over my arm and headed down two stories to the kitchen.

It was bright and noisy, as always, making me feel both comforted and on edge as I slid into an open chair next to my father at the breakfast table. He was staring intently at the newspaper in one hand while absentmindedly stirring his coffee with the other.

"Morning," I said to him. My voice was groggy from sleep and the twins were arguing loudly over who would do the maze on the back of a cereal box. My father didn't even blink his strained, puffy eyes.

Mother plopped an empty bowl and spoon in front of me. "Knock it off, you two! It's too early in the day for this," she was saying, voice elevating as she walked back around to the island counter. "I swear . . ." She waved her hand without finishing her thought and focused her attention on a hot-pink-covered paperback book. Novels were her addiction, and I'd never known her to be more than three feet away from one. They spilled off shelves, hid inside large purses, and poked out from behind couch cushions, nightstands, and heaps of unfolded laundry.

I liked watching her read, even though I knew that when she was staring at a page of words, she was worlds away. Her pretty face would change from dreamy contentment to wide-eyed excitement or furrowed curiosity with just a few page turns.

All six of her children were named after characters from the pages of her ever-accumulating mass of books. I sometimes wondered who the fictional woman Zylia had been, but my mother could never seem to remember the title of the story or where she had kept it. For a long time, I would flip through random books to see if I could find her, but the character always eluded me. Oftentimes I wondered if I was the imaginary one and the real Zylia was living a normal life somewhere on the other side of the pages.

"Oh my gosh, look at the calories!" Adonia widened her eyes, mascara-coated lashes reaching all the way to her perfectly shaped eyebrows. "I'm so not eating this." She slammed a box of sugary cereal back on the table.

"There's plenty to choose from; don't be so finicky," Father mumbled.

He was right. The long, scratched-up oak table held at least ten boxes of assorted cereals, most of them with colorful cartoon animals on the front.

The sight of food always made me ill in the mornings; ridiculous containers of happy, cheerful-looking creatures tried to make the processed puffs more appealing. I suppose it was really because my stomach was already in knots with the thought of having to endure another day of eighth grade at my worn-out, overpopulated, and downright intimidating school.

Last year hadn't seemed quite so bad with the comfort of knowing that my brother, Keane, was somewhere amidst the throngs in case I should need him. Not that I ever caught so much as a glimpse of him; it was just nice to feel connected to someone in the masses.

My younger brothers were present in the building, however, worlds away somewhere in sixth grade. They weren't a comfort at all, always getting into embarrassing mischief and causing trouble. The twins definitely didn't give me that sense of security that Keane emanated.

So now that my older brother had moved up in the ranks, somewhere with the well-liked Adonia in high school, I was completely on my own. Not that it was a new emotion—it was more like an acceptance that the hollow feeling within my chest was there to stay.

Father folded down a corner of the newspaper to glance at his watch. Then he aimed his gaze at the digital oven clock as if to confirm his shocking find. If he were more of an emotional person, he would have jerked or jumped or gasped at the realization that he was running seriously late. Instead, one sleepy eye twitched, and he quickly and fluidly stood to gather his briefcase and suit jacket.

My father was talking as he headed out toward the garage through the laundry room. "See you all tonight. Oh, and if there happens to be a bike in the driveway yet again when I come home this evening, I won't stop for it this time."

My twin brothers exchanged mischievous glances. They were always leaving their things out to be driven, kicked, or tripped over.

"Oh!" Mother stuffed her book tightly into the back pocket of her jeans, also becoming aware of the time. "Is your grandmother up yet? She has a doctor's appointment. I have to take her right after I drop Ivy off at school."

She wasn't really asking anyone in particular, as she was moving in the direction of the master suite where her mother resided.

The strange old woman my grandmother had become didn't really need all the yawning space of that big bedroom and bath. In fact, the hospital-sized bed she slept in, an old dresser, and a tiny desk were practically the only furniture she kept in there. To me the pieces look dwarfed and unfashionable, like old, mismatched doll furniture.

Thankfully, our house was big enough that there was room for all, with only some of us doubling up and sharing spaces. I always heard my mother say how the house goes on and up forever, but she usually only complained when she was cleaning it.

I could hear Mother now, talking loudly through the bedroom doorway. She always spoke up when addressing Grandmother, although I'm pretty sure the older woman didn't have any trouble hearing.

"Okay, kids, let's get a move on!" After waking Grandmother, my mother was back in the kitchen, clearing cereal bowls from the table. She took the clean, unused one from in front of me and commented cheerfully, "Wow, you were hungry! You usually eat like a bird in the mornings."

I started to say that I hadn't actually filled my bowl, let alone eaten, but decided it was really more effort than it was worth. Instead, I slung my backpack over my shoulder; on my way toward the hall, Ivy nudged me with her elbow. "Nice one, skipping breakfast like that," she giggled, her freckled nose crinkling up.

A small stab of fondness hit me, and for half a second I felt important. I smiled back at her but I didn't say anything, just watched her as she wiped crumbs off the table and into a napkin. She looked so small and cute in a pair of floral embellished jeans and a cotton long-sleeved top.

Ivy had the same caramel-colored hair as Adonia: thick and full of body. But Ivy's was straight and worn in an angled bob that appeared more youthful and innocent next to Adonia's flowing, wavy tresses.

"See ya after school," I said and slipped away from the morning bustle and out onto the sidewalk. I was the only child in the Moss family who walked to school. Adonia and Keane both rode a bus to the high school near old town, Mother drove Ivy to grade school every day, and Mace and Bram were forced to hitch a ride with Mrs. Edgar from two doors down. If it weren't for the woman's own two children, who took up the remaining empty seats, I would have been subject to the same fate every morning in her stuffy sedan that smelled of ripe underarms and faint cigarette smoke.

I didn't mind walking alone anyway; I'd been used to being on my own for quite some time. My mother had told me I was the only child of hers who could be trusted to be responsible enough to make it to school on their own. Of course, she was probably just saying that so I wouldn't feel slighted or insulted in some way.

Outside it was chilly and dim, with a hint of moisture in the air. I breathed deeply and felt the coolness pour into my lungs like a refreshing drink. It calmed me for a few steps along the sidewalk, but the familiar nervousness crept back quickly.

Two more blocks and I could see and hear the traffic noise beginning to pick up. My stomach ached with each step that brought me closer. I tried to distract myself with thoughts of soothing isolation and quiet. It didn't really help. You see, the thing about being invisible for most of my life is that I had never really learned how to be seen and heard in a socially acceptable way. And if I were to be seen, spoken to, or involved in some sort of meaningful human interaction, the most likely place was at school. Unfortunately, those interactions weren't usually positive.

People never acknowledged me when I was making straight As, letting kids cut in line, or keeping it secret that I had caught the pretty and fashionable Emily Andrews stuffing her bra in the handicapped bathroom stall. But somehow, I was able to suddenly materialize into view when doing things like tripping over chair legs, knocking over the ball cart in gym, or getting sick on the lunchroom floor.

However, this year I had been incident-free so far, and the anticipation of the next embarrassing encounter was eating away at my stomach lining. In fact, the expectancy was probably the worst part. I guess it's like the way I open a can of refrigerated biscuits. I tense up, clench my teeth, and hold my breath before I bang the soft cardboard cylinder against the countertop.

Then, when that underwhelming *pop* sound goes off, I realize it wasn't so bad after all. But I'm always aware that it *could* have exploded into my face and rendered me unconscious, so that's why I remain on edge, feeling the need to be mentally prepared for tragedy.

The last time I had been truly humiliated was near the end of seventh grade that previous May. I had wound up in this god-awful coed weight training class with sweaty, brawny boys and beefy, tough girls. My spaghetti limbs and I had no business being there, but apparently, I hadn't realized what I was signing up for when I thoughtlessly marked it as one of my desired electives.

Near the end of class one day, we were all finishing up our required lifting at separate benches. I was really struggling during my final set of bicep curls, sure that the silver number fifteen had to have been mistakenly stamped on my dumbbells. They had to be at least fifty pounds each, the way my arms were trembling and straining.

I had been losing weight since taking the class, not bulking up and bulging like some of the boys or becoming fit and defined like the girls. Instead I seemed to be shrinking away and becoming increasingly wispy in stature. It was due to this fact that my workout shorts happened to fall away from my bony hips and drop to the gym floor. I had tried to grab them quickly before anyone would notice, but the shock and embarrassment made me forget I was still holding the dumbbells; they went crashing to the floor, the clamor drawing all eyes to my flowery pink panties.

As the looming brown-brick building came into view, I wondered what new horrors eagerly awaited me. The building was tall, raised up on its foundation in a threatening posture, looking out over the street with rows of smudged, grubby windows.

Cars and buses were lining the sidewalk and congesting the street for at least a couple blocks in either direction. The school's massive double doors at the top of a flight of concrete stairs were open to allow in the throng of middle-school-aged children. As I waited to cross the street with a cluster of chattering kids, I noticed that the big, creepy building appeared to be an evil entity, sucking in the stream of students through its mouth made of oak and glass. I really wasn't in the mood to be digested today, but I found my way into the human current and yielded to the notion of being consumed.

I really thought I was going to make it, safe and invisible as usual. Maybe that's why during my last hour I started to relax and let my guard down as the monotone voice at the front of the class droned on; "So let's say Sam has five less three times as many pancakes than Oliver . . ."

In the refuge of the back row, I had taken out my notebook and flipped to the final pages, where artsy graffiti representing hours of boredom spread over the college-ruled lines in pencil and ink. I found a clear spot on a busy page, took a quiet breath, and started doodling whatever sprang into my mind. I had written *lonely* in large, curly cursive and began using my blue pen to decorate the dangling letter y with a twisting stem of ivy that wrapped around the word and flowered intermittently. I did something similar with the words *nobody* and *deserted* and was just tipping the page back to appraise my work when it was swiped from my hands.

It happened so quickly that I didn't have time to react before my notebook was being passed around the room from one snickering student to the next.

"Aww, poor little Zeea! Are you so very lonesome?" the tall blonde boy who had taken my notebook taunted from his seat next to me.

My eyes narrowed and I could feel myself bristling. He didn't even know my name. I knew that his name was Thomas Hodge, that he was an only child, that he was terrible at math, and that he had a chronically itchy scalp. I had never spoken to him, except for the time I asked him to please move his foot when he was standing on the strap of my backpack and I couldn't pick it up. Yet I knew something about him because I had sat silently beside him every math class for almost three months. And he didn't even know my name.

"Zie-*lee*-uh," I enunciated. "My name is Zylia."

The teacher turned from the chalkboard at that moment and eyeballed me over his thick lenses. The entire class followed suit. Suddenly, there were so many people staring, their gazes boring deep into me. It was such a foreign feeling to be scrutinized. I was used to being immune to the average line of sight, so to have that much attention was equivalent to being stripped of all clothing and gestured at with a pointing stick.

"What is all this commotion, Miss Moss?"

The teacher was speaking to me, the class was gawking, and my notebook was somewhere in circulation. I could feel my face burning as I answered, "I don't know." Hey, it was the best I could come up with.

My math teacher looked bored and fatigued with my comment. "Since you have taken such an interest in this class, I'm sure you won't mind completing an extra page of challenge problems along with your homework tonight."

Sure, I thought, *I'll do it! Just get these eyeballs away from me!*

He blinked several times before turning back to the chalkboard and finally resuming class. I watched as someone stretched out to toss my notebook into the wastepaper basket. The teacher didn't even flinch at the thudding sound it made when it hit the bottom.

Just like that, I had slipped back into nonexistence as if I had never been on display. I tested it once just to make sure, coughing severely into the crook of my arm. No one so much as peeked over a shoulder.

Well, I was back. My brush with humanity hadn't been so bad after all, or at least that's what I told myself to keep from crying once class was dismissed and I was digging my notebook out of the trash. The page was still open to my scribbling and I noted that over my ornate word *lonely,* someone had written *pathetic* in bold black marker.

I felt dizzy and the room was wavy, like I was seeing it from underwater. I held my eyes shut until the disconcerting feeling passed and all that was left was an agonizing ache in my chest.

Chapter Three

It felt warmer than usual as I set out on my walk home. Maybe it was just the heat of embarrassment, because the sky overhead was still dreary and filmy, with gray shadows slinking into view.

I was crossing the street when I caught sight of someone from the corner of my eye. It was the black jacket emblazoned with Korean writing on the sleeves that caught my attention. My heart raced and my stomach dropped. In that jacket was Josh Pierceton, who had been my one and only crush for five straight years.

I had been in love with that boy since he had picked up the pencil I'd dropped in Mrs. Edmonds' third-grade class, looked at me with those vibrant brown eyes and said, "I think this is yours, Zylia."

We'd never shared a class since then and although our entire relationship consisted of me sneaking looks at him from behind inanimate objects, I still felt a bond between us. I mean, what other eight-year-old would have been able to pronounce my name? Kids our current age and adults alike had a hard-enough time saying it correctly, so I felt it was quite an honor that he was observant enough to get it right.

Now he was standing alongside a school bus with a group of boys, his countenance animated and smiling as he held their attention with a story of some sort. I stopped on the corner and just watched him as he used his hands to gesture and indicate some great feat on the basketball court.

He was taller than most of his comrades by at least a few inches, and his skin was still a golden-brown left over from summer. Occasionally he would allow his friends a chance to talk, and I would see him nod politely and drag his hand through strands of silky black hair. I imagined that it would feel so soft and smooth that it would be almost weightless to my touch.

Every move he made slowed time for me in a mesmerizing fashion—like the way he shifted his backpack strap higher on his shoulder, making his neck muscles bulge. Or the way he shook his head when he would first start to laugh, as if in humorous disbelief of whatever was being said.

I wanted to talk to him so badly, wanted that beautiful smile directed at me. I felt myself relaxing, letting out a soothing breath, until suddenly the wind was knocked from my lungs and the cracked sidewalk rushed upward, encompassing my vision.

"Whoa, watch where you're going!" I heard some kid say.

"You just came outta nowhere!" another voice sounded into my confusion.

A hand reached out to help me up, and another pair of arms scooped up my books and pressed them into my chest.

"Um, thanks," I said, still a little stunned from the collision.

"Yeah, just be careful next time." Both kids—a boy and girl, probably siblings—were struggling not to laugh.

"But . . . I was just standing here," I objected as they started to walk away. "I wasn't even moving. You ran into *me*." As usual, my words didn't seem to weigh enough to carry sound. The two of them kept walking on ahead, their steps in sync.

I suddenly remembered Josh as I was pulling myself together. He must have boarded a bus or rounded a corner, because he was no longer in sight. I was relieved, though, because the last thing I would have wanted him to witness was me sprawled all over the sidewalk like a squashed bug.

The rest of the walk home was virtually uneventful, save for the tears burning at the backs of my eyeballs. I knew that they had something to do with the pain and embarrassment of being publicly humiliated, the affirmation of my chronic loneliness, or the stinging where my hands had scraped the sidewalk.

Whatever the case was, I didn't want to go to school ever again, but the thought of going home made me ill as well. I compromised by plunking myself on the porch steps of the house that neighbored ours to the south. It was almost identical to our own, but the paint was a much more cheerful bluish color and the tiny lawn was outlined with a prettier, low stone wall made up of irregularly rounded rocks.

I dropped my bag and books alongside me and leaned back on my palms. I wondered what it would be like to live in that house instead of my own—a parallel life, the same, yet different.

I imagined that the wallpaper and paint inside were in better condition, the stairs didn't squeak, and the garage door didn't stick at the midway point between open and closed. I dreamed that if I lived there I would be an only child, adored and fawned over by my parents and spoiled beyond belief.

"Zylia!" a voice called, bursting into my daydream. It was Ivy, standing on our front lawn and waving me over. "Hi! Come see what I made in school today!"

She was so content and cheerful that I couldn't help but smile back at her. I felt guilty as I gathered my belongings and headed toward the house, because I had forgotten to add Ivy somewhere in my daydream. She could have at least been my esteemed maid or something, but I had left her out completely.

Saturday morning, I woke to the sounds of Mace and Bram playing in the yard. I had been sleeping in my bed on the third floor, yet their squeals and laughter were loud enough to float in through the drafty windows and penetrate my dreams.

I felt tired and annoyed as I made my bed and then pulled on a long-sleeved t-shirt, running pants, and heavy socks. I could hear the shower running and Ivy's cheerful humming, so I went downstairs to use my parents' bathroom.

Their bedroom was directly below the one I shared with Ivy, and the door stood ajar. Inside, it was dark and stuffy—at least ten degrees warmer than the rest of the house. Mother had forgotten to shut off the space heater again, so I flipped the dial to off and pushed back the drapes. A dull, gray light shone into the square space.

My parents' room was crowded with oversized furniture much better suited for the master suite on the first floor, but I had always liked the coziness and safety I felt in there. The smell had been the same for as long as I could remember: a mixture of my father's musky cologne and my mother's assortment of lotions and soaps. That scent always reminded me of crawling into bed with them when I was little, after they were already asleep. I would rest soundly for a few peaceful hours and then I would sneak back into my own bed before they could wake and find me there with them.

I used the bathroom quickly and was about to leave the room when I caught sight of the king-sized bed with its rumpled sheets and heavy comforter hanging off the end and dangling on one side. On impulse, I smoothed the sheet over the giant bed and spread the blanket and comforter neatly over the top. I then arranged the pillows just the way I knew my mother liked them and stepped back to view my work.

"Perfect," I said aloud, and then looked around self-consciously, hoping no one had been walking by and heard me talking to myself.

Downstairs, the house was alive with a ruckus that would jangle even the steeliest of nerves. My mother was at the stove, making pancakes and barking orders, while Adonia was sitting at the breakfast table painting her toenails and talking on the phone. Beyond them, in the keeping room, my father had his laptop open on the ottoman while Keane was watching cartoons at an unnecessary decibel.

"Margaret, those boys are going to tear up the porch!" Grandmother was complaining as I entered the room.

"I know, Mom," my own mother sighed, then went on to yell, "*Mace! Bram!* Get *in* here and wash up for breakfast!"

The commotion on the front porch continued nonetheless, so I stuck my head out the front door to see Mace spinning around with a baseball bat while wearing a bandanna over his eyes. Bram was delightedly ducking and dodging his wobbly brother, laughing like a hyena.

"Guys!" I stepped out onto the porch, closing the door behind me. "You're gonna break your face—or the windows, at least. Stop that!"

"Who's there?" Mace asked breathlessly. When he stopped spinning and came to a teetering halt, I noticed that his dark hair was sweaty and askew.

"It's just Zylia," Bram explained in an indifferent voice that seemed to encourage the game to continue.

Mace lifted the bat suddenly, then swung around and connected with his twin brother's ankle. A look of surprise crossed Bram's ruddy face before he careened into my mother's decorative spiral plant stand. Potting cups and planters were sent crashing to the wooden porch planks, soil spilling out in dry, crumbly heaps. A heavy ceramic flowerpot busted wide open, small pieces of it rattling at my feet before landing.

Mace ripped the cloth from his eyes. "Oh no!" he said quietly, his hazel eyes darting around nervously. "Mom's gonna kill us!"

"It's not like she planted anything in those dumb things anyway, right?" Bram reasoned. "I mean, they're just full of dirt."

"But the pot is broken!"

"Yeah, yeah . . ." Bram leaned over and stood the plant stand upright.

I watched them for a few moments as they scooped dirt back into smaller, unbroken pots and put them back into their places. Most people outside of our family couldn't tell my eleven-year-old brothers apart. In fact, sometimes I would catch even my mother or father taking a second or even a third glance just to be sure they knew who they were talking to.

But I, on the other hand, was never confused about who was who when it came to either of them. Maybe it was that part of me that loved to draw, that place in my brain where I kept track of lines and curves and colors. Whatever it was, I was well-aware that Mace appeared heavier by at least five pounds or so, his nose slightly stubbier and his head shape more of an elongated oval than Bram's; Bram's head and face were rounder.

Both boys' eyes were a cloudy hazel, playful and mischievous, but Bram's lashes were thicker and darker like my own. Below the eyes they shared the same thinly contoured lips, but Mace's smile tilted upward and to the left instead of straight-on like his brother.

"Mace, go get the broom from the garage and sweep this up before Mother comes out here," I directed. "I'll be right back. I know where Keane keeps his modeling glue."

I slipped back inside, unnoticed by the rest of the family; I swiped the super glue from Keane's desk and was back on the porch in a flash.

I was breathing heavily as I squatted down. Together with the twins, I did my best to paste the flowerpot back together. There was one large chip that we couldn't find, but we turned the vase to conceal the damaged portion and had just swept up the black remnants of soil when the front door flung wide open.

"What is going on out here? Get inside for breakfast *now*." My mother's voice was low and strained, her green eyes narrowed.

The three of us avoided glancing in the direction of my mother's plant stand as we marched back inside the house.

Breakfast passed loudly with too much bickering, whining, and dish-clanking. Mother was barking orders about chores and homework while my siblings were all doing their best to be heard over each other.

The worst was Adonia. She was arguing about spending the day with her friends, even though she hadn't made her bed, taken out the trash, or finished her homework. She sat across from me at the table, gazing into a tiny round compact mirror at her makeup-coated features.

I watched her, entranced, as she blinked her thick black lashes, clumpy with mascara. Her skin was smooth, creamy, and without blemish. Her eyes were green like mine and striking in an altogether different way. If mine could be described as mysterious and soulful, then hers were flashy, sociable, and deceptively naive.

"I don't have time," Adonia said through glossy pink lips. "I promise I'll do it when I get home."

Ivy joined the table late, smelling soapy and fresh, instantly rolling her eyes when she heard what was going on. She disliked drama, disorder, or any sort of ruffle in her daily routine. She was the youngest of us all, yet probably the most mature.

"Not acceptable!" Mother shouted as she was piling dishes in the sink. Mace and Bram must have been feeling guilty about the vase, because they were helping her load the dishwasher without a single complaint.

Adonia flung her long, wavy hair over her shoulder and snapped her compact shut. "I gotta get dressed. Leah's coming to pick me up any second." She flounced out of the kitchen with an audacious air that I could never imagine having the guts to imitate.

"You'd better get dressed fast, then," my mother was hollering up the stairs as Adonia's footsteps receded overhead, "because you're not leaving until your chores are done!"

A knot was growing in my stomach. It always began as this wiggly feeling when tensions were high in the house, but it grew into a heavy lump once voices were raised.

Mother let out a frenzied sigh and stomped back to the kitchen. The twins scattered, and Ivy busied herself wiping down the countertops. My father and Keane were hastily finishing their pancakes and eggs.

Grandmother spoke up from one end of the table. "That girl's a spoiled brat."

My mother stiffened and said curtly, "Thank you for reminding me. I could always use a confirmation of my awful parenting skills." I thought her eyes looked a little teary, and she went upstairs without a further word.

My mother was frequently emotional, but it always sent a stab of pain right into my gut when I saw her that way. Since the knot was already there, I suddenly felt queasy. I looked around, hoping Grandmother would say something apologetic before my poor mother was out of earshot or that my father could at least mutter something comforting, but no one said a single thing.

Just then, when everything was quiet, the doorbell rang. I hesitated to move, and my father was first to walk into the hall and invite Adonia's friend Leah into the house.

"Oh, hello, there," my father said jovially. "Adonia isn't quite ready; would you guys mind hanging out for a few minutes?"

It should have crossed my mind that there was not just a lone visitor on the porch after my father's plural comment, yet I was still surprised as I saw multiple young people filing into the hallway. First there was Leah, a bleached-blonde beauty who had just turned eighteen, followed by a pretty, vaguely familiar-looking dark-haired girl. I could tell there was someone else with them, but my view was obstructed by the open door.

"And who do we have here?" My father was offering his hand in introduction.

Leah had a soft, squeaky voice that reminded me of the stereotypical popular girl. "Oh, this is my friend Jenny Pierceton and her little brother, Josh. They're tagging along with us today."

My heart stopped and I was sure that in my own house worlds were colliding. Realization dawned on me slowly as I heard his voice say, "Hello; nice to meet you, Mr. Moss." It sounded different than it did at school: a formal falsetto, with a crackly quality creeping in randomly amongst the syllables.

"What a polite young man you are, Josh; but around here, I'm just Phillip." I cringed at my father's embarrassing lilt. He tended to give his words a little twang when he was trying to be funny or interesting.

How had it happened that my ultimate crush was standing in the front hall of my own home? I hadn't even known that Adonia was aware of the Pierceton family's existence, let alone had befriended them!

It made sense, though. Jenny would have been in or around Adonia's grade, and pretty people had a way of finding each other. I hadn't ever gotten a close look at Josh's sister until now. She had the same dark hair as his, but hers was worn long and straight. Her almond-shaped eyes were similar as well, featuring her northeast Asian descent that I knew had come from her mother. Once I had overheard Josh telling someone that his mother was originally from Seoul and that they were planning a trip to visit some of his relatives. After that, I started researching Korea and developed a fondness for the bright culture, entertainment, and yummy-looking food that was so different from what I knew.

My father was closing the door, and in a moment of throat-tightening horror I stiffened, knowing I was standing just a few steps away, perfectly visible.

"The living room is just over here," said my father.

*Good, Daddy, **good**!* I thought. He was leading them the opposite direction. No one even so much as glanced my way. I caught sight of the back of Josh's hair; it was purposefully disheveled and glossy-looking from whatever product he had used. I noted that he was wearing the same jacket from the day before, and it looked even better on him up close. I tried to memorize the Korean symbols along the arms so I could look up what they meant later. I got a little distracted just before he disappeared around the corner, because I couldn't help but hope that Mace and Bram hadn't left an awful mess in there.

"Why don't you kids just have a seat? I'll see if I can find out what's holding Adonia up," I could hear my father saying. As he turned from the doorway just before he headed up the stairs, I saw the hospitable smile droop away ever so slightly. He was probably bracing himself for the public battle that my eldest sister and mother were sure to engage in.

What would I do if Josh became witness to some domestic display of turbulent mutiny? If Adonia and my mother flew into a rage, Josh would surely stay as far away from our crazy family as he could. I couldn't imagine life being worth living after a scene like that.

"Do I have visitors calling?"

I jumped, startled because I hadn't heard my grandmother leave her spot at the table and creep up alongside me in the hallway. "No, Grandmother; it's just Adonia's friends."

She turned to me with rheumy eyes and wobbled a bit, which always made me worry that she would fall. "My mother didn't tell me we were having company. I should put on my Sunday dress. You know, the pretty one with the blue trim?"

I thought things were heading in the direction of bad, but adding my delirious grandmother into the mix would make them way worse. "Yes, yes! That's a wonderful idea." I was guiding her back through the kitchen, my whispering words holding a slightly hysterical tone. "You really should get ready!" I knew mother would have never left her alone when she was in a confused state, but for heaven's sake, *Josh Pierceton* was in my living room!

I stopped short when I noticed the jam-packed garbage bin, but thankfully my grandmother kept shuffling off to her room. It only took me forty seconds to smash the contents deeper into the bag, tie it up, and heave it out the back door and into the dumpster. I dashed back and spent another fifteen seconds struggling to quietly open the fresh plastic liner that was glued shut by static electricity.

"Why do you do that, Zy?" Ivy asked me rhetorically when she caught sight of me trying frantically to finish our older sister's chore. She rolled her eyes and walked off as if she were disappointed in my goodwill.

I was breathing heavily when Adonia came prancing down the stairs with Mother hot on her heels.

I retreated to the keeping room, where I could still see what was going on while trying to stay out of the way and remain safely invisible. I caught sight of my reflection in a decorative mirror that hung alongside the fireplace and felt rather distressed. There was no way I wanted to chance Josh seeing me in my dreadful outfit and unkempt hair. I hadn't even brushed my teeth, and there was an oily sheen glistening along my nose and brow.

"Don't do this to me now!" Adonia was whispering loudly to our mother in the kitchen. "I barely even have any homework and I have all weekend to finish it!"

"I'm tired of your attitude, young lady. You have no appreciation for what your father and I do around here. All I ask of you is a simple . . ." Both my mother's eyes and Adonia's met the empty trash bin at the same moment.

"See there; I've done my chores." Adonia's expression was one of triumph as she gestured toward the bin. "I made my bed when I was upstairs. All I have left is the homework and I promise I'll do it tonight."

Grandmother emerged from her bedroom wearing one of her dresses that she used to reserve for Wednesday brunches with her sewing club. The polyester fabric hung away from her ever-shrinking frame, sliding off her shoulder on one side. "All right, then," she was saying over and over quietly as she made her way to the kitchen.

My mother's irate face morphed into the appearance of exhaustion and defeat as she caught sight of my grandmother. "Oh, Mom, what are you wearing? You're not even zipped up in the back." She was rushing to her aid, gingerly guiding her back to her bedroom.

"I'll see you tonight, Mom!" chirped Adonia, who seemed delighted that the attention had shifted away from her own disobedience.

"Not too late," my mother called over her shoulder. I think she had meant to sound stern, but the power seemed to have drained from her words. I watched her help Grandmother back into her bedroom and felt a pang of sympathy. I wondered if Adonia would ever be willing to help Mother like that someday. I didn't want to doubt it, but I did.

I had been distracted with my thoughts for a few moments, and suddenly I was stirred by the sounds of Adonia and her guests gathering in the hallway. I went back into the kitchen and stealthily inched closer to the wide passage that opened to the hall near the entryway. Even though it was desperate, I wanted to catch one last fanciful glimpse of Josh. I positioned myself in front of the big, ancient china cabinet that was along that same wall and peered around it with one eye.

"Make sure to drive safely," my father was cautioning Leah in the hallway. "I'd like my gal back in one piece."

Adonia rolled her eyes and made a perturbed clicking sound with her tongue, and I really couldn't blame her. The humiliating lilt was back in my father's voice. "Bye, Dad." She opened the door, and since they all had their backs turned in preparation of leaving, I felt it was safe to tilt my head and ogle the back of Josh's shiny hair with both eyes. He was stepping toward the doorway, his hands jammed into the pockets of an attractively snug pair of jeans.

"Oh, wait; I forgot my purse. I'll be just a sec." Adonia raced up the stairs, and the group lingered in the doorway.

I didn't have the time or cooperative motor skills to react before Josh had glanced into the kitchen and was looking my way. I jerked my head back, safely behind the cabinet, and dropped my gaze to the tile floor. I counted to three to calm myself while staring intently and mentally willing myself unseen.

"Oh, hey, I know you!" It was Josh's brilliant voice and he was standing in the entryway to the kitchen, speaking in my direction.

Oh, God. What should I do? What should I say? Can I pretend that I didn't hear? I started fiddling nervously with the sleeve of my shirt, subconsciously realizing there was an old mustard stain near the wrist.

"I mean, who could forget you, after all?" Josh went on, a little laugh in his voice. "You're the sixth grader who somehow managed to lock yourself in the office and take control of the intercom for what, like, ten minutes?"

In my enamored fog I hadn't noticed Bram standing near me. He spoke up with a grin, "Actually, that was Mace. I was the one who distracted the office staff long enough for him to get in, though. I should have won an award for the best fake seizure ever."

Josh was laughing melodiously now. "Oh, right, the twin team. You guys are awesome! Your brother's impression of Principal Gerard was perfect; I mean, spot-on perfect."

I didn't move, afraid that my veil of invisibility would fail and saddened that it was so effective.

My father peeked his head and shoulders into the room, trying not to smile. "Don't encourage them, please. I deal with so many parent-teacher conferences regarding those two that it could be a full-time job!" He was laughing, even though his words hadn't been nearly as amusing as he had probably thought they were. He ushered the group out the door, adding in a few more words of caution. Josh waved at Bram and joined the rest of them, never even noticing I was there.

My mother came back into the kitchen, looking tired and cheerless. "Mom's having one of her bad days," she explained. "I hope she sleeps for a while."

Father came over, kissed her on top of her head, and gave her shoulders a quick squeeze. He didn't say anything as he moved around her, his hand lingering between her shoulder blades before moving to the coffee pot and refilling his mug.

My mother let out a de-escalating sigh and smiled fondly at my father. "What would I do without you to keep me sane?"

My father was sipping his coffee and scrutinizing some mail that was lying on the countertop. "You'd be fine; better off, even," he answered teasingly as he always did when my mother made such comments.

"Oh, by the way, thanks for making the bed, darling. That was sweet and unexpected." She looked as if her spirits had lifted some as she began searching the kitchen with her eyes.

"Mmm-hmm," answered my father distractedly, still peering at some document while inadvertently taking credit for my deed.

"Where did I leave . . .?" Mother mumbled, looking all around.

On the china cabinet directly in front of me sat a paperback book; the cover was devoted to a long-haired man with a muscly, bare back and alarmingly tight jeans. He was looking at me over his shoulder with a cocky gaze. In his arms he held a beautiful woman with narrowed, lusty eyes whose blonde hair was flowing the wind.

I had the sudden urge to punch that fictional man in the face, but there were people around so I simply picked up the book and held it out toward my mother.

"Oh, there it is!" she exclaimed as if she were the one who had made the discovery.

I felt a gloomy cloud settle over me as I checked for my shadow in the stainless-steel refrigerator, just to make sure I was still there.

Chapter Four

Saturday seemed to drone on like some thick, bland book: tedious, uneventful, and markedly annoying. I wasted most of it replaying how I had seen Josh earlier, but imagining different scenarios where I spoke up and started intense conversations that made his brow furrow. Sometimes I'd throw in a spunky joke that would make his imaginary version fold over in laughter.

The house was so loud and alive that it was breaking into my thoughts. I found myself retreating, shrinking away to my safe spaces and alcoves that I had nestled into over the years.

My little hideouts were all over the big house, and some of the spots weren't even hiding places at all. In the dining room I had what was more of a *perch* in the built-in cabinetry that stretched along the back wall. There I seemed to magically blend in with the surroundings. The combination of open shelving and pull-out drawers below them stretched from floor to ceiling and were coated in a dark varnish. Near the center of the built-in display shelving was a long counter of polished wood. The surface divided the shelving from the drawers below it and was used as a buffet top.

Every drawer, shelf, and all counter space in and on that giant piece of furniture was crammed and stacked to the brim with decades of cutlery, clutter, and dust. It was so visually busy that no one ever seemed to notice when I would climb up on the broad buffet counter and squeeze my narrow hips in between the blue-tinted glass bowl filled with fake lemons and the giant porcelain turkey. From there I could slide back a little into the center square of the shelving unit, the only recess that was tall enough to accommodate my seated height. It was a bit quieter there; the television and voices were dulled and absorbed by the expanse of wood. Yet they were not so muffled and far away that I didn't know what was going on in nearby areas of the house.

From my roost I could gaze out over the whole dining room and just beyond, into the breakfast area of the kitchen. The kitchen itself was blocked from my view by a divider wall that my mother dreamed of having removed but that my father called "load-bearing" and therefore it had stayed. My mother had accepted the fact that it was permanent and had since devoted that side of the length of wall to her children's school photos.

I always took my time staring at the pictures, looking over them again and again as if I were viewing them for the first time. There was a series of them for each child, starting with Adonia, who had the longest line. Below hers, the rest of us had our own rows of mismatched frames hanging in almost straight lines along the makeshift gallery wall. It was interesting to see how my siblings and I had morphed over the years into what we were today. It was more fascinating still to imagine the lines of pictures extending farther down the wall and into the future.

My photos started with my sullen five-year-old self in braids that were accented with big, obnoxious bows. I always cringed and tipped my head to the side whenever I saw it, mirroring the expression I display in the portrait itself. My row of pictures ended with the one from this year that my mother had just recently put up. It wasn't very flattering the way my shoulders were hunched slightly down and inward as if I were trying to hide inside myself. My hair, however, had been sleek and shiny that day, and I had even managed not to blink. The smile wasn't quite right, though. It was just a tiny curve of my mouth looking forced and solemn.

It was no wonder I hadn't been able to feign a bit of mirth for the sake of one immortalized moment in time, with all my jeering peers hovering in line behind the photographer.

I could still hear them laughing as they coached me to smile or stick out my tongue or say *cheese*. There were so many of them, all staring right at me. I could feel their eyes like needles on my skin. The more they spoke, prodded, and taunted, the more I felt my features hardening to stone.

The photographer joined in at one point, "Give us a good smile for all your friends here." He was a small man with sparkling white teeth who obviously knew nothing about the difference between teasing and encouragement.

Friends? I couldn't find one face in the lineup whom I would have labeled as such. It was that thought that had struck me as tragically funny. That thought had bent my stoic face into that tiny, forlorn smile.

I gazed at those familiar pictures and wondered what my mother would do when she ran out of space along that particular wall. I was envisioning the frames branching out like vines climbing upward, outward and downward, being attached to the ceiling and fanning out over the carpet like an infestation. During this daydream I suddenly detected movement in my peripheral vision.

"Hmm," Grandmother was mumbling as she shuffled into the room. She was no longer wearing a dress, but was more appropriately clothed in cotton slacks and a flesh-toned turtleneck with a thick sweatshirt pulled over the top. Despite her warm attire she was holding tightly to a fleece blanket, wrapping it snugly around her shoulders.

I was a little surprised to see her there. The dining room was usually an isolated area of the house, only inhabited on special occasions. It wasn't even used as a pass-through very often since it was set off to the side of the other main rooms.

Grandmother worked to pull out one of the heavy dining chairs. It hadn't been moved in quite some time, so the legs were deeply planted into the thickly woven rug below. I felt guilty watching her struggling with it for a few moments but I was afraid to move down and help her lest she happen to see me and ruin my secret spot. Finally, she sat down and produced her latest crochet project from somewhere beneath the fleece blanket.

I watched her for a few minutes as she steadily worked with a pale blue yarn, her knobby hands moving with precision and familiarity. I had no idea what she was making. Her projects lay all over the house, from mittens and scarves to doilies and cozies. Even our television remote was bundled in its own orange-and-green cover. Some of the yarn had become fuzzy and worn, obstructing the pressing of several different buttons. It was annoying, but no one wanted to hurt Grandmother's feelings by removing it.

"Oh, there you are, Mother," said my own mother.

"Margaret?" Grandmother craned her neck to see who had entered the room.

I must admit that sometimes when I heard my mother's name spoken I had to stop and wonder who this Margaret person was. Her name was Mother to me, and it was hard to accept that there was a time in her life when her children hadn't existed and she had been only my grandmother's daughter.

"What are you working on?" My mother placed her hands on Grandmother's shoulders and peered at the yarn in her hands.

"I'm making a shawl for Angelica."

Mother sighed and a heartbroken look came into her eyes. "Angelica has been gone for years, Mother."

A wave of guilt rippled over me as I eavesdropped on this private moment. If my mother were to turn her face sideways, I would be in her line of sight. I imagined trying to explain what I was doing up there, wedged between the bric-a-brac, but every excuse I invented sounded awkward and phony even in my own head.

"No, Angelica lives upstairs with Ivy," Grandmother argued, sounding a little perturbed.

Mother furrowed her brow and I was pretty sure I knew why. Grandmother wasn't known to mix the past with the present, even when she was completely unaware of the current day and age. Usually she'd get caught up in some time or event from earlier in her life, reliving it and acting it out like she was walking about in a dream. But in those times, she'd imagine that we were people from her past, if she even saw us at all. The different periods would never overlap, so I could understand the concern registering in my mother's face. I hoped this didn't mean that Grandmother's illness was getting worse.

"Mother, Angelica was your sister. I think you're confusing her with Zylia. Your granddaughters share a room, remember? Zylia and Ivy."

My ears perked up at the mention of my name. The longer I waited, listening in on the private conversation, the more shameful I felt it would be if I were to be noticed. I held my breath, fearing discovery more than ever.

Grandmother went on undeterred, her hands moving the crochet hooks over her lap. "Angelica is so quiet and strange. She needs friends."

My mother moved to the side of the chair and tilted her head in thought. I could only see her profile now, but she appeared puzzled. "Didn't Angelica have many friends?"

"You see her every day; you should know! Of course, the girl has no one." Grandmother looked surprised. "The way she slinks about this house as if she's not part of anything; it's not natural for a young, healthy girl."

"Mother, how about we watch some TV? Doesn't that sound nice? Maybe we could even get Phillip to light a cozy little fire. It's cool enough for one now, I bet. What do you think?"

"If that girl's not careful, she'll fade away, right into the wallpaper. Blend in just the way that . . . where is Angelica?"

Mother sighed, said something under her breath, and forced a smile on her face. I could tell she was hurting and it made me feel a sudden, hollow ache. I watched her walk out of the room and wished I could reach out to her. I didn't even move, just waited in the silence watching my grandmother's busy hands while wondering idly about the old woman's sister.

Grandmother looked up just then, staring right into my face with those unblinking, birdlike eyes, and said, "Angelica, is that you?"

I tried to answer her, but my mouth wouldn't even open. Besides, what would I have said if my voice were to have worked?

"Answer me, *you*. Why are you always hiding from me?" She was peering so intently that the beam of her vision was surely searing my skin.

The feeling of being watched had always been a phobia of mine, the curse of someone who is used to being invisible. Icy terror washed over me, although I wasn't sure why. I was only sitting in the cabinetry, but if I hadn't known any better, it felt like I was being caught in the act of murder, knowing my punishment would be the end of my freedom and life.

I heard my mother's voice, fainter now, calling from the keeping room, "Your program's on. You know, the one with that detective you love? Hurry; it's just beginning."

And then, as if waking from a trance, Grandmother broke her fiery stare, gathered up her blanket and crochet paraphernalia, and worked herself into a standing position. She didn't bother pushing the heavy dining chair in; she just started off out of the room, her house-slippered feet making short, sliding strides like a preschooler shuffling on plastic training skates. She gave a lingering glance over her shoulder just once, looking as if she may have forgotten something, and I thought her gaze must have clamped on mine for a split second. She didn't wait around after that, but just left the room in her slow, rickety way.

I held my breath until she was completely out of sight, then waited a few more seconds before sliding off the buffet top and slipping out into the front hall. It wasn't until my feet were on the floor that I realized I was shaking.

I looked down at my pale, trembling hands and wondered what had spooked me the most about my grandmother. Was it the possibility that she was aware of my dining room hiding spot or that her description of her sister held an eerie likeness to myself? Or had she meant *me* instead of her after all? I was so confused. I wondered if this was how my grandmother felt all the time, muddled and baffled.

I slowly took the stairs up toward the third floor, thinking about my grandmother's sister—my great-aunt. I had never really heard that much about her, just that she had died young. I couldn't remember anything else at all concerning her.

When I got up to my room, Ivy was leaning back in her bed with her nose in a book that looked too thick and mature for her to be reading. On the cover, a large, bloody hand was reaching out, grasping for something in black space. I took two steps inside the doorway and she jolted upright.

"You scared the heck outta me!" she breathed, clutching the book against her chest.

"Maybe it's the book. You sure you should be reading that thing?"

Ivy narrowed her eyes. "Don't sound like *Mother*. I'm tired of all the baby books they make me read in school. I found this in Adonia's room. She said I could read it, so don't you go telling on me." Then Ivy laughed and rolled her eyes. "I'm sorry. I know you won't. You barely even talk to anyone, so of course my secret's safe with you."

I went over to my dresser and began looking through my clothes. I figured I would take a shower, so I would be squeaky clean when Adonia came back. If I were to see Josh Pierceton again today, I would be ready this time. Not that I wanted to look all done up; that would be trying too hard. I was hoping to look fresh and neat, my hair a touch tousled so it wouldn't be too obvious. Clearly, I was putting a lot of thought into making it look like I hadn't thought about it at all, and this was frustrating my sensibilities.

"You can read it after me if you want. I don't even think Adonia read it," Ivy went on. "I mean I've never *seen* her read anything unless it was assigned to her."

I picked through my t-shirts and lounging pants until I found a duo that matched well enough. "Okay. I'll probably read it," I mumbled, but I really wasn't thinking about the book at all.

Ivy was engrossed in the story again. I wondered how she could focus on the words with her face so close to the pages.

I left the room, went into the bathroom, and closed the door, alone with my dismal reflection. I felt a chill as I dropped my clothing in a pile on the tiled floor. I caught sight of my pale, bony flesh and just one glimpse of me was horribly depressing. I averted my eyes quickly, looking out the window instead, and that's when I saw the faint orange illumination coming from the house next door.

All the homes on my street were cookie-cutter replicas of one another, built tall and thin, each standing closely to the next. The floor plans were mirror images that alternated up and down the entire length of the road. That's how I knew that the light I saw would have been coming from the same third-story bathroom I was in now, but in the neighboring home.

The neighbor's house had been empty for so long, I didn't usually bother with the frustrating, tangled blinds over our bathroom window. But now that I'd seen the light, I began fiddling with the old strings, trying to get them to lower.

The more I thought about it, I wondered when the new occupants had arrived. I hadn't noticed a moving van, the removal of the "for sale" sign, or any hint of life whatsoever.

Could a real estate agent have turned it on? I wondered. Maybe the house had been shown earlier that day and it had been left on by mistake. But even as I thought up alternative reasons for the tiny, orange glow, I saw a distorted black figure flitter by. Whoever it was had passed by the window so quickly I thought I might have imagined it. But then the silhouette was moving by again and paused in its fluid motion to gaze through the window. I could make out a darkened face, close against the window pane, just before the form backed away and disappeared out of sight.

My focus changed, honing in on the reflection of myself in the long window, bright against the darkness behind the glass. It was then I became acutely aware that I was standing completely nude in a well-lit room and that someone had seen every inch of me from the knees up.

I panicked and dropped to the cold tile floor. I crawled on my elbows to the other side of the room, staying as low as I could manage, then reached up and shut off the light switch. The ensuing darkness was not as comforting as I had hoped it would be, the hazy green night-light near the sink shining like a beacon while my heart pounded in my chest. I redressed as quickly as I could, blindly pulling my clothes on from my spot on the floor.

I exited the bathroom as fast as I could, nearly scaring the wits out of Ivy once again as I burst back into our bedroom.

"Whoa! What's your deal?" she was asking as I peeked through the blinds in our room, trying to get a different view of the house next door.

I paced around for a moment without answering her.

Ivy complained, "Zylia! I can't read with you doing that. Can you . . ." But I wasn't listening, and before I knew it I was at the stairs, bounding down as fast as I could.

I wanted to find out just who had moved in next door so quickly and secretively. I felt wronged that my privacy had been invaded, even though I was pretty sure it had been mostly my own fault. In that moment I was so empowered by my anger that I was ready to walk right up to the neighbor's door, wait for that anonymous creep to answer, and accuse him of being a disgusting pervert.

My plans changed when I reached the last landing and saw my father opening the front door. "I was worried you kids were going to break curfew," he was saying, "but what a pleasant surprise! How was your movie?"

I froze. The group filed in, their features all animated with smiles and interest as they spoke of the action-packed production. I was immediately jealous but I didn't have time to register the emotion. One glance upward from any of them and they would see me and my frightened, haggard appearance.

I stepped back slowly toward the squat bay window nestled at the back of the landing. It was draped with thick, heavy curtains; as soon as I climbed into the seat, I was enveloped and absorbed into my surroundings like a chameleon.

I poked my face out of the curtains and watched from that spot as the social scene of goodbyes unfolded just out of my reach. I kept my eyes on Josh for as long as I could. He looked the same, except his hair was a little flatter against his skull, as if his gel or mousse had given out at some point during the outing.

I imagined him looking up at me to tell me goodnight with a dreamy smolder in his eyes. Instead he said, "See ya, Mr. Moss," and quickly departed.

Adonia was on her cell phone as she flounced upstairs, chatting away at an unbelievable speed. When she was pivoting on the landing, just before heading up the next flight, her face was a mere eight inches from mine and her hair grazed my cheek as she passed.

She didn't even notice me.

Chapter Five

Overnight, a blustery wind had kicked up; I was awakened by its howling against my bedroom window. The moment I opened my eyes I was wide awake, even though I knew it was too ridiculously early to be getting out of bed on a weekend.

There were no sounds from the floors below, the house calm and frigid. I sat up in my dark bedroom, flipping on the lamp next to me. Ivy groaned across from me in her bed, covering her face with an arm. She muttered a few indiscernible words—fragments of dream dialogue—before resuming her shallow, rhythmic breaths.

It was five a.m., and my mind was already darting about with questions, worries, and thoughts. I was wondering about my grandmother's sister, about the inner workings of Josh Pierceton, and most of all about this anonymous person who may have had a spotlight view of my naked body.

I wished that Ivy was awake so I could talk to her, but she would only be cranky and furious if I woke her at that time of the morning. Instead, I got up and dressed early, slinking about my room in the darkness. I didn't want to turn on the light in case I should either wake Ivy or draw attention from that mysterious person next door.

I poked my head behind the curtains a couple times to see if anything was stirring in that house that mirrored mine, but it was dark and still, without any signs of life. I was starting to get the feeling that I had invented the new inhabitant with my imagination.

I puttered around for what felt like ages, killing time by thinking while playing with a hair tie. I busied myself for as long as I could stand before I started making noises that were intentionally too loud. First, I coughed like I was hacking up some giant hairball, then I pretended to trip over a stack of books while calling out *"Oww!"* very loudly. It wasn't until I began clicking my tongue persistently that Ivy bolted upright and yelled, "*What* is *wrong* with you?"

I cringed, hating for anyone to be mad at me, especially Ivy. "Sorry, was I too loud?"

Ivy rolled her eyes and swung her dainty legs off the side of the bed. "Give me a break. What do you want to tell me? It's obviously something. You're a *terrible* actress, by the way."

The last part hurt a little; although the coughing may have been a bit over the top, I had thought my yelp of pain was quite convincing. I cut to the chase. "Have you noticed that anyone's moved in next door?"

Ivy's tired expression went black. "That's what you had to say to me at seven a.m. on a Sunday morning?"

"Is it only seven? I feel like I've been awake for a lifetime. I'm sorry, I just . . ." I suddenly felt too shy to tell her that someone in that house had spied a glimpse of my naked body. "Have you seen anybody over there or not?"

Ivy rubbed her eyes and stretched her arms over her head. "I don't know; it's not like I've paid attention. Why do you care so much, anyway?"

Why did I care? I repeated the question over again, letting it bounce off my skull. I guess I wanted to at least see the face of the person who had seen so much *more* of me. It only seemed fair. But even then, I knew that an intrigue was growing within me that went far beyond reasonableness.

I had been thinking to myself for so long, Ivy gave up on getting a response to her question and left the room to shut herself in the bathroom.

By that point, I had been awake long enough that my stomach was beginning to growl. I knew that breakfast would be a while yet, so I figured I could scavenge up something for myself down in the kitchen. Every window I passed on my descent provided me a different view of the neighbor's house, but still no clue as to who might be inside.

I was quiet as I made the trek downstairs, trying not to squeak the floorboards too much as I walked. I didn't want the whole family angry with me.

The kitchen was dim and shadowy. I left the refrigerator door hanging open while I fixed myself a bowl of Kix by the illumination of the interior light. It seemed even darker once I had shut the door and was standing alone chewing the slightly stale cereal.

I used my foot to carefully sweep the area ahead of me while my eyes were readjusting to the low light. Eventually I found the table and plopped myself down.

I was halfway through my Kix when I heard the breathing. At first, I thought I had been sleepless so long that I'd become delusional, but when I stopped chewing I detected distinct inhaling and exhaling from across the table. It was then that I became aware of a shadowy figure at the end of the table.

"Who's there?" I wasn't sure why my heart was pounding with fear or why my voice shook as I asked the question.

"You know me, Angelica. Don't be silly."

I knew it was my grandmother's voice, but I still plowed recklessly through the darkness and fumbled for the light switches. The light seared my eyes, but I kept them wide open so I could see my grandmother sitting in her robe and slippers looking harmless and benign.

For some reason I was still afraid.

"What is it, Angelica? What's bothering you? Come closer."

I didn't move.

"I'm sorry I didn't listen to you when you told me you were leaving. I didn't believe you when you said you saw the shadow. You have to understand." Grandmother was getting emotional now, tears coming to her eyes. She looked so small and withered, but I was absolutely terrified of her at that moment.

"I'm not Angelica," I whispered.

"How can you blame me? How could I have known you would disappear?"

"Disappear?" My voice was still a tiny whisper. I was trembling, yet curious to see where this was going. "How did I disappear?"

"It happened so fast. The rest of them were wrong about what happened to you, but I knew the truth. I knew that you . . ."

"Hey, is everything ok?" I hadn't heard Mother come down the stairs, but there she was in her sweats, speaking through a yawn. "You two are up early!"

And just like that, my grandmother was transported back to the present. "I was thinking waffles sound good for breakfast. What do you think, Margaret, dear?"

"Sounds delicious," chirped Mother in a sleepy voice.

To keep my eyes away from my grandmother, I watched my mother move around the kitchen, mixing ingredients and heating up the waffle iron. She kept pushing her golden hair behind her ears and yawning.

Before I was asked, I jumped to action and began setting the table. I made accidental eye contact with Grandmother exactly three times and each time I could swear I saw a clandestine twinkling in her birdlike gaze. It was a secret message aimed directly at me, I was sure.

"What a gloomy day outside," Mother said, pulling open the black-and-white café curtains that covered the window above the sink. "I think I heard that it may snow by this evening. I better get the grocery shopping done early."

Every other Sunday, like clockwork, my mother made a trip to the nearest discount club and stocked up on food and toiletries in bulk sizes. Oftentimes, I would go with her and help her load the cart. None of my siblings ever cared to go, but I took a secret delight in scavenging around in that giant concrete and metal store.

"Mother, do you think anyone has moved in next door?"

"Hmm? Oh, next door?" She was gazing out the window as she rinsed flour from her hands. "I don't know, honey. Have you seen anyone?"

"What? No, not me. Nobody's seen me. I mean . . . I haven't seen anyone." I was tripping over my words and my grandmother was narrowing her eyes toward me.

I was relieved when my father entered the room. "Mmm, smells good in here. Has anyone gotten the paper?" He ruffled my hair with his large hand. Weeked mornings usually put him in a good mood.

"I'll get it." I was dressed anyway and needed escape. I swiped a coat from the rack in the hall and jogged to the front yard, where I found the Sunday paper covered in a damp, bright blue plastic wrap.

Small flurries were making their way down from the gray dome overhead. I was getting quite chilled, so I turned to go in, and that's when I noticed that the neighboring home's "for sale" sign had been removed. So, it was true—someone must have been occupying that house.

I froze in my tracks, feeling somehow exposed to the darkened windows like so many eyes staring back at me. I tried not to move too quickly lest someone watching think I was afraid.

I fiddled with the paper nonchalantly and strolled up to the porch leisurely, hoping my acting skills had improved since my big fiasco with Ivy.

Once I was inside our covered front porch and safely out of view, I bolted indoors and rubbed my arms and shoulders until I stopped the shivering that was based more on my anxiety than my temperature.

"The realtor sign is gone," I announced as I reentered the kitchen and handed Father the paper.

"What sign?" he mumbled over the top of his coffee mug.

"Oh, you mean next door? Hmmm," Mother said, doing a terrible job at sounding interested. She changed the subject, and just when I was trying to bring it up again, Ivy came downstairs. I knew she would think I was obsessed or something, so I decided to hush up for the time being.

I hung up my coat and suffered through breakfast in silence. Mace joined the table when I was almost finished; I had heard Keane yelling at Bram from upstairs, so the household was finally coming alive.

Mother dismissed herself, saying she was getting ready to go shopping and that anyone who wanted to go with her needed to be ready in thirty minutes. I knew I was the only one who wanted to go, and I think she did too, but she always left the offer open to all of us.

Since I was already dressed and ready, I had thirty minutes to kill, so I made my way up to Keane's room on the second floor. I wanted to ask him if he knew anything about our new neighbors, but his door was shut and he didn't answer my knock.

I did notice that the door to the bedroom that Mace and Bram shared was standing ajar, and inside Bram was tossing a small rubber light-up ball against the wall.

"Hey," I said, poking my head inside the room. The laundry basket just inside the door was overflowing and the whole area smelled of that peculiar, stuffy "boy" smell.

"Yeah?"

"Oh, um, just wondering if you've caught a glimpse of anyone, possibly, moving in next door. Just curious." I felt so stupid all over again.

Bram was using up far too much concentration on that ridiculous ball. He was now bouncing it from the floor to the wall and catching it mid-air. "What?"

"Next door. Have you seen anyone move in?"

I counted the rubbery-sounding bounces of each impact and I got to six before he finally answered, "Nope."

Someone must have seen something, I thought as I ascended the stairs to the top floor. People were in and out of our house at all times of the day. It seemed impossible that my whole family was completely blind and unobservant.

Upstairs, I heard a sniffling that made me pause. It was coming from Adonia's room. I felt that familiar plummeting feeling in my stomach that was becoming a part of the jittery, stressed-out person I was developing into. I didn't know how to be consoling, but I did my best at making my voice sound kind and clear as I called through my sister's door, "Are you coming down for breakfast?"

The sniffling ceased instantly and a slightly delayed answer followed, "Um . . . no. Not hungry. Did Mother send you to get me?"

"No . . ."

"Well, good, because I'm sick of her forcing calories down my throat every second of the day!" Adonia's sadness seemed instantly replaced with anger.

"I never noticed . . . does she really?" I'd heard my mother and Adonia arguing about food before, but it had never reached my consciousness until that moment.

The door swung open, and Adonia stood with one hand braced against it and the other resting irritably on her jutting hip. She was wearing what I called her "cute girl" pajamas, which consisted of a tight white camisole that accentuated her ample breasts and a pair of tiny cotton shorts that rested so low below her navel that just glancing at them would compel me to pull my own pants up.

"You've never *noticed*?" Her eyes were puffy and red and her hair was swept back into a ponytail. I could tell she was mad, and chances were her fury would be directed at me since I was conveniently located.

"Well, now that you mention it . . ."

"Every *single* day it's all I hear." Her voice went up in a mimicking falsetto as she said, "Adonia, eat this, eat that; you're not anorexic, are you? Why haven't you touched your food . . . and on and on and *on*!" She looked me up and down suddenly and added, "We aren't all like *you*, you know. Not all of us got mom's glorious skinny gene. Some of us have to actually work on it. It's totally unfair!"

I was flabbergasted. My beautiful, voluptuous, movie-star-ready sister was jealous of my twiggy, flat-chested body?! It didn't add up in my mind. I wasn't sure how, but I knew that nothing I said to her would matter. I wouldn't be able to convince her with my words that she was attractive—stunning, even. So instead I asked, "Since when is it so important to you to be skinny?"

Adonia turned and walked back into her room and flopped down on the edge of her full-size bed. Somehow her body language had invited me to follow her. Her room was cluttered and colorful, and I was almost never allowed inside. I moved a pile of clothing to park myself on a hot-pink butterfly chair. I tried to sit comfortably, without looking awkward and out of place.

"Since forever, I guess." She positioned herself on her stomach, facing me, and rested her face in her hands. She bit her lip as if trying to stop the words, but they came out of her mouth anyway. "Since I started getting teased anonymously."

"What do you mean? Teased how?" I felt that defensive, tingly sensation you get when a sibling or family member is the target of something cruel, the one that makes your hands ball up and your ears burn.

"Oh, God, why am I telling you? You better not say anything."

"Adonia, I never tell anyone anything. And even if I did, no one would hear me."

Ironically, I didn't think Adonia had heard that comment of mine, because she had jumped off the bed and was frantically digging around in her top dresser drawer. She produced a purple folder and thrust it at me.

"I started getting them in my locker this year. Someone folds them up and shoves them through the vent." She was acting out her words with forceful gesturing.

I opened the glossy folder gingerly, as if it would fall apart in my hands, feeling honored to be confided in. Inside was a collection of notes, mostly sheets of college-ruled paper, crinkly and folded, with a fringe of torn edges where they had been ripped from a spiral notebook. Big, blocky words covered the pages in black, blue, and oftentimes a glittery purple ink. The lines had been written and traced over again so that the ink dented and tore through the paper in places, as if the author's handwriting was an expression of his or her own violent intent.

The words I read and traced my fingertips over made my chest tighten and my throat ache. Each page held the same message, sometimes in a phrase or a lone, ugly word. *Obese whale . . . Jiggles the Dumpy Clown . . . The Cupcake Queen . . . Go on a diet, I can't see around you . . . Fatty . . . Blubber Buns*

. . . *Hippo* . . . I didn't get any farther before Adonia snatched the folder right back and held it against her chest.

"You get the idea?" she asked irritably. "It's not just that. This troll is leaving messages all over my social media from fake accounts. I'm so sick of this evil witch."

I couldn't remember ever having felt such anger and injustice for another person. "Someone wishes they could be you," I stated. It seemed obvious to me.

Adonia looked down at the folder thoughtfully, considering. "No, did you even read these?" She replaced the folder to its hiding place. "It can't be that. This person is really disgusted by me." Glassy pools were building up in her eyes. "You don't get it. Just get out of here."

I obediently stood and slipped silently out the door. There were so many words I could have uttered, but they all seemed shallow and useless, so I didn't say anything at all.

When I left Adonia's room, my mood had crumbled entirely and I felt like weights had been strapped to each of my limbs. I could have weighed a thousand pounds as I trudged aimlessly downstairs. Before that day, I had thought my big sister had this perfect life that was only marred occasionally by bickering between herself and Mother. Perhaps being invisible was not as bad as it could have been. At least I wasn't on display to be picked apart and dissected by cruel eyes.

I planted myself at the kitchen table with a pencil and paper while I waited for my mother. I was doodling an image of my cartoon self-standing on a pedestal. As the minutes ticked by, the drawing expanded to include a crude audience with thought bubbles hovering over their heads. I filled them in with words that featured my worst physical attributes.

"Her mouth is much too small," said a lady with squiggly lines for hair.

"The knees are terribly knobby," said a large-nosed man.

"I really don't like gazing upon such an ordinary face. It's almost homely, wouldn't you say?" asked a floating head whose body I had abandoned drawing.

I sat back and took in the rudimentary sketch that wasn't even close to my best work. I tried to imagine really being up there in front of everyone, absorbing those critical comments like a dismal sponge.

"Are you ready, Zylia? Let's get going before the weather gets any worse," my mother called from the entry hallway where she was putting on her coat and gloves.

I wadded the page into a ball and tossed it into the trash on my way to the door without a second glance.

I didn't usually mind being in that giant, cavernous store that smelled like a mixture of faint disinfectant, metal, and cafeteria food, but on that particular day, it held a drab and unwelcoming aura, much like my doctor's waiting room.

Mother plunked down her massive purse in the child seat section of the oversized cart and drove her arms inside. She made a muffled shuffling sound as she used her hands to swim through a dense pool of receipts, novels, hand creams, and wrappers of all varieties.

I smiled uneasily at an older woman in a vest who was greeting people and checking for discount club cards as they entered the store. She was gawking right at me with big, beady eyes, her hand stretched outward impatiently.

"Ah, here it is." Mother handed me the card and I quickly gave it to the woman.

"Oh, my," the woman gasped, holding my mother's card against her breast. "Where did you come from, young lady? I didn't even see you standing there!" She glanced at the card and handed it back to me in awe. "How utterly bizarre, indeed!"

I looked to my mother for comment. I'm not sure what I expected her to say to validate my existence to this woman, but I lifted my chin and smiled conspiratorially, hoping she would offer something profound and enlightening.

Instead, my mother was humming intermittently and perusing the grocery list she had found in the great hunt through her purse. I envied her delicate disconnect from reality. "Hmm, let's start with . . . no, let's go this way," she mumbled aloud. The cart squeaked and her low-heeled boots clacked against the concrete floor.

We meandered through the aisles, weaving in and out through the human traffic of other shoppers. My mother was placing a freakishly huge bottle of hand sanitizer into our cart when a familiar voice caught my attention.

"Really, Mom, does it matter which one?" the voice was saying from behind me. It was a female voice, young with a hint of whimpering. As I turned my head, it registered in my memory who was attached to the vocals before I even saw Emily Batton balancing a large package of disposable cups in each arm.

During the summer between third and fourth grade, Emily had had a big pool party for the kids in our grade. Her mother had been in charge of the invitations and had followed the list of students in our class right from the school directory. Her indiscriminate invites were probably the only reason I had managed to get that aquamarine flier in the mail that read *Start summer with a splash!*

Instead, I had started that summer with a nasty sunburn, a swimsuit that rode up my backside, and low self-esteem from being the only kid too afraid to jump off the high dive.

There I was, standing in a discount store, and I could still hear the taunting ridicule of my fellow classmates echoing in my ears. I could almost feel the sun on my back and see the wavy water far below me as my schoolmates lined up along the edge of the pool, flapping their elbows and chanting that I was chicken.

"Well, Margaret Moss, is that you?" Emily's mother was driving her cart up alongside ours with a seemingly endless smile on her face. Emily herself hung back, studying the floral designs on the paper cups in mock interest.

Mother blinked a couple times before she made the connection. "Oh, *Gayle*! It's been so long since I've seen you. How have you been?"

I didn't focus on the conversation but let the mildly annoying falsetto tones fade into space as I stared at Mrs. Batton's face. She would have been a very pretty woman with her thick brown hair and matching coffee-toned eyes, but her oversized nose seemed to ruin it all. The surface was shiny, with visible pores and blackheads, and I couldn't take my eyes off it no matter how hard I tried. It was only the conversation between her and my mother, filtering back into my consciousness, that broke my acute gaze.

". . . Zaylee or something?" Mrs. Batton was asking.

"Zylia," corrected my mother.

"Oh, right! How is she doing?"

"Pretty good, pretty good." Mother was nodding her head a lot as if she were running out of vocabulary and this was the only means of communication she had left.

Neither of them seemed to notice that I was standing at the foot of the cart and that the question could have been directed at me. Emily, however, seemed well-aware of my presence and was doing her best to avoid eye contact. I wondered just how long she could feign curiosity in the uninteresting paper cups and the price tags below them.

"So nice seeing you," I was relieved to hear my mother say and our cart was in motion again. I stared at Emily's face as we passed her. It was a bold impulse and I imagined that my eyes were screaming, *look at me!*

She never did, though, and I felt downright sullen as I helped my mother pack the rest of our items into the cart and then load them onto the conveyer belt at the front of the store. My only solace was in the edgy, dark-haired checker with a lizard tattooed on the knuckles of his right hand. I couldn't take my eyes off his ear gauges, spiky hair, and overall captivating look as he swiped our items over the scanner in a mesmerizing rhythm. He paused for a second, glanced at me with intuitive eyes, and winked quickly before resuming his work.

The whole ride home I wondered if tattoos and piercings make a person more noticeable to others. Maybe everyone I'd seen wearing them were the invisible kind of people, like me. There had to be some motivation for enduring such pain and possible infection. One of Adonia's friends had opted for a tiny black heart on one of her lower calves, but wasn't old enough to have it done professionally. I would never forget the sight of that girl's red, puffy ankle after her older brother had practiced his first homemade tattoo on her when their parents had been away for the weekend.

Maybe I would get one someday—from someone who knew what they were doing, of course. Perhaps a soaring bird or butterfly; stirring and whimsical, but also something that denoted freedom and power. However, with my luck, they would use invisible ink and I would go through all that pain for nothing.

Moist gravel crunched under the tires as Mother drove the van through the wide alley behind our house and pulled into the cement driveway that led up to our garage.

"Do you mind jumping out and moving those, sweetie?" Mother gestured ahead with a flick of her wrist over the steering wheel at the slab of concrete littered with Rollerblades and helmets. "I'm tired of those boys leaving their things everywhere! It's like they don't even . . ." Her sentence trailed off as it so often did.

I waited for her to finish, motivated by a mixture of politeness and procrastination for the upcoming chore.

She jerked her head toward me so fast, her dangly earrings made a sweeping arc through the air. "*Now*, please, Zylia."

I leapt out of the van and shut the door a little too harshly, the slamming sound echoing ever so slightly. I hurried to remove the sporting debris, shoving it all into a pile just inside the garage, well out of the roadway.

As my mother inched the van into the garage slot next to my father's car, I stood back, feeling my eyes moving over the low iron fence that separated the space between our house and the neighbors'. The homes were situated close together so that the fence divided the grass into two ribbon-shaped strips of land, very long, thin and not evenly leveled throughout the length.

From that spot I could look all the way up to the top of that mysterious house that mirrored our own. I stood there gaping as a cold breeze kicked up the air around me, and I could almost feel the house staring back.

I blinked as a chilly drop of rain kissed the tip of my nose. I looked up at the darkening sky, where a gray cape of clouds was pulling its dark fabric over the atmosphere. I heard a dog barking and it brought my stare earthward, my gaze landing level with the neighbor's kitchen window. There was a face—only half of it, really—peeking through the curtain. In a single blink it was gone. It was there for such a short amount of time that I couldn't even tell if it had been male or female. All I knew is that it was the same face I had seen before, the face that had seen me upstairs in the bathroom.

"Zylia, it's starting to rain; what are you doing out there? Get in here and help me with all this!" My mother was giving me a disgruntled look as she lugged an oversized bottle of laundry soap from the back of the van.

As the freezing rain hit me, I could feel the stares of my mother and the mysterious neighbor smoldering on my skin. I longed for invisibility. At times like this, the very curse that plagued me was also my protection.

Chapter Six

I greeted Monday morning with a severe case of anxiety and a queasy tummy. The nausea only worsened as I watched Grandmother chew and swallow her oatmeal, smacking it against her tongue and licking it from her dentures' pale pink, artificial gum line. Even the metallic clicking of her spoon as it tapped, then scraped along the bottom of the bowl was as obnoxious as Mace or Bram sticking a wet finger in my ear.

"All your brothers and sisters are done already. You'd better finish up there; that's brain fuel," Grandmother directed, pointing at my own untouched bowl of oatmeal. There was a gooey clump of her breakfast adhering to her chin, and for a horrifying minute I couldn't stop looking at it.

I felt my intestines slither and I closed my eyes, waiting desperately for the sick feeling to pass. It was then and there that I decided the worst annoyance ever was someone talking to you—especially about food—when you were about to blow chunks.

"So, have you spoken with the new neighbors?" asked Grandmother.

My focus changed suddenly, and my stomachache seemed remote. "No; have you?"

"Of course, I did. I wasn't going to be rude."

My eyes widened. I felt relieved that someone had made contact with our wraith-like neighbors, proving them to be more than just the illusions of my lonely mind. "Who are they?"

"Our new neighbors, dear. Isn't that what I said?"

Mace burst into the kitchen and swiped Adonia's iPod from the counter. She was yelling at him to give it back.

I tried to speak to Grandmother over the ruckus. "No; I mean *yes*, that's what you said . . ." I was so flustered, and Mace had begun singing in a high-pitched falsetto with Adonia's hot-pink earbuds shoved in his ears.

"Break it up, you two!" shouted Mother. "It's time for school! Get a move on, kids!"

"What I meant was," I went on after the din died away, "what were they like? What were their names, that sort of thing."

"Didn't you hear your mother?" asked Grandmother. "You'll be late for school."

My stomach had finally started to settle as I reached my third-hour class and sank into my cold plastic chair rather gratefully. Careful not to make eye contact, I examined the grooves and scuffs on my laminate-topped desk as other students filed in and seated themselves around me. I only looked up once the grating sounds of chair legs being scooted on industrial tile had ceased.

The English teacher was a young, trendy woman with short, textured blonde hair. Her voice was pleasant to listen to, but she intimidated me with her mirthless smile and spiky high heels. She opened her pink lips to begin speaking, but was interrupted by a latecomer.

I turned my head in unison with most of the class, all our curious eyes landing on a girl peeking in through the doorway. One hand was resting on the door frame, her head and neck peering inside. Through the glass-and-wire panel beside the entrance I could see that she was carrying a heavy-looking purple backpack and had a wrinkled page in her opposite hand.

"Not sure if I'm in the right place . . ." The girl's brow furrowed as she glanced at the paper in her hand while she spoke. She had a deeper, stronger voice than I had expected.

The teacher helped to inspect the page before smiling and sweeping her arm in a gesture of welcoming entry. "Class, this is Terra Grant. She's new to our school, so let's make her feel like she belongs."

I felt a pang of sympathy for what this newbie must be experiencing up there in the limelight at the front of the class. I imagined a spotlight focused on her while I cringed at the thought of what would happen next. Even though I was nervous for her, I felt acutely relieved that it wasn't me in her shoes.

I was afraid to know how many in the room were curiously attentive to her, perhaps searching for original ways to damage her self-esteem. I wondered where they would start and began taking in her appearance, making mental notes.

Terra Grant was nearly the height of our teacher, probably pushing five feet five inches. Although she was tall, like I was, she didn't have the same thin, wispy frame that lacked curve and dimension. Instead, she was a bit thicker and more muscular than I, and the budding bumps under her white t-shirt made me unwittingly cross my arms over my own flat chest.

"Um, so where should I sit?" the new student asked. She hitched up her backpack and rested it against the curve of her hip, where a pair of black jeans hugged her snugly.

"Just find an empty spot and claim it. No one here bites," the teacher assured with that unhappy smile. I didn't know how she could make such a presumptuous comment with that air of certainty. I had no doubt that any one of these kids were perfectly capable of latching onto my skin with their sharp and recently acquired permanent teeth.

Terra Grant threaded a path through the obstacle course of protruding knees and backpacks until she reached an empty desk that was in front and to the right of mine. She flopped down in what was surely meant to have been a fluid motion, curling one leg below her before crossing the other over top, but her bag got hung up behind her and the extra girth of it made the desk slide forward quite noisily.

I held my breath, waiting for the peals of laughter and ridicule that were sure to follow her clumsy maneuver. Much to my surprise, no one seemed to take any interest, and before long the class was underway just like any normal day.

I peered at Terra from behind, watching her carelessly twist a glossy strand of amber-colored hair. Her wrist was adorned with many homemade bracelets of dark-colored thread, and there was writing in blue ink on her forearm, but I couldn't read the words from my vantage point.

I watched, mesmerized, as she surreptitiously pulled a well-worn notebook from her backpack and began scratching at a page with her pencil. I craned my neck until my collarbone began to ache and, finally, as Terra flipped over to a different page, I caught a brief glimpse of her artwork and knew instantly that it was better than mine. In only that blink of a moment I had taken in a detailed sea of dark, underwater creatures, shaded with a brilliant combination of pencil and ink. I wanted more than anything to flip through that book and see what else her imagination was capable of creating.

The rest of the class flew by in what seemed to be mere seconds. I had become so thoroughly absorbed in the new student that time had lost its effect on me. I felt a little silly watching her so intently as she scooped up her belongings and fished around in the pockets of her jeans for the page she had been holding upon her entry. She bit her bottom lip and scrutinized it for a few moments before joining the horde of students exiting the classroom.

I was nervous about going home, but the uneasy feeling was made up more of thrilling anticipation than dreading fear. I was walking so quickly that my breath was coming out in panting gasps that were visible in the frigid air. The predicted snow had never come the night before, only a cold, slushy rain that hadn't stuck around, so today the pavement ahead of me was clear and dry.

I was feeling a bit too breathless, so I slowed my pace and slid my backpack off my shoulders, carrying it by one strap with both hands in front of me instead. I bounced it off my knees as I strolled along, looking at the neighborhood around me.

I was close enough to home by then that all the houses on either side of the street looked almost identical to mine. As a younger child I had been mesmerized by the long line of stately homes that mirrored one another. But now I noticed for the first time how weary and bleak our street appeared below the sinister entanglement of mature oak and maple branches. It could have been the perfect setting for a horror movie, or maybe that book Ivy had been reading.

As I was prone, I let my imagination roam free over this subject and it was no time at all before I was frightened to my very core. Had our neighborhood always been so silent and still? It was like the muffled quiet brought on by a coverlet of fallen snow. Weren't there usually other kids walking along the sidewalk or families making a commotion as they arrived home? I had almost convinced myself that I was either on the wrong street or in the wrong dimension when I heard a twig snap somewhere behind me.

I spun around, and my heavy backpack caused me to lose my balance and stumble backward a few steps. There was no one on the sidewalk behind me for as far as I could see, yet I felt positive that I was under someone's surveillance. The only motion was a gray sedan turning onto the street a couple blocks down. I waited, watching the driver as the vehicle passed me. I recognized her as Mrs. Edgar from two doors down. She wore an intent expression below her furrowed brow, and behind her I saw my brothers Mace and Bram packed in on either side of her son. They had ornery looks on their faces and I knew they were probably driving the poor woman batty. No one in the car so much as glanced in my direction, which wasn't surprising considering the history of my life up to that point.

I exhaled as soon as the vehicle was out of sight, realizing only then that I had been holding my breath in the first place. I was just happy that the sight of familiar faces had brought me out of my twisted musings.

I ran the rest of the way, ignoring my pounding chest and laborious breathing. I paused, leaning against a tree in front of my neighbor's house. A slamming sound instantly caught my attention. *The* neighbor, mysterious and elusive, was home. Or at least someone was, because I both saw and heard the porch door bounce a couple times on its hinges before settling shut. It was impossible to see beyond that door, because unlike our own porch's framework consisting of transparent glass behind iron bars, this porch was made up of some sort of dense screen material with a trellis affixed directly over the top of it. The lattice design was braided over with gray, dormant vines like kite strings tangled in a thousand knots.

Maybe whoever was home was standing just inside the porch, staring at me. I looked away, ill at ease, and decided it was time to go inside where sly eyes couldn't reach me.

Aside from the fact that I wasn't in the mood to be the object of some real or imagined scrutiny, I had the intense desire to communicate with someone about all these strange feelings. It wasn't something I did very often. I was usually too embarrassed to even consider sharing pieces of my inner self. I felt that doing so would expose me like a deer in the crosshairs.

But today was different. I felt like I was drifting aimlessly, like I would lose myself whether I spoke or not. I could almost feel myself blowing away.

Inside, I dropped my coat and books just alongside the doorway. I heard voices and followed the sound into the breakfast area of the kitchen. Ivy was at the table, which she was apparently using as a makeshift craft station. Bottles of glue and glitter, along with packages of wooden sticks that looked like tongue depressors, were lined up neatly and accessibly around her. She was hunched over a rudimentary frame made up of the wooden sticks, her honey-brown bob grazing the table as she leaned forward to concentrate on making a perfect line of glue.

Mother was standing behind her, looking on with rapt interest. "That's really turning out quite nice! The birds will love it—after your teacher's done displaying it, of course."

I sidled up alongside them, startling my mother. "Oh, Zylia, how was your day?" she asked me while rubbing her throat with her fingertips. I knew she was trying to hide the fact that I had spooked her.

Terrible! I think I'm becoming a paranoid lunatic obsessed with our new neighbors! Also, I don't know if it's occurred to you or not, but I'm almost ***completely*** *invisible to the naked eye!*

Of course, I said none of it, only thinking the words at full volume, feeling them rattle around in my brain. "Good," was all that emerged from my lips.

Mother patted my shoulder with a sweet, although somewhat superficial smile before mumbling something about needing to start dinner and moving toward the fridge.

I slid a chair out and sat next to Ivy, mistakenly jostling her arm. She didn't seem to notice; her brow was scrunched in focus and her eyes were narrowed. I waited for a few seconds to see if she would say anything. Finally, I heard, "You're breathing on my arm," in an irritated tone.

I straightened up, not realizing how close I had been. "Sorry."

"Why are you breathing so hard anyway?" Ivy asked, not looking away from her project.

"I was running."

Ivy made an irritable smacking sound before asking, "Running from who?"

"Nobody," I answered quickly. "Just school."

Ivy didn't move her head, but flicked her eyes at me in a brief, aggravated look. I should have known not to bother her when she was working. My little sister was a perfectionist, and while she was intent on a task, any attempts at conversing would be useless.

I got up as quietly as I could and slipped down the hall toward the living room, where I heard wacky clatter and jangling noise coming from the television. I peered around the wide entry arch and saw all three of my brothers lounging in front of some energetic animated program teeming with goofy sound effects. Keane and Mace were sprawled on the sofa that had once been a rich brown and had faded over the years to a plain tan. Bram was seated in the old recliner that was covered in one of Grandmother's brown-and-cream crochet covers. His cheek was pressed into the palm of his hand and he shared the same glassy-eyed, spellbound look that the other boys had on their faces.

My eyes moved to the wooden coffee table in front of them. It was littered with mini chip bags, crumbs, and deflated juice pouches. I wondered if they would clear away the mess before Mother got onto them. I knew they couldn't have done their homework yet, and Mother had probably been too busy helping Ivy to notice them slacking.

I couldn't bring myself to disturb them, and I wasn't sure what I would say even if I did somehow manage to get their attention.

I couldn't think of anyone else left to talk to, and I definitely wasn't used to this desire to verbally unload on someone. Father was still at work and would no doubt be weary and sober upon his return. Grandmother was not only losing her wits, but had been downright frightening to me as of late. The only person left was Adonia. Since I hadn't seen her, I figured she was probably shut away in her room at the top of the house doing crunches or something. Approaching her was nearly the last thing I wanted to do at that moment. She had her own worries to deal with, and I wasn't even sure she liked me all that much.

A wave of sorrow washed over me and I wasn't completely sure where all the gloominess was coming from. I'd never had anyone to talk to in the past, so I couldn't figure out why it was bothering me now, after all this time.

"Zylia!" I jumped when I heard Mother call my name. "Can you help me for a minute?"

I followed the sound of her voice back into the kitchen where she was struggling to tie up a bulging trash bag. "Oh, there you are, sweetie. Would you mind taking this out to the dumpster for me? I just can't work in a filthy kitchen."

I wordlessly lugged the sack out the back way and hit the garage door button. I groaned when I noted that the dumpsters hadn't been pulled back to the side of the garage, but were still at the end of the driveway on the edge of the alley. My skinny arms were trembling from muscle strain by the time I finally got the sack over the rim. After it had plopped to the hollow bottom, I was about to pull the dumpster carts toward the house when I heard a rustling from behind them.

My body went rigid when I spotted the glossy black nose sniffing the ground between the two carts. There wasn't much space, merely a two- or three-inch gap, but I could make out part of a white-and-black face attached to that nose. I was almost positive it was a giant skunk bound to spray me or infect me with rabies, so I started backing up very slowly, heart thudding in my ears.

The animal leapt out into view and cocked his furry head before I could get very far away. He was most certainly not a skunk, but a beautiful dog like the kind I had seen pulling sleds on movies. His vast frame was covered with dense fur that was a snowy white all along his legs, underbelly, and face; the top of his back, head, and ears were charcoal black in color.

Even though I was relieved to discover that he wasn't a contaminated skunk, my anxiety did not dwindle altogether. I had never spotted this dog in the neighborhood before, and it was only a week prior that I had overheard a classmate speaking of a pit bull who chewed fingers off as a greeting. There was no way to tell if this dog was equally aggressive.

"You're beautiful," I whispered, wondering if flattery worked on dogs.

There was a *whap-whap* sound as the dog's plume of a tail whipped against one of the garbage cans. I was fairly certain tail wagging was a good sign, so I inched closer, speaking soothingly, keeping my gaze level with the dog's ice-blue eyes.

He sat, quite regally, and pointed his nose in the air, waiting for me to approach. I patted the well-behaved animal and rubbed my hands in his soft fur.

"Where did you come from?" I asked quietly, noting a golden, bone-shaped tag dangling from a thin leather collar. This disappointed me to some degree, because I had already been entertaining fantasies of adopting him as my own, even though I knew Mother would never allow it.

I tilted the tag until I could clearly read the name "Kale" pressed into the golden surface.

"Kale." I said the name aloud but then heard it repeated in a different voice, loud and irritated.

"*Kale!* Oh, there you are!" came a voice from beyond the dumpsters. "What's gotten into you? Since when don't you come when I call? I hope I don't have to start . . ." The voice trailed off as the speaker came fully into view.

I couldn't help but inhale so quickly that my chest lurched in a hiccup. Terra Grant, the new girl from school, was standing near my dumpsters.

"Oh, hey," she said coolly, taking me in with her narrow hazel eyes. "I know you."

I felt giddy and overjoyed that she had recognized me. "Yeah, I know you too. I wasn't even sure you saw me in class but . . . *hiccup* . . . I'm glad you remember."

"Oh, we have class together? I'm sorry, I didn't know. I recognized you from the window the other night. You look a lot different with clothes on."

Chapter Seven

"You . . . *hiccup* . . . live next door?" I felt heat rush to my face and neck as realization dawned on me.

"Yeah . . . that wasn't exactly what I expected to see when I was trying to figure out where the draft was coming from. It's freezing cold up there and I was trying to figure out why."

I took a deep breath to delay any more hiccupping. "I know what you mean. My room's up there." I nodded, using my chin to subtly point upward at my house.

"Terra Grant," she said formally, extending her hand.

I shook it, and after my chest lurched yet again in a hiccup, I said, "I'm Zylia Moss." I said my name slowly and clearly, so she wouldn't have to ask me to repeat myself, as most people did.

"Zylia, huh? Cool name. Bet there's a long story behind it or something. Well, this is Kale, but I guess you two have already met." She turned her attention downward to the dog, patting him on the head. "He's kinda nosey."

I was delighted. Not only could she pronounce my name, but she had guessed that there was a story behind it. Of course, she had no idea that the story was, in fact, an actual novel read by my mother at some point in her pregnancy with me, but I was dying to tell her. I was anxious to inform her all about me, the proof that I existed.

Terra shivered and rubbed her arms. "Well, I guess we better get back inside."

"Oh, okay." I tried to sound impassive, but I was crestfallen.

She turned to leave but then paused, adding, "I'm gonna start walking to school. I like to head out early. Feel free to join me if you ever wanna." She patted her leg and Kale followed her. The dog was almost prancing, looking back toward me every few strides with his tongue lolling happily from the side of his mouth.

The next morning my eyes shot open and I was up and out of bed in less than an instant, carelessly knocking over a mug of pens on my side table. I was halfway to the bedroom door when Ivy jolted upright, sucking air into her lungs as if she had just surfaced from below a tidal wave.

"Holy cow, Zylia! Gosh, what's your problem?"

"Sorry," I called over my shoulder, leaving quickly, then shutting the door behind me before my sister could pelt me with some random object.

In the bathroom, I tied my hair back in a low knot to avoid having to wash and blow-dry, then I quickly showered, wrapped myself in a towel, and left to ponder my half of the closet.

Ivy gave me a narrow-lidded, huffy stare as she walked by me, and once she was in the hall, I could hear her slam the bathroom door.

I was too mentally preoccupied to worry over my sister's feelings just yet. I rummaged around for a while before I finally pulled on a black-and-gray striped tunic over a faded pair of skinny jeans.

Next, I scrambled around, locating my shoes, books, bag, and jacket before I zoomed down the stairs so fast that I was bouncing against the walls as I turned at each landing.

Mother and Grandmother were the only ones up, looking sleepy and far from lively. I slid past Mother where she was standing at the counter starting a pot of coffee and pulled back the curtains to get a peek at Terra's house. It was still dim outside and I could see lights on in the main level.

"What in the world are you up to?" asked Mother. "And you're dressed so early!"

I was relieved that she went back to her coffee, seemingly uninterested in an explanation of my behavior. Yet Grandmother's probing eyes and tremulous lips did nothing to put me at ease, so I moved past them both and into the keeping room. There was a window on the far side of the fireplace. I set my backpack down on a nearby ottoman and moseyed over, trying to seem casual and indifferent. I was disappointed that the view from that spot was no better. I still couldn't see the driveway at the back of the neighboring house and I couldn't be positive if Terra would emerge from the front or the back door. All I was certain of was that I didn't want to miss her.

I became a little edgy as my siblings shuffled down one by one for breakfast and the clock crept closer to seven-fifteen. I didn't know how early Terra left for school, but the last thing I wanted to do was lose a chance at walking there with her.

I decided I couldn't risk waiting another second, so I quietly dismissed myself and exited onto the front porch. I was worried that someone in my family would become suspicious of my leaving so early, but no one even shot me so much as a glance before I snapped the heavy door shut.

I walked slowly to the front path, shivering at the moist chill in the air. Suddenly, I realized that I didn't know which way Terra was going to walk to school. Did she want to take the sidewalk in front of our house or would she be more apt to traipse down the back alley that ran along behind our dwellings? I could easily miss her if I took the wrong path, and an absurd fretfulness was taking over my senses.

Deciding I must have chosen incorrectly, I made a dash down the thin strip of lawn that separated our two lots and stopped for a quick breath at the garbage cans. I couldn't see any sign of movement from Terra's house. I supposed I would just have to run back and forth until she emerged from one end or the other and hope that I wouldn't miss her. While I was hoping, I should have probably wished that no one happened to be looking out a window and think me utterly deranged. I imagined that I looked like a dog testing the boundaries of an invisible fence.

Just as I propelled myself forward, I heard the rumble of the neighboring garage door opening. I halted, but my heavy backpack was still soaring ahead and it was all I could do to keep my balance. After a few stumbling steps I saw Terra sauntering out toward the alleyway.

I jogged up to her and said, "Hey there!" In my head it had seemed chill and nonchalant, but the words came out in the form of breathless relief.

"Sure is cold," Terra shivered, pulling her hood over her ears and crossing her arms in front of her chest. "I'm not used to this weather. It never got this cold where I lived before."

I found a pleasant sensation in the pebbles crunching below my feet and my backpack bouncing against my hip as I watched and listened to Terra talk. I saw the white air escaping from her throat in misty curls and thought, *this must be what having a comrade feels like.* I wasn't even nervous about travelling down the sinister alleyway with this confident girl by my side. Maybe this was what *normal* felt like.

Everything was different—better somehow. The world surrounding me seemed like reveal day on one of those home makeover shows my mother would watch. The very air around us was cleaner and newer. The cracks, chips, and grime on my school might have been charming, even—adding character instead of detracting from beauty.

The throngs of students trudging into the great mouth of the school seemed far less wolf-like and wicked with Terra at my side. I walked down the hallway with her, feeling on top of the world. I could even have conquered the universe!

At least I could have for about a second before I heard Terra say, "Oh, look, there's Josh Pierceton! He helped me find my health class yesterday. Let's go say hello."

It took a few seconds for my eyes to land on Josh's beautiful profile. He was leaning against a locker with his head turned in conversation, listening to a schoolmate while slowly blinking sleepy eyes.

"Josh!" called Terra. "Hey, Josh!"

I saw those drowsy brown eyes become more alert, scanning the crowd for the voice that was calling his name. In that moment I panicked, backing up and pressing my spine into the opposite wall.

"Watch it, klutz," someone barked rudely when I inadvertently smashed his toe with my foot. I didn't even have time to apologize before the student was swept away in the current of people. It might have hurt my feelings if I weren't looking desperately for an exit.

There it was, a girls' restroom, not more than fifteen feet away. I slid down the wall, against the flow of middle-schoolers, and ducked inside with a fervor that suggested I was taking cover from a deadly aerial attack.

"Whoa!" a blonde girl yelped, jumping out of my way before she could leave the restroom.

Another girl was standing at the line of sinks washing her hands. Our eyes locked for a second in the mirrored reflection before she flicked them downward, blinking rapidly and coughing.

I didn't need to use the restroom, but out of fear of looking even stranger than I already did, I walked into the farthest stall and latched the door. I risked germs by leaning against the metal handrail and distracted myself for a couple of minutes by reading what female students had etched into the metallic paint of the stall walls.

The writings were mostly phone numbers, vicious slander, and opinions on who the hottest guys were, but it was enough to pass a full five minutes before I started thinking it might be safe enough to leave the restroom. I was pretty sure that by then Terra thought I was a lunatic and would never speak to me again. I wondered if I had washed my only chance at a best friend right down the drain.

I started to open the stall door, thinking it was time to face my angst-ridden behavior, when I heard a plastic thumping sound coming from nearby. Up until that moment I'd believed that the bathroom had cleared out, and I was curious about who could have crept in without my noticing.

In that particular instant, unlike any other, I was actually appreciative of the slightly too-wide crack alongside the door—it gave me the perfect view of a short girl in a soft yellow sweater standing very close to the paper towel dispenser. Her shoulders were bouncing up and down, moving the locks of strawberry-gold hair that cascaded down her back in shiny waves.

It took me longer than it should have to realize she was crying, a paper towel pressed into her face to silence the sobs. A stab of empathy shot through me and I looked away, flushing the toilet to warn her of my presence.

When I came out of the stall, she was gone. I washed my hands while wondering who she was and what traumatic teenage ordeal she was enduring.

"There you are, Zylia!" Terra burst into the bathroom just as the five-minute warning bell went off. "How in the world did you disappear like that?"

"I'm sorry; it's just that . . ." I didn't know how to explain my paralyzing fear-and-awe combination connected to Josh Pierceton.

Terra put her palm up in a silencing gesture, pulling back her chin as she did so. "Hey, it's totally cool. When nature calls, you gotta go, right?" She smiled and punched me playfully on the shoulder.

After school I spotted Terra at her locker, bundling up for the walk home. I sidled up next to her and said, "Hey, at least it's warmer than it was this morning."

Terra crammed some books in her bag and slung it over her shoulder with a good-natured grin. "Yeah, yeah," she said as we merged into that familiar human river of students and didn't stop until we reached the crosswalk.

"You know, I can't believe this Ms. Beck of ours," said Terra as we waited for the picture of the orange-red hand to change into a glowing white silhouette of a person in mid-stride. "Does she think we're some kind of machines, giving us homework like that today?!"

"I know; it seems impossible," I chimed in, surprised to hear the conversational quality in my voice, "but at least the book report part isn't due until next week."

"Yeah, no kidding; we'd be *totally* screwed then!"

We complained about teachers and homework for the entire walk home. I was sad when I could see the edge of Terra's house peeking through tree branches. I didn't want the time with my new friend to be over. I thought about inviting her to my house, but I couldn't get up the nerve.

"Well, I guess I'm gonna head in," Terra said nodding in the direction of her garage. "I'd say we should hang out, but I promised my dad that I'd make dinner tonight; plus, as you know, I've got a buttload of homework to do."

I smiled. "No problem; some other time." I could hear Kale barking from somewhere inside her house as I walked away and up to my own home.

Inside, the house felt warm, and I was pleasantly surprised that someone had started a fire in the keeping room. Adonia and her friend Leah were sprawled out on the faded paisley rug, basking in the crackling warmth. Adonia was lying on her back, knees bent, giggling over something on the screen of her phone; across from her, Leah was meticulously painting her fingernails a bright pink color. The lacquer aroma mixed with the smoky fireplace and scents of home were welcoming and agreeable, stamped forever in my olfactory's comforting memories.

I stood there, just taking in the scene for a moment. If I had been witness to that very display only a day prior, I undoubtedly would have felt an envious grief that would have saddened me to the depths of my soul.

That day was different, however. Instead of cold jealousy and emptiness, I felt a fuzzy glow within me as I laid eyes on my sister and her best friend. I knew that it was now possible for me to share in the beautiful sensation of friendship. The concept didn't seem so foreign anymore, and the line between me and the rest of the world was suddenly less distinct.

Adonia peeked over the face of her phone. "Hey, Zy."

Leah turned her blonde head toward me as well, looking me directly in the eyes and smiling.

Even with my newfound optimism, I was still startled that they had noticed me. "Hey, what's up?" I said back, liking the sound of my voice as it resonated in the real world outside of my head for a change.

Chapter Eight

The next morning, I timed my departure perfectly so that I walked out my garage door, down the driveway, and fell into step alongside Terra in the alleyway.

"Morning," I said all too cheerfully. I couldn't help it; my mood was soaring high above the overcast sky.

"Are you as exhausted as I am?" Terra asked in a laborious voice. When she looked at me, I noticed her eyes were puffy and slightly encircled in gray.

Personally, I felt energized. My previous evening had ended on a high note, with me zipping through my homework and chores with time to spare. However, I wanted to relate with my newfound friend so I said, "Yeah, I'm pretty beat."

Terra sighed and shuffled forward, her arms wrapped tightly around her torso. She didn't say much, and the chasm of silence left a wide-open opportunity for me to speak.

"Hey, I'm sorry about disappearing on you when Josh showed up yesterday," I began. "Honestly, I didn't have to use the restroom at all."

Terra slowed her pace and looked at me with squinty, perplexed eyes.

I wasn't sure why I was explaining this to her when I had been home free of all doubt before, but the thought of someone else sharing in my secret felt comforting in a way I had never experienced. "I freaked out," I went on bravely. "I was nervous because I've always had this . . . well, *crush* . . . on Josh."

Terra stopped short with the sound of pebbles skidding under her sneakers. Her eyes were wide and suddenly awake as she asked in a half squeal, "Why didn't you *tell* me? I had no idea at all!"

"Yeah, I know. It's stupid, though, because he's barely even aware that I exist."

Terra hooked her elbow into mine and prodded me forward at a bouncing pace. "Oh, Zylia, you should totally talk to him!"

Horror shot through my spine and traveled an icy path up to my skull. "Oh, no . . . no, no, no, I couldn't *ever* do that. I'll ruin everything."

"Ruin everything? Like what? Do you guys have this great friendship I don't know about? Is it like a secret code through body language or sign language or something?"

I sighed. "No . . ."

"Then why not talk to him? What's the harm? Come on; we can make a plan. Hey, actually, I have a great idea!"

"I don't know . . ." I felt like I had somehow boarded a runaway train and there was no way to exit before the whole thing crashed to a fiery halt.

"Okay, when you were cowering in the bathroom yesterday, Josh was telling me that he and some friends were planning on heading over to that ice cream shop a few blocks away today after school. What's it called?"

"Candy's Creamery?" I'd heard of kids hanging out there before, but of course I'd never been invited.

"Yeah, that's it!" Terra snapped her gloved fingers as if the name had just come to her spontaneously. "We should meet them there—you know, make an appearance and strike up interesting conversation and stuff."

"I can't. I didn't ask my mother, so she'll worry if I'm not home right away, and I don't even have any money on me." I was spilling out every excuse I could think of.

"Zylia!" Terra was beginning to sound frustrated with me and that only made me tenser. "Come *on,* when were you grounded last?"

I thought about it, and within a second the memory came to me.

Last spring, Mother had made her celebrated spiced Bundt cake with drizzled cream cheese icing for Ivy's school's bake sale.

She had let me help her that afternoon, and it was fun working alongside her as partners. As an invisible girl in a very large family, I treasured any one-on-one time I got to spend with my parents, especially my mother.

That day had been sunny and breezy, and Mother had opened the windows to let in the outside air as we baked. She hadn't even flinched when I'd asked to run the mixer or lick the silicone spatula, just nodded encouragingly.

Time had seemed to move by far too quickly before we were placing the cake in the oven. Shortly after, the kitchen had become overly warm and the scent of spicy sweetness hung in the air, spilling into the keeping room and entry hall. I had dozed off in Father's recliner amid the cozy, bakery-like atmosphere. When I woke, the light had changed considerably to the glowing shades of evening, leaving long shadows across the floor.

I heard moaning coming from the kitchen, and I realized it was that sound that had woken me. Ivy was standing at the center island counter taking bites from something in her cupped hands.

I stretched and slid off the recliner, moving stiffly toward the kitchen.

"I didn't even see you back there," Ivy said around a mouthful of cinnamon-colored cake. "This is so good; have you tried it?"

I could only stare for a few moments at her sparkly, sugar-encrusted lips, knowing that she would be in trouble for diving into this dessert. "That cake," I finally managed to articulate, "was for your bake sale at school. You know, the one you begged Mother to enter?"

Ivy's eyes filled with tears almost instantly, which began spilling over her freckled cheeks. "I didn't know," she cried, holding out the half-eaten, crumbly cake in her palms. "It just looked so good and I forgot all about…"

I put my index finger to my lips in a silencing gesture and scooped out the remnants of the cake from her hands. "Go wash your hands and face," I told her.

Ivy stood there sniffing quietly and looking pitiful. Her soft, adorable features looked even more childlike and vulnerable with remorse written all over them.

I tried to smash what was left of the cake into the gap where it had been cut, finding that there was no foreseeable way to even out the discrepancy with such a crumbly cake. "Ivy, go wash up before Mother comes back. You have evidence all over your face."

The words moved her to action and she scrambled around me, vanishing into the little powder room next to the laundry area on the other side of the keeping room.

I stared at that Bundt cake, wondering if there was any way I could use icing to camouflage the offense. I hoped to find some excess frosting stored away somewhere as I did my best to pat the dessert down and even it out. I started scanning the room a bit frantically when I caught sight of a figure in the entryway to the kitchen. I took my time meeting my mother's eyes.

"Why would you do that?" Mother's green eyes were mystified and utterly dissatisfied; her full lips were parted in incredulity. "You *knew* what that cake was for; you helped me make it, after all."

I stood silently before her, afraid of her displeasure but also fearing the idea of ratting out my favorite sibling.

"You have *nothing* to say?" Her voice was getting louder.

"I didn't . . ." I started to tell the truth, but Ivy's broken-hearted eyes were burning in my memory, ". . . mean to eat so much. I thought I'd just taste it and it sort of fell apart."

Mother slapped her hand against the face of the refrigerator, startling me. "It's late, and now I have to make another cake." She tapped the toe of her brown leather flat against the kitchen tile in aggravated thought. "You are *grounded*. No television, no . . ." I thought she was about to say, "no friends" but realized that wasn't even remotely an issue for me. She struggled to think of something else. ". . . no . . . *drawing*! Seriously, not even a doodle for a whole week!"

I had tried to convince myself that the punishment wasn't so bad, and later that evening when Ivy had given me an indebted hug and offered to clean my side of the room, I knew it had been worth it.

"It's been awhile, I guess," I answered.

"Well, then, you're due for a good grounding." Terra laughed as if the matter were resolved.

I wasn't so sure. Both disappointing people and embarrassing myself were the two main causes of my frequent stomach upsets, and it seemed that whichever choice I made would result in one or the other.

That day in school I felt more undetectable than ever. I walked through the crowded hallways like a human pinball, careening off one person and bouncing into another. My shoulders and arms were stinging when I finally made it to my locker just before my third-hour English class. I set my bag on the floor and began riffling around for some new pencils when the metal door crashed into my face, my head bouncing sideways with the impact. The contents of my locker were springing around in my blurred vision as the tinny, rattling sound of the locker door faded away, leaving only a dim ringing in my ears. When I finally managed to stand upright and glance around me, it was impossible to tell who the clumsy or careless culprit may have been.

"What happened to you?" I heard a voice from behind me ask.

I swung around a little too quickly and tripped on my bag. I was thankful to see that it was Terra standing there; she grabbed my sore arms to steady me.

"You have a big red mark on your forehead," she declared, squinting and cocking her head to inspect it.

"Rough morning." I wanted to tell her what had happened, but tears were welling up and my throat was clenching shut painfully.

Terra picked up my backpack and slung it over her free shoulder. She then snapped my locker shut and guided me by the arm to the class we shared. It was strange how when Terra was with me, the flow of students parted and a polite "excuse me" or "pardon me" was mumbled by someone every couple feet or so.

Terra didn't let go of my arm until I was planted safely in my chair. She patted my shoulder jovially—which made me wince—before she took her own seat.

After the final bell rang at the end of the school day, I stood on the stoop considering my options. I figured I could attempt to make a dash for home before Terra caught up with me, but that may leave her confused and angry. My mind raced crazily as I mentally ticked off the possibilities. If I escaped, I could tell her later that I waited but couldn't find her or that I'd gotten sick and had to rush home immediately or . . .

"Hey there!" Terra's voice from behind brought on an unpleasant tightness to the back of my neck. "Are you ready for this? I hope so, because it is on!"

"Actually, I'm not sure about this." I couldn't even force a smile, and thought I might puke.

"C'mon, this is gonna be so fun." Terra took me by the arm and led me down the school steps in a chummy fashion. I was getting used to being maneuvered by her physically, but I could also feel her persuasion creeping into my brain as I fell into step alongside her.

It was strange not to go straight at the crosswalk and begin the trek homeward. Instead we went right, taking the sidewalk directly along the school front. The next few blocks seemed to morph from tall, closely set houses into brick buildings of various heights.

I felt like a hamster who had escaped from its cage, treading my little paws on foreign sidewalk under the well-clipped branches of unfamiliar trees. The cross-streets that intersected our current path were more congested than the sleepy streets around my neighborhood, and the crosswalk signals seemed to have longer cycles before letting pedestrians cross.

"So, you know where this place is, right?" Terra asked. "I'm counting on you, because I have no idea where I'm going in this town."

I'd never been to Candy's Creamery, but I knew where it was because the nearest branch of the public library was only a couple blocks away from it. Often my mother would park in one of the ice cream store's customer spaces when parking on the street was bad and she was desperate for her books. But honestly, I hadn't paid much attention to the route my mother had used to reach the location, since I tended to daydream while riding around in the van. Now, as I looked around me, I felt disoriented and confused.

"I think we turn right at the next light," I speculated.

"*Think?*" Terra repeated nervously. "That doesn't sound good."

"Well . . . I think I remember that . . ."

Terra interrupted me by pointing, jumping, and shouting, "Hey! Look, there they are! That's Josh!"

Almost a block ahead of us I could make out three young boys. One of them was jumping up, playfully swatting an advertisement sign dangling from a light post. I instantly recognized the black jacket with Korean writing on the sleeves. My heart fluttered like a butterfly having a seizure.

"Let's catch up to them!" Terra grabbed my sleeve and jerked me out into the roadway even though the light was presently warning against crossing.

In mid-jog I heard the deafening blare of a horn; upon turning my head I realized I was practically nose-to-grill with a black Cadillac Escalade. I never even looked at the driver, but as Terra pulled me safely to the other curb, I thought I heard a woman shouting something at us. It was probably good that I couldn't make out the words.

My legs were as stable as wet spaghetti and my heart was on the verge of explosion. Near the same place where I stood composing myself and fighting back tears, Terra was slapping at her leg in laughter.

"You shoulda seen your face! It was like you just knew you were gonna die!" she said through guffaws. "You take everything so seriously." Terra started jogging suddenly, still laughing. My nervous system was too ravaged to command my body to keep up with her. She rounded the block ahead of me, and when she left my vision I considered turning around right then and there.

Instead I kept walking, not even bothering to rush. When I turned the corner, I immediately laid eyes on a brightly lit sign that read *Candy's Creamery* in letters comprised of little pictures of peppermints, gumdrops, and chocolate squares. The glass door below the sign was swinging shut, so I knew I couldn't be too far behind my friend.

My heart was slowing as I reached the storefront. I felt numb inside, like my body was producing its own anesthetic. My mood may have been lackluster, but for the moment it felt better than sheer panic or taut nerves. I peered into the window, but I couldn't focus past my filmy, unsmiling reflection.

The door jingled obnoxiously when I entered the ice cream shop, but nobody glanced up. Even the young, apron-clad girl working the register didn't seem to notice a new customer. She was busy counting change back to Josh and his friends, so I couldn't even completely chalk it up to my invisibility syndrome.

"I know, right!?" I had just caught the tail end of Terra's conversation with a blonde boy standing next to Josh. Whatever she had said, it had the boy laughing and smiling.

Terra turned to me as if I had been standing there the whole time, not missing a beat. "So, what sounds good?" she asked, pointing up at the extensive menu that had silly item names like Hot Fudge Heap, Lemon-Berry Landslide and The Peanut Butter Boat. "Pick something, it's on me."

I couldn't imagine walking up to the counter and repeating one of those juvenile flavor names, let alone put anything against my dry, apathetic taste buds. "Could you get me an ice water?" I asked, trying to sound polite, but my voice came out sounding utterly hollow and piqued. Although I was still feeling comfortably anesthetized, I was pretty sure that somewhere within that tone had been my true feelings trying to escape the indifference.

"You sure that's all you want? Check out the Chocolate Caramel Moat! It looks like pure happiness in a waffle bowl."

"Just an ice water," I repeated.

"Okay, okay. Bor*ing* if you ask me." Terra ordered quickly and handed me a clear plastic cup with a bright pink straw.

The three boys had wandered off to find a spot to sit. I didn't look at them directly, but from the corner of my eye I could see them settling into a booth by the window. Every now and then I could hear Josh's voice above the others. They were speaking excitedly about something that had happened in gym class earlier that day, but I couldn't focus on the conversation. Instead, I was wondering where I would sit since the small booths only comfortably accommodated four.

I gulped the cold water so fast I got a mild frozen sensation deep within my head. I hadn't even realized how parched I had been.

Terra turned around with a heaping serving of ice cream drowned in toppings and syrups. It made me a little ill looking at it. I followed her over to the booth, where I stood awkwardly to one side while she noisily pulled an unoccupied chair from an adjacent table and parked it at the head of the booth. She then settled on the vinyl bench next to a boy in a red hoodie, leaving the extra chair on the end open for me.

She had probably thought I would prefer to sit closest to Josh, who was across the table from her on the outside of the booth, but as I slid into the chair I felt as if I were dangling on the edge of the party. I sipped my water knowing I was a fifth wheel, if that was a thing—useless and unwanted.

"You guys all know Zylia, right?" asked Terra.

The boy in the red hoodie shook his head and said, "No, I don't think so. I'm Taylor."

"Hey," my voice came in a whisper.

The boy opposite Taylor was Joel Knells. He had been in both my third- and fourth-grade classes and I was well-aware of the fact that he and Josh had been friends since way back then. In fact, my mother had given Joel and his mom a ride home once when their car spluttered to a stop in the grade school parking lot. I remembered sitting in the backseat next to him wondering if there was any way I could befriend him, imagining being able to enter the social circle where Josh existed. But the ride had ended before I'd mustered up enough courage to say a single word to him.

Now Joel was looking at me, his dull, gray eyes not registering me at all. "I'm Joel," he introduced himself, apparently unaware that we had ever met.

I didn't say anything in return. What was the point if there was no way I'd leave an impression on his memory?

Josh looked at me and smiled. I couldn't remember the last time I had been so close to him. I found myself memorizing his mouth: white teeth almost perfectly straight save an incisor that was slightly askew, all between full lips that held a tiny droplet of vanilla ice cream at one corner.

"How's it going, Zylia?" he asked me with those beautiful lips.

I blinked a couple of times, hope momentarily replacing the numbness I had felt. I imagined taking a napkin and gently wiping his mouth as I responded with something witty that would make everyone laugh. But instead I sat with my elbows glued rigidly to my sides and hands clasped tightly around my cup as I said, "Good. It's going . . . really good."

"Hey, what was the deal with Mrs. Peterson?" asked Joel. "Wasn't that weird how she just rushed out like that?"

"I heard she has health problems. You know, like, of the mind," inserted Taylor.

"No, that can't be right," said Josh. "She got a note on her desk; didn't you see?"

Terra swallowed a huge bite of ice cream before she chimed in, "Yeah, you're right. I saw that. It was like whatever was on the note really spooked her. Maybe a family emergency or something!"

I had no idea what they were talking about, since I didn't have any classes with Mrs. Peterson. Not being able to contribute to the conversation left me feeling even more alienated from the group, even though I probably wouldn't have jumped in anyway if given the chance.

"Oh, I can find out, though; trust me," assured Terra. She was eating like one of the boys: hunched over her bowl, shoveling spoonfuls into her mouth. I was suddenly annoyed by her and how she had forced me out of my comfort zone.

"Really? How? She's pretty tight-lipped about everything," Joel said.

"I have my ways." Terra's hazel eyes were glinting deviously. "I know for a fact she's friends with the nurse, who *is* quite the blabbermouth."

"You're pretty quick for a noob!" Joel complimented.

As I listened to them talk, I experimented with my imperceptibility by slowly pushing my chair backward, away from the table. I did it little by little, sometimes squeaking the legs against the scuffed tile floor, but no one even glanced my way. Then, when there was quite a distance between me and the table, I simply stood up and waited there for a full minute.

The boys had erupted into laughter at Terra doing an impression of the school nurse. They were seemingly mesmerized by my new friend, and a surge of aching jealousy passed through me. I counted thirty more seconds in my head as I loomed over them until I simply walked away.

I dropped my cup into the trash bin by the door and secured my backpack tightly over my shoulders. When I opened the glass door, the little bell didn't even tinkle to broadcast my departure. I looked up and saw that the little brass chimes had become tangled at some point after I'd entered the store.

Outside, clouds were passing in front of the sun and the cool air stung at my eyes. Feelings were rushing in now, making up for their brief absence. I had to get away from them before they overtook me completely. That's when I started running faster than I ever had before, feet pounding rhythmically against the frigid sidewalk.

And for the life of me, I couldn't stop running.

Chapter Nine

When I reached my house, I buckled over near the dumpsters, sucking icy air into my lungs as if I had just surfaced from an invisible torrent. I was barely aware of the small pebbles poking into my knees and then my hands as I leaned forward against the ground.

Without warning, my stomach heaved; I stuck my head between the two garbage cans and spewed my belly's contents all over the ground. I coughed and choked for what felt like an hour before I managed to catch my breath and lean back on my heels.

I sat there feeling my heart begin to slow as I watched greasy, yellow-tinted liquid seeping out around one of the trash cart's wheels. In my last class of the day, the teacher had surprised us by wheeling in an old-fashioned popcorn cart. We were allowed to feast on the buttery treat while watching a mind-numbing movie about our solar system.

It was peculiar to see the popcorn all shriveled, dandelion-colored, and mushy, looking nothing like it had going into my mouth. The sight was revolting, but I couldn't look away until I managed to find the strength to pull myself off the ground and head for the house.

I was weak and a little unsteady on my feet. To my shaky arms, my backpack felt like a five-gallon bucket filled with bricks. I dropped it at my feet the moment I entered the back door. I walked through the short hall and into the keeping room, the warmth of the house overwhelming me. My face and fingers had felt frozen, but now an uncomfortable tingling sensation was settling into my skin from the drastic temperature change.

Grandmother was seated in her recliner, humming shrilly as her hands moved around her crochet project. I moved past her silently and lumbered through the kitchen, where Mace and Bram were munching cookies at the table.

I rounded the corner into the front hall, thinking I might make it up to my room without being spotted—but Adonia was hanging up her coat next to the front door and accidentally brushed against my arm.

"Oh, hey . . ." she said, startled, giving me a weird look that I couldn't decipher.

"Just where have you been?"

Adonia and I whipped our heads around toward the staircase, where our mother's voice had come from. She was standing on the landing, arms akimbo and eyes smoldering with irritation.

"Why weren't you on the bus with your brother? Keane's been home for at least half an hour, if not longer. Where have you been?" Mother demanded.

I had thought I was too exhausted to feel any more emotion; yet when it sunk in that Adonia's absence had been noted and mine had not, distinct anguish overtook me. I had been fully prepared to be grounded or at least get a stern lecture. I should have known to expect the possibility of my unperceivable presence kicking in.

I was no one. I was nowhere.

I used all my remaining energy to trudge up the stairs past the ensuing mother-daughter argument that I had no part in. I went all the way up to the third floor, but I didn't turn right at the top of the stairs and plop down in my bedroom, which had been my initial inclination. Instead, I unfolded the sturdy plastic step stool that was always kept there, leaning against the wall. I climbed atop, stretching to reach a dangling cord with a large, old ring tied to the end of it. Once my fingers clasped the cold metal, it was only another moment before I was unfolding the ladder-like attic staircase.

I didn't venture to the uppermost part of the house very often. The attic was cramped, dusty, and dark, with low, sloped ceilings and plenty of cobwebs. In fact, the Moss kids weren't technically allowed up there due to an incident involving Mace somehow having managed to stick his leg through Adonia's bedroom ceiling. I'm still not sure just what my brother had been up to that day, but afterward Father was furious. He was grouchy for days, especially after he had hired some men to repair the hole and replace some planks in the attic. I could still envision him standing with his arms crossed as he stared up at the work being done with eyes that could have lit a match.

I refolded the step stool, placed it back against the wall, and quickly climbed up the squeaky stairs. When I was all the way at the top, I pulled a little chain and was pleased to find that the light bulb hadn't burned out in the windowless attic. I pulled the stairs back up, which took all my strength and effort. I didn't want to leave any evidence that I was breaking the rules and trespassing onto forbidden territory. However, I didn't let the folded staircase snap shut completely out of fear that I wouldn't be able to get it back open. I could just imagine being stuck in the attic, dying of dehydration, while my family lived out their lives in the floors below—completely forgetting that I had ever existed.

I found a sturdy-looking box and sat down amongst years of accumulated clutter that had been demoted to the secluded and forgotten space. I don't think I had ever felt so drained or weary. My muscles were sore and shaky, and when I lifted my shirtsleeve I noticed that there were a couple bruises forming on my shoulder and arm from where I had been ping-ponged around the halls of my school.

That's when the tears suddenly came, heavy rivulets of salty water blinding me and sliding off my chin. I didn't even bother wiping at my eyes as my shoulders bounced erratically along with the quiet sobs. After a few minutes, my weeping slowed; I leaned my head against a nearby crate, taking long, slow breaths.

I started looking at the objects around me and realized that with my head slanted to the side I could see beyond Grandmother's old sewing table covered with hat boxes and into a portion of the attic where some contents had recently been shuffled around. There were fresh lines and footprints in the dust on the old floorboards around the familiar stacks of boxes labeled

Books. I could see some sort of furniture piece sticking out from behind them, far back against the wall where the angled ceiling met the floor.

I slid my thin frame into the narrow space between the boxes and wiggled my way inch by inch closer to the wall, trying to get a look at what was hiding back there.

Throughout the years I had been in and out of the attic, searching every box that I suspected might contain the novel Mother had read when she was pregnant with me. The one that had a character named Zylia within its pages.

I had painstakingly opened, searched, and re-taped all my mother's boxes to hide my snoopy progress. I was always careful to put everything back just as I had found it in case she was to get suspicious. I read countless blurbs and jacket covers of all kinds, flipping through many dusty pages, scanning them for my elusive name. Sometimes I'd get a really hopeful feeling about a book and take it downstairs with me to read, but the mysterious character had never been anywhere within the pages.

Throughout all that hunting I had become familiar with the attic and its contents. I could always tell when Mother had added something new or taken something away. That's why it was so strange when my eyes fell upon the edge of a dark wooden box of some sort. There wasn't much illumination on that side of the attic, but from what I could tell, I would have guessed it to be an antique trunk like the one Grandmother kept in her room, full of crocheted blankets.

It must have been hidden away for quite some time. Nothing was disturbed right around the trunk itself, only some items and boxes several rows in front of it. I was pondering how I could have missed seeing such a possible treasure when I heard the doorbell chime faintly from below. The bell was wired so it could be heard on all three floors, but it still sounded muffled from my spot in the attic. I even wondered if I had fabricated the chime from memory, because the melody was repeating in my mind like an imagined echo long after it should have ended.

I knew it was going to take a lot of work to get to the trunk. I shrugged my way out of the tight spot between boxes and examined the situation, mentally plotting out how and where I would move the boxes and junk without forgetting the order that the items were in. I was sure it would be a project that would consume all my time and energy, and in my present state of mind and body, I wasn't up for the task.

I heard someone calling from down below. I put my ear close to the crack in the attic staircase, where it was slightly ajar.

"Zylia! Someone's here for you!" It was Ivy's voice.

I waited for a few seconds until I heard footsteps descending and growing fainter. When I felt it was safe, I climbed down out of the attic and folded the stairs back into the ceiling. I wiped at my eyes, hoping they weren't as puffy and red as I suspected, and dusted myself off as quickly as I could.

On my way to the main floor, it struck me that I had been summoned because of a visitor. It felt ominous in a way, because I wasn't accustomed to having guests come calling for me. In fact, it was so out of the ordinary that it had been over a year since it had last happened.

It was the first week of school the previous year, and I had made an acquaintance named Hannah. I don't think I had ever even learned her last name—or at least it hadn't stuck in my memory. I did, however, remember in great detail that warm day that she had walked home with me. I knew from her chatty conversation that she had had much more interest in my brother Keane than she had in me, but I was so happy to have a companion that I pretended not to notice.

I had walked her proudly in the front door and introduced her to my family with an over-eagerness that didn't go unnoticed by Adonia's rolling eyes. I wish I could have used her better-honed social skills to predict and possibly prevent the disastrous outcome of that day.

In the end there was no way I could have known that Mace would insult her, Bram would scare her, Keane would be rudely aloof and take absolutely no interest in her, and at some point, she would excuse herself to use the restroom and never return.

Mother had called her house once we'd caught on to her disappearing act. I remember watching her expression go from concern to relief and then fade into embarrassment by the time she had ended the phone call.

I begged her to tell me everything. I could tell she felt bad as she said, "Hannah's father says she won't be visiting us again. Apparently, her feelings are quite hurt."

Hannah had avoided eye contact with me for the rest of that week of school, then abruptly she was gone. I had heard from others that she moved away because her father had lost his job, but I always imagined they had left because of that painful visit to my crazy household. I would never find out for sure.

And now someone else was risking that same fate to come see me. I knew who it had to be before I saw her, but I was still surprised to find Terra standing in the entry hall. Ivy had taken her coat and was hanging it on the coat rack as I came down the last flight with heavy footfalls.

"Hey, there you are!" Terra sounded both friendly and concerned. "I didn't know where you had gone. One second you were right next to us, and the next you had disappeared without a trace. How did you do that?"

"How did I do that?" I repeated her question with my brow furrowed. I wanted to ask, "How do I not do it?" but I was pretty sure she wouldn't understand.

"Zylia's like that," Ivy informed her. "She can sneak up on you or vanish into thin air."

My mother poked her head through the kitchen entryway. "Why don't you invite your friend to stay for dinner? I'll have it ready in about an hour."

I had nightmarish visions of another failed attempt at having a guest over flash through my head. I wondered if Terra would use the same escape tactic Hannah had sometime before the evening was over.

"I'd love to; thanks," Terra accepted politely before I could even say anything.

Ivy winked at me and announced that she was off to finish her homework. I knew that hers was probably already finished and that she was doing her best to give us some privacy.

Once Ivy was gone, Terra leaned in close to my ear and whispered words that sucked the pain right out of my achy bones and wretched emotions. "*Josh was the first to notice you'd gone.*"

"Really?"

"Yeah. He couldn't figure it out. None of us could. After I checked the restroom and didn't find you there, he actually jogged ahead to look around the corner for you." Terra glared at me suspiciously. "Did you take a different route home?"

I was totally uninterested in her question. "Are you making that up? He *looked* for me?"

"Zylia, focus! I'm not kidding here. How did you get home so fast? There's no way you got that far ahead."

"How do you know when I left?"

"You were right there . . . and then you weren't." Terra narrowed her eyes in thoughtful skepticism. "I guess I was pretty wrapped up in that ice cream. I think it was better than I realized."

I knew from the way Terra was looking at me that she couldn't mentally let go of what had happened. It didn't add up to her, and I think it bothered her that she couldn't figure it out. She was onto me. Perhaps she was suspicious of my invisibility affliction. Other than Ivy, I was pretty sure she was the first to take note.

"Hey, what do you say we knock back some homework and watch some TV?" Terra asked, patting her backpack.

I knew that Mother didn't approve of distractions like music or TV while studying, so I suggested we go into the living room where we were out of her view. "Just have a seat anywhere," I said, but Terra was already flopping onto the faded brown sofa, so I made myself comfortable next to her. I reached for the remote control and handed it to Terra.

"I like your house," she said as she flipped through the channels. "It feels better than ours."

"Feels better?" I couldn't imagine what she was talking about.

"Yeah, you know, it just feels better; homey and cozy or something."

"You mean messy and lived in?" I laughed.

"I like it."

I didn't argue the point further; my eyes caught the television screen where Terra had landed her channel search. It was a trendy, energetic show geared for preteens. The attractive, makeup-coated stars made me think of Adonia and her popular friends. I usually didn't fall prey to the snare of young pop fashion or fads, but some secret part of me that yearned to be accepted and admired was guiltily intrigued.

We spent most of the next hour zoned out to the television, briefly snapping out of it to do bits of homework during commercials. By the time Mother called us to the kitchen table, we had skimmed through most of our work in what was likely a less-than-productive method.

"Mmmm, it sure does smell good in here!" Terra chirped as we made our way to the table.

Mother, always warmed by a compliment, paused and smiled before she went back to rummaging around for the giant wooden salad fork and spoon. I couldn't even spot a paperback anywhere near her, so I assumed she had paid careful attention to detail in making this meal.

Ivy was setting the table with our good dishes, which were a simple white, but it was the only matching set we owned that had survived our rowdy bunch. The rest of the family was slowly filing in and taking seats around the long table. The old piece of furniture was only meant to seat eight and having Grandmother with us pressed the capacity to nine, but my Father was squeezing in an extra chair for my guest nonetheless.

I slid in next to Terra as Mother and Adonia were placing the salad, bread, and lasagna on the table. We had to share one corner of the table, leaving our plates at odd angles and without much space, but I didn't mind. It looked like a feast and I hoped Terra would think we were all so organized, well-behaved, and hospitable every day.

As we passed the food around, I noted that Bram had a mischievous gleam in his eye as he scooped salad onto his plate. I started to panic, wondering what he was plotting. My mother must have noticed it as well, because she cleared her throat and said in a serious tone, "Bram, I hope you remember what we spoke of earlier."

This seemed to extinguish his impish spirit, because he nodded somewhat dejectedly and passed the salad without incident.

"This is really good!" Terra marveled as she plowed through a hefty square of lasagna. I wondered how she had so much room after that giant serving of ice cream she had had earlier.

The entire family agreed that the meal was delicious, and my mother sat at the other end of the table beaming. I looked from her and around at everyone else and thought, "I did this." Somehow the astonishment of me having a dinner guest had brought the whole family together at our very best. It was the perfect evening, like one you might see on an episode of the television series that Terra and I had just watched. It was funny how they were those same annoyingly hip shows that I had previously mocked, but was now reluctantly opening to.

Grandmother dropped her fork and it clattered against the tile floor. The metallic clinking was a portentous sound that brought silence to the room. Each person at the table turned in attention to the older woman, but Grandmother's gaze was leveled with mine alone.

She can see right through me, I thought as I matched her stare. Those dark, sunken eyes of hers seemed more shadowy than ever before, and she was so still I thought she may have been catatonic.

Somebody say something, I begged internally, feeling frozen and mesmerized. *Somebody say* ***something.***

My grandmother opened her mouth, and I regretted my irrational wishing. "Angelica, you're *back*! How did you make it through the shadow?" Her voice sounded odd. It was still raspy with age, but a higher, lighter note resonated through it as though her vocal chords had shed a few years.

My mother stood up and quickly walked around the table behind my grandmother. She placed a hand on her shoulder and said quietly, "Mother, are you feeling well?"

"Well, of course I'm well! Angelica's back! Isn't it exciting?" Grandmother lifted her arm and pointed a knobby finger at me. "She's here with us. Right there." I stared in dread at her trembling hand and the brittle nail at the end of her targeting index finger.

"Mother's just a little tired today." My own mother's voice was apologetic. "It looks like you're done eating, so how about you lie down for a bit?"

"No!" Grandmother shouted, slamming her palms against the table and tossing the rest of her silverware to the floor. "Don't you see? She could disappear again! She'll go away if we let her! We have to pay attention!"

I couldn't remember having seen Grandmother so out of control. It was chilling to watch, like another more commanding being was exploding out of her.

"You're getting yourself worked up over nothing," my father spoke up. He stood as well, swooping in and removing her plate and glass from before her the way a parent might do to prevent further damage during a toddler's tantrum.

I didn't dare turn my head to look at Terra, but I could sense that her form was rigid and alert beside me. I was positive she was regretting her visit and plotting her escape.

"Hold on to her! Hurry before she disappears again. *Angelica*! Don't go, Angelica! We miss you so much when you're away!" Grandmother's eyes were wide and frenzied, her arms gesturing madly. She tried to stand but there was a tremor that seemed to rock her body from head to foot.

My parents each took an elbow and pivoted her away from the table and toward her bedroom. The old woman fought against them feebly, but her frail arms didn't do much to alter her course. She kept her bird-like gaze aimed at me for as long as she could until it became too awkward or uncomfortable to extend her neck in my direction.

We could still hear muffled ranting coming from Grandmother's quarters even after she was out of sight.

"Whoa, that was so weird," commented Keane in one long exhale.

"I've never seen Grandmother act that way before," Ivy chimed in. She looked frightened and there were tears sparkling at the edges of her eyes.

"I bet we're all gonna be that loony when we're old," Bram said rudely with an exaggerated chuckle.

I heard Terra speak up, "This is the most exciting dinner I think I've ever been a part of—no offense." I turned toward her and noticed she was grinning from ear to ear.

I laughed in a combination of nerves and relief. "Sorry about that."

"Maybe we should clean up after dinner because Mother will be upset," Ivy suggested empathetically.

No one objected. We all brushed shoulders in a quiet dance around the kitchen, scraping food into the garbage disposal, rinsing dishes, and putting away the leftovers of what had almost been our perfect dinner.

"I should probably go," Terra said once the dishwasher was humming and my siblings had scattered.

I felt a stab of worry in my chest. "Please don't think this will happen every time if you decide to come more often."

Terra giggled. "Don't sweat it. I had a great time, really. It's just that I promised my dad I wouldn't stay too late."

"Okay," I said, walking her to the front door. I waited while she put her coat on and gathered up her school bag.

Terra was about to leave when she whispered, "Who's Angelica, by the way?"

The question had caught me off guard, making me realize just how curious I was about the person myself. "She was my grandmother's sister a long time ago."

"She isn't anymore?"

"Well, she died, I guess."

"Oh, really?" This seemed to intrigue Terra even more. "How did she die? And why do you think your grandma thinks you're her?"

"I . . . I don't have any idea." Suddenly I knew that I would do my best to find out all I could about the late Angelica, and I couldn't wait to start.

Terra shrugged. "All right; well, see you tomorrow."

I watched her walk out the front porch and then pressed the door closed, feeling a bit melancholy at the thought of going back to being alone.

"Oh! The kitchen's clean!" I heard my mother exclaim and figured that Grandmother must have finally settled.

I walked back into the kitchen and saw my father kissing my mother against the hair. "I'm headed up to bed," he said in a drowsy tone that was seemingly unmoved by the sanitary kitchen.

"I'll be up in a second," Mother said after him.

I waited for him to leave before I boldly asked her, "Why does Grandmother think I'm someone else?"

Mother gave me a tired smile. "Oh, darling, don't worry about that. Her mind isn't right. It's getting worse lately."

"But why me? Why Angelica?"

Mother cocked her head in thought. "I really can't say, except that the two of you look rather similar. If I ever dig up some old photos I'll show you, but tonight I'm heading upstairs to relax."

"How did she die?" I threw the question out quickly before she could escape to her bedroom.

"Your grandmother hasn't really talked about it a whole lot, at least not until recently . . . but," she paused, her face scrunching up as if she didn't want to tell me after all, "one morning when she was around your age, her family couldn't find her. I think your grandmother was the first to notice her missing. Her bed hadn't been slept in, and something like a week later they found a blue dress of hers tangled up at the edge of that stream that runs through Nightingale Park, a couple miles away from here. You've been there, I'm sure. Your father used to love it there so much I hadn't wanted to spoil it for him or anyone else by telling what had happened. I can't recall when he found out."

I had only a foggy memory of what must have been the park. It seemed that Father had taken us children picnicking there once as a special treat. I could faintly recall the warm breath of summer as I lay on the checked cloth and stared up into what I thought had been a forest canopy. It had certainly been more verdant and lush than any of the parks close by in our own neighborhood. I remembered asking to go again after that, but as far as I could remember my pleas were ignored; over the years I had forgotten about the place completely. I doubted that I would have felt so enchanted with that lovely patch of earth had I known the story of my great-aunt's demise. I wondered if the tale had ultimately deterred my father from taking us there.

"She drowned?" I asked, wanting to make certain.

"Well . . . apparently, I guess. I mean, she couldn't swim, and she was always wandering off," Mother said, growing wearier of the conversation with each word. "They never found her little body, though."

I shuddered visibly and uncontrollably.

"It was before my time. I really don't know the whole story." Her sigh was dismissive. "Well, I'm off to my room, sweetie. We'll talk some other time, okay?" Mother patted my head and ascended the stairs.

I followed her at a fraction of her pace. My mind was moving quickly through past, present, and possible futures. In my tornado of thoughts, questions, and ideas there was an image forming—a great shadow in the shape of me. Was I the same as my great-aunt Angelica? Would I disappear just like her, the way Grandmother feared?

On the second floor I paused, hearing my parents' muffled voices from behind their bedroom door. I couldn't hear the actual words they were saying, but their tones sounded fretful and anxious, leaving me with a cold trepidation in my tummy.

If I hadn't paused to listen I wouldn't have seen the heavy language arts book fly out of Keane's bedroom doorway and slam against the hallway wall. I gawked at the spot where it had landed; its pages had fanned open and tangled under the weight of the hardback cover. I moved across the floor to pick it up, smoothing the cool pages.

I could see Keane through the open doorway, sitting at the end of his full-size bed, arms folded angrily across his chest. He brusquely snatched the book out of my hands when I took it to him, but I knew the frustration wasn't meant for me.

Keane was a star student when it came to math or science, but in the last couple years he had begun to struggle in other areas like vocabulary and writing. I had heard my mother say once that it was simply because he had no interest in those things and his difficulties had nothing to do with his ability. As I looked around his cluttered room at all the model airplanes and spaceships, posters of the galaxy, and his grotesque bug collection, I tended to agree with her. He had no patience for anything he wasn't completely absorbed in.

"What are you working on?" I asked quietly, not wanting to anger him further.

"Nothing anymore." He wouldn't meet my eyes, but he didn't yell at me to go away either. After a minute or two he flipped the book open, turned the pages so rambunctiously I thought he would tear them, and finally smacked his palm against a page.

I sat next to him on the bed and gingerly slid the book onto my lap. It was a chapter on prepositional phrases, and it began with a short list of practice exercises. I figured out the answers after quickly perusing the questions above the asinine example sentences.

"Wow, can you believe some of these sentences? They are so ridiculous!" I commented, trying to make light of the situation. "Listen to this one. '*Judy slipped on a banana peel.*' Or here's another. '*Billy stood in the potato sack and jumped with all his might.*' Who comes up with this stuff?"

Keane let out a short, huffy sigh. "Yeah, I know. Stupid, huh?"

"If you want, we can start by going over these," I offered. "You know, just to see how silly this stuff gets."

"Um . . ." Keane scooted closer to me, looking at the book over my shoulder. "I guess that'd be okay . . . thanks."

By the time I left Keane's room, his homework was completed, and I added mental exhaustion to my list of physical complaints. I trudged up to my room, feeling utterly depleted. It was only eight-thirty, but I flopped onto my bed, and my pillow never felt so soft and cool.

"Are you going to sleep already?" Ivy spoke up. I hadn't even noticed her sitting crossed-legged on her bed, peering at me from over that sinister book of Adonia's she had been reading.

I let out a moan that was muffled by my pillow. My teeth had yet to be brushed, I was still fully clothed including my shoes, and I was lying atop my comforter, but even so my limbs were paralyzed with fatigue.

"Why haven't you told me about Terra?" asked Ivy. She was leaning forward with an animated twinkle in her eyes. "I know you don't talk much, but I thought for sure you would tell me if you . . . Are you listening?"

"Mm-hmm," I mumbled.

"She seems really nice. I'm so happy you made a friend! I mean, not that you don't have friends . . . I just . . ." Ivy waved her hand in the air as if to swish her words away. "So, tell me about her. What is she like? I bet she's funny, but sort of in like a cool way, right?"

I could hear her speaking, but I was too tired to respond. The room started appearing wavy in my vision, the colors blending to make crimped rainbow designs. Soon I was fading in and out of consciousness and slipping solidly into the dream realm.

I could see a young woman in a long, blue dress with ebony hair flowing down her back. She was facing away from me, exiting through a door that jingled. It was the door to the ice cream shop. I followed her outside but suddenly we were in a long, wooden-planked hallway, and she began to run.

"Wait!" I called after her, reaching out to try to grab the tail of her cascading, filmy dress.

I ran harder, extending my hands so that I could just touch the smooth, lustrous fabric; but when I did, the threads turned to powder-blue smoke on my fingertips.

The hallway ended and opened into an emerald-green meadow. It was so sunny and bright I could barely see her ahead of me but I did my best to keep up with her elegant bound.

When she came up upon a sparkling creek I shouted, "Angelica, *no*; you can't swim!"

I heard the most melodious laughter, like soothing birdsong. She was leaning forward, clutching her middle, thoroughly amused. Straight black hair covered her face.

I had finally caught up with the woman. I was standing directly in front of her, but I didn't dare to touch her lest she turn to smoke. "What is so funny?" I asked.

"You called me Angelica." Her voice was clear and sweet. She turned toward me then and I saw my own face looking back at me. "But Angelica is *you,*" she whispered.

And in a single leap she splashed into the creek ahead and disappeared into the shallow water. I rushed to the water's edge, wading in to my knees. *"Angelica!"* I kept shouting.

In the place she had gone under, the liquid began to ripple, bubble, and froth; soon the blue dress emerged on the surface of the water. I reached out to retrieve it and instantly my eyes were open, and I was lying in my dark bedroom.

It was much later, but I hadn't moved since I had first closed my eyes; my entire body was cold and stiff. I kicked off my shoes, trying not to wake Ivy, and nestled under my blankets. I shivered, waiting for sleep to overtake me again as the whispered phrase *Angelica is you* echoed throughout my drowsy mind.

Chapter Ten

Art class was usually my one great pleasure involving school, but today my mind was miles away from the still-life charcoal shading we were practicing on thick cardstock. I was supposed to be reproducing the bowl of fruit perched on a stand at the front of the class into an art form, but when I looked down at my smudgy black-and-white picture, an altogether different image was emerging.

The fruit bowl itself was too blocky and large for the page, and where I had started to draw a banana peeking out of the top, it happened to look more like the shadow of a thin person.

It took me a few seconds before the illustration came into focus, and I realized I was staring at the trunk in the attic with a figure hovering over it. Perhaps my subconscious mind had been controlling my hand while my thoughts were elsewhere.

In truth, I hadn't thought much about the attic and its newly discovered contents since I'd shut my eyes the night before. Instead, my mind had been filled with visions of the strange dream involving my great-aunt. I could still see her running ahead of me, evading me. More than ever, I wanted to know everything there was to know about her. I imagined that she was just like me, having faced the same problems and issues in an altogether different generation.

The more I looked intently at my drawing, the more I knew that it was no bowl of fruit mirrored on the page. I had to find a way to search that trunk—the real one in my attic. It wouldn't be an easy job and I doubted whether I could even accomplish the feat by myself, especially with my sore muscles.

"Let's all start cleaning up before the bell rings." My teacher's voice jolted through my internal contemplation and brought me back to the present. "And let's not forget about our special project for the art show during open house. Those of you whose artwork for the show is still in the craft closet may feel free to take it home to add any finishing touches you might like. Oh, and make sure to check with me before borrowing any supplies. You'll have to sign on the loan sheet first."

Panic made a zigzag throughout my intestines. I had known about the project for weeks. We had started it in class and were allowed to take it out whenever we had an empty, unproductive chunk of time left over near the end of the hour. It should have been easy enough since the requirements were so wide: a piece with the subject and media completely of our own preference as long as it wasn't offensive or disturbing in any way. The only other stipulation I could remember was that the teacher desperately wanted the artwork to show off something her students had learned so far that year in the class. It was a flexible assignment that counted for a good part of my grade, and in all honesty, I hadn't even begun. The only effort I had put forth was to choose an eight-by-eleven-inch cut of pale blue matte board and decide that my drawing should take place on it.

I recovered the board from the craft closet and held it against my chest in case the teacher should notice that it was completely devoid of diligence, save my full name scrawled on the back and a tiny scuff mark of unknown origins in one corner.

I kept catching glances of some of my classmates' projects that made my heart quicken: a painted mountain landscape, a colored-pencil drawing of a ladybug, and some sort of intricate three-dimensional abstract design.

I couldn't figure out why I had procrastinated so long, but as the final bell of the day rang, I suddenly knew exactly what I would draw. It would be a scene from my dream—the eerie, elusive woman in the blue dress. Maybe putting her on paper would make her real somehow. I imagined her springing to life, returning from the oblivion into which she had disappeared.

I shook myself from my reverie, left my last classroom, and headed toward my locker. Simply deciding had sharpened my thoughts to some degree, and I was already making a mental plan as I loaded up my backpack with the books I would need for my homework.

I had to get into that trunk, but it was going to take some effort. In my head I played out the shifting of boxes like one of those parking lot puzzle games Keane would play on his tablet. I remembered how some cars would only move vertically and others only horizontally until you found the combination that would clear a path for a single car to drive down the center and exit the lot. Keane had convinced me to play a few times, and the game both challenged and frustrated me. Each level increased in difficulty until finally I would give in to Keane persistently telling me he could do it for me.

Now I wondered if there was a sequence or arrangement that would help me to make it back to that trunk without tipping over or plowing through everything in the path and alerting Mother to an attic intruder.

I felt a tap on my shoulder. "Hey, you." I turned and saw Terra giving me a goofy face.

"Hi," I said back. I had been glad that morning on the way to school that Terra hadn't brought up my grandmother's behavior even once. It was as if she had graciously dismissed the subject from her mind completely. "You ready to head home?"

"Yeah, but actually, I meant to tell you my dad's picking me up today. I have a dentist appointment," said Terra, her face changing to disgust. "I'd much rather be going home with you; trust me."

"Oh, okay. Hopefully they leave you with a few teeth." I was trying to mask my disappointment by being funny, but I knew I sounded like my dorky father.

"Hey, whatcha drawing?" Terra was trying to peek at the front of my blank piece of artwork that I was preparing to cart home.

"It's supposed to be for the art show. I haven't exactly started."

"Glad I don't have to do one. I have the class, but I transferred to this school late enough that she isn't going to make me do it. Sucks to be you," Terra laughed. "What's yours gonna be? Maybe I could help you with it."

I smiled at the offer. "When you have some time, I'd love to tell you all about it."

"Okay, sounds good. I better take off. My dad's probably waiting." And with that she was on her way.

I tried to gather my things as quickly as possible, so I could walk out with her. I didn't want anyone plowing into me and bending my art paper, which was far less likely if I stuck close to Terra.

In addition, I felt mildly curious about my best friend's father, whom I had yet to even catch a glimpse of. I darted in and out of the crowd rushing for the door, spotting the back of Terra's amber-colored hair briefly before I lost sight of her again. For some reason I felt a foolish sense of desperation, as if she would be gone forever as soon as I lost sight of her. I tried to tell myself that I was normal in my feelings, simply nosy about seeing the man who had raised my amazing bestie. I wondered if he was rugged and handsome with a gravelly, movie-star voice, always ready to swoop in to save his daughter from trouble. Or maybe he was smart-looking in glasses and a suit and could teach her about anything from his impressive photographic memory. I had to know.

I knew that I was being ridiculous as I shoved my way forward on the sidewalk attempting to prove or disprove my harebrained imagination, my feet moving on unrestrained impulses.

It was my carelessness that caused me to smash into a much shorter girl, sending her careening to the pavement below. While students circled around, I stood there in dismay, trying to decipher whether I had indeed knocked someone down. I couldn't imagine that my nearly invisible self had done such a thing. I mean sure, I had been shoved, knocked down, and even trampled over on several occasions throughout my life, but I couldn't remember ever doing it to another soul. I hadn't even known it was possible.

"I . . . I'm sorry. I didn't see you there," I said down to the crumpled girl. After a couple seconds it occurred to me to put my hand out in a gesture of assistance.

The girl looked up at me with confused, stormy gray eyes. She brushed her disheveled strawberry-blonde hair away from her face before scrambling to gather her scattered items. Even as she reached to pick up the textbooks and loose pages, random sneakers and shoes were flattening, creasing, and leaving footprints on almost everything.

I did my best to help her, bending down and scooping up what I could with my one free hand while I protected my matte board and absorbed a few careless bumps from passersby above. I noticed that the departing students were seemingly unaware of the both of us and it was a joint struggle to get back up on our feet.

"I'm really so sorry about . . ." I looked around me in all directions, but the poor girl was nowhere to be seen, as if she had disappeared into thin air. I suppose it was right about that moment when I realized where I had seen her before. She was the same weeping girl I'd spotted in the bathroom when I'd been hiding out from Josh earlier in the week. I hadn't placed her right away since it was my first time viewing her face, but that lovely, wavy hair was an eventual giveaway.

Knowing I had plowed into someone who was obviously already having an emotional week made me feel even guiltier. I walked home, trying to shrug the weight of the error off my shoulders by replaying the scene, analyzing and obsessing over it.

By the time I made it back home, I had a semblance of peace of mind over the situation—not because I had it all worked out in my head, but because my thoughts were shifting to my art project and my late aunt Angelica.

I felt that working on the project would help me get to the bottom of what had happened to her, maybe even of what was happening to me. In my dream her face had mirrored mine, but now that I was doing the drawing, I desperately wanted to know what the real Angelica had looked like. There was only one way I knew to find out, and although it scared me, I was prepared to try.

I quickly put my coat and school things away before launching into my plan. First, I took note of my surroundings, combing the first floor for occupants. I had spotted my mother reading in the living room, so I was fairly sure she'd be occupied for a while; the only other person in sight was Bram at the far side of the kitchen making a snack of animal crackers dipped in hazelnut butter.

I decided I could begin the first stage of my plot by sidling into the chair next to my grandmother in the keeping room. She was working her aluminum crochet hooks on a nearly completed doily; her eyes peered through thick glasses, lips moving rhythmically.

The television was tuned to the weather channel, but Grandmother had the sound muted. I watched a man with a furrowed brow and salt-and-pepper-colored hair silently miming with big gestures over a map of the United States. He looked a bit like an ape with his deep-set eyes resting in shadows and his arms sweeping from one side of the screen to the other. I kept looking on while I wondered what to say to my grandmother.

"Hmm? What was that?" my grandmother asked quietly.

"Um, I didn't say anything."

She peered at me with assessing eyes from over the top of her spectacles. "Well, why not? You've been sitting there long enough to make conversation, don't you think?"

This appeared to be the blunt and cynical grandmother I had known before the dementia had gotten bad. At least this seemed to be her for the moment, so I decided to take advantage of her mindset. "How was your day?" I asked.

"It was great if you like being old and weak and bossed around all day by the younger generation," she said, laughing with no humor in her tone.

I chuckled along with her until a stern look flashed across her face and silenced me immediately.

"What about you? How was your day?" she muttered once my laughter had ceased and the air around us fell silent.

"It was good, nice and . . . good," I faltered. I wasn't used to holding conversations, and every time I opened my mouth I was painfully reminded of this. I had never learned how to speak to my grandmother, especially. Even before her mind had begun to slip, I still saw her as a stern, unapproachable woman. Not because she had ever really been overly severe toward me, but because our generations were so vastly different that each interchange felt as if something were lost in translation.

I tried again with, "I'm working on a project for art class, actually. I was wondering if you might be able to help me with it a little."

Grandmother's hands paused over her lap and she looked at me curiously.

"It's—um—a drawing. I was wondering if you could show me some old photos from when you were a girl."

Grandmother smiled, the wrinkles on her face becoming more pronounced. "I haven't gotten those out in ages."

I felt giddy, but I was trying not to let it show for fear I wouldn't be taken seriously. "Do you know where they are?"

"Well, of course I do!" Grandmother had cast her crochet utensils aside on the end table and was scooting to the edge of her recliner. "Why don't we go and take a look?"

I was up in an instant, extending my arms and helping her to stand. Her bones popped and creaked in protest like the sound of twigs snapping. All at once I was reminded of the unsettling sound my old Barbie dolls' legs would make when I would bend and pose them. The poorly articulated joints below those rubbery knees were always a morbid interest of my twin brothers. I would often find my frizzy-haired dolls with their legs bent forward at the knee, looking like their limbs had been grotesquely broken.

I tried my best to push this image out of my head as I followed slowly behind my grandmother and headed into her bedroom. When we finally crossed the threshold, the drapes were all drawn so I waited while Grandmother fussed with the dimmer switch until an unflattering orange glow was cast over the gaping space.

I had always found my grandmother's room to be the most depressing location in our home. If the lack of light wasn't dismal enough, then the adjustable hospital bed that was pushed up against the far wall stuck out like a reminder of illness and old age. In addition, the musty odor of ancient furniture, well-worn rugs, and medicated vapor rub assaulted your nostrils immediately upon entry.

When I was younger, I remembered the place being much more intriguing, compelling me to peek into my grandmother's medicine cabinet to steal a glance at her highly fascinating floating teeth in a jar. If the glass happened to be empty, I might linger to press my fingertips into her gel candles to get at the elusive pieces of wax fruit embedded within. In recent years I had had no interest in her rooms; the once-enticing allure had changed into an overall avoidance.

"Here we are," Grandmother mumbled quietly as she stooped over the old trunk at the end of her narrow bed.

When I laid eyes on the battered cedar chest I asked, "Grandmother, where did you get that trunk? Do you have more than one?"

She paused, looking just as inquisitive as I sounded. "This old thing? My father made it for me when I was just a girl. I used to keep my dolls and playthings in here." She was fondly petting the shabby lid of the chest. "He made one just like it for my sister as well. I was always going to pass this on to your mother, but maybe you should have it after I'm gone."

I was glad she wasn't looking at my face as she spoke because the comment had made me feel awkward, and although I wasn't close to my grandmother, I couldn't fathom the thought of her not being a daily part of our family. I shifted my weight, trying to think of something respectfully appreciative that I could say. Nothing even remotely suitable came to mind.

I was relieved when she changed the subject and asked for my help to open the lid, directing me to search around inside. I moved my hands past layers of quilts and crocheted blankets until I touched the hard, cool surface of what felt like books.

"I think I've got something." I was shoulder-deep into the trunk, coarse yarn pressing against one side of my face.

"Oh, good; that's the one I was hoping you'd find!" Grandmother said excitedly as I produced a thick, brown leather photo album and handed it to her.

She shuffled over to her desk and sat in the straight-backed chair in front of it. There was nowhere for me to sit so I hovered next to her, watching as she cleared away bundles of primary-colored yarn, so she could open the large album.

"My mother and father didn't take a lot of photographs. It wasn't so easy back then as it is for you lot, with your newfangled devices and all. I'm so glad I taught *your* mother to do it more often." She paused, and her tone changed suddenly. "In the end, sometimes the pictures are all we have left to remind us that the memories we have weren't just dreams." Her eyes were distant as she spoke, her withered hands moving along the book edges. I couldn't remember ever hearing her use that voice with me before. It was like she had overlooked the fact that I was her young grandchild and was addressing me as a peer instead. It made me feel grown-up and gave me hope that I would finally get answers to my nagging questions.

I felt a little impatient as she flipped slowly through solemn-faced pictures of my great-grandparents and ancient relatives I had never seen or known of. I was only listening to about half of what she was saying as she droned on about names, birthdates, personalities, and occupations.

". . . and he was quite the character," Grandmother chuckled as she tapped a crooked finger against a faded picture of a dark-haired man. She was still smiling and sighing as she unhurriedly turned the page.

That's when I saw her. A girl in a wrinkled photo at the bottom corner of the page beckoned to me with sullen, emerald eyes under a fan of jet-black lashes. She was perched on a chair in front of a frosty window, knees pulled up to her chest with bare feet peeking out from under the hem of a simple white dress. She looked so young and small, and there was something about her unsmiling expression that suggested she was timid of the camera. But as I peered longer I started to believe that her shyness was blended with astonishment, as if she were unaccustomed to being the object of attention.

I could see why Grandmother would think we looked alike. We had the same eyes and hair, but in the picture Angelica wore her long, dark tresses pulled away from her face with only a few flyaway pieces dangling down.

Her skin was pale, maybe even lighter than mine, and there were other differences as well. Her chin didn't come to a point the way I saw mine, but was rounded and shorter. Her lips were fuller and more pronounced, too, giving her an innocent pout instead of the thin, wary glower I displayed.

I couldn't wait for my grandmother's tedious dialogue to reach that photo, so I pointed to it, interrupting her by asking, "This is Angelica, isn't it?"

Her eyes caught the picture and her face drooped. "Yes, my sister. She reminds me of you, I must say." Grandmother's eyes turned to me and back to the picture as if she were comparing the two of us. "There should be more of her in here somewhere." She started leafing through the pages, searching.

"What happened to her?" I asked.

Wetness rose up along the rims of her eyes. "Everyone accepted that she had died, but I know that's not what happened at all. It's just . . ." She paused, gesturing at another photo of Angelica she had found. This one was older, and the girl appeared barely more than a toddler, peeking from behind a tweed-clad leg that belonged to an adult who was otherwise out of the shot. She was out of focus and her hair and clothes almost blended in with a dark paneled background, making her appear as a fuzzy apparition.

"You don't think she died?" I coaxed my grandmother, who had ceased talking and was only moving her lips nervously.

Her sparse gray eyebrows drew together as she examined me, making the skin in between them shift into a maze of leathery sand dunes. "Well of *course* she didn't die. But you know that already, don't you?" Her voice had lowered at least an octave, and it sent chills down my spine.

"Why would I know that?" was my whispered question.

"Because you've been there; I know you have. You've been to the place she went where no one else could see her." Grandmother stood upright, save the bend in her spine, looking me square in the face. "You are just like her. You fade away sometimes when no one is looking, right out of this world and into another."

I was trembling from the inside out. "I—I don't know what you mean . . ."

"Of course, you know!" Grandmother screamed. I couldn't recall her shouting at such a high decibel before, and it was quite paralyzing to experience. Even though she had raised her voice at us kids from time to time, it was nothing compared to the hysterical screeching of her vocal chords she was displaying.

I wasn't prepared when Grandmother shoved the palm of her hand dead center against the top of my chest, at the base of my neck. I lost my balance and staggered backward, my hands clawing at the air for balance and knocking over a basket of sewing supplies from the desk. It had happened too fast, and I was unable to steady myself in time before landing on my bottom against the thin rug.

"You tell me; you tell me *now*!" She was hovering over me, shaking a finger at me in rage. It didn't occur to me that her body was old and frail, but instead she seemed more powerful and terrifying than anything I could have dreamed up on my own. From my view, my harmless little grandmother had morphed into something sinister and villainous.

"Tell you *what*? I don't understand!" My voice came out quite audibly on this occasion, taking on an unhinged note of its own.

"Tell me where she is. Where is it that the two of you go? Where do *you* go? I've heard her voice calling to me from there but I don't know the way."

I spoke to her from my spot on the floor, "Grandmother, what are you saying? I don't go anywhere with Angelica! You're not making any sense." I didn't know I was crying until I felt liquid dripping from my cheeks. I was doing my best to wipe away the tears as the old woman rummaged around on the surface of her desk.

"Bring her back to me! I know you can do it," Grandmother commanded. When I looked up from rubbing my eyes I saw that she was holding a pair of sewing scissors menacingly, the sharp edge pointed at me.

Reality as I knew it vanished into a distant memory and the walls around me blurred and melted in my peripheral vision. The only thing I was acutely aware of was the demented old woman waving around a shiny metal weapon. In my head I was trying to hold off mulling over how the conversation had reached this violent outburst, and instead concentrate on an escape plan.

"You'll pay for taking her from me." She spat the words out at me, her voice icy cold.

Alarm rang throughout my skull and I quickly scooted backward toward the door, using my hands and heels in a crab crawl. My shaky limbs weren't cooperating like they should have been, and I managed to get my ankles tangled up, causing me to fall back against my elbows.

Grandmother kept advancing, slowly but surely shuffling toward me. *This can't be real; maybe she is only teasing me after all.* I rolled to my side, and as I was pulling myself upright I caught sight of Bram standing there gaping in the doorway. He must have left his snack to see what all the commotion was about, and his shocked, frightened expression did nothing to calm my own fears.

I had stood up so quickly that my vision darkened in a head rush, and it took a moment for my equilibrium to adjust. It was enough time for my grandmother to lunge at my chest with the scissors in a stabbing motion. I didn't even get the chance to scream.

Chapter Eleven

I didn't remember reaching for my grandmother's arm, but her bony wrist was suddenly in my grasp, and as the makeshift weapon turned, I was staring at my wide-eyed expression of horror in the reflective metal of the thick scissors.

"You . . . *forever* . . . why?" Grandmother's words were incoherent and breathless, and her eyes had the look of some rabid animal.

I heard strange squeaking noises, like something that would have emanated from a whimpering, distressed mouse. It was slowly increasing, becoming louder until finally I realized it was coming from my own lips as I struggled to keep the weapon away from my chest.

A scream resonated from the doorway behind me; next, there was a blur of brown sweater material filling my vision and the soft fabric of it pressing against my arms and face.

My mother had put herself between the two of us, and it didn't take long for her to wrestle the weapon from my grandmother. "Mother!" she kept repeating, horrified. The metal scissors were clenched tightly in one hand, held slightly behind her back while her free arm was extended in an appeasing gesture.

Grandmother still appeared wild and untamed. She was trembling and muttering nonsensical words while wringing her hands and backing away.

Mother's jaw was hanging slack as she looked back and forth between me and Grandmother. "Wh-wha . . . what . . . happened?" she stammered, trying to piece together how anything could have come to this.

I was sobbing by now, words choked up at the back of my throat, tears and mucus streaming down my face.

"*She happened!*" Grandmother suddenly answered. Her voice was an intimidating squawk, and her index finger was pointed accusingly in my direction. She looked as if she might pounce on me again at any second.

Mother grabbed my arm a little too harshly and ushered me through the door frame. By then Adonia and Keane were hanging alongside Bram, all with astounded and questioning expressions.

"Everyone upstairs!" Mother shouted. I could hear the anxiety in her voice, and it was about as far from comforting as anything could be. Mothers were supposed to be composed, controlled, and always have all the answers. The look of confusion in her frightened eyes was turning my world upside down. "Wait, not you, Adonia," she called after we had all begun to scamper like terrified bunnies. "You go get the phone and call your father."

Ivy and Mace appeared, curious to know what was going on. This time it was Adonia who shouted at everyone to get upstairs. No one argued, and minor collisions occurred in the stairway as we all ran to our rooms.

"Gosh, Zylia, what did you do to Grandmother?" Mace asked before he launched ahead of me two stairs at a time. "I think you broke her!"

I let everyone pass me as I tried to control my sniveling. With a waterfall of tears distorting my vision, I tripped on the stairs until I eventually made it up to my room.

Ivy was already there, standing at the door and ushering me inside with one of her thin little arms around my shoulders. The gesture was comforting, but I was too humiliated about my sobbing to sink against her slight frame. My baby sister must have sensed my unease, because she pulled away from me and came back a few seconds later with a wad of toilet paper in her hand.

I took it and sat on the end of my bed, dabbing and wiping at my eyes and nose. Ivy sat across from me on her own bed, politely waiting until my sniffling had completely stopped before asking any questions.

"What happened down there, Zy?" she inquired, framing the question softly and non-judgmentally.

"I'm not sure. Grandmother just went crazy. I thought she was going to kill me."

Adonia suddenly burst into our bedroom, hesitating in the doorway when she realized she hadn't knocked. She made a halfhearted attempt at rapping on the door she had already swung open.

I was not at all excited to see her. I wondered if she would scold me for upsetting our grandmother, and I didn't think my weak emotions could stand up to any more jolts. My back was tightening, and I felt like my shoulders were up around my ears.

"Hey," she said in a long breath. "How are you doing?" Adonia was looking directly at me, but I still thought maybe she was speaking to Ivy with those kind words. I didn't accept that they were meant for me until she came and sat next to me on the bed.

As far as I remembered, Adonia hadn't been in our room in a long time. Her presence in our space had always seemed to magnify the juvenile décor, making our matching lilac comforters and toy box full of Barbie dolls seem especially infantile. Instead of thinking of an answer for my older sister, I stared at that beat-up wooden box with an assortment of plastic limbs and fuzzy doll hair poking out of it and wished intensely that all of them belonged to Ivy. The truth was that most of them were mine, and every now and then I'd still get the urge to pull them out and play elaborate games of dress-up, house, and hopeful depictions of my future love life.

Adonia's palm waved in front of my eyes. "Zylia, are you okay?"

I forced myself to focus on her face. "It's all my fault. I shouldn't have asked Grandmother about Angelica. I don't know why I did it; I just wanted to know why she always calls me that. She thinks I'm someone else—some*thing* else."

"No, no, no," Adonia said soothingly. "She's just sick is all. She doesn't know what she's doing anymore. You know how it is; she gets all mixed up."

"I look just like her. She showed me pictures," I said quietly.

Adonia didn't hear me and went on, "I heard Mother talking on the phone. She was telling Dad that she didn't know how much longer she could handle the dementia."

"What did she mean by that?" asked Ivy, her freckled face filling with concern.

Adonia shrugged. "She's on the phone with the doctor now, or at least she was when I came up here."

"I wonder what the doctor will say," Ivy breathed.

I stood up and headed to the bathroom. No one said anything or tried to stop me, but I don't think it was because they hadn't noticed my movements. I had somehow evoked a tender pity from my sisters that was nearly tangible in the room.

I washed my face, trying not to stare too long at the red puffiness that had taken over. I was drying my face when I felt another wave of emotion overtaking me, so I pressed the hand towel hard against my mouth and nose to stifle the bawl. After a few seconds the feeling began to ebb; when I realized that no more tears were going to come, I calmly hung up the hand towel and smoothed my hair.

My sisters stopped talking when I reentered the bedroom, but I didn't really care to know what they had been discussing. "I think I need to lie down."

Adonia jumped off my bed instantly as if she had been spring-loaded. "Sure, yeah; you should. Come on, Ivy, let's give her some space."

I lay with my back to them, feeling a sense of comfort and relief when the door clicked shut and I knew I was alone. I didn't fall asleep; I just cleared my mind by visually tracing the familiar cracks in the old plaster walls. Sometimes I would see them as distant rivers or roads on a map, but they kept reminding me of the wrinkles in my grandmother's angry face.

Ivy called me down for a late dinner that night. All of us siblings moved silently around two boxes of pizza, soda, and paper plates set out on the kitchen island. I waited for everyone else to fix their plates before I picked the tiniest slice of pepperoni pie I could find and slid it onto a napkin. Afterward, I made my way to the table to join everyone else, looking over my shoulder cautiously every few steps. I kept imaging Grandmother jumping out at me again with that giant pair of scissors.

My father was the next person to appear in the kitchen, his features drawn into a tight, worried frown. "Kids, after dinner everyone goes back upstairs, understand? Your mother and grandmother are in the front living room, and we need to keep it as quiet as possible. She'll probably go her back to her room after you guys eat, but for now we wanted to keep her as far away from the action as possible."

I watched as all my siblings nodded, and when I found my father's eyes boring into my own face I quickly followed suit. He was probably angry at me for starting this whole mess.

"Is Grandmother okay?" Adonia asked.

Father nodded a bit hesitantly. "She's all right for now. I think she'll stay that way as long as no one disturbs her, and we keep it very quiet. Your mother is tending to her, so don't go bothering her either. I mean it." He put his index finger to his lips, further driving home his point about silence. "I'll be in my room if anyone needs me, but I think I can trust you all to behave yourselves—especially under these circumstances."

Once he was gone I chewed very slowly, watching my brothers and sisters as they wordlessly demolished every slice of pizza and retreated upstairs one by one.

It wasn't long before I was the only one seated at the big oak table littered with crumbs and greasy fingerprints. I packed the cardboard pizza boxes down into the trash can and ran a damp towel over the table. I couldn't hear anything in the rest of the house except for the faint whine of a toilet being flushed upstairs. I stood for a few seconds to take in the dark and quiet that felt so out of the ordinary.

I slipped back into the shadows of the keeping room, tripping once on the leg of an ottoman. I waited for a few seconds to see if the noise would rouse any suspicion, but the house was still silent, so I wasted no more time in darting into my grandmother's room.

I knew it was risky to turn on the light, but there was no way I could find the photo album or endure the sinister surroundings without it. The dim orange glow led my eyes to the album sprawled out on the floor near the desk. I wondered if it had landed there sometime during the uncanny struggle, but I couldn't be sure.

As soon as it was in my hands, I switched the light off and stealthily bolted upstairs. My footfalls barely made a sound, as if I were only a feather floating up to my room above.

Ivy was leaning against her headboard, eyelids closed and jaw hanging slack, with a book against her chest. She was startled awake when I entered the room, and the book slid to the floor with a thud.

"Hey, Zy," she said sleepily, sliding down and burrowing deeper under her comforter. "When the door opened at first you weren't there . . . I couldn't see you . . . at all." With that dreamy comment she was out like a light, snoring in her soft, dainty fashion.

I leafed through the album quickly, but could find no pictures of Angelica. The ones Grandmother had shown me earlier seemed to have disappeared. I thought I was just skipping over them in haste, but I located several blank squares where it was obvious photos had been before, aged brown outlines appearing in the adhesive behind the clear film.

I shoved the book under my bed and pulled out my largest sketch pad while I was on the floor. I grabbed some charcoal pencils and tried to find the ghostly image of Angelica in my mind.

Like a lunatic, I scraped pencil over paper, fast and harsh while the image in my brain was still fresh. I used my fingertips to blend and an eraser to clean and sharpen the edges.

After I had worked on the drawing for some time, I set it atop the desk, propping it up against the wall. Lying back on my bed gave me a good vantage point to examine it. The smeary charcoal blended and swirled in my vision, and I was falling asleep almost instantly.

There was sunshine lighting up the room when I opened my eyes, more than I could remember seeing in the gloomy weather of the past several days. I watched the illuminated dust particles dancing above my face as I gradually blinked myself toward a conscious state. The light was unstable in its glittering intensity, fading slightly grayer and then brightening again to a cheery yellow. I didn't bother looking out my window, but I knew that clouds must be drifting lazily across the sun.

When I sat upright, the drawing greeted my vision jarringly. Its black lines were striking and intense, outlining Angelica in a flowing dress, her head turned to look over her shoulder at the viewer of the sketch. Her hair was long, shiny and black; it appeared almost real, frozen in the midst of a swinging motion.

Everything looked right except for her face. It wasn't there. Only blank, white page stared back at me. I knew that this would be the rough outline for my school project, and although it was a good start, that face would have to come to me eventually.

There was a pounding on my bedroom door and I heard Adonia call, "Breakfast!"

Still wearing my clothes from the day before, I shuffled downstairs and found my family hovering and picking over a giant box of donuts. I knew my father must have been in charge of breakfast, because they were his favorite and my mother was never one to buy them.

Mace had crumbs all over his chin, and his cheeks were puffed out like a greedy squirrel. "Sugar rush!" he said too loudly, sending bits of cake donut flying.

"Hush!" said Father sternly. "We don't want to wake your grandmother. Why can't you keep it down when I ask you to?"

"Sorry," Mace said sincerely, but the word came out distorted through the half-chewed donut and sounded more like "Shaw-wee."

I felt a hand clamp down on my shoulder and looked up into the grave face of my mother. "Everyone needs to keep clear of Grandmother, but especially you, Zylia. I know you didn't mean for any of this to happen and it is not your fault, but I think it's best if you don't see her at all for a while. Understand?"

I felt like the whole family was staring at me. I knew that my mother wasn't really angry with me, just tired and drained from the situation, but her voice sounded so harsh that I found myself blinking quickly before tears could form.

In truth, I knew that I had brought on my grandmother's outburst. I had pressured her into showing me those photos, wanting to drag up the past. I couldn't leave it alone, even when I knew it was risky to her fragile mental condition. The cold guilt in the pit of my stomach was growing.

"Yeah, of course; I understand," I answered, my voice sounding a bit gravelly.

Suddenly I had to get out of the house as fast as I could. I ran back upstairs, hastily washed up, and threw on a pair of faded dark jeans and a long-sleeved gray t-shirt that was worn and soft. The shirt had an old ink stain on the breast, so I pulled on another smaller shirt over the top. It was short-sleeved and fitted with a black-and-white album cover depicted on the front.

As soon as I was ready, I bolted outside to wait for Terra. I knew I was early, but I didn't care. The cold morning air felt good in my hot lungs, and outside the burning of my conscience seemed to lessen some.

Time ticked by, but there was no Terra prancing out her back door at the usual moment. I kept waiting so long that being late for school was a risk, but I couldn't bring myself to care.

The neighboring garage began to open, startling me ever so slightly. I thought it must have been Terra, running late so I ran over and stood next to the drive. The garage door creaked and rumbled, even more than ours did, until it opened wide enough to reveal a dark, pine-green jeep backing out slowly. It stopped next to me, but I couldn't see anything except my own reflection in the tinted windows. I could hear a quiet mechanical hum as the window lowered and a face came into view behind it.

"Hi there! You must be Zylia. I'm Terra's dad, Roger," he said, sticking a muscular arm out the window and shaking my hand. "Terra wanted me to tell you she won't be at school today. She had some dental work done yesterday and she needs a while to recuperate."

I was a little surprised by his appearance, really only because he was not the hunky heartthrob I had envisioned in my daydreams. However, he was not unattractive, with a dazzling pair of blue eyes between a shiny, shaved scalp and a short, trimmed beard. I wasn't sure, but I thought he may have been a lot younger than my own father.

"Thanks for letting me know," I said politely. "I hope she feels better soon."

"She'll be back to herself in no time," Roger Grant assured me in a deep, manly voice. I felt he had the tone of someone who should be wearing a hard hat. "Well, I'm off to work."

I waited for him to back out into the alley the rest of the way before I started jogging to school. I was now feeling more concerned about being late and wished I hadn't dawdled around for so long.

I had so quickly grown accustomed to her presence that without Terra, school felt all wrong. She had become the only reason my classes were even bearable. I dreaded facing a whole day without her, but there was no way around it.

I was back to being bumped along the hallways like a pinball without my friend to make me visible. I was forced to move quickly, rushing from class to locker with lots of ducking and sidestepping.

My third-hour English class felt especially hollow. I sunk into my chair, feeling breathless from the physical challenge of the hallways; my eyes went right to the back of Terra's empty chair. I hadn't known her long, but already my life seemed intolerable and vacant in her absence. Usually by that time she would have tilted back in her chair to whisper something witty, offer me a piece of gum, or flash me her best smirk of a smile.

"Pop quiz, my peeps!" said the teacher, Ms. Beck. She was failing at trying to sound youthful and cool, and I felt a little embarrassed for her. However, I did not feel bad enough that I wasn't resentful of the ridiculous quiz that represented far too much of our overall grade by my standards.

Ms. Beck handed out a stack of papers to the front of each row and asked that each grouping of three stapled pages be passed back to every student. "I know it looks like a lot to complete, but you should be able to breeze through this in fifteen minutes," she said, scanning the classroom with a businesslike look on her face. "Yes, that is your time limit, so peel back that top sheet and begin."

Panic seized me as I heard a uniform rustling of pages and realized that the boy in front of me had never given me a copy of the quiz. I was frozen as the rest of the students hunched over their work and began to quickly scrape pencils across paper. Randomly, the sound made me think of Keane scratching at his itchy, dry scalp and my stomach turned when I imagined big dandruff flakes floating around the room.

Being distracted by the gross mental picture had allowed precious seconds to tick by. I had to force my mind away from the reverie before I jolted to action and tapped the broad shoulder of the boy in front of me. He didn't even look back; he only shrugged his one shoulder as if a fly had landed there and he was shaking it off.

I quickly tried again, this time tapping more insistently against his fleshy shoulder blade. He jerked his head back halfway over his shoulder, still not looking at me, and sighed irritably. "Knock it off, will you!" he whispered harshly.

"But I . . ." my voice trailed off. I knew I wasn't going to get anywhere with him, and I had already lost a couple minutes of test time.

I decided to raise my hand high in the air, trying to get the teacher's attention. She had sat down behind her desk and was fishing around in a drawer. Time was ticking by and no one seemed to notice my dilemma, so I waved my hand around a little frantically and cleared my throat loudly.

The room remained quiet, other than that horrid sound of pencils on paper and the occasional sigh or cough. At the head of the class, my teacher was no longer bent over her desk drawer, but now she was focused on rubbing a scuff off the pointed toe of her high heel.

I had already missed several minutes of the test by then due to my unassertiveness, and I feared there was no way I could catch up and have a fair shot at a good grade even if I did get my hands on those pages.

I pondered what to do next. I imagined myself yelling at the top of my lungs, *Hey! I didn't get a copy of the test!* I even took a deep breath and readied myself to shout it out, but I couldn't push my words into the outside world and they did nothing more than rattle around loudly inside my head.

For some reason I just sat there, letting time tick by, watching as my classmates began to put down pencils and lean back in their chairs. I was pretty sure that if I explained to the teacher what had happened, she would let me retake the quiz.

"Okay, that's your time," said Ms. Beck as she snapped her head up and tapped on her wrist. "I'd like everyone to come forward and make a pile right here." She indicated an empty spot on her desk with the flat palm of her hand.

I joined the swarm of students making their way to drop off their tests. The boy who sat directly in front of me reached the teacher's desk just before I did. He slapped his papers down and plowed into me with his ample shoulder on the way back to his seat. It was enough to send me reeling; I stumbled, reaching for the desk for support but knocking a stack of pages off it instead. I tried to catch them as they fluttered to the floor; as they fell, I noticed that they were blank copies of the pop quiz.

I was picking up the final fallen copy when my teacher asked, "Are you all right? What are you doing down there?"

I stood up and realized I was a little out of breath. "Yes, it's just . . . I need to take the test. I didn't get a copy in time . . ."

Ms. Beck interrupted, "You had just as much time as every other classmate of yours. It wouldn't be fair to give any one student extra time."

My stomach squirmed as I realized she had completely misunderstood me. I did my best to gather my thoughts, but I was instantly flustered and tense.

"Here, I'll go ahead and take that," the teacher said, reaching for the test in my hand.

"Oh . . ." I looked at the pages, feeling slightly confused as to how they had come to be in my hands. "No, this is blank; it's not my . . . I mean I didn't get a . . ."

Ms. Beck swiped the papers away from me. "Well, if it's blank, then I guess you get a zero, which is very unfortunate. Next time try to have your head in the game, okay?"

I stood in front of her for a few seconds, blinking wordlessly until I translated her expression to be a dismissive glare and forced my legs to carry me back to my seat.

When English class was over, I waited for everyone else to clear out before I trudged into the hallway. I did my best to numb my brain and convince myself that getting a zero on the test was no big deal. I was a good student, so I hoped my present grade had enough cushion to take a hit.

I was doing a fairly good job of putting the anxiety out of my mind when I spotted Josh ahead of me in the hall. We were walking in the same direction, so I had sight of him from behind, my view only occasionally marred by the herd of students around us.

I wondered if I could catch up to him, maybe even strike up a little conversation. I felt excitement shoot through my gut. Terra would be pleasantly surprised at me if I did something so out of character—I just knew it. I was already imagining her elated expression as I told her.

I quickened my pace and tried to squeeze closer to Josh, feeling a rush of courage that bubbled forth from unknown sources. Two more large steps and he was within my reach. I stretched out my hand, ready to tap him on his shoulder, when I was distracted by a light-haired girl moving in next to him. She looped her arm affectionately around his and leaned in to whisper something in his ear. Josh responded by bursting into laughter and shaking his head, thoroughly amused.

I slowed down, letting the crowd rush around and ram into me. Long before the painful jarring had come to an end I had decided I never wanted to come to school without Terra again.

Chapter Twelve

During the solitary walk home after school, my senses were overcome by a numbing depression that I could only imagine was like being in mourning. It felt like all the life within and around me had shriveled up and died, reduced to shades of gray in my peripheral vision.

I stood in the alleyway behind my house and gaped up at it with droopy eyes, backpack slipping off my shoulders and down my back, dangling at my elbows. It really was a mammoth-sized house, like the others on this block, but the extent was upward instead of out. The peak of its roof pierced the silvery winter sky above the treetops. There were days when I felt our home had a personality—an aura, almost. That day, it was nowhere close to a warm and welcoming dwelling. It was as if the inhabitants' feelings toward me were soaking through the walls and warning me away. I was not ready to go in there.

I walked around to the front and veered onto the Grants' property. I wasn't sure if Terra would be up for company, but I decided to give it shot. After ringing the doorbell, I waited a full two minutes before knocking loudly. I was about to turn and go when the front door started opening and Terra stuck her head out.

"Zylia?" she said in a froggy voice, squinting at me. I realized she must have been asleep, because there was a red pillow line down the side of her puffy face and she seemed a bit dazed and disoriented.

"I didn't mean to wake you; I just couldn't go home." I suddenly wanted to cry when I heard my pathetic voice.

Terra opened the door wide and motioned for me to come inside. I was standing in a foyer identical in shape to mine, but that was the only similarity. The floor there was covered in clean-looking slate tile, and the staircase was a gleaming white with a strip of light-blue carpet up the stairs. To the side I could see partway into their front living room; boxes were stacked against the wall, waiting to be unpacked.

"The pain meds made me sleep all day." Terra touched her swollen jaw gingerly, and only then did it register to me why one side of her face was so puffy.

"That looks really painful," I said, trying to muster up some sympathy out of the uncaring depths of my depression.

"Two root canals. Not my idea of fun," Terra commented dryly, sounding like she was talking through a huge mouthful of gum. "Stupid Sweetarts are gonna be the death of me."

Beyond Terra, where I thought the kitchen must be, there were long sheets of thick plastic curtains draped from the ceiling and skimming the floors. A pale, muted light glowed through the dusty, opaque plastic.

Terra must have seen me gawking at it because she quickly explained, "The house is kind of torn up right now. My dad's remodeling. He's into all this DIY junk. We can't live in a place for two days before he has to start ripping down walls. It drives me crazy because there's nowhere to walk in here without getting a splinter or stubbing your toe on a hammer."

"That's kinda cool," I said, trying to imagine my own father as the construction type. Instead I could only think of the time when he had bought Mace and Bram a bunk bed set that had to be assembled from a large box. I clearly remembered him sitting amongst boards, little packets of screws, foam, and wrappers while staring with a baffled look at the instructions and repeating *Hmmm* over and over. The mental image was both amusing and somewhat of a letdown.

"Let's go up to my room," Terra said, and I followed her up one flight. In my own house, that room would have been my parents' room. I assumed that her father must sleep in the master bedroom that Grandmother occupied.

"Sorry, it's kind of a mess," Terra apologized. She moved a basket of folded laundry aside and gestured for me to sit down in a white wicker chair with a puffy cushion done in a black-and-white scroll design.

"It's not messy at all," I said, and it was true. Aside from the basket of clean laundry and a few pieces of homework stacked on her nightstand, it was only her bed that was not in perfect order—easily excused since she had been sleeping when I rang the bell.

Her whole room was done in simple, monochromatic colors that made me feel even more babyish about the room I shared with Ivy. I wondered how she had put all her stuff away so quickly. I had expected to see moving boxes everywhere.

My eyes caught a series of artwork along one wall. Three shiny, lacquered frames were displaying a striking image of an old, gnarled tree. Its knobby branches were reaching like desperate arms into the next panel, trying to catch leaves that were skittering on into the third picture. The tree was so lifelike and full of personality that I couldn't look away. I thought I might have even detected a vague face in the lines of the bark along the trunk.

"I did that last year," Terra informed me. "My dad thought it was just super and had it framed as a housewarming gift. He knows how much I hate moving around and flipping houses, so he wanted to get on my good side. That's why he always puts together my bedroom first. But it's not my favorite piece that I've done or anything. I mean, I see lots of mistakes in it where I could have done better, so now it just sort of annoys me up there on the wall."

I knew I could never create anything close to that marvelous piece of art, and hearing her critique it made me feel a bit jealous. "I think it's nice," I understated, realizing that it was, in fact, spectacular.

Terra crawled into her bed—which was much bigger than mine—and pulled the swirly black-and-white comforter up over her legs. She cast one last indifferent look at the masterpiece and shrugged.

A moment of silence passed. I looked down at my hands, took a deep breath, and then I told her everything.

I started slowly, telling her that I had mustered up the courage to talk to Josh only to discover that another girl had beat me to it, maybe a girl*friend* even.

I explained how my grandmother had lost it on me, possibly trying to kill me, and how I thought that everyone in the household secretly blamed me. I revealed that even if they didn't, I blamed myself.

I told her about my curse of invisibility that was becoming more apparent every day. I even disclosed that somehow there was a similarity between myself and the mysterious Angelica; that as crazy as my grandmother was, the old woman was onto something.

I finished off by telling her about the trunk I had found in the attic and that I was desperate to search its contents, but that I hadn't had the chance, was afraid of getting caught, and thought I might need physical help to do it.

I must have talked for thirty minutes straight and Terra was very attentive the entire time, only interrupting to ask a couple of clarifying questions and always prodding me to continue as soon as she understood.

When I was finally finished, I felt weary but calmed. It was like a poison had been drained from me and the emotional purge of it all was healing and therapeutic like an antidote.

Terra seemed to mull over all the information while she delicately caressed her jawline. After a spell she said, "I think we need to have a look in that attic of yours. There's nothing much we can do right now about your granny or about Josh, but we have the whole weekend to find out what's in that trunk."

It was direction—the beginnings of a plan—and it caused my heart to leap excitedly. "Will you feel up to it, do you think?"

Terra sighed, "I sure hope so. If I don't get out of this house, I'll go nuts soon. How about just plan on me coming over tomorrow after lunch? Will that work?"

My beaming smile was answer enough.

I stepped lightly back home, feeling my depression peeling away like layers of clothing being shed. I managed to make it upstairs without being detected by anyone and worked on my homework until Ivy came up to tell me it was time to eat.

Dinner was a quiet affair, the sounds of silverware tapping against dishes becoming an alternative to conversation. The food itself was proof again that Father was trying to be helpful. I figured he must have stopped at the grocery store on the way home to pick up the two boxes of fried chicken and the clear, round containers full of assorted sides, including green beans, mashed potatoes, and macaroni and cheese. It seemed my siblings and I all had the same preference, because when the latter was passed to me, there was only a disappointing spoonful or two clinging to the edges of the container.

Mother went back and forth between the table and Grandmother's room, doing who knows what. Her brow was always drawn until she reached the table, then she would give a feeble smile as she rejoined everyone.

I thought it was strange seeing my grandmother's empty chair at the table. The vacant seat was almost more of a presence than Grandmother herself would have been. I chewed my meager, rubbery serving of macaroni and cheese, wondering if the old woman had eaten dinner earlier. Maybe she took her meals in bed as of late, but I hadn't noticed Mother carrying any trays of food in since we sat down to eat.

One by one we finished up and trickled off to our own corners of the house. Everyone moved quietly, no one needing to be reminded about our grandmother's fragile condition.

Once upstairs, I pulled out my art supplies and scratched around on my picture of Angelica. I wasn't feeling very inspired, but I went ahead and started lightly sketching in where I wanted the facial features on the draft version.

"Wow, that's really good, Zy," Ivy commented. She was hovering over my shoulder and breathing annoyingly across my ear and face.

I scratched at my cheek where her hot breath had caused my skin to prickle. "Thanks," I said shortly.

"So, who is it? She sort of looks like you."

I was displeased with the face that was forming under my hand. Her features were too cheesy and cartoonish. I rubbed out my light pencil lines with an eraser and set out to try again on her face.

"Oh, why did you do that?" asked Ivy, a disappointed whine in her voice. "You were doing so good, too! If I could draw like that I sure wouldn't erase it."

I tried to ignore her and went to work outlining what should have been intelligent, wide eyes. I wanted them to carry a lack of expression and yet be full of emotion. When I was done they looked squinty and almond-shaped, as if she were laughing at a silly joke.

"You're erasing *again*?! Zy, what's wrong with you? It looks great."

I knew that she was only trying to be nice, but my failed attempts at capturing the essence of Angelica were really starting to get to me and I was becoming increasingly irritable.

"It's just not *right* yet, Ivy. You wouldn't understand."

Ivy leaned forward on the desk, fists pressed deeply into her cheeks. "Well, it looks right to me," she said, her voice muffled by the pressure on her face. "She looks like a princess."

"*A princess*?" I squealed. "Geez, maybe I should tear it up and start all over."

Ivy looked baffled. "Why? After all that hard work?"

She was breathing on my cheek again, and all I could do was hold my own breath to keep from screaming. I wondered how freeing it would feel just to let out an angry screech toward the heavens when I suddenly heard just that very thing.

Ivy and I stiffened in unison, our ears perking up at the sound of a distant wail coming from a lower floor of our house.

"That's Grandmother," Ivy said, looking scared and concerned.

I reached the bottom floor so fast that I couldn't remember the trip down. It was as if I had heard the scream and then had suddenly been transported to the hearth room, where my grandmother was wielding a crystal vase, swinging it in front of her like a sword. She must have been amped up on adrenaline, making her surprisingly limber and swift.

"Mother, please! No one wants to hurt you." My mother was speaking calmly, but I could hear an edge of dread in her voice.

"You all want to hurt me!" Grandmother yelled, her eyes frightened orbs. She made a slice through the air with the vase and said, "You can't keep me trapped here any longer. I have to get to her!"

"Mother, no one is trapping you anywhere. This is your home."

I heard my father's voice. "Let's all just calm down here. Mace, back up, will you?" He seemed nervous that my brother was in such close proximity to my grandmother. I wondered if he expected her to attack him too. The thought really shouldn't have been comforting, I suppose, but it would make things less personal if I wasn't the only target of her demented rage.

"Give me the vase, Mother." My mother held her hands out diplomatically, palms upturned, pink nails shining as they caught the light. I could see that the muscles in her arms were tense and I realized then that she was fearful.

"Never!" Grandmother shouted as she stepped to the side, wobbling slightly before smashing the vase against an end table. There was an iridescent explosion of glass as the vase shattered and sprinkled onto the edge of the rug and all along the hardwood floor.

"Kids, get out now!" my father ordered. All of us siblings retreated into the kitchen, where we would still have a good view of the dramatic scene.

Mother stepped closer to Grandmother, shards of the vase crunching below her casual flats. The older woman turned sharply and attempted to flee, but slipped on the mess and fell backward. I could see it all happening in slow motion as her feet flew out from under her and her thin arms went flailing. It was the sight of her head hitting the end table that would repeat over and over in my mind for days to come. I could hear a sickening cracking sound of skull against wood before she crumpled in a heap over the top of the broken glass.

"Oh God, *Phillip*!" my mother screamed as she leaned over to check on my grandmother. I couldn't see what had become of my grandmother with Mother blocking the view, but I saw my father's face go pale as he looked over her shoulder at the scene. "Call 911!" My mother's voice was laced with hysteria, and when she pointed in the direction of the phone I saw that her hand was covered in blood.

My father seemed to hesitate for a second before bolting to the phone. I felt dizzy and faint as I listened to the strange, hollow tone he was using with the emergency dispatcher. He suddenly barked, "Someone get towels, *now*!"

I couldn't move. My feet felt so heavy, I was sure they were bolted to the tile. Keane pushed past me, opening the kitchen towel drawer and grabbing an armful before rushing to our mother's side.

It wasn't the way I had pictured myself acting in an emergency. In my mind's eye I was far more heroic, swooping in and taking charge, amazing onlookers with my level-headed control and up-to-date paramedic skills.

In reality, I stood motionless with my mouth agape, wishing I hadn't passed up on that teen CPR and first aid class over the summer. They had been conducting free classes for young people and their parents at our neighborhood pool, but I had been too timid to sign up because of the dreamy instructor with his distracting abs and sunny locks of hair.

Due to my superficial decision-making skills, I watched my mother idly while she was hunched over Grandmother, pressing towels against the back of her head. Her hands were shaking, and I wondered if she was wishing she had taken that class as well.

Keane had backed away from the scene, gesturing for the twins to follow him as a siren sounded in the distance and quickly grew louder.

Father rushed to the entryway and threw the front door open, the phone still against his ear. "Kids, move; get out of the way," he said as I heard a rustle of heavy footsteps on our porch.

None of us were in the way but we all shrank back against the edges of the room anyway, our wide eyes watching the firemen swarm around

Grandmother. They were talking to her in loud, reassuring voices, but there was no response from the floor.

The paramedics arrived soon after. I listened to them ask my parents all the same questions the firemen had as they loaded the old woman up onto a narrow bed with wheels.

I scurried to the edge of the hall and caught a glimpse of my grandmother as they wheeled the gurney out the door. Her skin was ghostly white and there were gauzy bandages wrapped around her head, making it look swollen and huge.

I felt a pat on the top of my head and looked up into the friendly face of one of the firemen. At first,a I wondered if he had accidentally brushed against me, but I saw his eyes crinkle up in an encouraging smile meant for me.

Nearby my father was barking orders at Adonia. "You're in charge. Make sure everyone finishes homework and is in bed on time. I'm counting on you. We'll call you from the hospital."

There was a loud shuffle as the house cleared out, and then it was startlingly silent. At first my siblings and I just looked back and forth at one another until Adonia made the first sound. She covered her face and burst into hysterical sobbing.

Keane seemed terribly uncomfortable with the flow of tears and said, "Grandmother will be fine. Come on; Dad put you in charge, so *get it together*."

"B-but there was . . . *blood* . . . everywhere!" Adonia whined. "And look, it's *still there*!"

Keane sighed, taking charge in the blink of an eye. "Adonia, just go to bed. You're not doing anyone a bit of good freaking out like that. I'll go upstairs and help the twins with their homework and Ivy and Zylia can start cleaning up this mess."

I wondered if Ivy's stomach was turning the way mine was at the thought of mopping up our grandmother's blood. She didn't say anything, though, and obediently went to work grabbing a roll of paper towels.

I followed her, moving the trash can near to the site where broken glass twinkled among streaks and puddles of dark red blood. I carefully disposed of the larger pieces and used a combination of the broom and the vacuum to clean up the rest.

Ivy moved methodically as well, donning rubber gloves and sanitizing the area of bloodied hardwood floor with some sort of kitchen cleaner. She was scrubbing at a stain in the rug when she said, "Hey, what are those?"

My own eyes met the point of her gaze and I saw several crumpled pieces of paper-like material between the end table and Grandmother's recliner. I reached in, pulled them out, and was soon staring into the face of Angelica once again.

"Wow, somebody sure didn't want to look at those again," Ivy commented.

It seemed she was right, because most of the photos had been tattered and scrunched up beyond recognition. I smoothed out a couple that could be salvaged and put them in my pocket for safekeeping.

Once the mess was cleaned up, it was almost impossible to tell that anything tragic had happened there. If I inspected the hearth room rug closely, I could see a few drops of blood staining the lighter colors within the paisley design, but otherwise the room looked normal again.

No matter what appearance suggested, however, the feeling of unease in the house was nearly tangible. Ivy must have felt it just as intensely as I did, because she slid her hand into mine and gripped it tightly as we headed up to our room.

Her fingers were cool and clingy, and I knew she needed comfort. It had been a long time since my little sister had held my hand. The last time I could remember was when Mother and Father had taken us to the amusement park. It had been sunny, hot, and crowded and I was in charge of keeping track of Ivy that day. She had been eating a giant cloud of pink cotton candy, and her hand felt sticky and moist in my own. I had to keep reminding myself that the slight discomfort of sugar and spit was a small price to pay if it got me out of taking care of either Mace or Bram. That day she had been ordered by our mother to hold my hand, and she had done so begrudgingly, but now my sister was grasping it willingly and almost desperately.

When we got upstairs she finally let go of me, but as Ivy and I brushed our teeth and dressed for bed, my mind continued to wander idly over that trip to the amusement park. I think I was subconsciously trying not to think of Grandmother lying in a pool of her own blood.

My musings of fairground food and dizzying rides were shattered when Ivy asked, "Do you think Grandmother is awake yet?"

Suddenly I imagined her on a slender hospital bed, sitting upright and demanding to be discharged. It was humorous until I came to terms with the implausibility of it being true. "Probably." I tried to sound hopeful for Ivy's sake, but I was sure our parents would have called by now if things were okay.

Seemingly comforted, Ivy pulled the covers up to her chin and let out a sleepy sigh. I sat on the edge of my bed and watched her breathing become shallow as she drifted to sleep.

I wished that sleep would come to my hectic mind, but it was so far off that I didn't bother to lie down and try to force my eyes shut. I wasn't ready to face the anxious thoughts of my insomnia-ridden mind. Instead, I laid out the rescued pictures of Angelica and went to work on the face of my drawing.

Chapter Thirteen

"Zylia." I startled awake at the sharp whisper of my name, my eyes snapping open as quickly as my dreams receded from memory.

"Grandmother never came home." It took a few seconds longer than it should have for my brain to register that it was Ivy who had woken me and was speaking. "I'm afraid."

I was groggy from strain and lack of sleep, and my voice held all the evidence of it as I croaked, "I don't think they send people home that fast. I'm sure it's fine."

"Don't you remember when Aunt Mel had Lily? She was home the very next day."

"Um . . . well, babies are different than injuries, I think. If you get injured, they have to keep you for . . . "I paused, trying to think of the right word, ". . . surveillance." I knew that wasn't it, but surely Ivy wouldn't challenge it. "Besides, Grandmother hasn't even been at the hospital for a whole day, really."

Ivy's hands were clasped tightly in her lap and she was perched rigidly on the edge of her bed. I desperately wished there was something I could do to calm and reassure her, but I couldn't even convince myself that things were going to be okay.

"Do you want to see my drawing?" I decided to avoid the unsettling subject completely.

Before Ivy could answer, the home phone rang. Even though the sound was muffled since the nearest handset base was across the hall in Adonia's room, we both jumped. I was sure to have an agitated day if my adrenaline had been set off twice already before I'd even gotten out of bed.

"That's probably news about Grandmother!" Ivy deduced.

Since the phone had given off only one shrill ring, it became apparent that someone must have answered it immediately. We found Adonia's bedroom door ajar and her room empty. Wordlessly, we flew downstairs and followed the sounds of voices to the kitchen. Adonia and Keane were standing alongside the far counter near the phone base, leaning in closely even though our father's voice was blaring over the speakerphone.

". . . and you all need to try and get along since we don't know how long she'll be in here," he was saying in a weary, yet firm tone.

"But she's okay?" Bram asked loudly. I hadn't even noticed him at the breakfast table. He was sitting with his twin, and they both had a hand deep inside the same cereal box.

"Yes, she seems to be improving . . . physically. You kids don't need to worry about it right now, though. Let your mom and me take care of her and you guys just be good and hold down the fort."

I listened to the last couple minutes of the conversation where Adonia assured our father in the sweetest of tones that she would keep everyone in check. Even Ivy rolled her eyes at the sound of artificial sincerity.

Adonia had barely disconnected from the landline before she whipped out her cell phone and pressed it against her ear. She tapped her navy-lacquered nails against the countertop until someone answered on the other end. "Leah—hey! You have to come over right away. I'm stuck babysitting and I'm just *dying* here. Fine, fine; as soon as you can."

The rest of us were staring coldly at Adonia as she looked up from her phone. It was Keane who spoke up and said, "You're such a jerk, Doni! If anyone has to babysit, it will be *me* watching *you*!"

I watched Adonia's heavily lined lids stretch wide around her angry eyes as she said, "Ha! Father knew exactly who to put in charge, so just get to your chores."

"Right after you do *your* chores! Do you think we forgot how you freaked out last night? Some leader you are!"

Bram chimed in, "I think Adonia should do *everyone's* chores, since she's on such a power trip and all."

"Shut up, doofus!" Adonia yelled back at him. "Get this place cleaned up. I don't want Leah to see it all trashed, and she's coming over soon."

A sound brought our attention toward the center of the kitchen, where Keane was using his arm as a bulldozer to swipe stuff off the surface of the island counter. A large plastic fruit bowl went clamoring to the floor, while a group of slightly shriveled apples bounced along after it. "No, you can clean the place up," Keane said, his hazel eyes narrow and blazing behind his glasses. "And you can start with this. Or maybe even these . . ." Keane locked angry eyes with a messy stack of mail on the counter behind him, and before his older sister could stop him, he sent it flying through the air and raining down all around us.

I flinched, covering my left eye after a sharp envelope corner sailed directly into my lower lid, just missing my eyeball. That only slightly hindered my view of Adonia lunging toward Keane and shoving his chest roughly.

Keane, although thicker than Adonia, didn't have her height or adrenaline-infused mean streak, so the shove was quite successful in slamming him back against the pantry door. I heard wood cracking and splintering as everyone began shouting at once. I tried joining in the yelling, but my voice was absorbed into the collective din.

My shoulders jerked upward—almost to my ears—as a high-pitched scream sounded to my right. All the voices stopped, and we looked up at Ivy, who had climbed atop the island counter. "*Children*!" the youngest one of us shouted and then very calmly went on, "For Grandmother's sake, could we please *pretend* to be civilized? We all have our own chores," she said as she waved one small, soft and usually non-threatening hand in the general area of the house around her, "so let's all just get to them without any more trouble."

Almost everyone dispersed after that with nothing more aggressive than shrugs, sighs, and dragging feet. Adonia was the only one to try and extend the angst with mean glares and unnecessary door-slamming, but even she followed through with her chores without causing any more of a scene.

I watched Ivy examining the pantry door after our other siblings had gone.

"Good job breaking up the fight," I said to her.

She acted as though she hadn't even heard me. "Doesn't look too bad," she was mumbling as she ran her small hands along the wooden door, "just a little crack on the inside here. If I have Keane press it together with some glue, maybe the parent patrol won't even notice."

"Let me touch it and then they'll never notice. I'll put my invisible spell on it."

That comment caught her attention, but only slightly. "Hmm? What did you say?"

"I said you're probably right; you should have Keane work on it," I fibbed, feeling desperate to abandon my heavy cloak of invisibility. I didn't think I could wait for Terra to come over after lunchtime. That seemed too far away.

According to Mother's chart on the fridge, I had bathroom duty for us girls, so I rushed through the familiar motions until the top-floor restroom looked presentable enough and smelled harshly of lemon cleaner. The whole chore took under half an hour, and soon I was ringing Terra's doorbell.

Terra was still in her pajamas when she answered the door: a blue t-shirt and blue-and-green plaid lounging pants. Her hair was a little ruffled, and her nose and forehead were shiny. She took one look at me and said, "I thought I was coming to *your* house later on. Wasn't that the plan?"

"Yes, but I couldn't wait." By then I was shivering and wondering why I hadn't bothered to wear a coat. "Please, let's just do this."

Terra shrugged, "Works for me." I waited on the porch, moving my hands up and down my arms while I watched her through the doorway pulling on a pair of Converse shoes over her bare feet. She grabbed her cell phone off a nearby table and slung a coat over her shoulders.

"Things are wild and crazy at my house," I warned her as we started back home. I quickly filled her in on the events of the morning.

"It sucks being an only child. Nothing like that ever happens around my house." There was a ring of disappointment in her voice.

As soon as we entered, however, it was like the very house was trying to make a mockery of my warning. It smelled fresh and clean from the completion of chores and had an atmosphere of calm and quiet with everyone tucked away into their own spaces. I noticed that the disorder in the kitchen from Keane's outburst had been tidied up, and I hoped it wasn't poor Ivy who had done the work.

I could hear soft, high-pitched chatter coming from the living room. It was not clearly audible, but distinctly teenage and gossipy. I could envision Adonia chatting on the phone while twisting locks of her hair. I figured it was either that, or Leah had already arrived. However, I doubted that the girl could have even completed her makeup in the forty minutes or so since Adonia had called her, let alone have shown up already.

Terra followed me upstairs, pausing and looking around curiously as she did so. "You know, I think I've only been to the top story of our house once, and it was that first day I saw you. You know, *saw* you."

I could feel my cheeks burning with embarrassment. I tried to block out the emotion by imagining Terra and her father being lost inside that giant house. I wondered what it would be like to have all that unused space to move about, with no rowdy siblings or demented grandmother to fill it with insufferable noise.

Ivy met us at the top of the stairs. She was carrying a basket of laundry that looked too large against her barely existent hip. "Oh, hey, Terra," she greeted, peeking around her burden. "I was just going to wash my clothes and I'll probably read and stuff while I'm down there, so you guys can have the room."

I felt thankful for my considerate sister, even though I knew she was probably just thrilled that I had managed to maintain a friend for more than a day and was trying to assist me in keeping Terra around by giving us some space. Whatever her motives were, I was glad to see her vacate the floor because I didn't want her knowing we'd be poking around in the attic.

In our room, I rifled around in my desk drawer until I produced a mini-flashlight. Before I could get back out into the hallway, I heard a wooden thumping sound and found Terra jumping to reach the metal ring dangling above her head.

"Try this," I said, and pulled the plastic step stool into position.

"Or we could do it that way," laughed Terra, rubbing at her jawline. "All that bouncing made my mouth hurt."

"Save your strength, because we have a lot of work to do." I led the way up the ladder stairs, and once we were both at the top we worked together to pull the steps back up into their folded, accordion-like position. I felt a little nervous as they clicked into place, but I comforted myself with the thought that surely the two of us could force it back open if it happened to stick shut.

"Wow; no offense, but you guys might have some hoarding tendencies hidden up here!" She surveyed the cramped and cluttered area with her fingers laced around the back of her neck. I couldn't help but notice that even in pajama bottoms and unkempt hair, she looked far cooler than I ever could.

"Yeah, and the trunk is actually back there." I pointed toward the south wall. "It's wedged way back where the ceiling touches the floor." I found myself pantomiming a large angle in the dimness.

"You have got to be kidding me." Terra tipped her head to the side, peeking around the sewing table and taking in all the stuff behind it.

"I'm sorry; I know you're not feeling well." I worried that she would back down, but instead she just shrugged and started inching the heavy sewing table slightly toward us.

I rushed over to assist her, and a cascade of hat boxes toppled down, some of them popping open. "You remember how those were stacked, right?" Terra laughed.

I joined in, but my laughter had a nervous edge to it. I feared there was no way we'd ever get everything back exactly as it was, and I didn't want to leave any evidence of my trespassing.

Half an hour passed with the encounter of one minor splinter, two fits of sneezing, and three spiders, but we had finally reached the trunk. It took us another few minutes to clear up the space needed to slide it outward and examine it.

Terra flopped down on the nearest surface, slightly denting a cardboard box with her backside, and breathed heavily. "Thank goodness it isn't padlocked."

I reached for the rusty latch and pulled the lid open. I wasn't sure what I expected to find inside—something magical, maybe, that would cause a rainbow of light to illuminate my face and reflect colorful beams in my eyes.

"Where's that flashlight?" Terra asked. "I can't see a thing in there, it's so dark."

I pulled the light out of my pocket and shined its meager glow inside. The small, yellow circle of light trained and bounced along various fabrics until it glinted off a long-lashed eyeball.

My arms jerked involuntarily, and my shoulders leapt up to my ears just the way they did during the shocking segments of suspenseful movies. I could hear Terra snickering, and I didn't even realize I had dropped the flashlight until she shone it in my face. "It *is* a creepy doll, I'll give you that much," she giggled, reaching in and pulling out the plastic monstrosity. "Who would have ever played with this thing? Freaky children, I bet."

I brought another doll out of the chest. It was like the first, with dark, wiry curls, beady glass eyes, and a faded gingham dress. "It must be very old," I remarked as I noted the scuffs and scratches marring the pale-peach plastic skin. I wondered if the childhood version of my grandmother had played with these dolls. I had to work hard to picture her as an unwrinkled, fresh-faced child brushing the frizzy doll hair that must have once been glossy and new.

It was much easier to picture Angelica as a small child, since circumstances had halted her aging process not far beyond the time when she'd have played with toys. She was related to me, after all, so there was a good chance that she had even carted the pretend babies around with her up until the time she had disappeared.

"Blankets . . . clothes . . ." Terra was sifting through the trunk impatiently. "There isn't really much in here—nothing interesting, anyway."

I felt my heart quickening in panic. I had been so certain that this trunk held all the answers, but now I wasn't so sure. I couldn't accept the fact that we had done all that work—and I had built up so much hope—for nothing.

"Oh, this is cool." Terra had produced a small, glass-lidded case that displayed an intricately decorated silver comb, brush, and mirror set. "It doesn't even look used. Bet this is worth something," she remarked, holding it up and wiggling it in a gesture that heightened her point but made me nervous that she'd drop it. "It's actually kinda heavy." She was shaking the case a bit, and I could hear the contents jostling together. I had almost worked up enough assertiveness to ask her to put it down when she decided on her own she was done fiddling with it and abandoned it inside the chest. It landed against the wood with a hollow plunking sound.

I would have been irritated at her manhandling our family heirlooms if I had not been so suddenly curious. "Did you hear that?" I asked. "I think this trunk bottom is much shallower than it should be."

Terra tipped back, her bottom against her heels, and examined the exterior. "You're right!" she exclaimed. "Look how much larger this thing looks on the outside."

Together we emptied the contents of the chest and used the mini-flashlight to peer at the bottom. The wood along the base looked different than the reddish-brown planks that made up the sides of the box. It was lighter in color and looked like a million splinters all mashed together and smoothed out. I remembered seeing wood like that before, under the carpet in my parents' room; it seemed like such a makeshift choice for a beautiful old chest.

I trailed the point of light along the rectangular bottom edge, stopping when I reached one corner that had a notch just big enough for my finger to slide into. I pulled upward and the thin, false bottom lifted easily enough.

"Jackpot!" Terra declared. She eagerly helped to move the board aside.

The flashlight beam showed heavy dust in the air and a thick coating of it lining the hidden depths of the trunk. A small leather book was wedged into a corner; it was the only item stored in the secret space.

Terra grabbed it before I could react and flipped through the pages. "This is some kind of diary. 'Angelica' is written on the inside."

Goosebumps sprang up across my forearms and between my shoulders. It was more than I could have hoped to find. I ran my finger down the ridged spine before I snatched it away from Terra. Cradling it against my chest, I said, "I want to be able to really look at this, but let's clean up first. I don't wanna get caught."

"Good idea; we've been up here for a while," Terra said with an approving nod.

We set to work on placing everything back exactly where it had been—or at least in the vicinity—which was a lot more work than pulling it all apart. The whole time we were working I kept thinking I was going to lose sight of the leather diary. I was afraid to let it out of my view in case one of us accidentally knocked it off into some random box, gaping crack in the floor, or unseen corner. Most of all, I worried that it would disappear and fade into dust, becoming nothing more than something I'd dreamed up.

However, as we closed the attic, I held the book safely in my hands. Ivy didn't seem to have returned upstairs, since our room was still empty; I was thankful that there were no sounds coming from Adonia's room either.

I brushed my drawing pencils aside to make room on the surface of my desk and laid the book down. Terra was hovering over my shoulder as I opened the cover delicately, a slightly impatient breath escaping her lips. I was treating the leather volume as if it were some ancient manuscript that was prone to crumble under even the slightest pressure.

"See, that's where she wrote her name," Terra said, pointing to the upper left corner of the inside cover. The name Angelica was written in small, curly letters. "This isn't like any other diary I've ever seen, though. There aren't any dates." She flipped through some pages. "Look at this . . . snippets of poetry, sketches, doodles, and nonsense. Most of it doesn't make sense."

I pointed to a line on the first page and read aloud, *"Today my family walked right through me. It didn't hurt nearly as much as I'd have imagined."*

A buzzing sounded, and Terra reached into the pocket of her well-worn plaid pants. I noticed then that she had black smudges on her face and hands. "Sorry, it's my dad; hang on," she said to me as she placed a slim black rectangle against her ear. I could only hear her side of the conversation. "Hey . . . Yeah, I did . . . Well, I thought I did . . . *Seriously?* . . . Okay, okay; I'll clean it up as soon as I get home . . . *Really?* . . . Okay, fine . . . Yes, I'm coming home *now*."

"You're leaving?" I asked in a deflated tone as soon as she moved the phone away from her face.

"Apparently I forgot to let Kale out today and he made a mess in my dad's toolbox. Of all the places . . . how am I going to clean that up?"

I waited anxiously for her to ask me to come and help her. I knew I wouldn't be able to just refuse after all the assistance she had given me in the attic, but I was working hard to think up an excuse to stay behind. I wasn't trying to be a useless friend; I was just exceedingly eager to get a better look at the journal, and the thought of dealing with dog poop instead was revolting from any point of view.

"I hate to do this to you," Terra looked at me sincerely, "but I have to go. My dad's pretty mad, and I might not be able to come back today. Actually, after I deal with Kale's mess, I might lie down for the rest of the day. My teeth are pulsing, and I'm pretty worn out. Looks like you're on your own from here; I'm really sorry."

"Oh, it's ok." I tried not to sound relieved. "I'll catch you up on whatever I find. Thanks for helping and I hope you feel better."

When I had said goodbye to Terra and was shutting the front door, I heard the garage opening. I glanced toward that end of the house and inadvertently began wringing my hands.

"They're home!" announced Ivy, who had been reading with her feet propped up in the keeping room. She hopped up and ran to open the back door.

Adonia came prancing out of the living room with Leah as her hesitant shadow. "Who's here? Who is it?"

The mystery was solved when Mother came in from the garage. Her hair had an oily sheen and she was wearing the same white sweater I'd seen her leave for the hospital in. There was a smear of blood at the waist, dark brown against the snow- colored fabric.

She answered our hugs and greetings with feeble pats and fatigued murmurs. I noticed dark circles below what should have been her bright, reflective eyes. Instead they were sober slits smudged with day-old makeup that hadn't been washed off.

"I'm only here for a while, darlings," Mother said quietly, her arm around Ivy's shoulders. I was sure she would have fallen over if she hadn't been using her youngest daughter as a crutch to advance toward the kitchen. "I need to shower and rest for a bit, and then I'm headed back up to the hospital for a while."

"Oh, can't you stay?" Ivy whined from the crook of Mother's arm.

"Please don't pester me today. I have a raging headache. We'll figure out some dinner before I go and then I'll be back again later. Your father will be staying at the hospital tonight without me so I can be here with you kids. But for now, I need a hot shower and some aspirin."

"I'll get you some, Mother," Adonia said, leaping for the cupboard where the drinking glasses were. Before my eyes, she seemed to have transformed into an adult as she filled the glass with cold water from the fridge door and located the correct bottle of pain reliever from the rotating tray atop the microwave. I was nearly convinced that her sudden act of helpfulness was more out of concern than a showy display intended to impress her guest.

"Than-koo." Mother's words were distorted by the round, flat pills on her tongue until she swallowed them with a labored gulp. "I'm going upstairs for a shower. I'll be back down after a while."

Once Mother had started up the stairs I looked down at my hands, realizing they were red and white from twisting them. When I released my palms from my own grip, I felt remorse take over. It was my fault, after all, that Grandmother had been injured; surely my mother was angry with me. Why couldn't I have just ignored my curiosity and left the poor old woman alone?

I thought over a long, scripted defense and repentant confession in my mind as I stood alone in the front hall. It took quite a few minutes to formulate, and I practiced it in an undertone on the way up the stairs. In my mind's eye, I delivered the apology with sincere tones, heartfelt words, and just enough tears to evoke kindhearted pity from my maternal listener.

My parents' bedroom door was halfway open and I could hear the shower running in the adjoining bathroom. "Mother?" I rapped on the door, but she didn't hear me. I entered the room and sat on the edge of the bed. The mattress was high off the floor and only my toes reached the carpet.

When the water shut off I called out again, "Mother."

"Mmm-hmm?" came her hollow-sounding response.

"Um, I just wanted to talk to you for a second. I'm sorry; I know you're tired."

Mother came out of the bathroom wearing a fluffy white robe, and a puff of steamy, soap-scented air followed her. She moved to her side of the bed and fiddled with the bedspread momentarily before giving up, slumping over and rolling on top of it glumly. "Those hospital recliners are a joke," she said through a yawn. "Not to mention it was so cold in that tiny . . ." her eyes closed and her lips went slack. After a few seconds I thought she was out completely, until she abruptly resumed her disjointed statement. ". . . and the nurse kept forgetting to bring in an extra blanket."

"That sounds awful," I sympathized. "How is Grandmother?"

Mother's breathing had taken on the slight rasp of a snore. I slid off the bed, deciding it was time to abandon my apology mission for now, and in doing so caused the bed frame to creak.

"Hm?" Mother moaned sleepily, none too cognitive. Her eyes were still closed, and I wondered if she were speaking during sleep.

"I just asked how Grandmother is doing," I repeated quietly.

After a few more seconds of snoring, Mother muttered, "She'd be better if we could keep Zylia away from her."

Chapter Fourteen

I thought that looking over the diary would help to take my mind off Mother's words, so I sat at my desk and tried to pretend I was thinking only of Angelica.

I opened the book to a random page, somewhere near the center. I first noticed an elaborate sketch of a dark-haired girl looking into a mirror. The scene was drawn in pen and I was impressed by the detail, wondering if my artistic interest had been inherited. Only a small wedge of the girl's face was in view, her head turned mostly away from where she peered into an empty mirror. I wondered if Angelica had meant to draw her reflection in the glass but had abandoned the small clip of artwork for something else, as I so often did. It seemed strange that she would purposefully leave the mirror empty in an otherwise meticulous drawing—unless she had meant it to be just that, a girl with no reflection.

Above the picture Angelica had written the words: "*Something strange is happening to me. I've known it was coming for a long time.*"

I kept reading the sentence over and over; but even as I read those words, different ones were echoing in my head. The words my mother had uttered that my mind was trying to repress.

I knew that my mother had been speaking in her sleep and would not have meant to intentionally hurt me, but the expression she used no doubt came from truth. She truly believed that Grandmother would be better off without me around. And it was true, of course. All her episodes had been triggered by me and my resemblance to Angelica.

Angelica. Who was the girl whose creative markings I held in my hands? I had once imagined her as a kindred spirit to my own plight—someone understanding, though misunderstood herself. But what if she were a foe instead? Ever since learning of her, my life had grown more complicated and harrowing. Maybe she was the poison infecting my existence and it had nothing to do with me.

I knew I was simply looking for someone to assume the heavy burden of blame. It was too much to undergo on my own. Tears were blurring my vision, sliding down my nose and making reading nearly impossible. I was worried my weeping would drip onto the pages of the journal, so I closed it, forgoing the idea of studying it any further at the time. Perhaps I could pick it up again later when I had my emotions in check.

I curled up on my bed and held the book tightly to my chest. I could feel the impending sobs rising in my throat, so I turned to face the wall in case Ivy came in and saw me. I didn't move for the rest of the evening.

I think it was the howling wind, entering my dreams like a mournful dirge, that woke me so early Sunday morning. Or it could have been the frigid chill that had brought me out of my slumber, limbs shivering and stiff.

I rolled away from the wall and realized I was still cradling Angelica's journal. I tucked it under my mattress quietly, careful not to wake Ivy, but when I glanced at her bed I realized it hadn't been slept in. Our bedroom light had been left on, and I knew if my sister had come to bed the night before she would have turned it off. Since it was a little before five a.m., the absence roused my curiosity a bit.

I rubbed my left arm vigorously where it was tingly from the way I had been lying on it. It was then that I happened to glance at my window and realize the culprit of both the shocking lack of heat and the dreadful howling noise.

The double-hung window was old, and the top sash had slid down a couple of inches on one side, creating a gap where the cold air was piping through. I used all my strength to thrust it back into place. It kept slipping back down until I engaged the lock, which seemed to work to hold the window where it should be.

When I moved my hands down away from the window I caught sight of my reflection in the glass, bright against the black morning beyond. I couldn't contain the audible gasp that sounded in my throat. I had expected to see the slightly translucent representation of my face mirrored on the pane, but instead I saw an ivory haze where my features should have been.

I probably wouldn't have found it so odd if I couldn't have seen everything else in the room mirrored around me in perfect clarity. I could have blamed it on the window or the lighting if it hadn't been that I could clearly read the word *lilac* in thin cursive letters at the bottom of the poster that hung alongside Ivy's bed. I could even make out each individual tiny purple bloom that adorned the bush in the picture, yet my own face was a filmy distortion.

I looked away from the window and frantically groped at my face. My skin was cool and a bit oily, but it otherwise felt normal. I scampered out into the bathroom and bravely peered into the mirror.

I laughed out loud, a guttural cackle that may have qualified as hysteria. My mirror image was just as it should be. I looked exactly the way I had expected to, aside from the puffy, red eyes that were the result of my prior evening of whimpering.

I walked back to the window, feeling a spirit of boldness now that I had seen my face intact. Strangely enough, my reflection in the pane of glass was evident; it was only slightly indistinct, as expected, where dark silhouettes of treetops and housetops were showing through slightly. I blinked a few times, watching the detail of my dark lashes bat slowly. Was it possible that my eyes had been playing tricks on me only moments before?

I tilted my head inquisitively and touched my hand to the cold glass. I checked the surface for condensation or fog that could possibly have distorted my vision in one specific area, but my fingertips found nothing.

I took a deep breath and tried to shake off the eerie feeling that had overtaken me. The only explanation I could satisfy myself with was that I had been imagining the whole incident. Hallucinations didn't bode well for my logic or sanity, but it was the only thing that made sense to me at all.

My throat was dry, and I didn't like being alone after such a weird happening, so I ventured downward into the shadowy house. I took the stairs, cold on my feet even through my socks, to the second floor. I noticed that my parents' bedroom door was halfway open, so I poked my head inside.

I heard the faint sound of breathing, and it comforted my uncanny loneliness to know there was life in the house. My eyes adjusted to the dim room, and I could see a small, slender arm dangling off one side of the bed. The rest of her body was hidden under a mound of covers, but I recognized the appendage belonging to Ivy. She must have crawled in bed with Mother since Father was away at the hospital.

I felt a little relief knowing that the mystery of Ivy's whereabouts could be simply rationalized without the likelihood of a mental disorder on my part. I was comforted enough that the memory of the ghostly reflection was beginning to fade, and I felt a little silly for being so distressed by it.

In the kitchen I downed two glasses of water, barely stopping for a breath. It seemed that the loss of all those tears the night before had dehydrated me. I stood at the sink breathing heavily, my belly feeling hard and full while my mouth still craved more fluid.

Once my breathing had quieted, I heard a noise at the back of the house. At first my brain merely dismissed it as an insignificant cough or sneeze, but I started to wonder why someone would be in that part of the house so early in the morning.

I set my glass down silently on the countertop and took a few steps out of the kitchen and into the keeping room. The only illumination I saw was coming from the far side of the room, where yellow light was spilling out from Grandmother's doorway.

The hairs on my arms were standing on end as I inched myself closer to the light. Could Grandmother have come home overnight while I was sleeping? I had gone to bed very early and had even missed dinner, but wouldn't Ivy have woken me to tell me the good news if our grandmother had returned? On second thought, it wouldn't be the first-time events had transpired without anyone thinking to inform me. I couldn't even count all the times I had been forgotten.

I heard the sound again, and now that I was closer to it, I recognized it as feminine sobbing. I didn't realize it was my mother until I peeked one eye around the doorjamb.

She was sitting in the middle of the floor with her back turned toward me, stacks of folded clothing on the rug beside her. I couldn't see her face at all; her head dipped downward toward her lap, only the back of her hair and her heaving shoulders visible. I was struck by how young and vulnerable she appeared, and it sent a stab of pity deep into my heart.

In the back of my mind I knew something terrible must have happened to Grandmother. What else could make my mother this distressed?

"What's wrong?" I asked. "What is it?"

Mother just went on crying for several minutes, as if she were the only one in the room. I wondered if I had spoken aloud or just imagined that I had. I watched her hands move to her face a couple times, and her shoulders began to settle. She folded several more articles of Grandmother's clothing, her long fingers gently smoothing and pressing down the outdated fabrics.

I moved closer to her, reached my hand out, and held it over her shoulder. I wanted to pat her and tell her everything would be all right, but instead I yanked my hand back as if the air had burned me. I knew she was unaware of my presence, and touching her could be startling instead of consoling. I backed up and stepped lightly out of the room.

I didn't see my mother again until breakfast. She had assembled us children at the table by means of the sweet smell of maple bacon frying. It had drifted tantalizingly through the air, and all who caught a whiff of it had ended up in the kitchen with a plate and fork.

Even *my* mouth was watering and my stomach growling eagerly. Normally my appetite diminished under such great strain, but I had missed a meal or two since Grandmother had been hospitalized. The little that I had eaten had been provided by my father, not the quality food prepared by Mother.

It had been several hours since I had come across my mother in Grandmother's room, and now there was only a slight sign of her emotional breakdown in the dark: puffy circles below her eyes. Otherwise, she was wearing a warm-hearted smile and a crisp button-down shirt that would normally have suggested a cheerful mood.

Mace and Bram, who were typically not outwardly affectionate, each gave Mother a hug around the waist before taking a heaping serving of waffles and bacon. I recognized that my little brothers were feeling the strain that had come into the household and were doing their best to lift it. I felt a small flare of jealousy and regret that I hadn't thought to do something so kind and simple.

"I wanted to talk with everybody," Mother announced as she poured orange juice into the twins' glasses.

"Is Grandmother all right?" Adonia asked, passing up on the waffles and handing the plate on to me and Ivy.

"Oh, yes; yes, she's fine," Mother quickly piped up, relieving the pounding in my chest. "Well, her head is healing nicely, but her dementia is getting worse. I'm sure you all realize that by now, of course."

"So, she'll be home soon?" Bram asked impatiently.

"Well, no. Actually, that's what I wanted to talk about. I don't think your Grandmother will be coming home. I mean, not here with us. It's just not safe for her . . . or anybody else." Mother's gaze promptly flickered to my spot at the table, and then in a mere blink, her eyes were back to being focused on the juice carton.

"Where will she live?" Ivy asked, sounding intensely concerned.

Mother's voice brightened. "We've looked up some lovely places, but we can't decide for sure until we know how much care she'll need after her hospital stay."

"Do you mean one of those old people homes that are sorta like a hospital and sorta like a jail at the same time?" Mace chimed in. "A boy in my class told me all about it. He said when he grows up that's where he's putting his father."

"Um . . ." My mother looked perplexed about how to answer. She busied herself putting the juice back in the refrigerator and when she turned back around, her face was a little gloomy. "No, nothing like that at all. She will most likely have her own little apartment and we'll be able to visit her and everything."

"You mean everyone but Zylia," laughed Mace naughtily.

I froze, fork in midair, and the few bites of waffles that were resting in my tummy began to shift uncomfortably.

Mother was truly shocked by the comment. "*Mace*! That was a very unkind thing for you to say and you need to apologize." She lingered over her chair, almost sitting down before hastily changing her mind. She said to no one in particular, "I'm going to watch the news in the living room. Make sure to clear away the dishes."

Mace didn't say anything to me or even glance in my direction; he only continued chomping his breakfast apathetically. Even though his words had hurt me to the core, I couldn't find fault with them. It was true; I was the origin of Grandmother's lunacy.

Ivy patted my shoulder supportively. "Don't listen to him," she whispered.

I knew Ivy was just trying to be nice. Underneath her kind words, she surely felt the same way as everyone else. My mother had defended me, but the words she had spoken in her sleep the day before had revealed her true feelings.

"He's right," I said to Ivy, but she didn't hear me. She was clearing dishes away from the table, including my own sticky plate of half-eaten waffles. I was still holding my fork, but even so, she had deduced that I was finished. I couldn't fathom eating another bite until my intestines stopped twisting with emotion.

I left the kitchen feeling woozy with hurt, and my unbalanced footsteps led me into the front hall. I leaned against the door for support just as someone on the other side rang the bell.

My nerves were too fried to be startled, so I simply pulled the door open in a dispassionate motion and looked into the merry, hazel eyes of Terra.

"Hey, you!" she greeted me brightly, the apples of her cheeks well-defined above a wide smile. She appeared chipper and smartly dressed standing on my porch. She was holding tightly to the ends of her colorfully striped scarf while tipping forward eagerly on the balls of her feet.

Her cheerful disposition should have been a breath of fresh air, but the gust wasn't quite enough to propel my mood upward. I stared at her for a few seconds before I asked, "What are you doing here?" Cold air was surging into the entryway, but I couldn't even put forth the effort to shiver.

"Well, I was hoping to take you to the mall. What do you think?" Terra hopped up and down in her sheepskin boots, either to keep warm or a display of her excitement.

"Um . . ." I wanted to decline. I couldn't picture myself forcing a smile and doing normal teenage stuff with the sensation of electric anxiety jolting through my limbs. I also knew that over my shoulder was the yawning maw of my uninviting home. The sense of unwelcome behind me seemed to come from more than just the people alone. It was as if the very walls wanted to spit me out like some foreign object accidentally trapped in its jaws. "How would we get there?"

"Oh, my dad's taking us! He can even meet your parents if that's a problem." Terra cupped her hand around one side of her mouth and lowered her voice slyly, "And don't worry; he's not one of those fathers who follows you around and embarrasses you in every store. We'll barely notice he's there. This way maybe we can have a look at that diary of *you-know-who's.*"

"All right; let me ask my mother." I let Terra inside, realizing I had left her on the porch too long, and asked her to follow me to the living room.

I was hesitant about asking my mother if I could go out with a friend and have fun on such a sad day. It didn't seem right that I should enjoy myself when I was the cause of poor Grandmother not being able to come home.

Mother was sitting on the sofa, her bare feet up on the coffee table where a steaming mug rested. The television was on but the sound was very low, and her eyes were peering at a paperback book instead.

I entered the room in my usual, silent way and Terra trailed in behind me almost as quietly in her rubber-soled boots. It took a moment for Mother to notice we were there, and when she did her shoulders suddenly leapt as we gave her a start.

"Oh, girls . . ." She swung her legs off the table and her feet landed on the floor with a thud. "I heard the doorbell ring, but I thought it was the boys playing around."

"Is it okay if I go with Terra and her father to the mall?" I blurted out quickly before I lost my nerve.

Mother blinked a couple times in thought.

"My dad's outside," Terra informed her. "He can come in and meet you if you'd like. He said he sure is sorry he hasn't gotten over here sooner, but he was afraid of just barging in."

"Oh, well, how sweet of him. Actually, I should have welcomed you and him to the neighborhood before now, but we've been having some family issues. I guess you've witnessed a bit of that." Mother blinked some more and brushed a lock of gold hair away from her face. "I think it would be fine for you girls to go. Please tell your father that I would love to meet him soon but I'm just not . . . myself today."

I waited, thinking that the consent had come far too easily. Perhaps Mother was just thrilled to have me out of her sight after all the hassle I had caused over the last few days.

"We'll be back later this afternoon." Terra was guiding me out of the room by my shoulders.

Back out in the hallway, I looked down at my old blue jeans and well-worn cotton shirt and wondered if I should change. "I'm just gonna run upstairs and grab the journal," I whispered. "Be back in a flash."

Upstairs, I decided to hide my outfit under my favorite hoodie, so I wouldn't have to worry about my fashion choices. I shoved the diary in the large front pocket along with my wallet, and dashed back downstairs.

Terra's father was waiting in his jeep on the street outside our house, warm exhaust puffing white clouds into the cold air from the back of the vehicle. It was so gloomy out that the jeep appeared black in the hazy setting, even though I knew it to be a dark green.

At Terra's direction I climbed into the back seat with her, grateful for the warmth inside. Her father was chatting through his hands-free device, but nodded back at me politely before returning to his conversation.

I fastened my seatbelt and watched Roger Grant through the gap between the two front bucket seats. He used his large, muscular arm to shift into drive and I couldn't help but notice that his bicep and my waist probably shared the same circumference.

As we drove, I listened to the bass tones of his voice and to his occasional hearty laughter before he finally ended his phone conversation a few minutes away from the mall.

"Girls, I know you're going to hate me for doing this," his blue eyes caught mine playfully in the rearview mirror, "but I gotta head over to the hardware store to check on something I ordered. I'm just going to drop you off at the main entrance and come back for you later. Hope that doesn't completely crush the both of you. I know you were really looking forward to my chaperone services," he laughed jokingly.

"Thanks, Dad!" Terra exclaimed.

"I want you to text me every twenty minutes, okay? Just a word to let me know no one scooped you up and murdered you, all right?" Roger Grant spoke the words lightheartedly, but they still gave me a little chill.

"Come on, Dad. Don't be weird in front of Zylia. We both walk to school every day and we haven't gotten in trouble so far."

"If you don't text, I'll call. If you don't answer, I'm headed back over here in a flash, and then if I can't find you right away when I get here I'm calling the cops." His tone was suddenly much more serious, and I wished Terra would stop being so obstinate and realize what a cool parent she had. My mother would have probably followed our every move and dictated the entire shopping experience.

"Jeez, okay, okay," she relinquished, "I'll text you."

"I shouldn't be much more than an hour anyway, then I'm coming back to drive you nuts," Roger said jovially. I could hear the smile in his voice, even though I could only see his eyes in the mirror.

I noted, regretfully, that he seemed so much happier and engaged than my own father. I couldn't imagine the slim, uptight man with a briefcase who lived in my home reflecting such inner childish mirth the way that Terra's father did. Even the crease at the base of Roger's bald, shaven head looked like a friendly smile from where I sat.

The jeep stopped in front of the mall's main entrance, a two-story wall of sparkling glass between an archway of blocky stonework. It was probably a good thing Terra's dad was letting us out in front of the building, because the parking lot was crammed full of cars and I wondered if there would be a place for him to park his vehicle when he came back.

"You girls behave. Stay together and don't . . ."

"I know, I know: stay alert, don't talk to strangers, don't pick my nose and so on," Terra sighed. "I'm going to text every twenty, so stop worrying." She slid across the bench seat and gave me a nudge. I fumbled with the door handle and heard the blare of a horn from someone behind us.

"Love you, Terra Bear. Don't get lost," Roger called in a teasing tone as we bailed out of the jeep.

Terra groaned and rolled her eyes as we darted through the cold air and into the cavernous plaza beyond the glass doors. I struggled to get warm, tucking each fist under the opposite armpit as I trailed after Terra. She was already prancing across the glossy tile toward the nearest escalator, her shoulder-length hair springing in time with her high-spirited steps.

I caught sight of my shadowy, hooded figure in the reflection of a store window. My dipped head and hunched shoulders were starkly contrasted against the pompously posed, headless mannequins who were confidently wearing up-to-the-minute styles.

I straightened up and followed Terra to the mezzanine story, where she finally stopped along the balcony wall to lean out over the floor we had entered. "Isn't this great? It feels like freedom," she said in a breathy tone.

I could only feel my nerves constricting horrifically, imprisoning me inside my own body. I knew nothing of freedom and couldn't understand how Terra could feel so carefree amid all these strangers. Any one of them would need to use only minimal force to topple her over the edge, the way she was bent out over the railing on her tiptoes. I was particularly leery of a shifty-eyed security guard having an intimate conversation with a muscular girl who had metal bone-shaped piercings above each eye.

I took a deep breath and tried to calm my nerves. There was nothing to worry about; I could be normal. What was I so afraid of, anyway? Here I was at the mall, where all the typical kids went to experience completely commonplace rites of passage. Maybe it would be different at the mall than at school. Maybe I could blend in without becoming invisible but be mindful enough to avoid sticking out like a sore thumb.

I was beginning to feel composed when Terra started speaking. "Let's have a look at that book now." She turned to look at me, her amber hair gliding off one shoulder and hanging in space, high above the lower floor.

"Now? I mean, right here? Don't you think we should find a more private spot?"

Terra ignored my suggestion, reached into the front pocket of my hoodie, and swiped the diary. "Let's see . . ." she mumbled, holding the book in front of her over the railing, reading to herself.

"Terra, please don't do that. You'll drop it!" I pleaded in a frantic whisper, my hands going numb.

Terra looked at me like I was crazy. "I'm not gonna drop it; what are you freaking out about?"

My whole body felt tingly, as if it were me suspended in midair and not a lifeless book. "It makes me nervous; please, let's sit down with it somewhere."

"*Okay*, all *right*; here you go." Terra handed me the diary and I reached out eagerly, grateful to feel the weight of it in my hand. But as soon as the leather touched my skin and I heard the approaching hubbub behind me, I knew I had made a mistake.

A group of hyper teenage girls encumbered with a hodgepodge of large shopping bags was rushing by, all gossip and giggles. One or more of them rammed into me, jarring my ribs into the railing. Time seemed to slow as I watched the diary sail from my fingers; the cover splayed open and pages fluttered wildly like the effect of some doomed, forced fledging. The book may have fallen for an eternity before finally landing behind a kiosk near the base of a potted palm. The distant slapping sound was the only thing I could hear when it hit the tile, amplified and echoing in my ears.

Chapter Fifteen

My eyes went blurry trying to focus on the remote object, and I felt my hope of ever holding it again drain away. Was I imagining that heads were already turning, fingers were pointing, and feet were advancing on the location of the journal?

Terra's mouth was hanging open in disbelief. "Oh, Zylia! I can't believe . . . Come on, we have to hurry before someone swipes it first!" she ordered, confirming my fears.

The sound of my heartbeat was hammering in my ears as we took the opposite escalator back down. We stepped over the large, rubber-ridged stairs faster than the slow and steady rate they would carry us on their own. We were making great time until we got stopped up by an enamored couple locked in an embrace, riding the stairs leisurely downward.

Once beyond them, we reached the main floor and I swung around, trying to get my bearings. The tent-topped kiosk I had seen from above had an all-new appearance from this lower angle. I couldn't pick it out separately, but I had spotted a row of booths just ahead, down a half flight of stairs and into a sunken center of the mall. I dashed toward them and ahead of Terra, looking up at the mezzanine above to try and place the spot the book had fallen from.

The dazzling lights, bold colors, and resonating sounds were like an avalanche overtaking my senses. I couldn't think around all the sensory stimuli coupled with my heightened alarm.

An arm was suddenly pointing over my shoulder. "*There*, by those plants! The man selling watches has it!" Terra told me victoriously.

I followed Terra to a small booth surrounded with large potted plants. A stocky young man with curly blonde hair tapped the leather diary against his beefy palm.

"That's ours," announced Terra. "Thanks for picking it up."

"You really could have hurt someone, you know. This thing whizzed right by my head!" The man recreated a more melodramatic demonstration with the book, causing it to pass by his head so closely that it grazed his well-oiled curls.

Terra snickered. "I saw where it fell, sir. It wasn't quite that close, but we do apologize. It was an accident, after all."

The man furrowed his thick, light brows and leaned back on his glass display case, holding Angelica's book farther away from us. "Are you making a joke out of this? I could report you to mall security. Where are your parents?"

"Have you made a mistake before?" I asked him, making sure my voice was audible. I even allowed the desperation I felt to seep into my tones. "Have you never *once* caused an accident that could change your life completely?" I didn't even understand what I was saying, but I thought it sounded passionate enough.

The man looked at me, his shoulders jerking in fright. "Where did you come from? It's like you popped up out of nowhere!"

Terra ignored his strange reaction to me and reached out her hand assertively. "That's all this was, sir: an *accident*. Now please return our property."

The curly-haired man handed the book over quickly, placing it in my hands instead of Terra's and staring at me as if he'd been spooked by a ghost. His eyes, wide and curious, continued to follow me even as we walked away.

Terra was giggling so hard she had to stop and lean against a wall, grasping her abdomen. "Can you believe that?" she asked through uncontrolled chuckles. "And *you*! You spoke up for once! I don't know what you said, but you spoke up!"

I gave a nervous laugh, clutching the diary close to my chest and taking note of several onlookers who seemed mildly interested in Terra's debilitating state of amusement.

I waited for a few minutes, until she finally straightened up and wiped her eyes where tears of merriment had trickled out. "I'll never forget that as long as I live," she sighed contentedly, guiding me forward by the elbow. "Can't you just see us in *mall jail* for something so silly?"

I wanted to ask if there really was such a thing as a mall jail without sounding too sheltered and naive. I decided not to and said, "All I can picture is your dad being furious with us."

Terra waved off my comment. "He'd be laughing with us, I bet."

I was starting to relax a little as we rounded a bend and the mall opened into a deliciously scented food court. We stopped at a coffeehouse storefront and picked up a pair of hot chocolates, their steamy tops laden with whipped cream.

"How about we sit over there?" Terra pointed to the center of the food court where a large wishing pool gurgled invitingly. "It's out of the way and I promise not to hold the diary out over the water. Plus, I need to text my dad before he freaks."

I ignored her playful smirk and nodded approvingly. We found an isolated bench partially masked in shrubbery alongside the pool and claimed it quickly. I sipped my hot drink and eyed the oversized fish-shaped fountain in the center of the shallow, tiled basin. It was carved from pale stone and adorned with a variety of colored glass pieces. Its stone mouth was open grotesquely wide and a stream of water poured out from it, thinning into rivulets over a path of rust-stained stone before continuing down a series of embankments and splashing into the coin-littered pond.

"My mother left me here once by mistake," I said aloud.

"Here? By that hideous fish?" asked Terra.

"It was the end of summer and we were shopping for school clothes. I was getting ready for third grade and all my siblings were with us. I guess we were all too much for Mother to keep track of." I gazed up at the artistic eyesore, lost in the memory of scooping out loose change and tossing it back in the water, using each coin to wish my family would come back for me. I'd gone through at least twenty dollars' worth of wishes before I saw the group of them exiting a nearby shoe store. I rushed over to them and rejoined the group, who—naturally—hadn't been aware of my absence. I was so relieved that I didn't even make a fuss, resigning myself to shove my feet into the previous year's shoes. I wore them through most of the winter until one day I couldn't take the pain anymore, and I used my allowance to buy a bigger pair.

"I got lost at the zoo when I was five," Terra shared. "Well, not lost, exactly; I just jumped off the tram and my dad didn't realize it right away. But when you're an only child you get noticed pretty fast if you're gone. You're kinda lucky that you can just blend in."

Maybe she had a small point, but I didn't feel lucky. I knew Terra couldn't understand the vacuum of oblivion that was always tugging at my reality, threatening to swallow me into its blank void.

I set my drink down on the lip of the pond and used the diary to fan myself a couple times. After dashing around in my thick hoodie and sipping a piping hot beverage in the temperate food court, I was beginning to feel a bit overheated.

"At least the book held up in the fall," Terra pointed out positively. "I was so sure the pages would rip apart on the way down."

I held the book between us and let Terra flip through it. She stopped on an interesting page I hadn't noticed before—not even briefly—when fanning through the book on my own. With it laid open, I could see curls of smoke drawn in the blackest ink encompassing the edges of both pages and growing inward in a circular pattern to fill most of the space in the center, save for a small alcove with a few written words.

Terra read the words aloud: "'*If I'm one day gone, you'll know it's here that I go. Into the black darkness that has become my foe. No one will look, and no one will ever find. My memory will only exist in the broken mind.*'" She paused after reading the entry and then traced her fingers along the edges of the page. "There are more words written under the blackness. You can just barely see that they were words, but I can't make them out well enough to read."

When I realized what the drawing was depicting, I thought I would feel horror-stricken and petrified, but a strange calm had settled over me. I said, "This blackness was in my nightmare. It was coming for me to take me away . . . and I was running, trying to escape."

Terra squinted at me. "This black blob? I could draw this in like two minutes; almost anybody could. There is no way you could *recognize* it from some silly dream you had. Don't be paranoid."

"But the words . . . they're like my fears coming true." I didn't care if she believed me or not. I was certain that whatever fate had befallen Angelica, the same was destined to happen to me. Perhaps it was a mysterious blight specific to the both of us and no one else would ever understand it. Something awful that was passed down and inherited.

It was then that I realized the reason behind my calmness. Even if Angelica was gone by way of drowning, being overtaken by a black nothing, disappearing, or any other reason, she had *understood* me at one time. She might be the only one to empathize with the pain of being invisible to everyone, especially the people you love. Just having her words at my fingertips was a comfort to me, even though I knew I could never meet her.

"I'm a little worried that your granny is getting to you." Terra pulled the book onto her own lap as if it were unhealthy for me to view it any longer.

I sighed and leaned back on the bench. Maybe I did need a break from all this crazy talk that had recently become a normal part of my vocabulary. If I wasn't careful, I could scare away my only friend with this madness. I let Terra look over Angelica's diary in peace while my eyes became mesmerized with the cascading water from the fountain. My ears soon became spellbound as well by the pleasant gurgle and splashing sound it made, echoing in the vast, high-ceilinged court.

"Listen to this," Terra said, holding up the book. "'*I opened my eyes to the quiet place again, neither asleep nor alert. That disjointed moment of rippled reality that settles over you in wispy waves. It's not long enough before it starts to come back. Never long enough. First the emotion, always before the memory. Feelings tickling my inner senses like dark poetry. I brace myself for the pain. It's never enough to dam the waters. Never enough. The quiet place is gone and I feel sick. It all came rushing back in a devastating instant, a brick through my glass sanity. Open or closed, my eyes can't avoid the vision of shady, obscure skin and vacant eyes. The quiet place could be mine forever if I let it overtake me, soothe me in its smothering cocoon. I let the thought of it make my lips curve into a tiny smile. Perhaps giving in would bring relief.'"*

I felt heavy-hearted as Terra stopped reading and looked up at me. I didn't know what to say as I let the words sink in.

"You know the two of you share the same genes, right?" Terra was mumbling and running her finger down one of the pages. "Well, it looks like you share the same low self-esteem too. What if that's all it is? Maybe you remind your granny so much of her sister because the two of you looked and thought alike."

I glanced over at Terra, not wanting to break my calm mood with any of her downplaying, speculative diagnoses. I wasn't sure if I had low self-esteem or not, but I wasn't going to take the word of a fellow thirteen-year-old peer. She had probably only recently heard the terminology and was eager to repeat it.

I made no comment on the issue and tried to focus hard on taking deep, soothing breaths. I was glad when Terra went back to reading the book on her own instead of pretending to be my psychiatrist.

I was in the process of wondering just what a real doctor of psychiatry would make of me when the loud plop of a coin plunking into the water sounded to my left. I couldn't see the person who had dropped it in due to a dense row of potted greenery, but I could hear a feminine voice whisper aloud: "I wish I wasn't alone."

The words tugged at my heartstrings, and I stood up from the bench in hopes that I'd get a view of the discouraged wisher. A tangle of foliage still blocked my line of sight at that height, but I could make out a pair of stormy gray eyes blinking at me through glossy green leaves. Pale lashes closed over the eyes in slow motion, but they did not look away.

"Hello," I whispered instinctively.

Instantly, the gray eyes went wide and I saw a flash of cinnamon-gold hair before a high-pitched scream from behind me caused me to look away.

A pudgy boy of about three was yanking at his mother's fingers, trying to pull her toward the fountain while screeching indistinguishable pleas. The two of them were mere inches from Terra, and she looked at me with an insulted expression and put her hands over her ears.

The boy let go and ran to the edge of the fountain, splashing the surface with a naughty look on his face. Water droplets were hitting Terra, and a few landed near my feet. I gratefully watched her lean over to protect the diary from the soggy assault.

"No, *no*!" shouted the boy's mother as she did her best to pull him away from the fountain. It seemed that the toddler must have been much stronger than his weary mother, because he was able to wriggle free almost instantly and leap into the shallow pool.

Suddenly he was jumping with the full force of his winter boots, causing water to spray through the air. I heard Terra let out a yelp and jump up right before a splatter of water hit me in the cheek.

The mother was now frantically shouting threats and reaching as far as she could over the lip of the pool without having to step inside. "*Gregory Luke*, you come out of there *right now* or you'll have to miss your play group this afternoon!"

The boy was laughing delightedly, mischievously rubbing his plump hands together. He hopped twice more before circling to the other side of the fountain, out of our view, and—thankfully—our splashing range.

I saw a security officer with an irritated expression zooming over on a segway while the disobedient boy's mother was rushing around to the back side of the large fish.

I assessed the water damage while the disruptive scene continued out of our view. Terra had absorbed the brunt of the waterworks, leaving a few soaking locks of hair, a wet stain on her beige coat, and a few drips on her purse. She had managed to conceal the diary completely, and it emerged from the incident dry as a bone.

As soon as I remembered, I looked back through the shrubbery; but the mysterious eyes were long gone. I walked around the row of plants, still taking note of the audible interchange between the frazzled mother, her child, and now the security guard.

Terra followed me, using her fingers to comb through her wet hair. "Can you believe that?" she asked. "I'm going to the mall with you more often. It's like never-ending excitement!"

As we walked, I spotted another bench on the other side of the plants. It was identical to the one Terra and I had occupied, but I was pained to find it empty. I scanned the nearby area but I could only find an older couple, a pair of mothers with strollers, and a man in a suit on his cell phone. It appeared that most of them had gathered to watch the scene in the wishing pond unfold, and no one that I saw could have belonged to those curious gray eyes.

"Did you hear a girl make a wish?" I asked.

Terra furrowed her brow. "Are you kidding? Who could hear anything over that noise?" She gestured toward the fountain with her head.

"No, I mean before all that—right before."

Terra gave me an exaggerated look of confusion that not only aggravated me, but twisted her features unattractively.

I tried my best to explain calmly, "I heard a girl make a wish, and she looked right at me through these plants."

Terra leaned in conspiratorially and whispered mockingly, "Was it Angelica?"

I sighed, feeling supremely frustrated. "No, of course not."

"Then why are you so worried about it? Why do you care?"

For a moment I was unsure. It seemed silly when facing questions about why I would so desperately want to find some stranger I had eavesdropped on. But suddenly I knew the answer. "Because I know her."

Chapter Sixteen

I couldn't believe I hadn't placed her sooner, but something clicked in my memory and I recognized the girl as the same one I'd spied crying in the restroom and then accidentally bowled over later outside the school.

"You *know* her?"

"Well, not exactly *know*. But I recognize her from school."

"Oh, well, why didn't you say hi or something?" Terra's interest was obviously fading. She had begun looking around, distracted, and barely met my eyes.

"I did." It felt pointless to go on. I wasn't sure what I was expecting Terra, a new student herself, to tell me about this mysterious girl. Surely, she hadn't even met her and was unlikely to know much about her.

Right then, I wished so badly to be acquainted with this peculiar girl, even though I'd barely given her any thought before. I sensed a familiarity between us that I wanted to explore.

Terra handed me the diary and grabbed my arm. "Come on, let's take a break. We're at the mall so we may as well shop, don't you think?" She was grinning broadly as she led me away from the fountain and all its mayhem.

It occurred to me that I was being selfish, wishing to befriend the strawberry-blonde stranger. I had gone from zero friends to one amazing comrade in such a short period of time that it had blinded me to the loneliness I'd felt only a few short days before. I decided to put a little effort into having fun with Terra, lest life somehow punish my greediness.

I tried my best to be cheerful as we walked into a girls' clothing store that boasted all shades of pink and had spunky adolescent pop music playing overhead. I felt a little out of place in my dark winter clothing, but I followed Terra's lead and browsed the hanging racks, metal hangers giving off high-pitched, birdlike squeaks as we slid garments along the circular frames.

I happened to catch my reflection in a long mirror and was surprised by my own relaxed posture and the pleasant curve of my lips. By the time Terra's father showed up, I was sporting a full-scale smile.

When Monday came around looking dull and bitter, I had only cold leftovers of the high spirits I'd felt the day before. I did my best to seize every remnant of the mood, letting my haggard emotions feed on the day-old joy.

Maybe the marked shift in my thoughts was because I was staving off the anxiety surrounding my grandmother. Or it could have been because of my chronic loneliness and the possibility of my disappearance that my mind was going south again.

The nearly obsessive line of reasoning my inner voice used against me was still in full swing, but it seemed to have a new target altogether. No longer was I focused solely on Angelica, her cryptic words, and her profound implication in my own life. My brain seemed to be giving that fascination a short rest. Where I normally would have been daydreaming about long, ebony tresses, I was instead musing on blinking gray eyes. I could see them so clearly in my mind, their lashes practically translucent and a light spattering of freckles on the nose bridge between them.

During the brisk walk to school Terra had begrudgingly promised me to keep an eye out for a girl near our age with reddish-blonde hair and gray eyes. Even though she hadn't said so, I feared she was starting to view me as others did when they happened to notice: abnormal and strange.

I couldn't explain to her why I was so curious about a stranger, because I wasn't exactly sure myself. If I went out on a limb and tried to express the tangible force of empathy and understanding I had instantly felt for this nameless girl, then I might risk alienating Terra even further.

During the first passing period I checked the nearest restroom and kept my eyes alert in the hallways. I was energized when I spotted a ruddy-blonde ponytail disappear around a corner. I ducked low and forced myself around the students in front of me, feeling overwhelming nervousness about losing sight of her.

When I next locked eyes on the ponytail it was swinging like a pendulum as its wearer bounded down a wide, windowed hallway that connected to the next building. I had never had any classes in that section and wasn't familiar with the remodeled part of the school, so I did my best to keep up, fearing the girl would take a quick turn that I wouldn't be able to predict.

I was only five or six students behind her when she started to slow and made a turn to the left en route to a bank of lockers. She had stopped at a shiny metal one that looked far newer and less chipped than the one assigned to me. As I got closer to her, I started to panic. I hadn't rehearsed what I would say once I found her, and I internally chastised myself for not planning it out.

The girl's head was ducked inside her locker mere inches from my own face. Surely words would come to me and I would know what to say by the time she looked up. But the girl was only at the locker for a moment before she snapped it shut and turned to face me. It was the first time I had seen her from the front, and now a pair of startled and alert blue eyes were blinking at me quizzically.

"Can I help you?" she asked suspiciously, holding a Spanish textbook tightly to her chest.

I wasn't sure how I had mistaken her for the gray-eyed girl. She was taller, younger, and even her reddish-blonde hair that had lured me in the first place was obviously an artificial color. "I . . . um . . ." I suppose I could have told her then that I had simply mistaken her for somebody else, but my mind had gone blank and my flight instincts had taken control.

With a swift turn on one heel, I fled the scene and hurried on to my next class. I ended up being a few minutes late due to my detouring, but the teacher didn't even glance up as I entered.

I took my seat and couldn't help but smile to myself as I envisioned that unknown girl I had followed. I wondered if she was still standing, mouth agape and eyes baffled, trying to figure out my bizarre interchange with her.

I tried to be more observant and a little less hasty after that. By the time third hour rolled around I was as close to being calm and level-headed as was possible for someone of my tense disposition.

I was glad to see Terra enter the room and slide under her desk with an elfish grin aimed at me. It was just enough to let me know that she hadn't given up on me or secretly labeled me with an undiagnosed personality disorder.

I spent my English hour sketching lightly in my notebook with a sharp-tipped pencil. I was drawing a fair girl, her face hidden in her hands and exaggerated streams of tears dripping out from between her fingers. I knew exactly who she was supposed to be, even though I tried to tell myself I was scribbling a random picture.

I wished I knew what made her sad and alone, wished that I could help her. Most of all I just wanted to learn her name. It didn't seem like too much to ask for, and surely it was the simplest, most basic step in learning about someone.

All I had to do was introduce myself and I'd be well on my way to deciphering this mystery girl. But first, I had to find her somewhere within the cold, cruel sea of students.

When the next bell rang I stayed close to Terra, listening to her chat about the absurdity of Ms. Beck's complex homework assignments. I strained my ears to hear her above the hubbub of other students, enjoying the sense of normalcy and recognition that walking alongside her gave me. I could almost forget about the strawberry-blonde girl with my attention focused on my best and only friend, putting my curiosity on the back burner of my brain.

I was starting to feel proud of my personal restraint to the point that I felt an inward smile heading fast to my lips. But just as I felt the apples of my cheeks begin to rise, I saw her.

I was certain it was her this time. The familiar crimson-tinted hair fell in waves all around her shoulders as she hopped and scampered to the side of the hallway like a delicate, flightless bird trying to avoid a stampede.

I hooked my elbow around Terra's arm, managing to slow her stride slightly. We were still a few paces behind the girl and I watched intently as she stopped at a large bulletin board filled with colorful fliers and announcements. I saw her pale, dainty, hand reach up toward a blinding yellow page and tear off a small tag from the fringed edge.

We were so close to her now, and I opened my mouth to interrupt Terra's venting and tell her so when a person swooped in on my left side and began guiding the pair of us to the other side of the hallway.

I felt frustration setting off a grimace in my face, but my voice had died, and I wasn't able to express any of it vocally. I felt the smooth, cool bricks that made up the hallway walls against my shoulder blades before I realized that the unknown arm had gently moved me against the wall.

"Hey, I haven't seen you guys for a while. Where've you been hiding?"

I inhaled sharply as all the expression slipped off my face. It seemed like I'd lived three lifetimes since I had seen Josh last, even though I knew it had been near the end of the prior school week when I'd spotted him in the hallway.

"I was out with some dental surgery," Terra answered, touching her jaw where the tooth had been worked on. "I thought I would die, it hurt so bad."

"Ouch; yeah, that sucks. Sorry to hear that." He turned to me and said, "What about you? Where've you been?"

Josh was searching my face now, his bright brown eyes seemed to be looking for a response from me. I felt my face sizzling with sudden heat that spread down into my chest. I couldn't match his acute gaze, so I stared at the tip of his nose, noticing that it was just a touch shiny, as I babbled, "Me? I wasn't hiding or anything. It probably just seems that way since I'm so hard to spot." My words sounded silly but at least there was actual sound coming from my throat. I giggled nervously, adding to the ridiculousness of my statement.

Josh laughed, probably thinking I was trying to make a joke. He said smoothly, "We'll have to hang out again really soon."

Terra smiled at me deliberately, a slight tease in the arch of one eyebrow. I worried her face would convey too much about my feelings for Josh, so I said quickly, "Yes, we should." My words were completely drowned out by a passing student speaking loudly about a basketball play. The student was not only loud but large, and he jumped as he passed by, indicating a slam-dunk to his friends, and landed too close to me. His bulk jarred against my side and the brick wall crushingly melded with my shoulder.

"*Hey, man, watch where you're going*!" Josh shouted after the boy.

"Oh, sorry 'bout that!" the boy called back insincerely over his shoulder.

"Are you okay?" Josh asked me, concern now reflecting in those eyes.

I nodded my head up and down while numbly rubbing my shoulder where it ached. I was trying to decide if I was dreaming or not. Was it possible that someone—that *Josh* Pierceton, of all people—had actually stuck up for me? Was I in the right universe?

"He hit you pretty hard. People need to pay more attention," Josh commented, sounding irritated while he said it.

"It actually happens all the time." I must have mumbled the words, because Josh leaned in closer and asked me to repeat myself. All at once I felt a surge of emotion welling up behind my eyes. It was a combination of the pain in my shoulder and the result of the unexpectedly kind consideration shown to me.

My voice was frozen and I was unable to repeat my words. I simply gave him a small smile, hoping he would ignore my comment and move on before uncontainable tears sprang out of me.

Terra seemed to sense that I was about to lose it and quickly took over the conversation. "We'll get back to you about hanging out. I'll text you later."

Josh nodded and I felt his eyes linger on my face for a half second more before he headed off to his next class.

"Oh, my gosh, he totally likes you!" Terra squealed, putting her arm around my shoulders and squeezing the very place that hurt the most.

"How do you know?" I shrugged her arm off, feeling irritable.

"Trust me, I can tell. He couldn't keep his eyes off you."

"He probably likes *you*," I opposed her, "or that other girl I saw him with. Don't forget about her." I just couldn't let myself accept a compliment right then; the flattering words were alien and my mental wall refused to open its gate and allow them entry.

"We better get to class, sourpuss," Terra ribbed. "We're going to be late if we just hang out against the wall."

Terra was right; more time had passed than I'd realized. The hall traffic had dramatically thinned down and only a few stragglers were shuffling their feet along the low-pile, threadbare carpet. Now I had a perfectly clear view of the bulletin board and the sight of it jogged my memory, previously suppressed by the fluttery, smitten sensation I had felt within my entire body. In the short interchange I had with Josh, I had somehow managed to forget about the strawberry-blonde girl completely, and she had long since disappeared.

"Are you coming?" Terra asked, since I hadn't responded to her tugging on my arm.

"No . . . not yet," I said quietly under my breath as I moved toward the bulletin board.

"Zy, what's up with you? Did talking to Josh melt your brain?" Terra giggled.

I smiled at her, trying to look normal and unruffled. "I just want to check something. You don't have to wait up." I didn't want to tell her what I was really doing, so I was relieved when she went on her way without any more questions.

The board was cluttered with fliers promoting after-school classes and clubs. There was a smattering of supportive pages on subjects like teen pregnancy and drug abuse. It was one of these that caught my eye—bright, yellow, and missing only one tag that would have reflected the same toll-free number in bold, black ink that the other seven fringed pieces showed. I had seen the mystery girl reaching for that very paper.

A silhouette of a bent head leaning into a palm was prominent on the page, blocky pixels showing up in the poor print job. Next to the image were large words in curvy letters that read: *Are you sad? Anxious? Hopeless? Depressed? Do you have thoughts of hurting yourself? For caring, confidential advice and assistance please call the number below. You aren't alone. We can help.*

I read the flier three times and it kept playing over in my mind after that, echoing not in my own familiar inner voice, but one that sounded like some middle-aged woman that I'd heard on an annoying medication commercial.

Melancholy settled over me as I realized the strawberry-blonde girl must be in deep emotional pain. I wondered what had happened to her to make her feel so sad and alone. I hoped that she would call the number and find help, but I worried that the anonymous adult on the other end of the phone wouldn't be able to understand her suffering, too far removed by the passage of years to recall the magnified anguish of adolescence.

By the time lunch period rolled around, I was a nervous, muddled mess. My stomach quaked with dread at my efforts to deposit a sphere-shaped scoop of mashed potatoes into it. The coagulated potato flakes felt grainy and slightly cool on my tongue, a temperature and texture that added an instant bonus to my queasiness.

I knew Terra was already somewhere within the crowded cafeteria, but I couldn't see her from my spot on the bench alongside one of the many fold-out tables. It made me gloomy to think that although we had lunch at the same time we weren't allowed to sit together, forced instead to squeeze in with our respective fifth-hour classes.

There wasn't a single friendly face at either of the long tables that seated Mr. Gnash's math class. I was almost positive none of them knew my name or even the fact that I was part of their class. No one had bothered to slide down at all when I'd brought my tray to the table. I was forced to perch on the end of the bench, left with only enough room for half of my tiny bottom on the seat, and I had to turn my tray diagonally to get enough of it on the tabletop to support it. One wrong move and I'd launch out onto the scuffed synthetic flooring, still striped for its original purpose as a gymnasium.

I gave up on eating and tried hard to concentrate on a plan to find and help this mystery girl who was possibly contemplating the end of her life that very moment. I knew I was probably the only one who took notice of her, and so the responsibility of saving her life surely rested on my shoulders.

My forehead began to feel damp and my ears were being assaulted by the din of the cafeteria. I'd never been accountable for someone's life before, aside from babysitting Ivy, and she certainly had never shown any signs of hopeless despair. I was completely at a loss as to how I could help, let alone find this girl.

A woman's voice from the office came over the intercom system. It wasn't the first time the meal period had been interrupted by the loud, crackly speaker, but for some reason I took notice as the voice announced: *Melanie Greene, please report to the office.*

Three tables away, the strawberry-blonde girl rose like a beacon above the mass of seated students. I couldn't believe my luck as I watched her speak briefly with a teacher on lunch duty and then exit the cafeteria.

So, most likely, her name was Melanie Greene. I said it repeatedly under my breath, feeling as though it might slip my mind easily. *Melanie . . . Melanie . . . Melody . . . Mallory . . .* Panic gripped me, and I wondered if that was how people struggled to remember my own name, saying it over until it meant nothing and became another word entirely.

Melanie Greene. I tried hard to focus but I could feel myself becoming giddy with exhilaration. Then, for no clear reason, I stood up, disposed of my tray, and slipped out of the lunchroom. If anyone had seen me they didn't let on, and before I knew it, I was standing in an empty hallway.

There was no sign of Melanie, but I knew where she was headed and hoped in my powers of invisibility to get me there unseen. The office was located at the end of a meandering hallway in the newer part of the building. The first year I had attended, it was an overheated, square-shaped room at the front of the school that would have better functioned as a cubicle. Nowadays the office had been relocated and expanded to a more functional size that featured its own reception and waiting area with a high, glossy counter and a windowed front wall. It was convenient, because I would be able to see inside without getting too close or having to enter.

As I neared the office, a saggy-eyed teacher materialized in my vision. I could hear a heavy, metal door close behind him and the dull thud his loafers made as his steps advanced toward me.

I held very still against the wall and closed my eyes. Like an ostrich with its head in the sand, I mistakenly believed that if I couldn't see the man then he wouldn't notice me.

The footsteps stopped and I could hear a heavy sigh before me. I'm not sure what emotion hindered me, but I was unable to open my eyes.

Chapter Seventeen

"Excuse me, young lady, but is . . ." The gravelly voice stopped, sounding unsure of how to form the question. I kept my eyes tightly shut and listened to him mutter irritably, "What exactly are you doing out here? Do you have a hall pass?"

There were a million things I could have told him, loads of excuses I could have made up, but all I could do was slowly open one eye and then the other, taking in his weary, bespectacled face.

"Well?" he prodded.

I stared and blinked, swallowed, and blinked some more. Words and language had become a foreign concept to my petrified lips, and even my limbs felt frozen and positively stationary.

"Miss, are you listening to me? What is the meaning of this . . . this bizarre behavior?" The teacher was becoming impatient.

I tried to pull myself together from the inside before I slipped entirely into some catatonic stupor. My nerves were coming awake, buzzing below my skin. A single tear trickled from my eye and I managed to form the words, "I'm sorry. I don't have a pass."

The teacher clasped my shoulder in his palm, more concern than reprimand showing behind his thick glasses. "Why are you wandering the halls without one? Are you all right?"

I ignored his first question but nodded vigorously in answer to the latter, hoping I was at least somewhat convincing.

"I suppose I'll leave off the written warning for today." He was searching my face, leaving me feeling vulnerable. "I sense there are some things you need to talk about. Maybe you could discuss them with the school counselor? It's just a suggestion, of course. We have three great counselors, and their room is located behind that door next to the main office." He pointed with a thick finger. "Walk-ins are welcome, but you won't get to choose who you speak to that way. There's a number posted if you want to make an appointment with one of them specifically."

I was desperate to get away from him and his scrutiny so I said what I assumed he wanted to hear. "I'll check into it; thanks."

The teacher smiled warmly and let go of my shoulder after patting it once. "Good girl; now back to class."

I wondered what emotions had been painted all over my face to make that teacher believe I needed professional help. I was edging toward insanity and becoming transparent in more ways than one.

I couldn't very well stand in the hallway and wait for Melanie to exit the office, since the teacher was waiting on me to make a move. I quickly told him that I was headed to my sixth-hour art room, and he escorted me most of the way there. I wasn't sure if the accompaniment should make me feel like a delinquent or a mental patient, but for the remainder of the school day I felt like a little of both.

During the walk home after school, Terra commented, "You seem morose."

"Morose?"

"It means sad or glum," Terra said just a little too quickly, as if she had been eager to educate me.

"I know," I lied, unwilling to let her make me feel even more brainless than I did. Indeed, I was suffering from the unfamiliar adjective that sounded too pretty of a word have gloom as its meaning. It seemed to be a despair that had no foreseeable end.

"You should be on cloud nine after that brush with Josh!" Terra giggled and nudged me.

I wavered between telling her or not telling her about Melanie. Part of me desperately wanted to spill out an excited explanation, but the other part feared the feedback I would receive. "Oh, I am, it's just . . ." I searched my mind for something to say that she would accept, ". . . I feel like I totally blew it. I always say something stupid in front of him."

"No, no way; you were fine," she said with conviction and spent the rest of the walk home assuring me that I hadn't ruined anything with my muddle-headed words.

Morose or not, I knew that I was fortunate to have a friend like her, bolstering me up when I needed it and giving me tactful rebuke when I was getting carried away. I felt an inward guilt in regard to our friendship, as if I weren't holding up my end. I seemed to need her far more than she would ever need me and I no longer felt satisfied with that. Maybe it was some irrational pride that caused me to harbor the thoughts, but I was completely caught up in them when I heard Terra gasp.

"What is it?" I asked, snapping free from my thoughts and following Terra's gaze. I was so preoccupied I hadn't even realized we'd reached the edge of her driveway until just then.

Terra was frozen, staring into her garage with a stricken look on her face. The interior of the garage, empty of her father's vehicle, was visible due to the large metal door being partway open. It looked as if a part of the mechanism had caught and stuck during the descent, leaving it buckled and uneven. The crumpled opening in the doorway looked to me like the old house curling its lip into a snarling, foreboding expression.

"Did someone break in?" I asked, jumping to conclusions. Sometimes our own garage door was known for sticking, but it had never looked as folded as that.

Terra ducked into the garage under the lip-like door, and I could hear her calling for her dog. I followed her hesitantly, because not only had I not been invited, but I was increasingly afraid of burglars or boogeymen lurking inside.

Terra bolted into her house so fast that the interior door bounced against the hallway wall. I was met by a slight puff of warm air from the inside before the door ended up nearly shut again. I noticed the large dog door built into the base of it, the plastic flap nearly opaque with smudges.

I could hear Terra calling her dog's name inside the house. The outcry became quiet and distant, then much louder before she was back out in the garage with me.

"Kale is gone," she said breathlessly, sounding more irritated than concerned. "My dad must have left thinking the garage door had shut but it broke or something, because there's no sign of intruders. I mean nothing's missing or ransacked." She was pounding on a yellow-lit button, but it did no more than cause the garage door to rattle and squeak vigorously.

"Maybe you shouldn't push that," I suggested quietly, but I don't think my words were loud enough to be heard.

"He can't have gone far." Terra stalked back out into the open and called, *"Kaaaaaaale,"* in a bright, cheerful voice. "You can't let him know he did something wrong. He'll hear it in my voice and get skittish."

For the time being, I positioned my school things into one corner of Terra's garage and followed her lead by calling for Kale in my friendliest, singsong voice. We walked up and down the alleyway and then cut through the side yard to the front of the house, calling for him all the way.

When there was still no sign of the husky, we took off in opposite directions down the sidewalk along the street out front. After four blocks, all I had to show for my efforts was a distrustful look from an elderly woman and the answering bark of at least half a dozen neighborhood dogs that were now inadvertently accounted for. The drapes at the front window of one home began to ripple wildly as I passed and I could hear a deep, throaty growl that made my heart quicken.

I stopped calling for the dog and turned back, feeling the cold numbing my nose, cheeks, and airway.

Soon I could see Terra's figure walking back toward me as well. Her stride was irregular as her head darted around above her shoulders, looking in all directions.

"Any luck?" she shouted to me when we were close enough.

"No," I called back, using an exaggerated shrug with upturned palms to signal my disappointing failure.

When I came near enough, I was instantly aware of an almost tangible anxiety emanating from her. Her already narrow eyes were squinted tightly with only a glint of hazel peeking out, and her two front teeth were chewing away at her bottom lip. "I don't know what to do. I'm not sure how long Kale's been gone. If my dad came home for lunch, that would-be hours ago, but if he got out first thing this morning and has been gone all day then Kale could be *miles* away," Terra fretted, balling up her ungloved fists and shoving them under her armpits.

In my eyes, Terra had always been smooth and cool as concrete, but seeing her distraught was like noticing tiny cracks in that sturdy exterior. I ached for her sympathetically while at the same time, somewhere deep inside of me, I was reassured by her display of humanity.

"Has he run away before?" I asked.

"Not like this," she answered, her normally strong voice sounding strange and small.

As soon as I recognized that she was close to tears, dread lumped itself in my gut like a rotten apple. I could barely deal with my own emotional displays, and I certainly didn't have the foggiest idea how to manage someone else's.

In the past, comforting my siblings' cries seemed only to arouse their anger, while comforting my mother's infrequent tears had only created embarrassment for her. The closest I'd ever come to successfully calming someone's waterworks was in the fourth grade.

During recess I had been sitting alongside the tall chain-link fence, where a row of boxwood shrubs poked through the diamond-shaped links from the other side. I was alone, as usual, twisting a blade of parched grass between my fingers and humming a bouncy tune I'd heard spilling out of Adonia's earbuds on the way to school that morning. I was doing my best to bide my time and ignore the small grouping of rowdy boys whose dodgeball game was edging closer to me as it went on. It wasn't until a dispute erupted among them that I began to watch from the corner of my eye, and when they all started taking turns pelting a single dark-haired boy with the big red ball, I allowed myself a full-fledged gawk.

The poor boy had been a newcomer to the school that year, but otherwise there didn't appear to be any obvious differences between him and the other boys. There were only a handful of them playing, and all varied from light to dark in shades of skin and hair. I couldn't help but speculate as to what set this boy so far apart from the others, simultaneously wondering the same about myself.

I spotted both recess attendants on the other side of the schoolyard, looking a bit ridiculous as they tried to untangle a long segment of rope for double-dutch. I hoped they'd take notice of the bullies before the harassed boy was physically injured. All I could do was look on as the boy held his arms over his face to guard against the rubbery blows. My muscles were spring-loaded, ready to take some sort of action that my brain hadn't yet given the okay for, but before I could react, the assault ended abruptly.

I watched the group of boys saunter off, sending cold, jeering remarks over their shoulders at the lone boy, whose arms were still caught up in the air, protecting his face. He eventually lowered his elbows and wiped his eyes on his shirtsleeve. I could see his chest heaving in and out as he moved toward the fence and clamped the fingers of one hand around a segment of the chain link, using it to brace himself upright. It sent a ripple through the flexible metal pattern that lapped and stilled behind my back.

"They're just jealous," I said to him at full volume, not wanting my voice to get lost in the air. It was a phrase my father had often vocalized in various situations, using it to explain almost anything away. He had told me it was the reason I had a hard time making friends; assured Mother it was the cause of her book club members not complimenting her new haircut; and I had even caught him saying it once when a group of teens in a convertible blasted around our minivan. I was sure it was perfect for this occasion and tried to insert that knowing, consoling tone that was always present in my father's voice when he said it.

The boy's heavy breathing and flow of tears stopped instantly and he stared at me with wide, spooked eyes. He rubbed a palm over his brow and tried to form a question, but the words were indiscernible.

"Those boys, I meant," I went on confidently, "they were just jealous of you."

After a few seconds he stated, "I know." However, the clueless look in his eyes read like volumes of confusion, and he sprinted away from me like I posed a possible threat.

I wanted to do better than that now, for my friend. I swore to myself that if tears started spilling down over Terra's cheeks, I would not somehow accuse Kale of being jealous of her.

"Does your father ever take him along in the car for a ride?" I asked. I didn't know much about dogs, but I'd often seen them riding around in cars and trucks, tongues lolling and looking like they belonged there.

"Not usually, no. Sometimes . . ." She looked as if a thought had blinked on behind her eyes. "Oh, I should call him." She dug her phone out of her back pocket. I noticed her hands were shaking a bit as she brought the phone to her ear, but I wasn't sure if that was due to the cold or her stress.

I stepped quickly to keep up with her as she suddenly launched into motion. She headed back through her side yard, the wind rushing through the small shaft of space between our houses, making Terra's end of the conversation barely audible. By the time we got around to the back of the house again, she was wrapping up her call and shoving the phone back into her pocket.

"He's coming home to help look. He'll be here in twenty minutes or so," Terra told me. "You don't have to wait with me. I'm sure you have better things to do than chase after my dang dog."

I felt dimly flattered that she would think I'd have anywhere more important to be right then. I tried not to make eye contact with the clear rivulet of snot that was running out of her left nostril and said, "I want to help. Let me just put my things away and I'll be back over."

I scurried back into her garage to get my things and raced them back over to my house. Our garage was empty of cars, and if any of my siblings were home from school, they were quietly tucked away somewhere upstairs. I wasn't sure how long I'd be with Terra, so I thought I should leave a quick note on the dry erase board, on the off chance that someone noticed my absence. I picked up the marker but couldn't find a clear space to write without the risk of the ink bleeding into mother's chore chart, grocery list, and various scrawled numbers.

I abandoned the idea of leaving a note and rifled around in the pantry for half a minute before rushing back over to Terra's with two packets of hot chocolate powder in my hands.

I found Terra in the alleyway, still calling for Kale. She looked like a nervous, searching bird, her eyes darting wildly while her head turned and dipped and bobbed in jerky motions. I imagined that when I called her name I'd spook her and she'd spread her wings and fly away.

"Terra," I called anyway, and she came jogging back. "We should go inside and warm up while we wait on your father. I brought something hot to drink." I dangled the packets in front of her face.

"Okay," she agreed reluctantly. "I hope Kale doesn't show up while we're inside, though."

The warmth inside the Grant home was a bit of a shock to my skin, leaving my hands and face feeling numb and tingly. I passed through the nearly empty keeping room and into the construction zone of a kitchen, where Terra filled two Styrofoam cups full of heated water. She wordlessly mixed in the chocolate while glancing restlessly out the window.

I hovered over my steaming cup, letting the waves of heat defrost the tip of my nose. Terra sipped at hers, unable to keep still. She kept pacing in front of the kitchen cabinets. They were stripped bare of countertops and doors, leaving the sparse interiors in plain view. I spotted a few pots and pans, some mismatched Tupperware, and a substantial supply of peanut butter.

Terra was muttering under her breath as she paced. She absentmindedly tripped over a metal tray of tools and not only sloshed her hot chocolate but sent an array of screws and screwdrivers rolling in all directions.

I thought I had heard a sound coming from the back of the house that hadn't been a part of Terra's clumsiness. "I think your dad might be here now."

Without delay, Terra plunked her cup down on top of the microwave and bolted out the back door. I quickly followed suit, struggling to keep up with her.

Terra's father had hopped out of his jeep and was pulling on a cord dangling in the garage. "Hey, baby," he said when he saw Terra. "Still no sign of Kale?"

"*No*, he's *gone*," Terra replied in a whimpery and dramatic voice. Tears had started streaming down her face and all I could do was marvel at this side of her, wondering if she was capable of an all-out breakdown right there in front of me.

"Hey, hey now, it's okay." Roger pulled his daughter close, pressing her head against his thick gray sweatshirt. "We're gonna find him; go get in the car." He patted her hair and I felt a stab of something in my chest. It was an emotion close to yearning as I tried to imagine my own father in a hands-on, comforting role. The mental image I conjured up was more comical than consoling and I felt a faint sense of resentment for the lanky, distant man that was my father.

"Zylia's coming too," Terra announced, hooking her arm in mine and leading me under the door and to the vehicle.

I hopped in the back seat behind Terra, and through the windshield we watched Roger yanking on the garage door. He managed to unfold the door and close off the garage, but not without a couple muffled curse words flying into the wintry air, barely audible through the closed doors over the low hum of the engine.

"This crazy dog," Roger breathed as he climbed into the car and backed out into the alley. "Where should we start looking?" One hand was on the wheel and the other he dragged across his short beard.

"He could be *any*where by now," Terra moaned.

I tried to add a helpful comment. "We looked up and down Orchid Street and the alleyway but couldn't find him."

"Well, we'll start on the next block over then, how about?" He hit a rut as he maneuvered the jeep out of the alley and we all swayed in unison. "Keep your eyes peeled."

Terra and I focused our gazes out the window and silence settled over the cab of the jeep as Roger drove up and down the next few blocks. I peered into driveways, yards, and even made sure to check porches for any sign of the dog. Once I saw a dark, fluffy tail poking out from behind a trash bin and I held my breath excitedly, remembering my first encounter with Kale. When we got close enough I was frustrated to find that the coloring was too pale and that the tail belonged to a large, round-eyed cat.

I wanted so badly to spot the dog. If I could be the one to find him for Terra, it would almost be like proving myself as a valid part of our friendship. I so vividly imagined succeeding in catching a glimpse of him that I didn't quite believe my eyes when I saw a familiar pair of perky ears raise up over a low brick wall.

"There he is!" I shouted as we came closer and I was certain.

"It is him!" Terra confirmed, relieved.

Roger put the brakes on sharply and Terra opened her door, calling the dog's name. Kale looked wild-eyed and skittish, his pink tongue dangling to one side. He hesitated in responding to Terra's call so Roger hollered, "Kale! Get over here!"

The outcry spurred the canine into action, but unfortunately, he sprinted off down the street in the opposite direction. "No; come back!" Terra yelled after him. She seemed to be beyond the tears and had moved quite quickly into anger. "Dad, why did you have to sound all gripey? You scared him off!"

"Calm down; we'll get him." Roger gestured impatiently for his daughter to get back in the jeep. Her door hadn't even snapped shut before he was driving forward. I caught a glimpse of Terra in the side mirror and noticed her lips were tight and her cheeks an indignant red.

Kale took us on a trip beyond our neighborhood and far into the next. The houses were large, but unlike ours, they stretched out instead of up; the yards between them seemed broader as well. The dog snaked through a few well-manicured, unfenced plots before foolishly darting across a road. I cringed and listened to both a horn blaring and Terra gasping.

"He's all right; he made it." Terra's father said calmly. My eyes had clamped shut in horror, but I opened them and saw that Roger's face was stony and his neck muscles were tense. "See him over there? He's headed for that park. Let's give him a little space and maybe he'll come back."

"But we'll lose sight of him!" Terra said worriedly.

Roger let out a sigh as he pulled up to the intersection. He looked both ways, crossing the road far more cautiously than the dog had, and maneuvered the jeep into a little gravel lot where a small number of other vehicles were parked. I saw a square, white sign on a metal post that read *Recreational Area Parking, 6 am to 10 pm only*.

"He's gone into those trees!" Terra emerged from the jeep as soon as the tires had stopped.

Beyond the lot, the frozen land rose slightly, then smoothed out before meeting up with a front line of large, old trees. The leafless branches looked nearly black in color where they pointed their gnarled and twisted fingers at the cold, gray sky.

I jogged after Terra, who had taken off down a paved path that led into the grove. From behind us Roger yelled, "Don't get lost, you two!" When I looked back to give him a polite nod of acknowledgment, I noticed that he was barely out the jeep and in far less of a hurry than his daughter. I slowed a little myself and swung my head back to face forward, my eye catching a weathered sign adjacent to the path. It was slightly hidden behind a tangle of scrub and brushwood, but I could make out chipped letters in white paint over a cracked and splintered surface that read *Nightingale Park*.

Recognition didn't sink in right away, only a vague familiarity. I jogged onward, scanning the tree line for Terra or Kale. The trees became denser the farther I went, and an ominous feeling settled down around me.

It was an intangible warning that seemed to take the form of a frigid current of air, brushing over the earthen floor and whispering around my ankles.

I looked over my shoulder furtively. The parking lot was no longer visible through the trees, but I could see Roger coming up the path slowly. I thought for a moment he was laughing to himself, but then I saw him touch his ear and knew he was having a phone conversation. His presence reassured me and I picked up my pace, running until the cold air burned my lungs.

The trees opened on the right side, revealing a contemporary plastic-and-metal play structure in the center of a poured rubber circle. The play area would have been cheerful and vibrant in the sunlight, but under the gauzy sky it looked lonely and ice-cold, void of any children. On the left the trees continued, following the lip of a stream. There were frozen chunks of ice caught up in places along the water's edge, but I could hear the liquid flowing below, unimpeded by the temperature.

Somewhere in the distance I caught the faint sound of Terra beckoning for Kale. Her voice seemed to dart and dance about my ears like a jittery hummingbird, coming at me from no single place, but many directions instead. I concentrated, trying to hone in on her location; but the wind picked up again, and by the time it had died down the distant calling had ceased.

The paved path continued ahead but I branched away from it, onto a beaten-down strip of ground that descended toward the stream. Part of a colorful striped scarf was coiled loosely along the shoreline, brightly contrasted against the dull brown earth. The rest of the scarf was soaking, undulating slightly in the cloudy water. It was Terra's scarf, and when I saw it I felt ice in my stomach and my breathing became labored.

I had worried that my fate and Angelica's were intertwined and nearly identical, that I would meet with the same demise. But now the evidence seemed to laugh at me, that mirthful, multi-hued yarn. It may as well have been a blue dress.

I knew that Terra was gone forever, just like the mysterious Angelica, disintegrated into cold nothingness. This knowledge wedged itself into my chest, keeping the air out. I gasped as deeply as I could but was unable to fill my lungs. My heart went wild. I could hear it pounding in my ears as I clawed futilely at my throat, trying to loosen the cords of my hood. My vision darkened, and I collapsed to my knees, the dreary sky above swirling.

Chapter Eighteen

I felt something like a tiny, wet sponge being pressed against my forehead and then a larger, somewhat warmer one was being rubbed along the side of my cheek. I opened my eyes and they slowly focused on a furry, white face and pair of ice-blue eyes.

Absentmindedly, I patted Kale on the head and used my free hand to wipe dog slobber from along my jaw. My breathing was returning to normal as I got back up on my feet, and my racing heart had begun to slow down.

The sound of Terra's voice brought clarity and sanity to my unreasonable mind. "Yes; you caught him!" She was panting as she hustled over and stooped down alongside the dog. "I almost had him back there but he looped back and headed this way. He thought it was just a big game." She clamped one hand around his leather collar and used her other to glide back and forth over his coat.

For the next couple minutes Terra was so busy covering Kale with kisses and pats that she didn't notice me staring at her with extreme relief while I recovered from the anxiety attack.

Roger caught up to us a couple of minutes later. We were bringing Kale back up to the path when he called, "That dog is in big trouble!" I could tell by his tone of voice that he wasn't really angry, and when he was close enough, he rubbed his large hands affectionately over the dog's back.

"Here, dad, hold my scarf so I can keep a good grip on him," Terra instructed, extending the soggy, dirty article.

"What on earth did you do to it?" Roger held the scarf away from his body exaggeratedly, as if it were contaminated. This made Terra giggle, and when he looked at me and grinned I knew I should laugh politely too, but all could produce was a forced smile and a breathy hiss.

Terra and Kale joined me in the backseat of the jeep for the ride home. The latter seemed wholly unaffected by the adventure but was obviously enjoying the extra attention from his owners. Terra's earlier display of agonizing concern had now been replaced with mock scolding and high-pitched banter directed at her dog.

It appeared that everyone had fully recuperated from the incident except me. I was still a bit shaken, and I let my eyes linger over the dormant treetops as we pulled away from the sinister park. It was silly, of course, that I'd let myself get so emotional about a scarf dangling in water that had such a gentle current and was probably no more than waist deep at the most.

If Angelica had wandered into that same water so many years ago, then surely, she had never expected anything dire to come of it. Maybe she had gone into the stream in pursuit of something she'd dropped or something she was trying to gather. I let my mind tick off the possibilities: a coin, a shiny rock, or an endangered kitten.

Once, when I was younger, I had reached far out over a mud puddle to retrieve an exquisite feather that had caught my attraction; it was dark gray, edged with iridescent teal. I'd liked the way it glinted in the sunlight and imagined I might be able to clean it up and wear it behind my ear. In my effort to claim it I had slipped and landed on the knees of a brand-new pair of tights into the grimy muck.

What if Angelica had done something similar? Maybe in some quest of fancy she'd gotten tripped up and tangled, lost her balance, or hit her head. She could have struggled free of her dress if it were encumbering her but lost out to the water in the end.

I wasn't even sure where she had gone into the stream. Perhaps it was wider and deeper in another area of the park. I even wondered if the path of water was the same as it had been all those years ago; I was pretty sure that seasons, droughts, or dams could change a watercourse over time.

My mind was turning until a question interrupted it. "Would you like to come in? I could whip you up a decent meal. Seems you deserve it for helping us find that mutt." It took me a second to realize Terra's father was speaking to me and another to notice that the jeep was already parked in their driveway.

"That's nice, but I probably should get back home." I fumbled with the door handle. "Thanks, though."

"Well, some other time, then."

"You don't want to eat Dad's cooking anyway. It's so gross!" Terra laughed as we all got out of the vehicle. Her father simply shrugged and gave me a grin before ambling over to tinker with the garage door.

"Bye," I waved before making a beeline for my house, hoping to appear at ease.

The keeping room was dim, and I was startled by a basket of clothes sitting in Grandmother's recliner. For a second I had thought it was her and that things were back to the way they used to be. I stood motionless, staring at the chair before my mother spoke up from the kitchen, "Zylia, don't go skulking about. You startled me. I thought you were upstairs."

It was odd since I had slammed the garage door on entry, using far more force than I had meant to, but apparently that sound had alerted no one. "Oh . . . sorry."

"What sounds good for dinner: stroganoff or meatloaf?" she asked me as she searched around in the pantry.

Both sounded awful to my testy stomach. "Either."

"Well, that's no help," she mumbled grumpily, digging farther into the food cupboard. I didn't mind so much if she was in a cranky mood, because it was better than seeing her cry.

"Do you need any help?" I asked, trying to be considerate.

She sighed irritably and waved me away.

I gratefully retreated to my bedroom, where Ivy was dusting her bookshelves and tea sets. "Would you like me to get your side when I'm done?" She paused in mid-wipe of a sparkly teacup to gesture toward my cluttered and dusty end table. "I don't mind."

"Sure," I answered, rifling around in my bag for Angelica's journal. "Thanks." I settled onto the bed and stared at the cover, hoping Ivy would wonder what it was. I wanted to share my secret with her. Right then, I needed to talk and release a torrent of emotions.

Ivy's little hands moved meticulously with the dust cloth, her eyes distant as she hummed an unrecognizable melody. I opened the book to a random page. At some point I knew I'd make myself read it from cover to cover, but for the moment I was too listless.

I took a few deep breaths and moved my fingers along the side of a page where a series of teardrops were drawn in dark ink. I guessed that at least a hundred words were written all over the center of the page in a combination of print and cursive, big and small lettering, following no line or order. They stuck out at angles and overlapped each other so that it was hard to make out each word individually. I singled out *imperfect, desire, wound,* and *stupid*. I looked harder to find *despair, want,* and a word that might have been *distraught*. The words were so stacked and jumbled that a headache quickly developed behind my eyes from trying to decipher them separately.

The collection of words formed a sorrowful theme that prompted me to recall the bright yellow flier I had seen at school. The journal seemed to prove that Angelica had been truly depressed. All the words, poems, drawings, and phrases were those of a miserable girl. What if she had been unhappy enough to go into the water on purpose?

I shuddered, the question making my skin prickle. I pictured her in my mind walking out into the stream with a stoic look on her ivory face: eyes closed, her abundant lashes resting against her cheeks. The movie in my imagination played on and I saw her sink down into the water, letting it cover her face and saturate her hair. Her body gave in, relenting to the current, and was carried away gently. I could see her in the blue dress floating off into oblivion until a clanking sound startled me from my musing.

"It didn't break; don't worry." Ivy was at my bedside table, dusting a crooked ceramic vase I'd made in sixth grade. She held it out sheepishly, showing it to be intact.

"It's okay." I wouldn't have cared if she broke the vase or anything else in the room at that moment. I was completely unconcerned with anything material, my head given over to things elusive and indescribable.

My thoughts jumped from theoretical visions of the past to possibilities of the present. I was following a trail of associative images in my mind that started with the muddled words on the page in front of me and ended with the memory of Melanie's hand reaching upward to take the number for the depression hotline.

Melanie's tormented face filled my mind's eye. For as little as I knew of the girl, I was aware of something significant—crucial, even—about her. I might be the only one who knew, the only one who could change her course of unhappiness.

I was fully aware that I was making a presumptuous leap, dreaming up baseless possibilities and conclusions, but if Angelica had taken it upon herself to end her misery, then I feared Melanie doing the same.

I recalled a line from the depression hotline flier: *Do you have thoughts of hurting yourself?* Did Melanie feel that way? How could I stop her?

I couldn't quit thinking about it. With my body on autopilot, I went through the motions of a normal evening: homework, dinner, and chores. Inside, I was wondering and calculating, resolving and settling my thoughts, then beginning the process anew. The exhausting cycle went on well into the night and continued in my dreams, when I had finally surrendered to sleep.

The next day, just after lunch, I had the seed of an idea. Instead of using the limited time between periods to scrounge up my books and fight the crowd on my way to my next class, I headed directly to the counselor's office. I remembered that the teacher who had caught me in the hallway the day before had said something about there being a list of numbers on the door. Maybe I could work up the courage to call one of the school counselors and ask his or her advice on helping Melanie.

When I finally reached the wood-colored metal door, I saw the list that the teacher had been referring to. It was a laminated sheet with three names, a number, and a big smiley face at the top with the words *call for questions and/or appointments* typed next to it. Below the sheet was a clear plastic, tiered pamphlet holder filled with an assortment of subjects ranging from college and career preparation to abuse and addictions. I had just plucked one out with a heading on suicide prevention when the door opened, pulling the rack of brochures away from me.

"Goodness me!" came a startled, high-pitched voice from the doorway. I recognized the older, heavyset woman from around the school, but I wasn't sure of her name. "Sorry; you startled me." She grasped for her glasses that were hanging over her abundant bosom from a thin, metal chain and placed them on her slightly crooked nose. I saw her looking at the pamphlet in my hand when she asked, "Are you wanting to make an appointment with a counselor? I'm the only one here today but I can answer some questions for you; whatever you need."

"Oh," I hadn't expected to run into an actual person and hadn't yet prepared what I would say. "Well . . . I . . ."

The woman smiled, warmth emanating from her tangerine-painted grin. "My name's Miss Levie. I was about to take my lunch, but you know, I'd *rather* have a chat with you."

"Oh, I can't. I'm going to be late for class as it is," I said quickly, finding my voice.

"Nonsense; we'll just take a few minutes and then I'll write you a note to give your teacher. No worries at all." Miss Levie stood aside and ushered me beyond the doorway.

She motioned to a wooden chair with a padded seat, and I obediently sat down while she seated herself in an identical chair next to me. I stared at the small gap of space between us. There was a small end table displaying an old-fashioned ticking clock, a box of tissues, and ceramic coaster with a log cabin painted on its surface.

Unsure of where to look, my eyes roved the rest of the room like a caged animal looking for a potential escape exit. The office wasn't large, and the only other door besides the one we had entered was on the back wall behind a cluttered desk, standing between two jam-packed bookcases. It was probably a closet of some sort, but I felt better imagining it to be a shortcut that led directly out into the open air outside the school.

"What's your name, dear?" asked the counselor sweetly.

"Zylia Moss," I whispered.

"What an interesting name!" she exclaimed in a quiet, soothing tone, perhaps intending to match my own hushed modulation. "How do you spell that?"

As I noted each letter individually, I watched her dragging a pen across a notepad she'd produced when I wasn't looking, her left hand curled inelegantly around the ballpoint utensil.

"I bet people have a hard time remembering that," she commented.

I could have gone on and on over the extent of her understatement, I thought, but kept quiet about it, simply nodding in agreement.

She asked a couple more basic questions about my age, grade, and contact information, and handed me a sheet of paper that covered her professional policies. Then she leaned back and folded her plump hands. "I think that you and I would get along great. We could really swap some stories, chew the fat, or even shoot the breeze; you know what I mean," she said with a soft laugh.

I knew she was trying to be nice, but I really had no idea what she was talking about.

"But if you wanted to," her big, disarming smile turned serious as she went on, "we could speak of important things as well. Do you have anything important we could talk about, something that's been on your mind lately? We could set up another time to talk about it, but if you give me an idea today, then maybe I could be more prepared for our next visit. What do you think?"

Her gentle, soft-spoken prattling was somehow calming to my nerves, and I discovered I could open up a little. "All right, yes, I do have something important. It's not for me, though; it's about a friend."

"Oh, I *see*," Miss Levie said, winking at me for some reason. "Would you like to give me a hint about it today and then we can schedule you in for later this week? I bet I could even get you out of your least favorite class if we work it just right." She nudged me with her elbow, a playful and conniving look on her face.

I nodded and explained, "It's about suicide." The last word came out louder than I had expected and landed with a great weight into the room. Before that moment I don't think I had ever used the word out loud, and it had the striking effect of a curse word against my ears.

The more I thought about it, I couldn't remember a time the word had ever been spoken in my household. There was once, when my mother and father were discussing a news report over breakfast, when I knew my mother had meant the word suicide, at least. She only mouthed it, though, using her lips exaggeratedly in front of her teeth as if it were inappropriate to say aloud.

Miss Levie blinked, nothing at all registering on her face. "I see. Maybe you should tell me just a bit more. Have you been thinking a lot about suicide?"

"Yes, I can't stop thinking about it. I think my friend is depressed and I worry it will make her want to hurt herself."

"Your *friend* . . ." Miss Levie pursed her lips in thought before continuing, "Why do you think she is depressed and could potentially harm herself?"

I heard the bell ring in out in the hallway and the shrillness of it coupled with the reminder of my tardiness made me tense up. I said nervously, "She's very lonely."

"Lonely," Miss Levie repeated contemplatively. "How do you know she's lonely to such a great extent?"

"I know everything about lonely," I said with sober conviction.

"I *see*. How would *you* describe loneliness?" asked Miss Levie.

"Some people think it means you're by yourself a lot, but it doesn't have anything to do with being alone," I told her, finding myself able to speak of it freely. "I could be surrounded by people and it's like . . . well, it's like I'm desperately shouting for help in the middle of a crowd and no one so much as turns their head to check on me. At first, I might think they don't care and that's why they don't bother to look, but then I realize that I only wish that were true. If the people in the crowd didn't care, at least it would be some sort of emotion toward me, but it's not that at all. It's like . . . well, it's worse than that, because they don't even know I *exist*. They can't see or hear me and I mean less than nothing to every one of them. I can touch things without ever leaving a mark or break things without making a sound. *My* loneliness is having no proof that I was ever even alive in the first place." The verbal purge of feeling had left me a bit breathless and surprised at myself.

Miss Levie opened her mouth halfway, closed it, and then after a beat opened it again to say, "Such passionate loneliness would certainly make anyone feel desperate. It's perfectly understandable for you to feel concerned about this, and I'm glad you chose to speak with me." She repositioned in her chair and posed a new question that caught me off guard. "When your friend thinks about hurting herself, does she have a plan to bring that about, or does she just kind of think about it every so often with no real idea of how to accomplish it?"

"I'm not really sure . . . I don't know her that well, actually."

"Ok, well, what about you? When you think of seriously hurting yourself or suicide, like you said, what comes to mind?"

Instantly I thought of Angelica and all over again I could visualize her pale form floating in the water, hauntingly serene. "Drowning," I said. "It makes me think of drowning."

Miss Levie's voice became warmer and consoling, and she touched my shoulder briefly. "Where do you think of drowning, darling?"

"I think of the stream that runs through Nightingale Park." As soon as I said the words I realized my mistake. "Not *me*, drowning, of course, someone else."

"Your friend," said Miss Levie with obvious skepticism.

"Uh, no . . . not her either. It just reminds me of something else." My explanation sounded absurd even though I knew it was the truth. The urge to flee took hold of me. "I better go," I said, quickly grabbing my bag and standing up.

"I know life can be painful, but you made the right decision about trying to get help." Miss Levie stood up and I feared her blocking my exit. "A very brave decision, actually. Now whether this is about you or your friend, I think it's important we continue this help."

Brave? Inside I was coming unglued. I had gone about this all wrong and this woman probably thought I was some sort of suicidal, depressive time-bomb waiting to implode. I'd never be able to help Melanie at this rate.

I weaved around the counselor, sidestepped through the open doorway, and went into the quiet hall. "Thanks so much for listening; it really helped," I lied, desperately trying to extinguish the concern in her eyes as I began to move down the hallway.

"You may feel like it, but you aren't alone, Zeela," Miss Levie called after me.

I kept walking. Surely the more steps I took away from her, the more likely she was to overlook her encounter with me entirely. I'd fade from her memory just like my name had already done.

"You forgot to have me write a note . . ."

I knew Miss Levie was still speaking to me and that it was rude to walk away. If my mother had witnessed my actions she would have felt disgraced, no doubt reminding me that she hadn't raised me to behave that way. Even though I could feel shame and mortification searing through me by way of my conscience, I was helpless to stop my feet from moving; they were locked into some evacuation mode. It didn't even occur to me to question where they were headed until they landed me in a bathroom stall.

Sixth hour was well under way, so the student bathroom was vacant—peaceful, even. There was no way I could inconspicuously merge into my art class at this point. I would have to face a tardy slip or go back to Miss Levie and try and get an excuse note. I couldn't decide which would cause more trouble so I simply did neither. Eventually, I heard the bell ring to dismiss sixth hour and the bathroom was flooded with racket from the hallway as girls were opening the door to enter.

I listened as stall doors banged shut, toilets flushed, and paper towels were swiped from metal holders. I watched an assortment of shoes occupy the stalls on either side of me as I caught snippets of useless conversation from random people.

". . . and the other one wasn't too bad. I mean it fit good and everything, but it was so puffy I couldn't move . . ."

". . . mine has a liner you can take out if it gets too . . ."

"*No freakin' way!* Aaron said *that?!*"

"No joke; I'm telling the truth!"

". . . a shiny blue wallet with, like, a silver claspy thing . . ."

"Geez, Martina! Pee a little quieter, will you?"

". . . because I didn't even read the book before I took that test . . ."

I should have come out of the stall then and joined the flow of students commuting to last hour. I could have sidled into my science class as if I hadn't ditched an entire period prior and maybe then I'd have slipped under the radar, but I couldn't inspire my legs to leave that stall.

After a while, the chatter ceased and the next bell rang. A few minutes after that, I grew bold enough to peek out the door of the stall and look around the beige-and-white-tiled bathroom. When I was positive it was empty, I walked up to the sinks and set my belongings on a dry part of the counter.

I was feeling grimy after occupying a germy bathroom stall for an extended period of time, so I washed and scrubbed my hands while eyeing my reflection. The girl in the mirror didn't look like me. I was alarmed at the wary crease in her brow and the darkened puffiness below her eyes. My mirrored replica also had her lips pressed into a hard, white line and there were tangles in her ebony hair.

Two summers before, Ivy and I had tagged along with Mother and Grandmother to the farmers' market downtown. Mother had grumbled and fussed about parking until finally paying to leave the van on the fourth floor of a shadowy garage. As we made our way to the elevators, a young woman had staggered out in front of us with outstretched arms. Her hair may have once been blonde under layers of dirt and oil, and there were strange scab marks up and down her arms.

"Do you have any spare change?" she had asked, her eyes wild and pleading. "Anything at all will help."

Mother had tugged Ivy by the wrist and motioned for me to move away as well while Grandmother put a green bill in the young girl's trembling hand.

Once we were safely in the elevator, my mother let Ivy's hand loose and said admonishingly, "Mother, you shouldn't open your wallet in front of desperate people. It's dangerous!"

Grandmother simply shrugged.

"You know what she'll do with that money, anyway."

"She was so terribly young," Grandmother commented while shaking her head.

"She looked *old* to me," Ivy put in rather cheerfully, and I had to agree with her.

"That's what happens to young people who break the law," Grandmother enlightened. "It's dreadful for your complexion."

I wondered if Grandmother's words were coming true for me currently. I had never skipped school before, and now that I had, there was someone older and more troubled staring back at me from the mirror. The more I scrutinized the likeness of myself in the glass, the less I was able to connect myself with it.

I blinked slowly and repetitively under the fluorescent lighting. On my fifth blink I opened my eyes to find that my reflection was no longer there, only the view of the stalls behind me. I clamped my eyes shut in fear, counting out a full sixty seconds before opening them again.

I was thankful to see that my reflection had returned, unchanged save a few beads of sweat above my lip and along my hairline. I averted my eyes and walked away from the mirrors, no longer able to deny that something out of the ordinary was happening to me. Whatever it was had chilled me to the core with the greatest fear I had ever felt.

Chapter Nineteen

When the last bell rang I reluctantly left the bathroom like a rabbit emerging from the safety of its den. The very atmosphere felt painful on the outside. It was as if I had undergone some sort of sensory deprivation and I was just now being reintroduced to color and sound. My limbs were erratic as I tried to merge into the student traffic, unable to find the sync of the passing crowd.

If I had been a real rabbit, surely, I wouldn't have survived all the toe squashing and shin kicks I endured on my way out of the school. When I finally met up with Terra on the steps out front, I had two red welts forming under my pant legs.

"Howdy, partner!" Terra greeted me with a cheerful smile that I couldn't match. Any delight I felt was due to her being in such a talkative mood that I wasn't required to say a single thing the whole walk home.

When we had almost reached Terra's back drive she asked, "Do you want to come in for a while? Kale wants to get to know you better."

"I'd love to," I lied, thinking fast. There was no way I could fake the social pleasantries it would require to hang out with my friend. "But I have to get to work on my art project or my grade's gonna tank."

"That's cool; some other time, then."

I smiled as wide as I could, but felt that it wasn't enough to make my eyes crinkle convincingly. Once we had parted, I raced to the haven of my vacant bedroom and attempted to mentally digest everything strange that had happened that day. It was like trying to eat a brick.

I kept reliving the hours I had spent in that hollow restroom like some prisoner recalling the long days of served time. Why had I been so fearful to leave that smelly place? It seemed so silly now, looking back, that I couldn't have just walked into my classroom and endured whatever punishment awaited me. If only I'd done that, then maybe I'd never have caught that scary moment in the mirror when I wasn't there.

I shivered at the thought of that glass, empty of my reflection, empty of me. Where had I gone for that short time? I had still been aware and could see and think, but I'd lost all human substance.

I laughed out loud, my voice sounding chilly and eccentric. When I heard myself, I was momentarily sobered. I reasoned that my mind was slipping and there wasn't much further to go. I had to get it together or I'd be in the same boat as grandmother: nutty and delusional.

After a while, I pulled out my rough sketch and the large page of matte board. Even though I had been fishing for an excuse to avoid being around Terra, it was true that I needed to get to work on the eerie drawing. It was due in three days and many of my classmates had already turned theirs in.

I let myself sink into the rhythm of the dark strokes I was creating on the page, the troubles and worries of my crazy world departing from my consciousness for the time being, bleeding into my art instead. I wasn't sure how much time had passed when my bedroom door burst open and I saw my mother standing in the doorway with an unclear expression on her face.

I couldn't remember the last time I had seen my mother in my bedroom. She almost never came to the top floor of our home except to occasionally deposit something in the attic, or when she was doing one of her deep cleanings that she couldn't trust to delegate to us kids.

It struck me as even more abnormal that she hadn't knocked before entering. I had always known her to give a signature three-beat tap with her knuckles and a vocal notice before coming in.

"*Zylia,*" my name had been caught up in her exhale, and I thought I could hear relief in her voice. "Didn't you hear me calling for you?"

"No." I had been completely tuned out.

"I was yelling and . . ." she trailed off and pressed her hand against her forehead. "Are you okay?"

"Me?" I answered stupidly.

"Of course, *you*, Zylia! What is going on?"

Was mother aware of the strangeness that was happening to me? Could she tell that I was fading from reality? Was my complexion already that bad?

When I didn't speak up soon enough, my mother blurted, "Your school counselor called. She said you spoke to her about some pretty serious stuff and then you skipped your last two classes."

I was a frozen block of ice, too horrified to respond.

"Say something, Zy," Mother prodded, her voice low and strained.

I said nothing.

"The counselor said you were . . . *suicidal*." She pronounced that last word in a quieter tone than the rest of her sentence and her mouth went all weird as if the word burnt against her tongue. "Is that true? I know things have been difficult around here with your grandmother but why would you feel like . . . *that*?"

I forced my paralysis aside and forced out the words, "Oh, no . . . I don't feel that way at all."

Mother was flustered and started blinking frantically. "What? But she said . . . you spoke to her, that you had a *plan* and everything . . . what is going on?"

I took a deep breath and searched my mind for the words to make my blunder right. "It was a mistake, something I was researching for someone else. The whole conversation wasn't about me at all, just a situation I made up. I shouldn't have talked with her. Then afterward I guess I felt embarrassed and freaked out, so I skipped class."

"You don't want to hurt yourself?"

"No, not at all."

"So, this was all a mistake? You're fine?" I could hear her tone slipping out of concern and into irritated disbelief.

"Yes."

"Let me get this right," Mother inhaled, then spoke very slowly. "You alarmed your school, endangered your grades, and *terrified* me all for no real reason?"

When she put it that way it sounded just awful, and intense shame caused my head to droop. "I'm sorry," I whispered.

"Sorry? *Sorry!*" The last word had been a definite yell and she started flailing her arms around as she shouted, her fingers stiff and almost claw-like. "What were you thinking? Are you totally ignorant of the stress I'm under lately? Your grandmother is in the hospital. The *hospital*!"

"I know, I . . ."

"I don't even know what I'm doing. I don't know where to put her." My mother was no longer talking to me alone. She was shouting at the atmosphere. "The waiting lists on the really good places are *insane*. Unless we pay through the nose; then maybe we could get her in somewhere halfway decent." She swiped some laundry off the floor at the end of the bed and slammed it into the hamper with a force that made me jump. "The thing is, she *wants* to come *home*. She doesn't even remember what she did to land herself in this situation. She thinks it's some scheme to get rid of her. She'll probably be too crazy to realize I care and die thinking that I gave up on her."

If my conscience was an organ, it was located deep in my gut. I could feel it come to life, prickling and burning me from the inside out. I hadn't imagined what my mother was feeling throughout this ordeal. I knew that she was stressed and concerned for her mother, but the strained look that screwed up her face was near hysteria by that time. I couldn't find any other words to express my remorse, and I was terrified to say the words *I'm sorry* again since they hadn't gone over well the first time.

"I didn't mean any of this," I said, but my simple words were washed out by my mother's shouting.

"You are in so much trouble!" Mother jerked her finger at me. Her eyes were narrow and flashing, her jaw clamped shut. I had never seen her look at me that way before. Even when she lashed out at Mace or Bram for their endless shenanigans, I don't think I had ever caught so much seething ire in her expression. "Your father and I will probably have to talk with the school," she went on, pacing in a figure eight pattern. "You'll have to explain yourself to your teachers and counselor and write notes of apology or something. God, they'll probably make us take parenting classes and send you to a psychiatrist!" I could tell she was making it up as she went along, unsure of what was going to happen or how to punish me. "You know, maybe I should make you walk around with one of those giant cards announcing your wrongdoing to shame some sense into you! But what would I even write?? . . . Oh, and your current chores will seem like a baby's job compared to the list of duties I'm going to think up for you for next week . . . no, the next two weeks! All of that is really getting off easy, Zy. You made me think you wanted to . . . oh I can't even *say* it! What an awful thing to do to your own mother!"

In the blink of an eye she was gone, slamming the door behind her. I listened to her angry footsteps fading downward into the lower parts of the house. When I couldn't hear them anymore, I allowed myself to breathe and wrapped my arms around my torso to brace against the violent tears I knew were coming. Seconds ticked by and they didn't come. In their place crept a growing heat that rose from my chest and into my face. My body temperature must have increased drastically, because beads of sweat were forming above my lip and along my hairline.

The air in my room felt sweltering as I breathed it in and out in ragged breaths. I pushed my sleeves up, trying to get relief from the heat; but it must have been coming from within me, because I felt like I was baking from the inside out.

I tore open my bedroom door like a lunatic, but the hallway air was just as stifling and had the sickening aroma of old wood and dusty heater vent. I pulled my hair up off my neck with my hands, noting that the long strands were damp around the collar.

I walked slowly down the stairs, stopping on the second floor. The heat I felt inside me was so intense that I feared melting. I could hear the twins goofing around just down the hall, a muffled song of thuds, mocking snickers, and a suspicious splintering-wood sound.

I imagined that nothing could interrupt their childish, untroubled play, not even finding their own sister melting into a puddle on the floor just outside their room. I could envision their sneakers delightfully splashing through my disregarded remains.

I tacked down the rest of the stairs, feeling wobbly and grasping the handrails tightly. If I didn't cool down quickly I would certainly burst into flame; the thought of it brought a terrifying remembrance to the forefront of my mind.

It was a scene from a movie my father had been watching while my preschool-aged self-had crept out into the living room and viewed it secretly around the spindle-shaped legs of a side table. The vision of a woman screaming and running out into the street would haunt me for weeks after covertly observing the age-inappropriate content. Her clothing and hair had been alight with bright, orange-yellow flames that were consuming her. She staggered and stumbled until falling to the blacktop, the camera honing in on her singed, bubbling flesh as she expired.

Now the snippet of recollection brought me fresh distress, and I could almost see the flames wafting up from my skin. Distraught, I stumbled into the front hallway and fumbled with the door, not bothering to be quiet in my escape.

The air outside was icy, and the sun had sunk low behind the neighborhood. The houses down the street were an ashy silhouette against the luminous, carrot-colored orb. Even in the cold outdoors, my mind could not escape being taken over by thoughts of burning heat.

At least I had cooled down drastically, and I was pretty sure my anxiety-fueled hot flash was subsiding. The frigid air was like a warning slap to my senses. I focused my mind and tried to think clearly. What was happening to me? When I had I become so . . . *unstable*?

I could see tiny pricks of light above, where the stars were starting to show against the darkening sky. I was breathing so deeply I felt I could have sucked the stars right into my lungs. My chest ached with the effort of it, but my mind felt calmer with all that oxygen.

Once my breathing and temperature had returned to normal, I dropped my gaze from the sky and let it fall toward my body, where my hands were moving brusquely up and down my arms. But my hands weren't there and neither were my arms; only the ground below me met my vision.

I squeezed my forearms tightly, feeling a definite pinch but seeing no evidence of the action. I frantically touched all over my face and legs. I could feel my appendages; my sense of touch conflicted with my sense of sight.

I felt a cold pain as my invisible knees seemed to collide with the ground and the frozen earth rushed up and took over my vision.

Chapter Twenty

I groaned and opened my eyes, dim shadows and a cluttered tangle of debris overwhelming my vision. I was lying on a pile of stuff over a dirty, wooden floor, my body wedged between boxes and crates. It took a full minute to realize I was in the attic.

Prior to that, there had been only a couple occasions where I had woken unsure of my surroundings. Once was on a family vacation when a dream had startled me awake in an unfamiliar bed. But all it had taken was a few seconds and a glance around the room before my senses returned and I could recall that I had gone to sleep in a roadside motel crammed into bed with my sisters.

I waited for the haze to lift and for my memory to return, just as it had then, but nothing at all came to me. My mind remained blank even as I scrambled upright and took long breaths of the stuffy attic air. I was standing in a bizarre, lumpy nest of unraveled fabric bolts, unfashionable bath towels, and a few stray pom-poms.

"How did I get here?" I asked aloud.

I looked at the dangling attic light bulb, grateful for its faint illumination. If it hadn't been left on, there would have been no way to discern my surroundings. Had I been the one to leave it on? *When and why did I come up here?*

I clawed my way through boxes in the direction of the ladder stairs, unconcerned of the mess I was leaving in my wake. My heart skipped a beat when I reached the spot where I would normally see a rectangular hole leading down to the third floor. The gap was filled in with the collapsible stairs, snapped firmly in place.

Being trapped in the attic was rated as number three on my top terror list, just below having to eat bugs to stay alive and being swept away in a hurricane. As I fought with all my frantic might to get the stairway open, I realized I might need to reevaluate my list, because it occurred to me that bugs might be my only option up there, and who knew what the crazy weather could bring? Being trapped in the attic could be an experience of all three of my worst fears at once.

When I became conscious of the fact that under the dim lighting I was not even pressing against the trapdoor, but pounding against the solid floor beside it, I was too relieved to feel sheepish.

I came down out of the attic quickly and clumsily, with so much force that I felt like the attic had spat me out like a bitter piece of food.

The door to the bedroom I shared with Ivy was open, and my sister's bed was neatly made. I could hear the shower running in the nearby bathroom and pounded on the door much harder than I had intended.

"Yeah, what is it?" Ivy answered in an imperative tone. My knocking must have created a frenzied sense of urgency that I hadn't intended to convey.

"Um, it's Zylia; can I come in?"

"It's unlocked," she called.

I entered the humid bathroom and closed the door behind me. It was no wonder I never got any hot water. Ivy had the room steamed up like a sauna.

"What's going on?" Ivy peeked out from behind the floral shower curtain, her sopping-wet hair looking browner than its usual honey color.

I wasn't sure, not in the slightest, how to answer Ivy's question. I was actually hoping she could have been the one to tell me and I think that was why I had invaded her privacy in the first place.

"Why are you just standing there?" she asked peevishly. "I have to get ready for school."

School? It hadn't even occurred to me that the entire night had passed. The blinds were closed and it was probably so early that it was still dark as night outside anyway. "I don't remember going to sleep," I said stupidly.

Ivy scrunched up her freckled nose and looked annoyed. She slid the curtain back in front of her face and was no longer visible. "You are being so weird, Zy," she said from inside the shower.

"Did you see me? I mean, did I go to bed last night?"

There was a clattering sound as a plastic bottle no doubt bounced off the tub floor and an irritated sigh followed it. "I don't know. I went to bed before you. I didn't see you when I woke up, though. I thought you got up early. Where did you sleep?"

I wasn't about to tell her, so I backed up toward the door, slipped out before she could launch a follow-up question, and snapped the door shut quietly behind me.

I felt grimy and in need of a shower myself, but I was eager to solve the mystery of my missing memory. I decided to drag a brush through my tangled hair and pull on fresh jeans and a long-sleeved cotton top before investigating further.

On the way downstairs, it occurred to me that this whole thing could have been some sort of prank pulled on me by my mischievous little brothers. Perhaps their devious ways had gone too far. Could they have found me outside? I remembered collapsing against the cold ground. Maybe they had worked together to carry me to the attic, thinking it would be funny when I awoke there all alone. The theory bolstered me slightly and I descended one floor to their room to find the truth.

Bram was dangling his pajama-clad legs off the edge of his twin bed when I found him. He looked half asleep, his dark hair ruffled and his eyes narrow and puffy.

"Where's Mace?" I asked from the doorway, surprised at my authoritative tone.

"Bathroom; why?" he answered sleepily.

"Nice prank you two pulled; real funny."

"What's wrong with you?" Bram asked, sliding off his bed and doing a little wiggle that told me he was waiting for the bathroom to free up. "What are you talking about?"

"Don't play dumb about the attic. You know what you did."

"The attic?" Bram looked both genuinely baffled and seriously close to peeing his pants. "Trust me, we've learned our lesson about the attic. We didn't do *anything* close to that place."

I had forgotten what a huge punishment the twins had gotten when, together, they had managed to bust a hole through the attic floor. Mace had nearly fallen right through the ceiling down into Adonia's bedroom.

Now that I thought of it, the twins might be wiry and strong, but were they really capable of moving my lifeless body indoors and up three flights of stairs, one being an awkward ladder-like contraption with no railing? It seemed even more outlandish after I factored in that the crazy mission would have had to go unnoticed by anyone else in the house.

"Why? What happened up there?" Bram asked me.

I stammered, "Uh-um . . . nothing happened. Just checking because I thought you might have . . ."

"Are you insane?"

"Quite possibly," I answered quietly, closing the door to hinder any further questions and to block the view of Bram clutching at his private area and bouncing around urgently.

Insanity appeared to be the most logical conclusion. Surely, I was suffering from a madness worse than my poor grandmother. At least her delusions had a known diagnosis and she had spent most of her life in a reasonable state of mind. What would my future be like if at age thirteen the lines between reality and imagination were already hazy? I was doomed.

Keane's bedroom door opened unexpectedly, and I was startled to see an unfamiliar shirtless young man standing in the doorway. He had light brown oily hair sticking up on one side of his head and a dim expression in his hazel eyes.

"Oh, hey," he said, taking notice of me. His voice was deeper than I'd expected it to be and I couldn't help but notice a fine patch of hair sprouting in the space between his nipples. "You must be one of Keane's sisters. You guys have a damn big family!"

I looked down, feeling bashful, but my gazed happened to land on the young man's drooping athletic shorts and the exposed band of underwear that clung to his thin frame. I felt my cheeks grow hot.

What was this scantily clad person doing in our house? He didn't look like any of Keane's friends that I'd ever seen. He didn't have thick glasses that made him look smart or heavy acne that made him appear geeky. Instead, he was rather attractive and no doubt somewhat older than Keane's fourteen years.

"I'm Brody." He stuck out a long-fingered hand in introduction and nearly crushed mine in his grip. "Do you have a name?" As he came nearer I noticed the faint scent of cigarette smoke wafting from his person. The scent was always foreign to our household, and was both repulsive and fascinating to my nose.

It took a second to summon my speaking faculties to answer, "Zylia."

"I should have known it'd be a weird name. All you guys have weird names." He laughed rudely, and I was ashamed that I felt captivated by his deep chuckle. "But yours is pretty, though, just like you. I like it."

An unidentified squishy feeling wormed its way through my insides and made my legs feel wiggly and unsupportive. It was a confusing, swirling blend of distrustful apprehension and tickled delight. What seemed like hundreds of responses played themselves out in my brain, but my tongue was unable to utter a single word.

It turned out I didn't have to say anything, because Keane caused quite an unexpected distraction as he came scampering up the stairs. He obviously hadn't expected anyone to be standing in the hall near his doorway, and he rammed forcefully into me. I tipped like a domino, and in the blink of an eye my cheek was pressed against the bare chest of the strange man-boy. His arms encircled me and I was distantly aware of their strength as they set me upright.

"God, Zy! What the hell are you doing?" shouted Keane.

I couldn't understand why he was so irritable when he was clearly at fault for the accident. Then I saw that he had dropped something in the shuffle that at first looked to me like a deck of cards. He did his best to hide the red-and-white label as he shoved the box into his shirt pocket. I stared in disbelief at the bulge it made inside his flannel breast pocket.

Keane shook his head. "Don't even think about it, Zy. You're no nark."

The young man named Brody nudged my brother and laughed. "Come on, Keane; she knows snitches end up in ditches. She wouldn't dare." He reached out and gently grabbed a lock of my hair as he added, "Besides, I think she likes me."

"Dude!" Keane punched the other boy in the arm. I watched as a pink mark spread over the area of impact.

The sensation that came to me next was completely unexpected and a little embarrassing, but suddenly, more than anything else, *I wanted my mother*. I knew that seeing her would be awkward and that it was likely that she was just as furious with me as she had been the previous night; but even so, my mother was still a comfort in my crumbling world.

Keane pushed his friend, both of his palms making a slapping sound against Brody's chest. "Come on; we gotta get going."

Brody was staring right at me, thoroughly amused by now, his guffaws ringing in my ears like an agitated donkey.

I couldn't take it any longer and fled the scene. As I propelled myself downstairs I couldn't stop repeating that phrase in my head over and over. *Snitches end up in ditches*. Since when did my brainy brother befriend that barbaric Neanderthal? And smoking? The idea of Keane purposely inhaling toxic fumes into his lungs really had me worried and unsettled. Next to Ivy, he was the last person in my family I could ever have imagined falling prey to that vice.

Mother would be horrified; that much I could envision crisply. I knew that I should tell her, but the thought of it was causing dread to creep up on me. It had nothing to do with the brutal, yet singsong threat I'd received upstairs. I was pretty sure that no matter how mad Keane might become over my tattling, he'd never have me murdered and tossed like garbage into a ditch. At least not over cigarettes, surely.

The reason I feared telling my mother was that I knew the information would crash-land into her sensitive soul, already paper thin and haggard by other stressors. I, myself, had added to her heavy load with my well-intended but blundering shenanigans, and now I couldn't see being the messenger of more bad news.

Downstairs, I braced myself for the sight of her. I knew I'd blame myself for any slump in her shoulders, circles below her eyes, or strands of hair out of place. I hated that I had caused her pain and I wanted more than anything to put my arms around her and tell her how sorry I was.

The kitchen was empty. I stood near the center island and looked around, noticing the subtle oddities that were like little clues to the cracks in our family. There was a stack of mail so tall that it had slumped over, making a cascading slope that ended in a pool of letters dangerously close to slipping off the edge of the counter. Nearby, the fruit bowl was empty save one black banana: sad, shriveled and bonding itself to the plastic surface. Overhead, at least one of the bulbs in the main lighting fixture was burnt out, leaving the room a shade or two dimmer.

I heard someone come up behind me and feared it was Keane's friend, following me to make sure I wasn't tattling.

"What's wrong with you? You're jumpy," Adonia said as she plunked her fabric handbag on the cluttered island counter.

"I'm . . . is Mom here?"

"No, she left just a minute ago. I think she said something about a meeting with a discharge planner or something, whatever that means. Something about Grandmother moving to rehab or . . . I don't know, I wasn't really paying attention," she shrugged as she rifled around her bag for her lip gloss.

As I watched her squeeze a clear, gel-like substance onto her lips, I felt surprised that my oldest sister had taken note of even that much information. It was unlike her to retain anything that didn't wholly interest her.

"Dad's gone too, so I hope you have lunch money. Mom forgot to put any on the twins' account, and guess who has to front the cash for them today?" Adonia pointed two pink-painted index fingers at her chest and rolled her eyes. Her dramatic display was especially irritating, since I knew she couldn't have been out more than six bucks and she'd probably get her money back from Mother or Father by the evening.

"Keane, we're gonna be late for the bus!" Adonia yelled, startling the wits out of me.

I heard a stampede coming downstairs and I slipped behind Adonia, feeling nervous about coming face-to-face with the strange guest from above.

"Hey, Doni," Brody said as soon as they were within sight.

"What the heck, Keane??" Adonia shrieked. "Did you sneak him over? Mother would have your head if she knew this dorkweed was in our house."

"That's hurtful," Brody chuckled in his donkey laugh.

"What's up with my goody-goody sisters ganging up on me?" Keane's cheeks were an angry red below his glasses. "Can you guys just gimme a break? Geez!"

"Goody-goody?!" The words exploded from Adonia's shiny lips.

I slipped around the group and made my way for the stairs. Brody caught my eye and gestured at me with his index finger and thumb in the shape of a gun. He mouthed the words bang-bang before blowing the tip of his finger and flashing a vulgar grin.

I had to run down the alleyway to catch up with Terra. When she heard me coming she slowed up and walked backward until I could fall into step alongside her. "I'd almost given up on you coming to school today," she said. "What happened?"

There was just no natural way to begin an excuse that consisted of waking in the attic with no memory of how I had come to be there. Even if I started at the beginning with the incident of my panic attack followed by my anomalous disappearance, it still had an extra layer of strange to it that I wasn't ready to share.

"Zylia, talk to me. You're not trying to avoid me lately, are you?"

"What? No! Of course not! It's just been a weird morning for me," I said, hoping she'd leave it at that.

"Spill it. Now."

There was one nagging issue I felt I could confide in her that surely wouldn't be lumped into a loony, paranormal category. "I feel a little weirded out because I caught my brother with a pack of cigarettes this morning."

"One of the twins?" Terra's eyes widened.

"No, no; *Keane*."

"Oh, well, that's a little better, at least."

"Better?"

"Well, it's not good, but you know what I mean. I mean the twins are—what, eleven?" Terra explained.

"Well, Keane's no adult. He's only a year older than me!" I defended a little too indignantly.

"Sorry; I wasn't trying to downplay it or anything."

"I just never would have expected it from him, you know. He's too smart for that." I was dragging my shoes across the pebbles, slowing my pace. "I think it's peer pressure. He's hanging out with some creep I've never met before."

"Maybe you should tell your parents?" Terra seemed uncertain of her advice.

"I know, but I just can't do it yet. My mother is freaked out with this whole Grandmother situation and I've been . . ." I quickly remembered that Terra wasn't aware of me visiting the school counselor, accidentally implying that I was suicidal, and then skipping two classes. "Well, I haven't helped her out at all with any of that stress. I'd just hate to add to it now."

Terra put her arm around my shoulders and I was pleasantly surprised at the gesture of affection. "You'll know when the time is right." She smiled, a twinkle in her hazel eyes before she added cheerfully, "And in the meantime, just remember: at least it's not heroin! My dad used to work with a guy who had needle marks up and down his arms."

I tried to keep my eyes from going wide to hide the fact that I was shocked by the comment. "Is there usually a connection between smoking and heroin?" I was horrified. I'd have to remember to keep an eye on Keane's arms.

"No, goofball; I was trying to be comforting." She dropped her arm from my shoulders as if her efforts had totally failed. "Come on; we gotta hustle before you make us late."

Chapter Twenty-One

As if my nerves weren't fried enough that day, the fire alarms went off during my fifth-period math class, scaring me so badly that I slid off my chair. When I landed halfway under the desk, the boy next to me laughed hysterically.

If it had been a real fire, there was no doubt I'd have been consumed in smoke and flame before I made it out of the building. It appeared that my lollygagging fellow students were in no hurry to evacuate. Most of them were slowly moving out of the classroom and into the hall, clustering up into inefficient groups instead of the neat, clean line we had been trained to form. Some were even smiling and talking over the shrill, intermittent blaring like it was some sort of field trip, even though we were supposed to be silently filing outdoors toward our predetermined spot near the basketball courts.

I put my fingers in my ears and narrowed my eyes against the blue strobe lights flashing in the exit signs. Even when we'd made it outside and the alarm was a little more distant, I could still feel the sound slashing into my skull.

I was grateful, at least, that I'd had the sense to grab my hoodie off the back of my chair. There were many students with their hands folded under armpits or rubbing them against bare skin to stimulate warmth. The same boy who had laughed at my frightened reaction was shivering and bobbing on his tiptoes in a thin cotton shirt. *Who's laughing now?* I boldly fantasized about saying to him, but I quickly and sheepishly averted my eyes when I accidentally connected with his gaze.

That's when I saw Melanie. She was lined up with a class along one of the school's outer buildings, no more than a few paces from where I stood with my group. Her hands were in the pockets of her jeans and her head was tilted forward, but I knew that strawberry-colored hair by now. It was a little frizzy, the cold breeze ruffling it up in a somewhat unsightly way. The day around us was gray, but Melanie looked a shade or two grayer than everything else, as if her gloomy personality had somehow muted her pigmentation.

I wanted to walk over to her, but Mr. Gnash was doing a head count of our class so I knew I had to wait. I couldn't risk even the tiniest of infractions for fear that it might result in a note or call to my poor mother.

A group of honking geese flew by overhead in a V-shaped formation. I watched Melanie's eyes glance up at them, lingering for a moment. When her gaze dropped back earthward, it happened to line up with mine. I instinctively waved at her, a little too vigorously perhaps, but I was elated to have her attention.

Melanie checked over each shoulder suspiciously before hesitantly lifting her hand to wave back. I knew that feeling, the surprise and disbelief that someone was addressing me. I'd lost count of the many awkward waves that had been meant for someone near me instead. Even more embarrassing were the extended handshakes or high fives left hanging in the air as I realized, all too late, that the approaching palm was en route for someone else.

I put my hand down, becoming aware that I'd been waving for far longer than what was probably socially acceptable. Melanie was smiling at me, trying but failing to hide the baffled crease in her brow. She must have thought I was a weirdo—or a stalker, even—but I had no clue how to initiate a normal conversation, let alone a friendship meant to save someone from the depths of depression.

I pointed at my chest and called, "I'm Zylia."

Melanie cupped a hand behind her ear and shook her head, indicating that she couldn't hear. It was no wonder, since the fire alarm was still squealing in the background and there was the hubbub of other students schmoozing and goofing around.

I took a tentative step forward, wondering if I should just walk up and introduce myself, when the screeching alarm stopped and a garbled voice came over the intercom, announcing that the drill was complete and that everyone could return to their classrooms in an orderly fashion.

Mr. Gnash clapped his hands together in a futile gesture to gain the attention of his class. "Form a line, please, everyone. We've had an unexpected chance to stretch our legs, so we should be all set to finish up our work back inside." He pulled the bottom of his sweater down that had risen up over his pudgy middle.

Across the short distance, I saw that Melanie and her class were also being rounded up and guided back indoors. She was no longer looking in my direction, mystified, but seemed to be avoiding the puzzle of me altogether by staring at her shoes with her hands jammed farther into the pockets of her jeans. Her group was in motion before mine, traipsing ahead in single file toward the nearest school entrance. I watched Melanie as she passed, hoping she'd look my way with the merest hint of a smile. As she was nearly past me, I decided I'd settle for a grinless glance if she'd only give me some evidence that she didn't think I was a socially odd loon or an all-out creepy stalker.

Her body language told me all I needed to know, though, even if I didn't want to decipher it. Her shoulders were scrunched, and her head hung low between them as if she were trying to shrink away out of sight, retracting into herself like a human turtle.

Was she trying to disappear from the world or was she just intent on avoiding me and me alone? Normally, I'd just assume that I had already disappeared from her mind, but something about the skittish vibes she was emanating made it hard to believe my invisibility was at fault.

"It's not like I purposefully did the wrong chapter review," Terra was ranting as we headed out of the school. "I mean if I had meant to skip out on some homework, I wouldn't have turned in *anything* at all! I worked hard on that pointless paper. That should be proof right there that I don't deserve a zero!"

"That's really ridiculous," I chimed in, trying to be supportive. "I've heard stories about how unreasonable Mrs. Allen can be. I'm glad I don't have her."

"Yeah, I'm so pissed right now," Terra huffed. "I'm gonna see if my dad will call and chew her out."

"Wow, would he do that?" I asked as we crossed the street at the stoplight. I pictured her strong, protective father swooping into the school and demanding to speak with the teacher who had wronged his daughter. In my mind's eye I added a cape for good measure.

Instead of answering me, Terra asked, "Isn't that your mom?" She was pointing to the long row of vehicles lined up on the opposite side of the street.

I spotted our dark-blue minivan with a mixture of dirt and old road salt crusted and spattered around the wheel wells. The driver's-side window was rolled down and my mother's head was poking out, strands of blonde hair hanging from her cable-knit beanie. "Zylia!" she called. "Over here!"

"What's she doing here?" I mumbled as Terra and I walked to the passenger side of the van, avoiding the traffic.

"Hey, sweetie," my mother chirped as she leaned over to assist in opening the passenger-side van door as if I were somehow incapable on my own. "I had an errand to run and I thought you might like to go with me." I didn't like the artificial cheerfulness forced into her tone.

"What about Ivy? Don't you have to pick her up?" I asked, feeling confused and a little suspicious. Was this some kind of trap? I remembered overhearing a classmate talk about how her mother claimed she was taking her to Disney World, when in reality, they were headed to the dentist. Was my mother capable of that kind of deception? What if there was really something sinister behind this mysterious *errand*?

"Your father took off work early; he's picking her up. Don't worry." My mother patted the passenger seat invitingly. I looked at Terra, sending her a message of apprehension with my eyes.

"Well, I guess I'll let you gals do your thing," my best friend said, patting me on the shoulder with her gloved hand and showing no indication that she'd detected my fear.

"Terra, we can drop you off you off at the house really quick before we head off. Climb aboard!" my mother offered.

"That's nice of you, but I could use the walk," Terra declined, much to my disappointment. I wanted to keep her with me as long as possible to stretch out whatever time was left before any uncertain fate could take hold.

"Okay, then; see you later!" my mother said with a wave, giving off a false, sugary perkiness. Soon after she merged into traffic, she began glancing over at me with a huge smile. I wondered if she was driving me to the mental hospital and wanted me to be in the best possible spirits when I arrived. Perhaps I was being dramatic, but there was definitely something out of the ordinary going on, and the suspense was the worst part of it.

I was relieved when she finally started speaking. "Zylia, I wanted to talk to you because, first, I need to apologize. I really lost my temper with you last night and I shouldn't have done that, especially with you in such a . . . fragile state."

I wriggled in the seat, trying to adjust the shoulder strap of my seatbelt but it was locked into place, keeping me pinned against the seat. I suddenly felt trapped, claustrophobic, and overheated in my heavy coat.

"It's understandable if you're depressed. I hope you won't hide it from me because I lashed out like that. You have to understand that I'm just going through a lot right now and I don't mean to take it out on my family, but I'm not perfect."

Was the heater on full blast? Why was I so sweaty? What was I supposed to say to her in response?

I flinched as a small sports car honked and went speeding around us after my mother glided into its lane without checking her blind spot. She was an alarming driver even on a normal day, often looking worlds away when behind the wheel. But it was so much worse when she was intently conversing with passengers. She was prone to lingering eye contact with her listener and releasing the steering wheel to make theatrical gestures in the air.

"Oh, sorry, dear; that little car must have been speeding. It came out of nowhere," Mother said to excuse her blunder. "Now what I was trying to say is this: I want you to feel comfortable with me, to be able to tell me anything. You aren't going to be punished for having feelings. I'm so sorry if I made you feel that way."

"It's ok, Mother; it's fine." I was desperate for the conversation to end. "Where're we going?"

"Zylia, please don't change the subject. I want to know if you're okay. I need to know if you're depressed . . . even just a little bit. Would you tell me, please?"

Oh my God, why was she acting so bizarre? I felt like I was being questioned on a witness stand in one of those crime shows Grandmother would watch. Any of the ways I imagined I could answer the interrogation sounded like lies as I quickly practiced responses in my head. *I'm fine. I'm good. Things are okay. I'm just tired. Schoolwork is really getting to me.* The words sounded like a sham because they *were* all falsehoods.

But what was the truth? I was either fading from existence or my sanity was slipping away, and I wasn't about to share either possibility with my mother. I was already concerned enough that she was going to drop me off in a padded room somewhere. I didn't need to make it a sure thing. I had to find some way to take my mother's focus and scrutiny off my mood.

I took a deep breath and felt thankful that I wasn't hooked up to a lie detector test before I said, "Really, I'm okay. I'm holding together pretty well . . . at least, I'm doing the best I can with everything that's going on with Grandmother. I guess it has been a little hard to be normal when I'm this worried about her."

Mother sighed, flicked her wrist, and engaged her left blinker. I could instantly tell she had fallen for my excuse, because relief was evident in her posture as she loosened and relaxed. It's not like I was really lying, anyway.

I honestly did care about my poor grandmother, whom I had played a role in pushing over the edge.

"I know, sweetie. I'm worried about her too," Mother said. "In fact, that's what this outing is about. We're going to tour a facility where she can stay after she leaves the hospital."

My mouth went dry as my fears on that matter were confirmed. "You mean Grandmother's not coming home?"

Mother shook her head and pretended to be intent on driving. She didn't know that I had caught her biting her bottom lip, a sure sign she was holding back tears. "We just can't . . . I mean, she's gotten to a point where we can't take care of her the way she needs."

I'm not sure why, but I suddenly felt that it was important to say, "You've been a great daughter, and Grandmother would tell you she was proud of you if she could."

My mother turned to look at me in surprise, leaving her eyes off the road for longer than I was comfortable with. "Oh, Zy, thank you," she said sincerely. Her voice cracked on the last word, and before I knew it she was sobbing.

"I . . . I'm sorry," I mumbled, feeling panicked. Watching her cry gave me a sense of impending doom. Here we go; the woman who cared for our family, my rock, was finally cracking. I was pretty sure the driver's seat had become ground zero for a Moss family apocalypse.

"No, no," Mother said, waving a dismissive hand at me and wiping an eye with the other one, leaving the van to drive itself for a horrifying three seconds. "You're very sweet. These are happy tears."

The rest of the trip I chose not to say anything else, even when I felt Mother was veering out of her lane a bit or when I noticed she was going ten miles an hour above the posted speed. By the time we pulled into the parking lot of a rambling, single-story facility, she was finally done sniffling.

"I guess this is it," she said, giving the building a squinty once-over before using the visor mirror to freshen her makeup. "It looked so much nicer in the pictures online."

While I waited for my mother to work with the cosmetics in her purse to conceal the fact that she'd been crying, I examined the building's exterior myself. The long, low structure that stretched across the lot like a winding snake wasn't much to look at. But where a snake would have bent in smooth curves that made the letter S, this building tacked in sharp L-shaped angles around the semi-circled parking lot. A large, wooden sign that read *Oakview Lawns* was affixed to the shabby, orange-hued brick.

When Mother was finally ready, we walked up to a stretch of dark-tinted glass that slid open automatically and led into a small, stuffy vestibule with an ancient-looking intercom system.

I tapped my toes while I listened to Mother speak into the silver device. "We have an appointment for a tour; this is Margaret Moss."

There was an obnoxiously loud buzzing sound before a wide metal door slowly opened into a green-carpeted reception area.

I followed my mother up to the front desk, which was really just a large window in a wall with a length of countertop installed in the opening. It had a curved edge on the patron's side, and perhaps it was only my mood, but to me it looked like a polished, wooden lip sticking out in a giant pout.

To my left, the room widened out into a sort of recreational area. There were tall, mismatched bookcases filled with a variety of reading material and a few tables and chairs. In a floral upholstered chair at one of the tables sat alone, elderly woman with curly, white hair. She had been gazing out a steamy window until she looked in my direction. She gave me a sweet little smile, but I noticed that above those withered lips, her eyes were watery; a sense of sorrow seemed to emanate from her. I could almost feel the emotion reaching out hungrily toward me.

I smiled back at her, feeling happy that she had noticed me; but I also had the urge to cheer her up, if only in the smallest of ways. I must have been beaming at her for an uncomfortable length of time, because soon she cast her eyes downward and adjusted the afghan lying over her lap.

"I was under the impression that the private rooms fell into this price bracket," I heard my mother say as I looked away from the old woman. Until then, I hadn't paid much attention to her conversation with the plain woman at the reception desk. She was leaning across the pouting countertop and looking at a pamphlet that the employee was holding out to her.

"No, no; sorry about that. I've noticed that a lot of people seemed to be confused by our website, so I'll have to have someone look into it. In fact, we only have shared rooms available right now anyway." The woman was nodding with a huge smile and a nearly imperceptible flinch on her face, as if she were expecting to be yelled at sometime soon. "They do tend to fill up quickly. Would you still like to see one of the open semi-private rooms?"

"Um, well . . ." I could hear the frustrated indecision in my mother's voice. "Sure, I suppose. And what other amenities do you offer? I'm not sure if I can trust that information I found online."

The woman behind the counter laughed nervously. "Can't fault you there. Well, let's see." She was pointing at the pamphlet again and pushing it toward my mother. "We have a lovely dining hall with quite an impressive menu, and each room has its own enclosed patio. For an extra fee we can offer cable TV, housekeeping, and laundry services, and there is even an add-on that includes salon services." The woman smiled as if she had just offered up a treasure trove of unexpected luxuries.

My mother was quiet.

"One thing the residents really seem to appreciate here," the woman went on, "is that the rooms are simply sun-drenched and inviting." She waved her hand in an expressive arc.

"Does that cost extra?" my mother asked in a monotone voice I wasn't familiar with.

"Excuse me?" The woman looked confused.

"The *sun*," Mother enunciated. "Does it cost extra?"

Chapter Twenty-Two

After leaving the care facility, I was afraid to say anything to Mother, who had an explosive look about her. I sat quietly in the passenger seat while she called Adonia and instructed her to find a frozen lasagna in the deep freezer and heat it up in the oven. I assumed she wanted to get a head start on dinner, but on the way home she swung the van sharply into the parking lot of Buster's Burgers and announced that we were skipping the lasagna and eating dinner out.

"I need a milkshake more than life itself," my mother said, winking at me. I thought she was looking a little more relaxed, at least, but anything might have seemed chill and easygoing compared to the way I was hooked to the armrest like a frightened, feral cat.

It felt weird walking into the little burger joint, just the two of us. In fact, I couldn't remember a time when it had ever been just her and me splurging on greasy burgers and oversized milkshakes. But that's where we ended up, sitting across from each other on bright-orange booth seats, struggling to make conversation.

"I'm sorry, Zy," my mother said around a mouthful of french fries, "this wasn't how I pictured today going."

I had been distracted by a loud, edgy-styled couple and their baby, so it took me a moment to make sense of her words. I tore my eyes away from the family and tried to focus on my mother. "What did you picture?" I asked.

Mother took a long draw from her vanilla shake and plunked it back on the table. "I don't know what I was thinking, really. I guess I figured I'd find a lovely place for your grandmother to stay and then I'd get you to open up to me about what's been going on with you. I'm such a dreamer."

It was obvious she felt she'd failed in both categories, so I was determined to say something consoling. I wanted her to believe that I was really baring my soul. And why shouldn't I? I was going through an internal hell that needed to be shared with someone.

"I'm sorry about Grandmother; I wish she could come home. I kinda feel like . . ." My words were interrupted by the shrieking of the ketchup-smeared baby in a wooden high chair. The young parents were giving flashy, pierced smiles and taking photos of the mess instead of soothing the baby.

"It's not your fault, you know," Mother said when the fussing baby had ceased. "I know I've told you that before, but I'm afraid you might not believe it."

She was right; I didn't.

"When that counselor called me, my heart just broke. I was—I mean, I *am* scared for you, Zylia. Even though you say it's nothing, I feel like I'm missing something very big. Something right in front of me that I can't see. You would tell me, right? If there were something going on, you'd let me know?"

So, this was what the outing together had been all about. I could see now that she was afraid of letting me out of her sight. It was as if I were on suicide watch, considered to be a walking danger to myself. I nodded as sincerely as I could, but it was difficult to swallow the lump of fast food in my throat.

"You know what I think? I think all this . . ." Mother went on, putting two clawed palms in the air in front of her for emphasis, ". . . dementia and nursing home mumbo jumbo has me thinking of myself, actually. Not in the selfish way like it sounds. It's just that this disease runs in the family, so I could put you guys—*my own kids*—through this ordeal eventually. It's a terrible burden. I hate to say that of the situation because it's like I'm saying that of *her*, like she's a burden. I don't want her to feel that way, but it's the truth."

And that's how the rest of the conversation went. I choked my food down as she rambled on, venting all her grown-up problems to my thirteen-year-old self. I knew she hadn't intentionally dominated the discussion, and as I looked into her distant eyes, I was pretty sure she had forgotten she was speaking to me at all. It was almost as if she had been journaling into space, just to get the words out of her system.

Honestly, I had stopped listening. The distance between us across the table seemed to grow into miles, as if I were looking at her through a tunnel. The sound of her babbling was muted, and she was tiny and blurry in my vision. I felt dizzy and I knew something was happening to me, but I was helpless to stop it. I didn't even try. I knew it wouldn't be long now before I'd slip away, and it just felt easier to accept it.

The school's art show open house on Friday evening somehow leapt into the present, and I couldn't believe it was already time to display the wide variety of pieces our middle school had worked on for weeks.

Our entire sixth-hour art class was spent working in the gymnasium to aid in getting it ready for the show. Much of the enjoyable work, like hanging streamers and lighting, had been done by some of the earlier classes and their teachers, so by the time we got there it was mostly sweeping up and tucking gym equipment under the stage and out of the way.

The most interesting thing we got to do was assist in hanging our work. There were several long rows of folding metal partitions out in the center of the glossy maple floor, but those were already filled to the edge with artwork from earlier classes so the walls around the side of the gym were being used as well.

I waited at the bottom of the ladder with the rest of Mrs. Braeburn's students as one by one we handed up our projects to the stocky custodian. He was using adhesive Velcro strips to affix everything from cardstock to canvas to the eight-foot blue padding, and it was taking an eternity. The art started at about five feet and went up to the top of the protective mat from there. I was annoyed that the art was random in size and media, leaving a trail of uneven rows along the wall. I felt like the whole thing should have been executed better, but I knew my voice was far too inconsequential for me to attempt to offer up any input.

Mrs. Braeburn called up to the custodian, "Are you sure that adhesive comes off cleanly? You'd think it would leave a residue."

He came down the ladder slowly, unlocked the wheels, and moved it over slightly. "It comes right off, clean as whistle," he assured with a wheezy laugh. "We did the same thing last year; no problems at all."

Mrs. Braeburn looked annoyed as she scanned the gym. "I thought we were supposed to get more of those tri-fold display centers. I hate that you have to crane your neck to see some of the smaller details."

"I guess that's what happens when you give the kids free reign to make anything from a banner to a notecard-sized piece of work," the custodian exaggerated, laughing again with that asthmatic sound.

Our art teacher was really irritated now and was doing her best to hide it. I watched her switch her weight from one brown ankle boot to the other as she clamped her hands behind her back.

I had been holding my drawing against my chest rather shyly, and when it came to my turn I had trouble letting go of it. The hard-faced custodian had to pluck it from my hands like a stubborn weed before he placed it along the very top row, adjacent to a classmate's impressive painting of an exploding volcano and above another student's strange and surreal picture of a green, triangular-shaped family. High on the wall, my charcoal Angelica appeared somber and misty in contrast to the color surrounding it. I felt self-conscious with it in view, carefully keeping my gaze focused on the floor.

"Is that a self-portrait?" asked a girl named Becky, who'd already had her color-penciled lizard hung farther down on the wall.

"Uh, no," I answered when I realized she was speaking to me.

"You sure? She looks a lot like you," Becky commented skeptically. "You're really good."

"Thanks," I said modestly.

"In fact, it's kinda weird, but," Becky squinted up at my drawing, "she looks more like you than you look like you."

Confusion consumed me and I asked bravely, "What do you mean by that?"

"You know, like, you're so quiet and stuff. It's almost like you're not there; you just sort of blend in." Becky was speaking in an upbeat voice, unaware of the depth with which her words were slicing me. "But the drawing—it pops right out, like it's real, ya know?"

"Oh, yeah; I see." Because I wasn't real, of course.

"Where's your label?" the custodian asked me.

"Oh . . . I . . ." I had completely forgotten I was supposed to make one.

"Everyone else gave me theirs," he said impatiently, tapping a scuffed black boot on the ladder step.

Mrs. Braeburn came to my aid, most likely because she was eager to get a break from the custodian. "Don't worry; let's pop over to the computer room in the library and make you one really quick." She turned and called to another teacher, "Miss Barb? Can you keep an eye on my class? I'll be back in a flash."

I felt Mrs. Braeburn's hand between my shoulders, guiding me away. "It really is a lovely piece. You have more talent than you let on. So, what's it called, dear?"

Since I hadn't planned a title for my artwork, I improvised with the first words that came to my lips. "Angelica, the Forgotten Girl."

"It's Friday and it's *my* day!" Terra sang as we walked home in step with each other. "Now, what to do with our glorious weekend?"

I smiled, but was unable to match her level of joviality. "Are you coming to the open house tonight?"

"Ugh." Terra made a disgusted noise. "I hate the thought of spending my freedom back in that prison!" she laughed, seeming very proud of her comparison.

"Yeah; me too." I would have bet that I wanted to be there even less than she did. Come to think of it, though, home didn't sound that appealing either. "My mother was talking about it this morning at breakfast, though, so I guess I'm going."

"Sucks to be you," Terra laughed, but then patted me on the back as if she were afraid I would take her words too seriously.

Once I was home, I entered the house quietly. I thought that maybe if I made as little noise as possible, I wouldn't be seen, and the school open house would be forgotten just like I so often was. I was startled when my mother instantly dropped her novel, clamped her eyes on me, and said cheerfully, "Hi; you're home! All ready for tonight?"

Why was she being so sugary, weird, and overly attentive? Almost every other day of my life I could have stamped, shouted, and done a goofy dance upon entry and no one would have noticed. "Um, I guess."

"Well, I can't wait to see your art. I'm kinda glad you didn't show it to me beforehand. It'll be a surprise that way." She jumped out of the recliner and waved me into the kitchen. "I've got it all figured out. Your father is at the hospital, so that's taken care of. We can have an early dinner and then the twins and Ivy will come along with us. The older two have plans, unfortunately."

"Mace and Bram are coming?" I was apprehensive at the thought.

"Well of course they are, sweetie; they have art in the show too."

For some reason it had slipped my mind that my brothers would have anything to do with the night's activities. I hadn't seen them working on any art projects at home, and I couldn't picture either one of them as artistically creative. Their imaginative abilities tended to lean toward planning escape routes and coming up with stories to get out of trouble.

"Don't expect me to give up my Friday for some amateur art!" came Adonia's voice as she slid into the room and opened the fridge. "Leah and I are hanging out."

"Oh, Adonia, don't be that way," Mother scolded.

"It's okay," I said assuredly. I didn't want to be a part of the stupid thing myself, let alone any of them either.

I helped my mother put together a salad while she whipped up a quick cheeseburger macaroni on the stove. I didn't like how she kept making a point of catching my eye and giving me an encouraging smile. I wished things could go back to normal when she was barely aware I was alive. With things as they currently stood, I felt like I was on parole of some sort. One wrong word and she'd probably have me jammed into a straightjacket.

Before I knew it, Mace and Bram were viciously fighting over the front seat of the van, tugging at each other's clothes and hair.

"*Hey?!* What are you two doing?" my mother shrieked in a frightening tone. I realized how close she had been to breaking the ultra-sweet character she was playing, frazzled frustration just below the surface of her demeanor.

I climbed in the very back, past Ivy in the middle row, and watched as Mace begrudgingly relinquished the front seat. He made sure to sneak in a punch to his twin's arm before quickly snapping the passenger door shut to avoid retaliation.

As he was crawling into the back with a grumble, we all heard some tapping on the side of the van and a voice asking, "Hey, do you mind if I tag along?"

I couldn't hide the delighted animation on my face when I realized it was Terra.

"Well, of course!" my mother said, trying to switch her fake, happy mood back on. "The more the merrier." She was laying on a smile so thick that her neck looked strained and her eyes held a hint of delusional euphoria.

I chose not to look at this clown-like version of my mother on the ride over to the school. Instead, I had my best friend to keep me company and make me forget that my family was crumbling all around me.

"What made you decide to come?" I asked her as we unloaded the van.

"I was bored," Terra answered with a wink.

"You just want some of those free snacks that were promised, I bet," I teased her as we followed my family inside the school. It was weird being there so late in the day, the tall, blocky building looking even more sinister near dusk.

"Dried-out donuts and stale crackers . . . how did you guess?" Terra giggled.

Just inside the doors there were a few staff members handing out pamphlets and fliers and helping to direct visitors to the gym as they entered. While Mother lingered a bit over the information table, Terra and I strolled into the gym with my siblings close on our heels.

"Wow," Ivy said. "This is really cool." She was looking up, taking in the streamers and twinkle lights woven above our heads in the school colors of blue and gray.

I couldn't help but look up and all around myself, listening to the classical piano music being piped in through speakers overhead. The perimeter of the gym was lined with tables covered in filmy gray cloths that displayed a variety of pottery, small statues of wood, and clay molds of all sorts. The folding display racks were spaced across the center of the gym, thin lamps affixed to their tops, light beaming down onto the canvases and prints secured along its surface.

The lighting wasn't quite as good for most of us, who ended up with pictures high along the walls, but it was all still nicely done with a few spotlights aimed up over sections of art. The well-decorated area was a little too much for my eyes to take in all at once, and I had to blink as light and color swirled in my vision.

I couldn't help thinking that all that beauty and expression was hovering over a floor that was infamous for causing bloody knees, concussions, and even owning a tooth every so often.

"Those display thingies would fall like dominoes," I heard Bram whisper to Mace and it sent a chill up my spine.

"You know, you're right," Terra chimed in, much to my horror. "I don't think they did the best job anchoring them. One wrong nudge and . . ."

"Please don't encourage them," I begged. "Seriously, don't."

"Oh, there you all are," I heard my mother's slightly breathless voice say from behind us. "I wanted to get in on that raffle and then . . . well, wow, this is lovely in here! They really went all out."

I felt my spine relax a smidge knowing that she was much better than me at controlling my twin brothers. Thankfully, they had become distracted anyway, seeing their art and wanting to show it off.

The group of us followed them over to one of the tables, and the boys showed us two carvings of dried clay. They were intended to go together as a pair, even though the twins didn't share the same art class. Bram's model was a green-painted, blobby-shaped, Godzilla-type creature with one foot high in the air.

"Now check this out," Mace said as he slid his model of a crushed car below the creature's foot, where a little dented nook in the smashed ceiling allowed them to interlock.

"Eww, did you paint blood streaming out the doors of the car?" Ivy asked in disgust.

The twins laughed in unison and high-fived each other.

Mother rolled her eyes and suggested we look at my art instead. Mace and Bram were still giggling as I led them to the opposite wall where my picture hung in one of the few shadowy, hourglass-shaped spaces made from the distance in illumination between the spotlighting. The gym was starting to fill up with visitors, and on the way over my mother got distracted by an old friend and lingered to talk with the woman a while.

Terra clutched my sleeve. "Did you see what I just saw?"

I feared turning around, imagining I would witness a disaster my brothers were surely causing.

"Josh," Terra whispered.

My spine went more rigid than it had been all night. "Where?"

Terra pointed at the gym entrance, and I desperately wished to retract my question so her attention-drawing hand would have stayed down. "See? He's over there with his sister and maybe his parents; I can't tell."

"Who are you guys talking about?" asked Ivy.

I jumped, having forgotten she was there. "No one."

"We should go say hi," Terra suggested.

"Oh my gosh, does Zylia have a *crush*?" Ivy looked skeptical and thrilled at the same time. I wasn't proud of it, but at that moment I wanted to shake her adorable little shoulders and tell her to shut up.

"Hey, I've got an idea." Terra placed a hand on my shoulder, and there was a twinkle in her hazel eyes that made my stomach flip. "I'll mosey over there and get a conversation going," she was gesturing flamboyantly as if she had to mime out the whole plan for me, "then I'll say we should come see your art. Eh? *Ehh*? Perfect, huh? No pressure on you. Be back in a bit."

She was gone before I could stop her. I watched the top of her amber-colored head bob around in the crowd before I couldn't bear to look anymore. I just wanted to get this night over with, minus any embarrassing or awkward social situations.

"Zylia, Ivy, there you are!" Did my mother always speak so *loudly*? I could swear she was using a megaphone and drawing all kinds of unwanted stares. "Sorry about that delay, but we," she had a twin on each side of her, "are very ready to see your art."

I, being very ready to evacuate the building, quickly pointed up to my drawing. "It's the charcoal one, beside that volcano." But as soon as I locked eyes on my eerie picture of Angelica, the matte board came loose from the wall and took a dive, landing facedown on the gym floor.

"Oh, no; was that yours? Let's grab a teacher who can hang it back up." My mother was already roving around in search. "Someone didn't do a very good job of sticking it up there," I heard her mumble as she moved away from the four of us kids.

I picked my drawing up and held it to my chest, feeling nervous that Terra might be back with Josh any second. My mother, however, had speedily found a helpful teacher, probably with that amplified voice of hers. They were already on their way back toward us with a cumbersome ladder equipped with rails and wheels that I recognized as the one the custodian had been using earlier in the day.

"It's funny how Zylia's is the only picture to fall. Figures, huh?" chuckled one of the twins behind my back. I just pretended not to hear and hoped that behemoth ladder could come and go so I could make a dignified escape.

The squeaking wheels came to a stop below the blank spot on the wall where my picture had been. The unfamiliar teacher smiled at me and said, "It's too early for malfunctions. Let's fix this up for you." As she held her hand out to take the matte board, a bald man tapped her on the shoulder and whispered something in her ear. "Oh, okay." She looked a little startled as she turned back to me. "I'll be right back, sweetheart," she assured me before taking off after the man.

A few minutes went by and the gym seemed to swell up with parents and children, but there was no sign of Terra or Josh.

"Hey, why is this ladder here?" whined a makeup-slathered girl I recognized from one of my classes. "It's completely blocking my painting!"

A woman who must have been the girl's mother—based on her bold lip color and over-highlighted contour—said, "Let's see if we can get someone to move this!"

"Someone's coming to take care of it soon," I heard my mother explaining.

I looked at the back of my drawing. All the little Velcro tabs were still in place and so were the ones high up on the wall. Maybe the custodian just hadn't pressed hard enough for the tiny teeth-like spines to lock in place. There was no reason I couldn't climb the ladder, affix it myself, and just get out of the spotlight before this scene got any bigger.

I didn't look to my mother because I feared her trying to stop me; I simply marched up the ladder, drawing in hand. I'm not sure how, but halfway up, a tiny signature caught my eye. It was odd that the small, curvy letters reading *Melanie Green* should draw my attention before the gorgeous colored-pencil creation of an ivy- encroached wishing well above it. The label below it disclosed the title simply as *I Wish*.

"I really don't think you should be up there, Zy," I heard my mother say from below.

"Well *someone* should do *something* about this ladder, at least!" That must have been Mrs. Cosmetics' irate tone, but I didn't bother turning to find out.

Instead, I quickly moved to the top of the ladder and braced myself with one of the rails. From the corner of my eye I became aware that I had risen above a sea of people and could possibly be the most visible person in the room. This made me feel intensely self-conscious, so I hastily reached up to press my artwork in place.

"You didn't even draw anything!" I could hear Bram taunting from below. "The whole thing is blank, you cheater!"

I flushed with irritation, thinking how my family members were experts at drawing unnecessary attention to any situation, but when I looked down I realized he was right. There wasn't even a single charcoal smudge on the entire surface. I flipped it over just to be sure it wasn't facing the wrong way, but the Velcro adhesive tabs were still clinging to the backside.

That's when I noticed my hands blink out of sight. Suddenly, I just couldn't see them anymore. And even worse, I could feel the matte board slip through where my hands should have been and fall to the floor yet again. It wasn't just my hands, though; it was all of me. I looked down at my body, and where I should have seen a navy sweater, dark-wash jeans and a pair of Chucks, I saw only the ladder. Beyond my invisible self, I saw a sea of horrified faces all staring up toward me, and I realized they must have seen it happen too.

It was Ivy's face I focused on, her eyes round, mouth agape. She looked very frightened, and it was only then that I felt my own terror infect whatever was left of my consciousness before I dissipated into the air completely—and everything went black.

Chapter Twenty-Three

When I awoke in my bedroom, there was no way to tell how much time had passed. To "wake" wasn't even the right expression, because I didn't just yawn and stretch, then open my eyes to the room around me like a normal person might have done. It was just suddenly *there* and I could see it somehow, even though I couldn't see myself.

I felt disconnected from reality, from tangible matter itself. How was I to get from one point to the next with no legs or body, just an empty space where I should have been? It was a mental exercise, if I indeed still owned a brain. I had to focus clearly to move around the room. It wasn't anything like walking or even floating, really; it was just sort of thinking myself from one part of the room to the next. Going over it bit by bit in my mind.

It happened very slowly at first. I thought intensely of the end of my bed, tangled sheets and comforter cascading into a rumple on the floor. If I had pores, they would have been sweating by the time I could see the end of my bed clearly. At least my visual arc had changed, letting me know I was advancing in space. My next out-of-body movement happened much quicker, somehow spurred on a little by fear. I thought of the small mirror on the dresser, the one that would hold no face for me, and suddenly it was right there in the forefront. I'd almost rather see a bloodied, disfigured reflection than see nothing at all. I tried not to look inside the glass because I knew the emptiness would haunt me. However, the pull was too strong; after much deliberation, I did peek. Seeing the reflection of my room that was devoid of me felt equivalent to seeing my face hacked to bloody bits. My feelings cringed in a similar response, recoiling at the sight of that terrifying nothingness. I had no facial features, no limbs or torso; I was simply invisible, just like I had known I'd become.

I forced myself to think of something different. The time. It must have been early, because when I thought of the window I could look out and see the very beginnings of dawn bleeding up into the starry sky.

I wondered where Ivy could be at such an early hour. Her bed was made—perhaps even unslept in. As I was gazing over the smooth, lilac comforter, a dark shadow entered my vision near the foot of the bed. I tried to turn and look at it directly, but I hadn't yet mastered turning my gaze with a neck that wasn't really there. By the time I could see where the shadow had been, it was already gone.

I heard the bedroom door snap shut and I knew I had to follow whomever or whatever it was. I thought hard about our bedroom door, about the residue of unicorn stickers that had once been stuck to its surface, still visible in the light at certain angles. I thought about the grains in the dark wood and the silver doorknob and finally I was there, right in front of it.

I thought about opening the door next and I was startled when I felt a distant impression of coolness where my fingers should have been touching the knob. It was as if I were feeling it through layers of fabric or gauze. I rejoiced that my sensations were back, however dampened they had become, certain that *I* would be back as well! But when I looked down I still saw nothing, and something about the shift in focus caused my hand to move right through the knob; I was unable to grasp it further.

Wait! I was attempting to shout, although no sound resonated. I was afraid the shadow would get too far away for me to ever catch up. I didn't know why, but I knew it was important somehow. That eerie, filmy figure had become my only hope.

I tried again with the doorknob, feeling more panicked and frustrated as time was ticking on. I instinctively knew I needed to focus, but despair was taking over. I could no longer touch the knob; oddly enough, it was becoming higher in the plane of my vision. I watched it going up and up until suddenly it occurred to me that I was sinking. I was so low that I could see quite clearly beneath the two twin-size beds.

Once I had made that alarming realization, my descent picked up speed. In an instant, I was through the floorboards and ceiling and into my parents' bedroom below. I scarcely had time to take in the fact that it was empty as well before I plummeted down another story, into the front living room. After the trauma of dropping straight through two stories, I was no longer concerned about the house being devoid of inhabitants and more preoccupied with how much farther I was going to fall.

It wasn't just the crawl space I feared, where a plumber had once removed a deflated, curled, and nearly mummified raccoon that was covered in spider webbing. As terrifying as that would have been on a normal day, I now had to worry about sinking through the very center of Earth and perhaps coming out on the other side. If I somehow emerged after that, would gravity reverse or would I drift up into space, falling straight up into the stars?

I looked down at the wooden floor covered with an old, trampled area rug and I knew it was getting closer, coming up at me. If I'd had a voice, you'd have heard my screams because they were the loudest thing in my consciousness, filling up anything that was left of me. A mute distress signal was what my essence had boiled down to.

Then there was a flicker of shade in the doorway of the living room; an indistinct silhouette beckoned for me to follow. I was trailing the shadow even before I realized I had stopped sinking. Somehow the task had interrupted my hysteria and given me focus in its place.

The floor was underneath me again, a bit fuzzy and remote, but just as solid as I needed it to be to track the tail of the hazy shadow that was staying just out of my view. I followed it through the main floor and out by way of the garage. I saw it shift through the metal door and disappear from my sight. Instinctively, I moved toward the garage door button, but quickly realized I didn't need it. It was the first time I'd moved through that giant door frame without hearing the squeaking and clicking of whatever gadgets and gears weren't functioning at their peak.

When I was outside, I realized a good amount of time had passed, the overcast sun now high in the sky. I was vaguely aware that time didn't seem to be following the same rules anymore, but I didn't linger over working it out because I could see the shadow again far off down the alleyway.

I thought myself over the pebbles, realizing that I'd be shivering by now if my skin hadn't been sequestered from the elements. When I saw the shadow again, it had disappeared into the walls of my school. I suppose I spent a little too long gawking up at the ominous old building without paying attention to my surroundings, because the next thing I knew a silver sports car rushed right through me. I felt no pain or sensation other than the vague idea of being hit by a powerful gust of wind. Next came a mild sense of being scattered about over the road before coming back together and bonding bit by invisible bit.

It was unsettling, to say the least, and afterward I made haste in entering the school. I had just assumed it would be silent and empty inside, because I thought it was Saturday. However, just inside the door and immediately to the right was the nearest classroom. The door was wide open, and a normal sixth-grade math class was being held inside.

I moved about the desks, staring at the students as if they were the bizarre aberrations instead of myself. What were they doing here on a Saturday looking normal as could be?

I passed by all the students, one by one, trying to reach out with my mind somehow to get their attention. I'm not sure how they could have helped me, even if they were to become aware of my ghost-like presence. Most likely it would have done nothing more than send a poor sixth-grader running in fright.

There was a girl with a high ponytail sleeping in the back row. I hung over her for a while, watching and wondering. If I couldn't reach people while they were awake, what if I could call out to them from a place of dreams? I'm not sure why I came up with the outlandish idea, but it didn't seem any more abnormal than my situation at present, so I figured I'd give it a shot.

I found myself thinking about her hair, long and sandy-colored. I tried touching it, and for a second I thought I could remotely feel coarse and frizzy strands. In fact, I noticed a slight movement where the hairs were grazing the surface of her desk. Her head popped up suddenly, and there was surprise registering in her sleepy eyes.

"Welcome back, Brandy," I could hear the teacher say. The words sounded muffled, as if I were hearing them from underwater. "I'm sure you've had an exhausting weekend like the rest of us, but you're on learning time now."

Wait, the weekend was over already? That's when I thought of the teacher's desk and noticed one of those tear-off calendars plainly displayed on the cluttered surface. According to the page it was indeed Monday, and if that were true I had lost two days somehow.

"*Zylia.*" I heard my name whispered from the doorway. I thought I'd imagined it at first but then I saw the shadow flicker in my vision, and I was following it again. I trailed it through the hallways and into the section of the school where most of my classes were located.

When somewhere far away the bell rang and the halls filled with students, I could no longer focus enough to find the shadow. I stayed there in the hall, feeling the rush of students flowing through me. In a way, it was a familiar feeling, the closest thing I'd felt to normal since I'd disappeared. I was used to being trampled over by a horde of students who didn't realize I was there. At least this time it didn't hurt.

When the crowd thinned out, I saw Terra leaning her shoulder against a locker and speaking to Josh. I was so overcome with happiness at seeing familiar faces that it took me a while to notice the tears streaming down my best friend's cheeks.

"I'm so worried," I heard her say in muted tones. "I've never made a friend so fast. It already felt like we'd been friends forever. I'm so afraid I'll never see her again."

I knew she was speaking about me and it sent a mixture of sweet warmth and melancholy over my consciousness. *I'm still here. Right here.*

"This is crazy," Josh said. Even muffled, his voice still sounded beautiful to me. "I can't believe it. I mean, she's always been there; I remember her from when we were little. Now I might never get to tell her I've had a huge crush on her this whole time."

If I had a heart, it would have leapt out of me. Terra gave an awkward chuckle as she swiped a tear from her jaw. "She'd have peed her pants if she knew that. She was crushing on you way worse."

Geez, Terra, make me sound like such a dork, why don't you? I thought, suddenly feeling desperate to be a part of their lives again. It was as if some sort of abstract webbing had cordoned me off, separating me just enough from the world around.

Terra! Josh! I thought myself to be screaming, but no words could be heard. *I'm right here! Don't give up on me!*

Terra gave Josh's arm a friendly squeeze. "I gotta get to class. See you after school."

No; don't leave! I watched them walk away and knew that I must be gone forever. I was being smothered right out of my life from something beyond. It hadn't occurred to me until then that being invisible, I wasn't putting out any breath. The sudden thought brought on feelings of claustrophobia and suffocation, as if the otherworldly web had tightened around the only thing left of me: my consciousness, my mind.

I did my best to fight and claw my way back to the life I once knew, but panic had taken over and colors were swirling and fading all around me. It was all turning into a great cloud of blackness, just like the one I had seen in my dream. The looming cloud of nothingness I had feared for so long was finally grabbing me, wiping my world dark and blank.

The darkness was thick and intense, an inky void that stretched to eternity in every direction. Eventually my panic burnt itself out and I simply stayed there in the dark, feeling as if someone had drained my adrenal glands. I was no longer responding to the dark with fear, but acceptance. In fact, curiosity was beginning to take over.

The longer I let myself stare into it, the less dark it appeared. After some time, I realized that it was all different shades of murky black and foggy gray overlapping and undulating, just out of focus. I blinked mentally and suddenly she was there, standing above me with concern etched in sooty-colored lines on her monochromatic face.

"It's okay, Zylia," I heard her say as I felt her use her arms to help me sit upright. That's when I realized my body was back, clad in the same outfit I'd worn to the open house. I'd never been so happy to see my twiggy torso and limbs and vowed to never complain about my lack of curves again.

But relief was turning to confusion as I took in my surroundings. "You're my grandmother's sister. You're Angelica," I said to the girl made up of raven colors. We were seated on a fancy couch in a sort of drawing room with a long hallway running off behind us. "What's going on? What is this place?" I wanted to stare at her and memorize her face, but I couldn't keep my eyes from darting around the intriguing room with its opulent, Victorian-style decor, all in ominous shades of gray and black. But it wasn't just the decor that was colorless. It was like I'd jumped into an old movie, long before they'd had the technology to produce color.

She spoke to me in a low, sweet voice. I could hear it clearly without the underwater filter that I was becoming used to. "Try not to feel afraid; there's still time for you to get home. I was hoping you wouldn't have to come this far. I thought maybe you'd gone back."

"Gone back? But didn't you lead me here?" I asked her suspiciously, feeling my fight-or-flight responses switching back on. "Weren't you the shadow I was following?"

"Yes and no," her sweet voice answered. "There's so much I need to tell you, but we won't have much time." She took my pale hands into her own gray ones and gazed at me directly. I looked into her pitch-dark eyes, nebulous and somber, and realized she wasn't a thirteen-year-old girl. She may have looked it on the outside, but her eyes were old and weary just like the ones I'd seen on my grandmother's face. "I'm not going to lie to you, Zylia; I do wish you could stay here, but I didn't bring you."

Angelica adjusted herself on the couch, smoothing out her long dress over her knees. "There are certain types of people who come here to this place. Those of us stranded here call it the *In Between*. Picture, it as a colorless carbon copy of the world you know, only here the rules of time and nature are quite different. In fact, sometimes they don't even apply."

I tried to let the information sink in, but it wasn't really registering. Since I knew I'd never understand this foreign place, I moved on to a different question. "I don't understand. How did I get here?"

Angelica looked over her shoulder and down the hall furtively. I think she had been trying to do it discreetly, but the motion was unsettling and made me feel she had something to hide. "Picture it like this: the *In Between* is a realm that floats alongside reality like a balloon—it carries no weight. There isn't enough substance here to pin it down, not even enough to color our world. But there is just enough to keep us here forever."

My head was swimming with questions, but I didn't know where to begin. "But none of that tells me how I got here . . ."

Angelica held up a delicate hand to silence me. "I'm getting there. This place—it sort of draws you in. It preys on people like us, isolated and creative souls who are full of unheard inspiration and unspoken ideas. People who think they have no one so they delve deep into their inner lives. Just like you and me—people who don't have their feet grounded in reality."

I felt so confused. "So, people who walk around with their head in the clouds? Maybe I'm just too *fanciful* for regular Earth?"

"It's so much more than that; but don't worry, you're not stuck here yet."

I looked around the well-decorated room for an exit but couldn't find one. Just her mentioning the word *stuck* had me feeling trapped and panicky. "So, there's a way out, you mean? How do you know I'm not stuck?"

"Look at you," Angelica said as she gestured gracefully at my lap, "you're still pigmented."

I couldn't believe I hadn't noticed before, but she was right. There were definite notes of dark blue in my sweater and my skin was the palest of peach. The colors may have been a little off—muted or something—but compared to Angelica and the rest of my surroundings I was a rainbow of color. I felt grief rush in as I asked, "So you're trapped here? You can't come back with me?"

Angelica shook her head forlornly. "It's too late for me."

My sadness was replaced with horror as a loud banging and simultaneous wail smashed through the quiet of the room. It was coming from down the hallway, where I noted a door rumbling on its hinges as if it were being beaten on from the other side.

"What is that?!" I asked, mouth wide open in fear, but my voice could barely be heard above the shrieking.

"No, no; don't be afraid!" Angelica tried to calm me, standing and blocking my view of the door.

As the demented roar became high-pitched and nearly non-human, it was way too late for me to be unafraid. As soon as I was overtaken by emotion, my world went black again.

Chapter Twenty-Four

I was disappointed to find myself invisible once more, but consoled by the fact that I was home again and could hear my family somewhere nearby. I followed the distant, underwater voices to Adonia's room.

Everything was so colorful in contrast after where I'd been, so my older sister's girly room looked especially vibrant when I peered inside. Adonia was on the bed, looking quite motherly with Ivy's head in her lap. Her friend Leah was cross-legged on the floor before them.

"It'll be fine," Leah said, sounding more disinterested than comforting. Maybe it wasn't that she was being callous, only that I needed to regain equanimity with the strange, diminished acoustics. I thought my way closer to try and make a better judgment.

"No, no . . ." Ivy moaned, raising her head up just enough to be heard. "How can you say that? She's gone. *Gone!*" As soon as she said the words, her shoulders were bouncing up and down in a violent, heart-wrenching sob. "Nothing will ever be fine again."

Adonia made a shushing sound and smoothed our little sister's hair. "Leah's right," she asserted, although her voice was cracking. "Everything *will* be fine because Zy isn't gone forever. She'll be back. She's never let us down before, has she? She always comes through."

"Nothing will be the same without her," Ivy cried, making my invisible chest ache.

Leah was rifling around in her purse. "Here; take this." She offered up a slightly crumpled tissue and accidentally overturned her bag as she was leaning forward. She sighed irritably. "We should really get out, you guys. It might cheer you up."

Ivy sat up and crossed her arms over her chest. Her weeping was contained for the moment, and a furious look set across her ruddy, tear-stained face. "How could we even *think* of fun at a time like this?"

Leah was cramming items back into her large purse huffily. "I didn't mean it like that; sheesh!"

"Let's just go downstairs for a bit, okay?" Adonia said softly, pulling Ivy in close. "You need to try and eat."

I watched as my oldest sister helped Ivy off the bed, supporting her small frame in a caring manner I'd never seen her use before. I tried to shut off my vision as they walked through me, but the effort was a futile one. How was I supposed to close eyes that were no longer there? Since the view was mandatory, I took the opportunity to check their faces for any sign that they noticed me as they passed through the remainder of my being, but there was nothing of the sort.

As Leah got up to follow them out, I saw something sparkle on the floor near the place she had been seated. It was a purple gel pen with a clear, glittery tube that must have fallen out of the girl's bag. Something was nagging at my mind but I didn't have a chance to entertain it, because suddenly I could see right through the floor and into Keane's bedroom.

From my top-down view I could see Keane lying on his bed, breathing out a puff of thick, white smoke into the air. Brody was sitting on the floor, one leg folded underneath him, and he had propped an arm across the opposite knee. After a croupy-sounding cough, he went back to taking long drags from the cigarette between his index and middle finger. I couldn't believe neither of them was worried about my mother taking note of the smell.

I carefully let myself sink down one story, feeling much more in control than I had on my previous plunge earthward. Once I was closer, I could make sense of their muffled conversation.

"I just don't understand it," Keane was saying. "It doesn't feel real." He looked so alien while puffing on the brown-colored end of a cigarette, adeptly tapping the ashes off every so often into an empty Coke can.

"Yeah, I get you," Brody nodded in agreement. "You should be smoking more than these plain-ass cigarettes to get that drama off your mind." I watched the lines of his sinewy neck and collarbone become more pronounced as he pulled air deep into his lungs.

"No, man; I don't wanna forget." Keane swung his legs off his bed and crushed the end of his cigarette against the top of the metal can before dropping it down inside the mouth hole. "The thing is, I can't even remember the last thing I said to her. It was probably something stupid or rude."

"I wouldn't worry about it," laughed Brody. "You got plenty more sisters, right?"

"What?" Keane raked a hand through his brown hair, which I knew to be indicative of his temper flaring.

Brody went on laughing and could scarcely get the words out around his amused guffaws. "Come on; there's so many people in this house, you should consider yourself lucky if one disappears!"

I watched in surprise as Keane lunged forward and stooped down to land a blow right to Brody's gut, then shoved him hard at the shoulders.

The older boy didn't even have time to react, uttering a feeble groan as he was brought to the floor. His cigarette fell onto his jeans and there was plenty of squirming and fumbling as Brody tried to keep from being singed.

Keane stamped out the embers with his sneaker against the hardwood floor, and I couldn't help but feel a rush of affection for my brother. I wanted to reach out and hug him, even though I had no arms; but as soon as I envisioned myself doing so, I was back in that strange drawing room, sitting next to Angelica as if I had never left.

I clutched at my throat, taking in ragged breaths and feeling around on my body, touching my arms and legs to make sure they were there.

"That's it; stay calm," Angelica soothed. "The gateway between worlds is very sensitive to emotion, especially fear. That's why you were pulled away from me so suddenly."

It took a split second for the memory to return. "It was because of the screaming. What was that? What's behind that door?" I dared to peek over her shoulder, but the door in the hallway was shut and all was quiet within.

Angelica's dark, ancient eyes took on a heavy sadness. "Do you know of Runa's illness?"

It took me longer than it should have to remember my grandmother's name. I'd only ever known her as Grandmother, but of course her own sister would use her first name when referring to her. "You mean the dementia?" I asked.

"That's what they call it there, in the colorful world, because they don't know what it really is. The *In Between*, it has a great pull, but sometimes only parts of a person's mind fit the parameters for this realm and it causes what appears to be a shatter in their sanity. Their minds can see a little bit into the shadow world while their bodies stay fixed firmly in the reality they've always known."

"That's how Grandmother knew things about this place," I realized.

"Yes; my poor sister. But sadly, there are people who have it much worse," Angelica said, flicking her eyes over her shoulder but then quickly looking at her hands in her lap as if she had accidentally given something away. I knew she was talking about whatever was behind the door. "Some make it here without all of their minds intact and others can't handle the fate of being trapped here."

"That's horrible," I shuddered.

"I've made it my job to help them," Angelica explained. "And I want you to tell my sister that so she doesn't worry. I want her to know I have a purpose here and that I'm okay. I fear she blames herself for my disappearance, but it was my fault all along for not realizing I was loved there."

"I would if I could, but I think I'm stuck here too. I don't know how to get back."

"Whatever you're doing so far, it's working," Angelica told me encouragingly. "Your tint is returning, darkening."

I looked down and saw that it was true; I was beginning to look more vibrant and alive in color saturation. "But how? I haven't done anything."

"You must have; people have made it back before and it always happens just this way," Angelica spoke with certainty. "Your color will grow and then you'll go back."

I felt hopeful at the thought. "Tell me what to do."

Angelica stood and began pacing in front of me, her long, black dress making swishing noises. "The ones who made it back—I think they had to recognize the impact they had on the world around them, believe that they were important and needed."

"I . . . I've never felt that way. That seems so . . . How would that even help?" I stammered. "But wait, that's why you led me to the school, isn't it? I heard my friends talking about me, missing me."

"I was hoping it would help to send you back." Angelica stopped moving abruptly and looked at me gravely. "There's something else, though. Some reason I couldn't make it back. If only I could . . ." her voice trailed off and she seemed to be mumbling to herself, lost in a memory.

I shifted uncomfortably before standing up. There was a possibility this dull-looking world could be my home forever, and it was a frightening thought. I tried to control my emotion because I wanted to learn as much as possible from Angelica. I was desperate to find out anything that could help me.

I moved over to a side table draped in cloth and covered with ornamental photo frames that were void of any pictures inside. I ran the tip of my finger over one of the light gray frames, and it felt cool and solid to the touch. It felt so real that I was struggling once again to swallow a lump of fright that had settled into the back of my throat.

"May I show you something?" Angelica asked, stealing my attention away from the side table and gesturing with a wide sweep toward the hallway.

I felt my muscles tense up a little at the thought of seeing what was back there, but I nodded and followed her down the long hall anyway. When we passed the door where I'd heard the bone-chilling shrieks earlier, I couldn't help but let my gaze linger over the wood-grained surface and wonder what lay beyond.

"It's just through here." She made a quick turn down a short leg of the hall and opened one of the many doors we had passed. Behind it was a wrought-iron gate, and Angelica immediately began working its squeaky latch.

The room beyond the gate was a sort of greenhouse that stood at least three stories tall. There was nothing at all green growing under the enclosure, just more of that monochrome coloring that made everything appear as if it were part of an old black-and-white photo.

Even without anything other than variations of black and gray, the great garden was stunningly breathtaking. Pale-gray light filtered in from foggy glass panes above the limbs and trunks of twisted and gnarly trees; branches reached upward like wanting hands. Below, a shiny, blackish grass covered the ground like a thick, soft carpet and just over the top of it hovered a wispy mist that was equal parts beauty and bleakness.

Near the edges of the room, the dark grass gave way to oversized rosebushes. Feeling unhindered, I walked over and touched one of the giant blooms. I'd never seen anything like it, the gray rose head being at least triple the size of anything I'd seen back home.

"They're lovely," I breathed.

"They're called Nightmare Roses," Angelica informed me. She snapped off a rose and handed it to me. "In fact, this whole garden is grown from loneliness and bad dreams."

I wasn't sure what she meant, but I loosely cradled the delicate, silky rose as if it might be deadly to the touch. Suddenly, there was a fluttering from within the bush alongside me, and a tiny bird flew out at me. As it flapped by my head and landed on a higher branch, I could see that it had the alert, long-beaked face of a raven, but its wings were shaped more like a butterfly and had a muted glow like dim fairy dust.

I gasped at the extraordinary sight, and before I could ask, Angelica said, "That's an Inkfly."

"I've feared this place for a long time—the blackness that I somehow knew would absorb me. And it is scary, don't get me wrong; but it's actually kind of wonderful in a way," I commented, eyes darting all around me. "All of this time I think I thought that I was meant for the dark, but now that I'm here, I know I don't belong and I want to go home."

Angelica's wise eyes widened and she looked me up and down. "You will be going back home very soon. All the way back."

I looked down at my body and saw that my color was returning, radiant and vivid against the ashen backdrop of the *In Between*.

"Listen carefully, please," Angelica said, a sober expression overtaking her features as she clamped her hands down on my shoulders so tightly that it hurt. "If you're like me, and I believe that you are, then you're going to go back and think this was all some kind of crazy dream. Then, you're going to resume your life just the same as it was before without changing a thing. You can't do that, Zylia. As much as I'd enjoy your company, if you do that you'll be brought right back here in no time. And then it will be for good."

I felt a growing trepidation, because I was already starting to feel the pull toward that blank space that must have been the gateway between both worlds. "What do I do? Tell me what to do!"

"You need . . ." Angelica was flustered, which didn't instill faith in me that I could escape this prison for good. ". . . to remember that all of this is real and that you must believe you're wanted, needed, and missed in the world outside this place. You must make a stamp, a footprint there. Make one that can be seen and heard and *felt*."

"But I don't know how to do that!" I was clutching at her shoulders as well now, and tears of fear and despair were burning my eyes.

"You have to try, at least. That's all I know. Others have made it, and so can you."

I wasn't satisfied and wished for a more competent guide—complete with a detailed map—to plan an escape route.

"Don't forget to tell my sister what I asked, please," Angelica begged me. I realized then that she was just as human and helpless as myself, maybe even more so; at least I had a chance at keeping out of this dungeon.

"I'll tell her," I promised, nodding firmly to convince her. Then, her tragic, ashen face blinked out and was replaced with the all-encroaching blackness of space.

Chapter Twenty-Five

So many voices filtered into my brain—more than I could distinguish. Male and female voices all overlapping one another in a hubbub of chittering noise. I wanted to open my eyes, but they felt heavy and I was afraid of what I might find if I forced my lids upward.

I felt some pressure, first on my head and then again around my arm. It gave some distant layer of my consciousness a twinge of joy to note that my extremities must be intact.

I decided to make sure this was true and finally attempted to open my eyelids; the light and colors were too intense, so I immediately squeezed them shut again.

"Can you hear me, Zee-luh?" The male voice overhead wasn't just annoying because it had mispronounced my name, but there was a nasally twang and an assertiveness layered into it that had me feeling a little on the defensive. "Can you wake up for me?" There was a series of beeps and a static sound, and I couldn't place any of it.

At last, I managed to open my eyes long enough to take in a narrow, metallic ceiling above me with a silver bar running down the center of it. In a shallow recess there were spotlights glowing, and alongside them I noticed a clear-faced cabinetry system dominating one wall.

I was trying to identify some of the unfamiliar packaged items inside the cabinets when a wide face hovered over me and that nasally voice said, "She's coming around, Mom; vitals look good."

"Oh, thank God!" I heard my mother's voice from somewhere nearby. "I'm here, baby; you're gonna be just fine."

My mother's voice, edged near hysteria, sounded beautiful and comforting to my tired soul.

"Where is she?" I asked and was surprised at my croaky voice. I tried to turn my head to get a better view, but I felt restrained and encumbered by unknown forces.

"Stay still, sweetie; Mom's up in the front of the ambulance," the nasally voice informed me. At that point I should have wondered why I was in an emergency vehicle, but first I was trying to work out why this man was referring to my mother as "Mom" instead of "*your* mom" as if he were a sibling I'd never met. "Do you know where you are?"

"You gave away spoilers."

"What was that, sweetie?" The man was talking in a tone that suggested I was under the age of six while he entered some kind of information on a tablet.

"You said my mother was in the front of the ambulance, so I'm gonna make a wild guess here and say I'm in the back of that same ambulance." I didn't feel any guilt related to my disrespectfully sarcastic comment; too much was going on in my brain.

"Well, Mom," the man said loudly so the people in the cab could hear over the engine, "I think this one is gonna be just fine. She's definitely got her wits intact!"

It was a few more minutes before the vehicle bounced and rattled its way to a stop and I was being hauled out the back on a squeaky gurney. I felt a little dizzy as I watched the concrete canopy of a carport change into the drop-ceiling, fluorescent-lit hallway just inside a set of automatic doors.

The man with the nasally voice was speaking to another person wearing a white coat who had appeared alongside him. "This is Zee-luh Moss, head injury with loss of consciousness for at least five minutes, laceration along the front left side . . ."

The voice trailed off in my mind as I tried to make sense of what was happening to me. The last thing I remembered was Angelica, but she was quickly fading like a figment, slipping away into the dream world.

"Do you know where you are?" the man in the coat was asking as he peeled back some gauze that I didn't realize had been wrapped around my head. He was looking at my scalp with a little light. "How many fingers am I holding up?"

I answered one asinine question after another as I waited for someone to explain what had happened in the span of time I couldn't account for.

"Yep; you're gonna need some stitches." The man in the white coat moved the beam of light to my eyes without warning and I felt a searing optic pain. "Let's put her in four and get her cleaned up," he went on.

I was self-conscious as I rolled by a large desk, feeling like the busy nurses had stopped their important jobs momentarily to look at me.

The ambulance workers transferred me onto a different bed in a room behind a curtain. As I was being lifted, I caught sight of myself in the reflection of a large metal lamp fixture overhead. In that brief second, I could see that streaks of red had made stream-like paths down one side of my head and face.

The doctor pulled the curtain shut, making a clinking, zipping sound as he asked some questions about my vitals.

I heard my mother's frantic, breathy voice asking, "Is she gonna be okay? There was so much blood that I . . ."

"Try not to worry. Head wounds tend to bleed a lot, but the cut itself is much more superficial than it probably looks to you. Since she was unconscious for a while, I'm going to order some scans just to be on the safe side." I listened to the man's soothing, clear voice and watched his eyes crinkle pleasantly as he offered my mother a calming smile. It was hard to imagine that they were talking about me. "I'll be back in a minute," he lied, because it was at least half an hour before we saw him again.

Soon after he left, my mother was at my side, squeezing my hand as a sour-faced nurse was methodically lining up instruments on a metal tray for my suturing procedure. I watched her set out separate bags containing scissors and thread, the plastic crinkling under her bright-blue gloved hands. When I saw the needle, I felt a wild flutter in my chest.

"Don't ever scare me like that again, Zy," said Mother between answering a string of standard questions about my medical history. None of it seemed relevant to my current situation.

"What did I do?" I asked sincerely. "How did this happen?"

"You really don't remember falling from the ladder and hitting your head on the corner of a table?" My mother's moist eyes were full of concern as they searched mine.

"Oh," I breathed. Was that what had happened? I remembered holding my blank artwork and watching my hands disappear; then, next I knew, I was transported to the *In Between*. It all seemed so silly now, a jarred-head-induced hallucination. Angelica and that world had all seemed so real, but here in this emergency room I felt foolish for ever believing it.

"Did anyone notice?" I asked, sounding pitiful.

My mother simply patted my hand and said, "Oh, sweetie," over and over, her voice quieting with every repetition. She was probably pacifying herself, but adversely it was agitating me.

My father arrived just as the doctor was injecting a mixture of lidocaine and epinephrine along the wound in my scalp. It was touching the way he swooped in looking haggard and pallid, the bags under his eyes pronounced, and the worry lines in his forehead deeply furrowed. "How's my girl?" he asked in a tone that was a blend of affection and concern.

I winced, sucking air in through my teeth, as the numbing agent stung my wounded scalp. I felt tears welling up in my eyes and it was hard to answer. "I'm hanging in."

"This is the worst part, I swear," said the doctor, a bit too jovial for my taste. "Once we get you numbed up it's smooth sailing after that."

Father hovered near the side of my bed, looking like he wanted to touch or hug me but seeming unsure whether the movement would disturb the man with a needle poised over my head.

My mother filled Father in on all the details as the doctor went about cleaning my wound; then, right before the sutures were woven into my scalp, she began talking to me to get my mind off what was happening.

"On the bright side, your art was stunning," she said.

"You could see it?!"

"Well, it's not like I was paying more attention to it than you, if that's what you're suspecting. In fact, I hadn't thought about it until now, but it fell right alongside you and I couldn't help but notice how lovely it was."

My mother had misunderstood me. I wasn't accusing her of taking notice of the picture when her attention should have been on her bleeding daughter. Rather, I was amazed and relieved that the portrait was discernable to the naked eye.

"It's Aunt Angelica, isn't it?"

I felt a strange pulling at my scalp, not exactly painful, but a bit uncomfortable and unsettling. I tried to go on as if my head wasn't being sewn shut. "Yes; how did you know?"

"Well, I'd forgotten how much you two looked alike until recently, at the hospital, your grandmother has been going on and on about the similarities," Mother explained. "She kept saying how Angelica was in black and white but Zylia's in color. Anyway, I thought she was talking nonsense until, in the ambulance, on the way over here, I realized she must be talking about your artwork. She must have seen you working on it at some point. I should have known who it was, anyway, because you're not the type to draw such a flattering picture of yourself."

"*Margaret . . .*" My father sounded appalled.

"Oh, but I mean that as a compliment, of course. She's so modest and humble, you know. Did that sound bad?"

"Yeah, a little," he said with a laugh. "I'm sure she knows you meant well, though."

Something felt off in my head, and it wasn't the agony of my cranial wound. It was the question of when my grandmother would have seen my artwork. I'd only ever worked on it in my room on the third story of our home, a place her frail frame had certainly never ventured. The only time I could remember taking it back downstairs was earlier that day, on the way to the open house, and Grandmother had long been in the hospital by then.

A memory of the *In Between* was returning, tickling at my awareness like an annoying feather. Even so, my mind tried to flick it away in order to continue believing it had all been an absurd dream. Hadn't Angelica said something about Grandmother being able to see into the colorless realm?

"I'll tell you what," Mother began, switching to a new train of thought that apparently required a bubbly tone, "there was a cute dark-haired boy who was *incredibly* concerned about your accident. He seemed familiar, like he's been to the house before. I think his name was Jason or maybe . . . Jacob?"

"Josh?!" All questions concerning my grandmother's unlikely knowledge receded to the back of my mind.

"Yes; that's him! He was the one who called 911 for me because I was too shaken to figure out my phone. It was like I was suddenly holding some alien device." Mother gave a quick laugh at herself. "Then, when people started crowding around to see what was going on, he ushered them back, telling everyone to give you some space. He was more helpful than the adults; it was amazing, really."

It might have been the blood loss, but I could almost feel myself floating above my body in a dreamy haze.

Four hours later, after a clear CT scan and seven stitches in my head, I was finally home. Mother didn't want me climbing upstairs, so she made a bed for me on the couch in the front living room and sent Adonia up to get me some pajamas. Next, she kissed me on the forehead and retreated to find some ibuprofen for my headache.

In the meantime, Ivy had brought me hot tea and crackers and rolled out a sleeping bag so she could camp out in front of the sofa to keep an eye on me.

Soon all three of my brothers had inched into the room and were gathering around me to ask how I was doing and to get a good look at my injury. It was weird to feel so much concern directed at me in such an obvious fashion.

"Does it hurt terribly?" Ivy asked.

"Well, *duh,*" Bram said rudely, "she's gotta freakin' slice out of her head; of course, it hurts!"

"Your picture looks even better now," exclaimed Mace. "Did you see it?"

"Oh, don't show her that; it'll freak her out," Keane scolded.

"Guys, give Zylia some space! She has a concussion, for gosh sakes!" Adonia shouted when she returned with a pair of my fuzzy pajama bottoms and a cotton top. Her loud voice had hurt my head more than all my other siblings combined. "Terra came by earlier," she informed me. "I told her you weren't back yet but that she could probably see you tomorrow. She seemed really worried."

Poor Terra; I hadn't even considered her reaction to my injury. I hoped I hadn't embarrassed her with my tumble.

Mace had retrieved my artwork from somewhere out in the hall and eagerly held it up for me to see. There were streaks of dried blood smeared diagonally across the matte board; grim burgundy blended into the bottom of Angelica's flowy dress. It was unsettling, adding a morbid, but not unappealing interest.

"Take that away," I heard my mother say, a groan in her voice. "Everyone off to bed—now. Scatter!"

There was a noisy shuffle before silence fell over the front room and it was just Mother and me. "You need to rest—doctor's *and* Mom's orders." She picked up my pajamas from the arm of the couch and held them out to me. "I'm really glad you're okay, Zy. You gave me a huge scare."

"Sorry; it wasn't what I was going for."

My mother tossed her blonde head and laughed quietly, but I couldn't think why. Maybe she was just relieved the whole ordeal was behind her. "You're a funny one, Zy, and that's just how I like you. Now get some sleep. I'll be back to check on you in a bit."

It felt strange to change clothes right in the middle of the living room. The long drapes were pulled over the windows, but I still felt exposed since there wasn't a door I could lock, and my father or brothers were free to come strolling through the open archway at any time.

I stripped my top half first, feeling some tenderness along my scalp as my shirt got caught up in my hair. I put on my nightshirt quickly, then went right to removing my jeans when I heard a crunching sound and felt a lumpy spot in the right pocket.

I couldn't remember placing anything in my pocket, so out of curiosity, I reached in and pulled out a handful of unusually large rose petals. For a few seconds I only stared into my palm, moving my fingers over the crumbling plant material that had dried to a deep black color.

I knew immediately that it had to be the rose Angelica had given to me. "Nightmare rose," I whispered aloud, my quiet words reverberating inside my ears. It still didn't make sense; none of it did. But if the *In Between* was real, then there were still things I needed to do before I was safe from that realm.

I lay on the couch and instead of resting, I roved the ceiling with my eyes. I didn't see the textured white plaster, but only that strange black-and-white world that I thought I had put behind me as nothing more than a bad dream. And what of the visits I had paid to my family and friends while I was there?

Angelica had said that time is different there and that I was going "all the way back." Maybe all those things I saw were what *could* have been, things that might have happened if I'd become trapped in that place.

Perhaps that was why the rose was already dry and brittle, now subjected to the spell of linear time—an effect that it had never been governed by. Time certainly hadn't seemed to touch Angelica the way it had my grandmother, so I didn't think it was a wild assumption.

As I lay awake, mulling over my next course of action, I inadvertently pressed and ground the rose petals to crumbs in my hand.

Chapter Twenty-Six

I must have slept, because I was wearing a quilt and I was sure I hadn't covered myself with it. I pushed the heavy blanket off me and black crumbles floated in the air around me like ashes, remnants of the crushed rose I'd forgotten I was holding.

The *In Between* was real; it had to be. Even if I'd dreamed the whole thing up, I figured it was best to do as Angelica had told me and make a stamp on this world so it didn't forget me and let me go. I just didn't know how to do it, and I felt pressed for time.

My mother walked into the room just then. "Oh, you're awake. Do you need any ibuprofen? I've left you a water glass there."

I nodded, realizing my head was throbbing. She already had the pills in her hand, predicting my needs. It was nice to be looked after so thoroughly, but I had to be careful not to become comfortable with this new attention. It could end as soon as I was better, leaving the invisibility to take over yet again.

"Would you like some lunch?" asked Mother.

"Lunch?" I was surprised to see that the clock read ten until one.

"You slept through breakfast, which is fine. You needed the rest." She almost ran her fingers through my hair but must have remembered the stitches and stopped herself; she froze mid-motion like a frightened animal, then pulled her hand back awkwardly. "I can make you a sandwich," she offered as she clamped her hands together tightly to keep them in check.

"Sure."

"Do you want me to open these drapes and let some light in first? There isn't much out there, so I don't think it'd be too hard on your headache, but it might help your mood a little."

"Okay," I agreed because I knew she wanted to open them. My mind was running a race from one thought to the next, but I found it hard to verbalize anything. I imagined that anyone I confided in would think that the bump on my head had knocked my brains loose.

The doorbell sounded as my mother was pulling the drapes apart; the hazy, cold light did little to illuminate the room. "I'll get that," Mother said to no one as she was pushing back the last of the fabric panels.

I took the pills and leaned back on the couch, feeling a toxic mixture of pain and hopelessness. The next thing I knew, Terra was bursting into the room so fast she might have ridden a slingshot from the front door to the spot where I was seated.

"Zylia!" She was breathless as she joined me on the couch, grabbing my hands in hers. "Oh my gosh, are you okay? I've been so worried!"

Her comforting concern brought a warmth to my chest. "I'm fine physically. I mean, I will be." I pointed to my head with a smirk.

I carefully moved my hair back, and Terra leaned forward to examine my wound. It seemed to be quite the attraction, as everyone who had viewed it lingered over the gruesome sight.

"Dang, Zy, that's nasty-looking!" Terra said bluntly before settling back into the couch. "I thought you were gonna die; everyone did!"

"Really?" I found it hard to imagine. "Was everyone staring? How will I ever go back to school now?"

"Are you kidding? It was amazing for your popularity! Now everyone's gonna know who you are! The best part is Josh," she said with an ornery grin.

My heart twitched at the sound of his name. "My mother said he called the ambulance."

"Oh, yeah; he was so worried about you. I couldn't believe how he just jumped into action. Not as worried as me, of course," Terra added. "No one could have been that scared. Although your mom was pretty much freaking out, so maybe it's a tie between her and me. Oh, but I forgot about Ivy," she continued to ramble. "She was sobbing like a baby—no offense. I almost felt as bad for her as I did for you. Even your bratty twin brothers were shaken up. It was wild, the whole thing. But back to Josh . . . he *hovered*, to say the least."

I couldn't help but laugh, feeling my friend lifting my mood already. "It's too bad I couldn't talk to him. Hey, at least I didn't run away! But I guess I didn't start a delightful conversation either, being unconscious and all."

Terra waved her hands dismissively, as if my words were silly. "He's totally crushing on you; I can just tell."

A memory flashed like lightning in my brain and I suddenly remembered seeing Terra and Josh in the hallway of the school, hearing them talk about me in that time or place that had never existed . . . or had yet to exist?

Was it possible that Terra's words could be true right here and now? Did Josh Pierceton truly like me? And was I really putting that question right up there with the enigma of time and reality, the confusion over my newly uncertain universe itself?

Josh did have perfect tawny skin, glossy black hair, and an adorably straight nose; but I didn't want to be so shallow, so I quickly refocused my thoughts.

"What are you thinking?" Terra squeezed her eyebrows together. "You don't believe me, do you?"

"Oh, no. It's not that." *Make a stamp on reality*. Angelica's words echoed in my mind. "It's just hard to imagine all those people noticing me."

"They did, though," Terra smiled. "More than ever."

Soon after, my mother re-entered the room with two plates of ham sandwiches, some purple grapes, and two cans of strawberry soda, the latter clenched between her elbow and side. "I was bringing Zy some lunch anyway and I thought you might be hungry too."

Terra sprang up to unburden my mother's hands and said gratefully, "Thanks so much! You must have heard my stomach growling from a mile away."

Mother smiled. "I'm just in the kitchen if either of you need anything," she reminded us before leaving the room again.

We munched silently for a few minutes before Terra blurted, "I'm jealous of your mom."

"Really? Why?" The question came out far more flabbergasted than I had meant it to be understood. "I . . . I didn't mean she isn't great; she is . . ."

"It's cool; I got you," Terra said with her mouth full after taking another bite of her sandwich. "I don't really have anything to compare it to, but your mom seems like the best. I mean she's got a whole mess of kids she obviously loves, and my mom couldn't even stick around for just me."

Pain, other than what was in my head, began to ache in me. "I didn't know; I'm so sorry."

"It's okay," she assured me even while her distant, watery eyes told a different answer. "I was seven and she told me I was a big girl and that I didn't need her anymore. I screamed and cried like a baby while she loaded her things into some guy's car. I thought it would make her stay, make her feel sorry for me, but not even close. She smiled and waved as they drove off, but it was in this weird way that's stuck in my head forever, like she could have just been waving at the mailman."

I had no idea what to say. "That's awful, Terra . . . gosh . . ."

"I can't believe I told you," she sighed. "I never tell anyone. It's so embarrassing."

"You know that's nothing for you to be embarrassed about . . ."

Terra interrupted irritably, "That's what everyone who hasn't lived it says."

I waited a few beats before doing my best to comfort her with, "When we first met, I was totally *naked.* I think we're past the embarrassment phase of our friendship."

Terra's jaw stopped working on a bite of sandwich and went slack for half a second until she burst into hearty laughter. We giggled until my stomach hurt and I thought my brains might explode from the pulsing seam in my scalp.

"I've never had a best friend before," Terra said after we'd settled down. "I'm not gonna be all mushy or whatever, but that's what you are to me."

My arms were wrapped around her before I even knew what I was doing. She felt a little rigid at first, but went along with my hug anyway. "This falls under mushy," she said over my shoulder.

"Sorry," I said with a smirk and let her shrink away from me.

"You could have died. The least I can do is let you hug me."

"Seems reasonable," I laughed.

Mother popped her head through the doorway. "It sounds like you guys are having a blast in here." She moved over to the coffee table and gathered up our dishes. "Don't overdo it, honey. The doctor said to really get some rest over the weekend."

"I'm so sorry," Terra said, standing up quickly. "I've stayed too long."

"Oh, sweetie, I didn't mean that," Mother tried to backpedal.

"No; it's fine, really. I'm supposed to help my dad with some stuff tonight anyway. Thanks for lunch!" Terra gave me a little wave with a chummy grin.

"Come back anytime; I didn't mean to run you off," I heard mother calling out the front door moments later.

When Terra had been with me, everything felt so real and true. Somehow, she had brought along with her the comforting sensation of believing that everything was going to be okay. Now that she was gone, the room seemed a little colder—duller, even—which made me feel a wave of dread.

I was tired to my core, but when Ivy and the twins asked me to play Monopoly, I couldn't resist. I had to bow out near hour two, however, because my headache was in full bloom. I was glad that they continued to play the seemingly endless game; the sounds of their jovial and slightly competitive voices were a welcome change in the loneliness of the room. It was funny how my head injury had caused a measure of peace to cascade over the household. Maybe the threat of possible death made my family realize what they truly had. Was it enough to keep me here in this reality? It was hard to believe I had to ponder a question as strange as that.

I suppose I would have been well enough to go upstairs, but instead, I ended up sleeping on the sofa Saturday night also. I wasn't ready to leave the safe little nest Mother had carved out for me on one end of the worn couch. She kept the side table next to it stocked with bottled water and mini bags of chips, plus she made sure I had plenty of blankets and ibuprofen when it was due.

My bedroom above seemed like a small, scary place, miles away atop some evil villain's castle. Even though there was no rain in sight, I pictured lightning flashing into our little room and Ivy having to deal with the storm on her own.

My thoughts would have seemed ridiculous before I'd visited the In Between. Now nothing felt like a fairy tale anymore.

As my eyes grew heavy, I couldn't help but wonder why my life had become so strange. Maybe it was because I was born from a woman who had spent every possible moment with her nose buried in a world of fiction. A child of two worlds, not belonging completely to either one.

I knew it was ridiculous, but I liked the sound of it, and with that thought I drifted off to sleep.

Sunday morning, I slept in late, and after a much-needed shower, my mother helped me wash my hair out with baby shampoo in the kitchen sink. She thought the mild soap would save my wound from stinging, but it was really the light tugging that became uncomfortable as my mother carefully brushed out the tangles. I could hardly escape it, though, when my hair hadn't received a proper washing since sometime before it had been matted in blood.

After realizing the tangles were more than she had bargained for, she brought me into the keeping room, sitting me on a pouf ottoman in front of her favorite chair. There she slowly and more delicately worked through my hair with a wide-toothed comb.

"How's my clumsy girl?" my father asked, bringing over his newspaper and sitting in the recliner alongside us. I felt like he was forcing a chipper tone into his normally dreary voice.

"I'm okay." The tangles were all out of my hair now, but my mother was still lightly combing the ends, leaving me feeling almost too relaxed to respond.

"All my kids have tough heads," he said with a little laugh and shook his newspaper straight.

"They get it from their father," my mother teased back at him.

A few moments passed, and I was nearly lulled to sleep when I heard my father ask, "Oh, Margie, did you call that new nursing home back? They need an answer by tomorrow or the room goes to someone else."

Mother gasped. "Oh, shoot, I forgot about that. I never even got a chance to tour the facility since . . . everything has been so crazy."

"I want to see Grandmother," I blurted out. I didn't even know I was going to say such a thing until the words were already there, hanging in the air.

"Oh, Zy . . . I think that . . . well, maybe when you're feeling better . . . both of you," Mother answered in a disjointed tumble of words.

"No, you don't understand," I voiced firmly. "I *need* to see her."

"Someone needs to check on her anyway," my father offered. "None of us have been up there since yesterday."

"Do you really think that's a good idea?" my mother asked in a low whisper. I found that amusing since I was practically sitting in her lap, easily within hearing range.

"You know, she's had a couple really good days. I spent a lot more time with her since you've been dealing with Clumsy, here, and I think you'd be surprised."

"Has she *really*?" Mother sounded shocked, yet delighted. "Why didn't you tell me?"

Father shrugged. "I just did."

"I mean before now, obviously." Mother sighed and rolled her eyes.

Father dropped his newspaper and swiped off his reading glasses in an irritated gesture. "Sorry; things have been a little crazy around here and I didn't feel like standing in line behind the kids to talk to you. Your mom's doing better. I thought you'd love to hear that; I didn't realize it would cause an argument."

Mother took a deep breath that must have calmed her, because her next words were disarming. "I'm sorry, honey; I appreciate you staying with her. I guess we're all a little on edge."

Father replaced his glasses, picked his newspaper back up, and said, "She's more—I don't know—*with* it. Far more alert and awake, even. She asked about you and the kids, apologized for being a burden, that sort of thing."

"Did she really?"

"Well, I'm not making this up! She was even cognizant enough to ask me how to go about filing a formal complaint against the hospital food service staff."

"Now that sounds like Mom," Mother laughed. "I wonder what's gotten into her."

"It's the nature of the disease, Margie. Good days and bad."

"So, can I see her?" I asked.

"Sure; why not," Mother relented. "You and I will go after lunch if your father is willing to hold down the fort."

I felt a rush of adrenaline. Maybe Grandmother was well enough to hear about my visit with Angelica. I knew it was risky, but I'd made a promise to pass on her message and there seemed to be no better place to do so than a hospital, should something go wrong. Besides, if I was lucky, maybe she'd know what Angelica meant by "making a stamp on this world." She might be the only one in this whole reality who could help me.

Chapter Twenty-Seven

Grandmother looked small and frail in that mechanical bed with her eyes closed and silver hair flattened against the pillow. Tubes were taped down to the back of her bony, blue-veined hand. They connected to a half-drained IV bag that was hanging from a silver rack to the side of her bed. I watched her hand as it slightly rose and fell from where it was rested against the chest of her faded hospital gown.

"She's sleeping," my mother whispered. Either she was in the mood to state the obvious or she feared that I might have mistaken the poor old woman for dead. "Maybe we should sit for few minutes; I just hate to wake her." Mother took the plastic chair nearest the bed, crossed one leg over the other, and whipped a novel out of her purse as quickly as an old western lawman would have drawn his weapon.

I was too antsy to sit down, moving over to the large, rectangular window instead. The paisley curtains were open, letting in cold, pale light and providing an undesirable view of another red-bricked wing of the hospital. Far below was a courtyard square, but I had to press my forehead against the cool glass and cast my eyes so far downward that they were nearly shut before I could get a look at the simple iron benches and rows of nearly naked trees.

"Knock, knock," came a voice from the doorway. I turned to see a short woman in blue scrubs applying hand sanitizing foam as she entered the room. Blonde hair hung over one shoulder in a loose side braid and she wore a pleasant smile on her pretty, round face. "I'm sorry to interrupt your nap, sweetie," she said to Grandmother while sending a wink my way, "but

I'm gonna get your vitals from you really quick, then I'll leave you alone for a while."

Grandmother's eyes began to flutter open as the friendly nurse took her blood pressure and listened to her heart. "Looking good," she chirped, entering data onto the wall computer pad.

"Hi, Mom. How're you feeling?" Mother was speaking in a falsetto and patting my grandmother on the hand like she was a toddler.

Grandmother grunted irritably.

"How do you feel on those new antidepressant meds?" Mother looked to the nurse and asked, "Has she had any side effects?"

The nurse looked away from her task at the screen with a smile. "I don't see any notes here that would indicate she's having issues with any of the medication Dr. Marks has started her on. She certainly hasn't said anything to me about side effects, and between you and me, she'd let me know." She shot my mother one of those practiced, diplomatic winks and continued working at the wall station.

"Have you eaten today?" my mother went on, sounding maternal and nurturing to the very woman who'd given birth to her decades prior. "Phillip said you'd been having problems with the food here."

"You try eating cardboard meatloaf and gummy potatoes!" Grandmother barked. "You'd have problems too!"

I heard a muffled snicker coming from the nurse, but when I looked over, she was all business. "I'll be clocking out here pretty soon and Nancy's up next shift, okay? You just hit your call button if you need anything."

"I know the drill," came Grandmother's grumpy response.

"Bye, Runa," said the nurse as she left, her professional cheer undeterred.

When the door clicked shut, my mother said cautiously, "I brought someone to see you. Zylia's been missing you and wanted to say hello." She waved for me to come closer and I did so reluctantly.

Grandmother took notice of me suddenly and her eyes went wide. I wasn't sure what to expect, but I'd be lying if I said I hadn't pictured her ripping out her IV and lunging out of bed at me, blood dripping from the needle site as she attempted to choke the life from my throat.

"Zylia! I'm so glad you came," she exclaimed with emotion glistening in her rheumy eyes. "Give me a squeeze; it's been too long." She held her thin arms out toward me and I couldn't help but be surprised.

I did my best to lean over the bed rail and give her a decent hug, but I was nervous about getting tangled in her IV tube or crushing her feeble frame. I ended up patting her gingerly on the shoulders.

She took my face in her withered hands, and I assumed this was the juncture when she would snap my neck or tear my face off. "I'm so glad you're okay," she said. "Your father told me there was an accident at the school and went running out of here. I think I was the last to hear that everything turned out all right."

"I'm sorry, Mom," my mother broke in with a big, apologetic sigh. "It was a crazy night for all of us. I'm sorry we didn't call you from the emergency room."

"You can make it up to me by getting me a Twinkie out of the vending machine," Grandmother said slyly.

Mother blinked a couple times. "Are you sure you're supposed to have those?"

"If they're out of Twinkies, get me one of those chocolate cupcakes with the curly white strip of icing down the center," Grandmother went on in a demanding tone.

Mother stood hesitantly. "Well, I suppose one wouldn't hurt . . ." She edged her way toward the wide hospital-room door. "Will you two be okay a for a couple minutes?"

"Take your time," my grandmother urged with a quick wink.

As soon as my mother was gone, I realized I had a limited amount of time to talk to her in private and I had no idea where to begin. Turned out it didn't matter, because Grandmother was the one to speak up first. "You've found her, haven't you? You've seen my Angelica?"

I nodded vigorously, tears coming to my eyes. I didn't care who thought she was crazy; I couldn't have felt closer to or more understood by anyone else on Earth. "How did you know?"

"I thought I saw you with her in the darkness . . . Oh, but I knew you would, anyway," she murmured, tears trickling down her cheeks as she stroked my hair fondly. "You're so much like her; I knew you could find her."

"She sent a message for you. She's trapped in a different place but she wanted you to know that her disappearance wasn't your fault, that she should have realized she was loved in this world." I struggled to remember her words. "Oh, and she's okay; she has a very important job and I think she's happy . . . well, settled, at least, with her life there. She misses you so much."

Grandmother was sobbing quietly and it was hard not to come apart myself. "I'm sorry; I didn't want to upset you. I wasn't sure how to tell you." I handed her a wad of scratchy, hospital-grade tissues from a nearby tray table and patted her arm uselessly.

"I'm not upset, dearie. I'm not even sad. I'm so very *relieved,*" she went on, letting out a little laugh mixed in with the tears. "I think I can see her sometimes, the way I saw the two of you. But even before that it was like I could witness things that go on in a different world. Sometimes it's a fleeting image, always darkened and grainy. Then other times I can hear things too. Snippets of conversations that don't make sense or the sounds of someone else's nightmares screaming. Everyone writes me off as crazy. They tell me it's the dementia . . ."

"It's not," I said encouragingly. "It sounds crazy, yes; but I was there, I was really there." I knew it myself for sure in that moment. "There's no color and everything's . . . so different." I couldn't find words to describe what I'd seen.

Grandmother's face went sober. "Angelica left once, but she came back; I'm sure of it. It was brief, but I can remember it. No one else seemed to know she was gone and then she was back a couple days later . . . or maybe it was only a blink or two; it's a little fuzzy now. But I know for certain she didn't stay here long after that. It couldn't have been more than a week later when she was gone for good. That means it could happen to you. We can't know you won't disappear again."

"I know." I clutched at my grandmother's worried hands. "Angelica warned me about that. She said I 'needed to make a stamp' in this world. I'm not exactly sure what that means, but I'm working on it. Do you have any ideas? Have you overheard anything that might help me?"

Grandmother's lips were moving rhythmically, as if she were thinking suddenly.

"I guess I need to stand on the roof and shout my name to the world or something," I said, laughing dryly at the notion.

My Grandmother didn't laugh. I could see by her distant gaze that she was still thinking. "I don't think that's it," she said. "I think Angelica is wrong or you misunderstood her somehow."

"What do you mean?" My ears had perked up.

"We all knew Angelica, knew how kind and generous she was. We all grieved for her when she left. She didn't need to make any more of a dent in our world to be important or needed or loved. People came out of the woodwork after her disappearance and then again when she was presumed dead. More people than would fit were crammed into that funeral parlor to say goodbye to nothing more physical than a memory. We *all* loved her, but she didn't know it. That was on us, not her. We lost her because we were too selfish to let her know how much she meant to us and now we're doing the same to you!" Grandmother was getting agitated, her eyes darting around the room and her body beginning to rock as she was sitting up in bed.

"No, no, it's okay; it'll be all right." I tried to calm her. "It goes both ways; I'll figure it out. It's not your fault. Remember what Angelica wanted you to hear; it was never your fault."

This seemed to settle her down because she suddenly became still, and the saddest little smile touched her lips. At that moment Mother came back into the room balancing an open book in one hand and a coffee in the other.

"Margaret," my grandmother snapped, scaring both my mother and me. "Don't you dare take this little girl for granted. She's the best of the bunch. Put down those books of yours every now and then and realize the story is right in front of you. Don't forget Zylia the way we forgot Angelica."

I cringed, worried my mother would chastise me for sending Grandmother into another agitated spell. However, she just stood there frozen, with her elbows held unnaturally high and her eyes opened wide. At first, she just looked stunned and unable to figure out why she was being reprimanded. But then her gaze moved to my face and her expression changed. Something clicked in her eyes and it was like she was noticing me, becoming aware of me . . . really seeing me.

She finally melted into action, leaving Grandmother's Twinkie and even her book and coffee on the tray table. Then, she kissed her mother, grabbed my hand, and walked out of there. She kept squeezing her fingers into my palm and looking at me all the long way back to the van.

"I don't ever want to lose you," was the only thing she said to explain her out-of-the-ordinary behavior.

I smiled up at her and said, "I love you too, Mom."

Chapter Twenty-Eight

Things started to feel different soon after that, even though life was beginning to return to normal as far as routines were concerned. I could almost feel a layer of my outer shell shed itself and let some light into my lonely soul.

I probably would have been good to go back to school by Monday, but I let Mother fuss over me for an extra day and enjoyed the attention. I'd never had so much one-on-one time with her, especially while she was being so *present,* so I was kinda glad to have it stretch out as long as it could last.

Besides, I was toying with an idea in my head about how I was going to deal with my brother, Keane. I waited until everyone had left for school and Father had gone off to work before I attempted to help Mother with the breakfast dishes.

"No, sweetie; I'll take care of these. Why don't you enjoy your last day of rest?" She clicked the dishwasher closed with her hip and punched a button. "Trust me; no one is going to judge you for wanting, oh, say . . . a bubble bath, or a nap, or . . . God, that all sounds so good."

"Maybe you're the one who needs a break. It's been really hectic for everyone; especially you, I'd imagine."

A fondness crept into my mother's eyes in the form of tears. "I'm so lucky to have you, Zy. I don't tell you that enough." She wrapped her arms around me and squeezed tightly. "Oh, guess what?" she suddenly remembered, a beaming smile on her face. "Your grandmother is coming home tomorrow! The doctors think she's ready for another try. It's kind of strange, actually; they don't really have an explanation for her sudden improvement. Now, of course, her dementia isn't healed or anything; but it seems she's got a few good days left in her, at least."

"I'm so happy. It's not the same here without her."

"It's not the same here without all of us," Mother rephrased.

Once I could politely extricate myself from my mother's physical affections, I went right upstairs to Keane's bedroom door. It was slightly ajar and I used my index finger to push it open a little farther, cautious, as if something might leap out and bite me. I waited a second, making sure my mother hadn't followed me upstairs. Keane's room was on the same level as hers, and surely it would be conspicuous if she caught me snooping in my brother's room.

When I didn't hear anything, I went inside the room and closed the door. I didn't want Mother sneaking up on me, and I'd seen enough scary movies to know the things that could happen when doors were left open.

Once inside, a single look around the room confirmed it: Keane was a slob. Before I began my search, I took a deep breath, noting that the room smelled strongly of fresh pine with musty undertones.

I waded through discarded jeans and shirts cast over loose stacks of playing cards and balled-up pieces of paper. I was sure Keane would have never left his room in this state just a few months before. I stooped down and unfolded a piece of crumpled schoolwork, smoothing it out over the hardwood floor. It was a science paper—his favorite subject—with a bright red-letter D marking the top. Whatever was going on with him was obviously affecting his grades along with everything else.

I knew what I was looking for, but I didn't know where to begin. Keane's room had a lot of clutter and possibly more furniture than my stuff and Ivy's combined.

I felt a pestering wave of guilt as I methodically searched his dresser, taking out the drawers to look behind them after carefully searching through the insides. I found nothing out of the ordinary—other than a disturbing amount of ripped and tattered boxers.

I moved on to his end table, desk, and the closet, following the same painstaking formula of attention to detail. By this time, I was getting a little nervous that Mother was going to come check on me, so I did my best to speed up the pace.

There was nothing under the mattress, I couldn't find any loose floorboards, and even his bookcase was a bust. The only thing that he should have feared someone might find was the overwhelming amount of tree-shaped air fresheners around the place.

That got me thinking. Cigarettes were stinky. If he had been smoking in his room, how had Mom never caught him before? Were the air fresheners just to cover up any scent left on his clothing?

As a last-ditch effort, I climbed across his bed and forced the old window open. I couldn't believe my eyes when I saw seven cigarettes lining the interior of the sill. I took two of them, my innocent thirteen-year-old hands feeling like I was holding the devil itself, before closing the window back down on the rest.

I did my best to leave the room exactly as it was when I'd found it, save swiping a pair of dirty jeans off the floor. I was pretty sure they wouldn't be missed, but just to be sure I used my foot to spread out various other pieces of dirty laundry over the space where the jeans had been.

I made my way downstairs silently, praying I wouldn't run into my mother. At the bottom of the stairs I slowly moved around the corner, and I could see that the kitchen was empty and the keeping room beyond was dark.

My shoulders relaxed as I realized it would be smooth sailing toward the laundry room. Mother must have been reading in the front living room, so I wouldn't have to worry about her catching me with the strange combination of cigarettes and my brother's jeans.

I passed the kitchen, moving quickly through the next room, when suddenly I spotted my mother sleeping in the recliner. My body decided to do an adrenaline dump into my poor, frail nervous system.

At least I didn't scream, I thought as I crept past her with my heart thudding uncomfortably in my throat.

When I finally reached the laundry room I shoved the cigarettes into the pocket of Keane's jeans and set them at the top of the nearly full wicker basket. I knew Mother would check the pockets ever since she had ruined my father's work phone in the washing machine. I turned to leave, but just to be sure, I turned back and pulled one cigarette high enough so that it could easily be spotted over the lip of the denim.

Now I had ratted out my brother without the consequences of being a nark. Even if there were suspicions, there were too many of us under the same roof for it to ever come back on me. This was a situation for my parents to handle, and I was leaving it in their hands.

Later that afternoon I was flipping through boring TV channels when I heard Adonia and her friend Leah burst into the front hall. Something in the tone of their voices made me turn off the TV in an instant so I could listen to what was being said.

". . . massively personal. You'll see; they're the worst ones ever," I overhead Adonia say as I moved toward the open doorway.

"Oh; hey, Zy," Leah said. How had she spotted me so fast? Was I becoming more visible? It was so startling that it took me a moment to realize that it was a good thing.

Leah came close and threw her arms around me dramatically. "How is this brave girl?" she asked, speaking to me like I was decades younger than herself. "I heard about your accident. You healing up okay?"

My sister followed her into the room. I could tell she was torn, as if she didn't want to be there, but didn't want me to know it. Whatever conversation they had been in the midst of was surely not meant for my ears.

If I didn't act fast, I was going to lose them both to the locked confines of Adonia's room. Without bothering to think it through, I blurted, "Yeah, I'm okay. But what's wrong with you, Doni? You look so sad." I gave my most mature, empathetic face and hoped for the best.

"Same old stuff; you already know about it," she answered evasively.

"Oh, Zylia knows about the notes?" Leah asked incredulously. "Well, you might as well show us the new ones you got today."

Adonia sighed. "Yeah, fine; but do it quick. I don't want Mom seeing."

I was surprised that my sister was so easily agreeable to sharing her troubles with me and even more taken aback that her friend was interested in including me. Maybe I still had the pity factor that had been working in my favor since the accident.

Whatever the reason, the three of us sat together on the couch; Leah swiped a familiar purple folder from Adonia and opened it. "So, these are the new ones?" she asked, pulling out a couple sheets of notebook paper with the same derogatory handwriting similar to what I'd seen when my sister had shown me before.

"Yeah," Adonia answered with a flat, deflated sound to her voice.

"'*Pencil skirts are made for pencil bodies,*'" Leah read. "'*Do yourself and the rest of the school a favor and hide yours completely.*'" She flipped to another page. "'*The world would have so much more space without you in it.*'" She glanced up briefly before reading the last one. "'*Diet and exercise or homeschool and cake, make a choice.*'"

I was reading along over her shoulder, noting that the words were scribbled in that harsh, heavy-handed style I recognized from the earlier notes.

"See what I mean?" Adonia asked soberly, and I worried that she was about to cry. "They're getting worse. They're not just mean and horrible anymore. They're almost threatening now."

"They are. They're personal," I said, and both girls looked at me. I pointed at the first page. "You don't wear pencil skirts on school days."

"Oh my God; you're right!" Adonia's face went white. "When did I even wear one last?"

It clicked in my mind almost instantly—the vision of my lovely sister in a black pencil skirt and dangerously high platform pumps. I remembered it well, since my mother had nearly flipped out at the sight of her looking so mature and alluring. "You wore one to that fashion club event," I reminded her.

A light went on in Adonia's greenish-blue eyes. "The fundraiser dinner!" She slapped Leah on the arm. "It has to be someone who was there!"

Leah's expression was flat. "Uh, like every high schooler we know who's anybody. That doesn't really narrow it down much."

Adonia looked deflated. "You're right." She sank down in the couch.

"So, it's a popular girl who's jealous of you," I said. "Someone who's been watching you closely."

"It's super creepy," Leah commented, handing the pages back to my sister.

I didn't have time to plan my next actions; they just sort of happened. I guess I figured that if I was wrong in my suspicions I could blame it on the head injury. "May I borrow this?" In an instant I had swiped Leah's black drawstring shoulder bag and began rummaging around inside.

"What the hell?!" Leah squealed, trying to grab it back.

I jumped off the couch, taking the bag with me, and poured its contents out onto the coffee table.

"Geez, Zy, have you lost your mind?" Adonia shot. "What are you doing?"

I pawed through loose change, tiny lotions, and an absurd amount of lipstick tubes before relief dawned over me. "Looking for this." I held up a purple pen with glittery ink.

Leah's face went white even before I snatched the pages from Adonia and used the pen on the surface, showing that the inks were a perfect match.

Adonia looked confused and then stunned. "Leah?"

She was instantly defensive. "What? It's just a pen; they're not hard to come by. What are you trying to say?"

"I'm saying that you're a jealous bully," I said, my heart pounding in my chest. If it hadn't been for my visit to the *In Between*, I'd never have been able to put together the clues. I remembered seeing the pen in that possible future and feeling that it was important somehow.

Flustered, Leah began shoveling the strewn items back into her purse. "I can't believe this. Are you going to let your bratty little sister talk to me that way?"

"Shut your mouth, you skanky troll!" Adonia spat out the words. "You don't even get to talk to her, let alone call her a brat; understand?"

Leah hooked her bag over her shoulder; her shiny lips retracted into a tight, angry circle.

"It all makes sense now," Adonia said, shaking her head.

"I . . . just . . ." Leah tossed her bleached-blonde hair in a defiant manner, but her lips were beginning to quiver.

"Get out," Adonia ordered while pointing in the direction of the door.

"Doni, I don't even have a ride." Leah was suddenly trying to sound sweet.

"You have a phone and a coat," Adonia answered coldly, causing some tiny cheerleader inside of me to swing her figurative pom-poms proudly with an abundance of glee.

"I'm sorry," Leah cried, tears finally escaping her eyes. "I don't know what's wrong with me. I'm so sorry."

My mother came into the room quickly, detecting the tension. "What's going on in here?"

Adonia was unfazed by her former best friend's tears. "Leah needs a ride home. For good," she offered as explanation. Then she walked over to where I was standing and enveloped me in the warmest, tightest hug I'd ever received from her.

Grandmother came home Tuesday, the same day that I was to go back to school. She had improved enough that it was deemed she wouldn't have to move into a nursing facility right away, that she could give staying at home another try. We were all so glad to have her back that we were reduced to competing in order to talk with her over breakfast, voices mingling and overlapping, one rising louder than the next. It was funny how no one in this family could really appreciate a person until they were gone for a while; I wondered if that were true of every family.

I would have liked to stay home and chat with her about Angelica and my strange adventure. I was longing to. But it wasn't a conversation for the breakfast table in front of the rest of my family.

I think she was eager to talk to me as well, because amidst Mace and Bram's stories of all the things she missed while she was away at the hospital, she kept flashing me intentional, knowing glances.

Even if I didn't get to spend the day with her, I was happy to see her more like herself, and I was grateful of our newfound closeness. I made sure to kiss her on her silver head before I grabbed my backpack and left.

Terra wrapped her arms around me and gave me a tight squeeze, my breath puffing out into the cold morning air. "I feel like you've been gone for a century," she told me, linking her elbow with mine.

"Really? You missed me that much, huh?" I tried to act surprised, but I felt it too. The space of time from my normal, invisible life to these new days where everyone was taking notice of me had seemed to stretch on much longer than three days. I knew that it was the weird gap in the middle that made it all seem so strange and infinite. The time in between worlds. The In Between.

I tried not to think about it. What else could I do to make myself any more real? How did I know when my existence in this realm was validated? I was doing my best to speak my mind and to help my friends and siblings, but if it wasn't enough I would just have to face my fate.

And I was almost ready to do just that, but there was one more thing I had to check off my list before I'd allow myself to give in. One more hint from my trip out of this world that had given me a glimpse of another loose end I needed to tie up.

"I'm talking to Josh today," I announced unceremoniously to Terra.

"Really?" A skip broke into her stride as a ripple of excitement shone on her face. "Finally! What are you going to say?"

What was I going to say? *I've been secretly crushing on you from the shadows?* Way too creepy. *I know we're only going on fourteen here, but I have our entire future planned?* Whoa, now! I was obviously going to have to think up something before I let my intrusive thoughts take hold of my tongue.

"I'm just going to talk to him—like a typical, non-invisible person would," I settled on telling her, even though I was fully aware that my brain wasn't functioning within normal parameters.

It turned out I didn't have worry about how to start a conversation, because by the time I was stuffing my coat into my locker, I felt a faint tapping on my shoulder. It was so whispery-soft that I thought I may have imagined it, but I turned to face Josh's almond eyes that were fixated on me.

"Hey, Zylia," he said to me. That was my name and mine alone, but I still fought the urge to glance over my shoulder and make sure he wasn't talking to someone else. "I'm glad you're feeling better. We were all worried."

"Thanks," I answered, my voice surprisingly calm. "I didn't mean to be such a klutz."

Josh laughed but then stopped himself short, as if he were concerned about hurting my feelings. That's when it occurred to me: *he* was nervous talking to *me*.

I felt energized and wanted to put him at ease, so I asked, "What do those letters mean on your jacket? I've always wanted to ask."

"Oh . . ." he looked down along his arm as if he forgot what he had been wearing. "It's something my mom made for me; kinda embarrassing, really. It's just what she has called me since I was little."

I watched him blush and my heart skipped a beat. "Like a pet name?"

Josh nodded and said the word in Korean. It sounded like a whiney "*key-oh-whoa*" to my American ears. "It means *cute*; she's always called me her cutie."

All this time I'd pictured those symbols related to something sporty and macho like *champion* or *warrior*. "That's adorable," I said with a laugh.

"Please don't tell anyone," he begged, looking nervous. "I can't believe I told you that."

"Your secret is safe with me," I said and meant it, even though I wanted to tell Terra quite badly.

"I guess I've wanted to talk to you for so long," he confessed, "that I'm saying too much up front."

Endorphins flooded my body with sensations I'd never felt before, like an explosion of happiness in my core that sent my brain floating right out of my head. The warning bell rang and interrupted the dreamy moment. Instinctively, I flinched as kids began rushing around us, but I was surprised when no one collided with me. Something had definitely changed.

"I better go, but I'm really glad you're okay," Josh said, looking like he wanted to say more but couldn't get his lips to work, just opening and closing them silently.

I was shamefully delighted by his unease. I'd never been on the opposite end of that feeling, so I allowed myself a measure of satisfaction before I wrapped my arms around him in a quick but tight hug. I had caught him off guard, and the books in one of his arms pressed uncomfortably into my chest; but I felt his other arm do its best to catch up and return the squeeze. "Thanks for looking out for me and calling the ambulance," I told him, noticing that his dark hair smelled of a strong, masculine scent: a soapy forest waterfall.

Even after all that had transpired—all the weird, out-of-this-world things that had happened to me in such a short span of time—I was walking on air after that encounter. The lighthearted feeling stayed with me all the way through Ms. Beck's third-hour English class, where we ended up in the school library.

I'd always liked that room of the school, long and broad and filled with row upon row of books. It was easy to be myself in the quiet space, surrounded by wood and greeted by the pleasant smell of old pages.

I was nearly asleep, my head hovering over a copy of *The Princess Bride*, when the dismissal bell rang. In my stupor, it was particularly jarring; my head snapped up and I realized that most of my class was already halfway out the door. As I was gathering my things, I heard the librarian, Mr. Watts, beckon me over to his desk.

I couldn't imagine what he wanted as I walked over to the cluttered oak surface. The balding man was rifling around in one of the bottom desk drawers. "I'm glad I remembered," he told me. "I found a dust jacket for an old hardback book and I wanted to show it to you. For weeks I've been trying to locate the actual book itself, but it's a mystery as to what became of it. I even tried to look it up online, but I couldn't come up with anything . . . ah, here it is." He passed a dust cover jacket that was titled *Zylia, The Shadow Girl* in curly, smoky lettering.

"I thought you might find it interesting," Mr. Watts went on. "I've never seen anything with a name like yours on it."

I tried to keep my voice from shaking as I asked, "Can I keep this, please?"

He nodded. "It's all yours, and I'll let you know if I ever stumble across the actual book itself."

"Thank you." I was out of the library before he could say another word.

Epilogue

I knew I didn't have enough time between classes, but I didn't care. I was going to take a moment to examine that book cover even if it got me suspended. It had to be the novel my mother had named me after, the very one I'd been hunting for years.

I weaved around the passing-period traffic and ducked into the nearest restroom. I was barely inside the door when I pulled the flimsy book jacket away from my chest where I'd been cradling it. The ends were frayed with small tears where the spine of the book would normally rest, as if it had been handled a lot over the years.

The face of the jacket was still glossy, and behind that hazy title was the shadow of a young girl, her features blurred and distorted by blackness. Dark green vines were all around her, pulling at her shadowy limbs and twisting around her torso.

On the inner flap there was a short blurb on what the missing book was about. I read it in an undertone, my mouth moving along with every word. *Follow Zylia, The Shadow Girl, in a tale of high adventure that leaves a tangled path from a cliff's-edge castle and into the Carnage forest beyond. Will her brave heart and sharp sword be enough to rescue her precious loved ones from the monstrous perils spat from the darkened realm? Join her in this epic battle against madness: one girl against the blackness of time and space.*

I let out a puff of air, realizing I'd been holding my breath. There was something spooky and exciting about being named after this particular fictional character. I forgot I was in the restroom and spoke aloud. "Man, she sounds pretty bada-*aahhhhh!*" I was startled mid-sentence to the point of screaming.

I hadn't noticed it, at first, but there was Melanie Green, standing right in front of me, adjacent to the sinks. "Sorry; I guess I thought the bathroom was empty."

"You can see me?" She sounded startled as well, her pale lashes reaching up to her eyebrows.

I nodded. "Yeah, I can . . . now," I said, gulping down a bubble of air. "Why do you ask?"

Melanie let a tear roll down her face and pointed at the mirror. I followed her finger slowly and saw my own reflection standing alone in the bathroom. I quickly looked back to her and saw that she was still there, in the flesh, but looked paler and faded.

"I'm not there, am I?" Melanie's hands were shaking as she brought them to her face. "I'm disappearing, aren't I? *Please*, help me."

I rushed over to her in an instant, clutching her hands in mine while accidentally crumpling the book jacket just a bit. "Don't worry. It's going to be okay."

And somehow, right then and there, all those years ago, I knew that it would be.

About the Author

Misty Mount has written since age five and was first published at fourteen. By day she's a caregiver, wife and mother to a young son but during the quiet hours of night she becomes a novelist. She resides in Wichita, Kansas.

CPSIA information can be obtained
at www.ICGtesting.com
Printed in the USA
LVOW03s1338070218
565640LV00002B/587/P